MW00637651

07/25/05   *15 months*

An Angel's Gift

❧ Hearts Soaring With Love ❧

a novel

by
Sherry Ann Miller

the sequel to

One Last Gift
Hearts Anchored With Love

Published and Distributed by:

Granite Publishing and Distribution, LLC
868 North 1430 West
Orem, Utah 84057
(801) 229-9023 • Toll Free (800) 574-5779
Fax (801) 229-1924

Page Layout & Design by Myrna Varga • The Office Connection, Inc.
Cover Design by Tammie Ingram

ISBN: 1-930980-98-1
Library of Congress Control Number: 2003101167
Printed in the United States of America

First Printing, March 2003
Second Printing, August 2003

10 9 8 7 6 5 4 3 2

To Sheila, whose unfailing trust and confidence
have encouraged me onward when I thought I
couldn't go forward any longer . . . and inspired
me to be a better person than I am;

And to Carol, who never gave up on me even when
I wanted to give up on myself. First my sister . . . for
all eternity one of my dearest friends.

May you both find your fondest dreams realized,
and the sweet memories cradled in your hearts ever after.

Prologue

*A*lyssa's dream intensified, and she could see herself speaking inside a swirling vortex to a stranger . . . a man with no face.

Her voice sounded surreal, like an angel with a soft, ethereal echo, as though she spoke to him directly from heaven.

"I love you with all my heart . . . ," she whispered, choking on the words, fearing them. The intensity of those seven words startled her.

Frightened, she looked straight at him, sensing in her heart that the man who stood inside the whirling dream was her fiancé, but she couldn't see his face. Although his green eyes appeared somewhat similar to Abbot's, they were different, more caring and less selfish somehow. He had no nose or mouth; she could only see a shadow where the rest of his face should have been.

"Who are you?" she asked timidly.

The man attempted to answer, but his mouthless face could form no words.

Alyssa demanded, "Who are you?"

Again he tried to answer, to no avail.

Terrified, she screamed, "Tell me who you are!"

The pitch of her own voice awakened her with a start. Gasping for air and striving to overcome the horror that clutched her heart, Alyssa trembled. Then she buried her face in the pillow and wept.

Chapter One

*P*utting one boot in the stirrup, Ed swung his leg up and over the back of the palomino stallion. From the saddle he made a clicking sound and gave Breeze a gentle nudge with his spurs. With little encouragement, Breeze galloped west toward Mountain Meadow, a mile-long stretch of the finest pasture grass in the high Uintas, where the Bar M black Angus herd grazed.

Ed noticed beams of sunlight peeking over the eastern mountains bordering the ranch. The rays of sunshine danced upon the young, dew-laden leaves of the quaking aspen, making them sparkle as though they'd been dusted with diamonds. Tall pine trees, interspersed among the aspens, stood like sentinels, guarding the meadow from marauders. To his left, a quarter mile away, a small plume of smoke wafted heavenward from a campfire. Down the length of the meadow Ed saw groups of black cattle stirring about as they grazed on the lush emerald grass.

Something in the sky caught Ed's attention and he pulled back on the reins. "Whoa!" he said firmly. "Whoa there, Breeze." The stallion, huffing in protest, responded to Ed's command and came to a full halt.

Tilting his head back, Ed looked at the sky above Porcupine Ridge. A small yellow Cessna made lazy circles high above him. Ed watched the plane curiously, wondering why the pilot kept circling the Bar M Ranch.

He didn't recognize it as one of Sky Patrol's planes. Ed would know about any rescue mission in progress because he worked part-time for Sky Patrol. He owned his own helicopter, but because he also managed the ranch, he had to limit his flight hours to emergency situations.

Squinting, Ed grabbed the binoculars from the saddle bag. Putting them up to his eyes, he watched the plane as it circled the Bar M Ranch. *It's definitely a Cessna*, Ed decided as he scrutinized the insignia on the wings. Then he saw the passenger door open.

"What the blazes?" he asked aloud, though no one could have heard him.

To his utter amazement, someone jumped from the plane, arms out to his side, in a daring free-fall. For several long minutes Ed watched in astonishment, confused and a bit concerned about the sky diver's lack of wise judgement. There was no place to land on the other side of Porcupine Ridge, yet that's where the jumper would eventually end up.

After what seemed an interminably long time, the jumper finally pulled one arm close to his body and attempted to deploy the parachute.

To Ed's horror, the chute failed to open. He gulped as he stood up in the stirrups, and an anxious knot formed in his belly.

The jumper's arms flailed, making him descend like a bucking bronco. Regardless of all his efforts, the parachute would not open.

In agony, Ed could only watch and wait. Beads of moisture appeared on his forehead, soaking through the rim of his Stetson, as he considered all the possibilities. If the jumper was extremely lucky or entitled to divine intervention, he'd hit some feathery pine boughs on the way down, slowing his fall. It might be enough that he could survive, but not without numerous broken bones. If not, Ed hoped the sky diver had made his peace with God. He didn't want to think about what would happen if the chutes failed completely.

"Pull the secondary!" Ed yelled with all his strength, even though he knew he would never be heard.

Then, as though he'd never been up in the sky at all, the parachutist slipped behind the mountain and out of view.

Ed swung the binoculars around and watched the camp. His three ranch hands were shouting to one another and two of them were mounting their horses. Satisfied that they, too, had seen the jumper, Ed tugged the reins to the right and yelled, "Git up!" while spurring the stallion sharply in the flanks. Breeze responded with a sudden lurch and galloped swiftly up the switchback path that led to the top of Porcupine Ridge. A spray of loose rock, kicked away by the palomino's hooves, tumbled down the steep mountainside behind him. It took nearly fifteen minutes to reach the top, and Breeze snorted from the effort.

If the parachutist managed to survive, a matter of seconds may make the difference in his ability to stay alive. Ed needed to get to him! Fast! To his relief, Ed heard his men not far behind him, following up the switchback trail. He didn't want to be the only one around to pick up the pieces. He'd never seen a body after a fall like that, though he'd heard that recovery was a rescue worker's worst nightmare.

From the top of Porcupine Ridge, Ed stopped long enough to search the steep terrain on the opposite side with his binoculars. A blue and white fabric that seemed to sparkle in the sunlight dangled in some tall pine trees several hundred yards down the mountainside. A feeling of relief, mingled with hope, coursed through him. The chute had finally opened! He didn't know whether to shout for joy before or after he found the jumper. At least now there was a chance he'd still be alive.

Spurring the stallion on, he started down toward a stand of tall pine trees where the parachute was tangled, but he had to wind his way between several trees to reach it. Fortunately, this side of Porcupine Ridge was less traveled, with little loose rock to impede their progress. Within a few minutes the stallion carried Ed to a spot just below the parachute.

The fabric, tangled in the pine trees, still had the dangling ropes tethered to it, but the jumper had managed to unlatch himself. Ed looked around quickly on the ground. A little farther down the mountain, behind a mound of scrub oak and almost camouflaged in the underbrush, were a pair of white boots facing toe down, with a pair of legs still attached. Imprints in the soil indicated the jumper had staggered a bit before falling forward. Ed's hope soared.

Slipping from the saddle he ran over to the jumper and knelt beside him. About the same time, he heard horses being reined in on the mountainside just above him.

"Whoa!" exclaimed Luke, the youngest of the two ranch hands, a Native American with a heart as generous as the Bar M, and a smile that matched. He grabbed Breeze's reins in his hand and held the palomino stallion in place for Ed.

"Is that fella' dead?" asked Sidekick John as he slung a leg over the saddle and jumped down.

"I don't know," sighed Ed. He turned the body over, being careful to keep the neck aligned properly, then removed the blue and silver helmet. To his astonishment, a woman's face, quite unconscious yet exquisitely beautiful, lay beneath it. Suddenly, and without expectation, he found himself almost spellbound by her striking beauty. It took him several long seconds before he could even speak.

"For one thing," he observed, taking in a deep breath to calm himself. "She ain't a fella'!"

She had skin the color of pale amber, with a faint sprinkling of freckles across the bridge of a fine, straight nose. Her eyes were closed, and her full, glossed lips parted slightly.

For a few brief seconds, Ed wondered if he should kiss her in order to wake her up. The thought brought him back to reality, and he shook himself out of the tantalizing spell.

Putting his ear close to her mouth, he could hear and feel warm air coming from her nostrils. His ears tingled as relief flooded over him. "She's breathing."

He felt for a pulse at her carotid artery, and found it steady and strong. Disheveled about her head was shoulder-length brunette hair that seemed to glisten like gold where the sun touched it.

Satisfied with her heart rate, Ed unzipped the blue and silver jump suit she wore and examined her neck, arms and legs to see if anything appeared broken. "She ain't broke up," he said, relief evident in his own voice.

"What should we do with her?" asked Luke, his dark eyes admiring her beauty every bit as much as Ed had.

"Can we keep her?" Sidekick John grinned and bobbed his head up and down, his long red hair brushing his shoulders.

"Wouldn't that be nice," Ed observed, shaking his head. He had to subdue a smile when he noticed Sidekick frown. Then Ed took charge of the situation. "She may have internal injuries. We'll make a travois and bring her back to the ranch."

Immediately Sidekick and Luke started looking for long, straight branches they could use for poles.

"We can use the parachute fabric and rope for the bed," Ed suggested.

Unexpectedly, the woman groaned, startling him. "Be still," he instructed. "You may have internal injuries."

She shook her head and gasped, as though trying to catch her breath. When she succeeded, she spoke softly, and her voice sounded like an angel's voice. "I'm okay. Really." She opened her eyes and sat up. "Besides, I can walk."

Shakily, the young woman stood up while Ed wrapped a strong hand around her elbow to support her. She swung her brown hair out of her face, then pulled her arm free from his hold and brushed her jump suit with her hands to remove some of the dust. "Please don't damage my parachute. It cost me a fortune!"

Ed tilted his hat back off his forehead. "Well, I'll be a one-eyed pole-cat! At first we thought you were dead. Now we find that you're not even injured."

"Just my ego," she admitted with a coy sniffle.

"You have a bump on your forehead, probably from your helmet when you fell face forward." Ed touched it with his fingertips. "Does this hurt?"

"No, I'm okay. I got the wind knocked out of me when I let myself out of the harness." She turned around and stretched in several directions, as though making sure that all her limbs still worked. "Is there anyway to retrieve my parachute without damaging it?"

Ed thought a moment, then decided. "Luke can fetch my climbing gear from the cabin. With a little effort, he should be able to dislodge it for you."

Now that he knew she would be all right, Ed grew wary. Why had she come? What did she hope to accomplish by parachuting onto the Bar M? He became a little suspicious of her motives.

"Thank you," the woman said, holding out her hand. "I'm Alyssa Kendal, and you are?"

"Ed Sparkleman," he said, shaking her hand. "These are my ranch hands, Luke Jennings and John Brandt."

Sidekick John shot forth his hand and shook hers before Luke had a chance. "Does this mean we won't get to keep her?" he asked Ed, his eyes twinkling in amusement.

"Excuse me?" she questioned with a hint of caution.

"Don't mind him," Ed suggested. "We call him Sidekick for good reason."

"Pleased to meet you," said Luke, shaking her hand. "What were you doing, dropping out of the plane like that?"

"Not what I'd hoped," she admitted. "I intended to land on the other side of this ridge, near your camp, to make my grand entrance."

"Then it's a good thing you landed over here," Ed scolded, irritation making the knot in his belly tighten. "If you'd landed on the other side, you could have spooked the cattle and started a stampede, putting my men and herd at risk. Disregarding that danger, there's still the fact that this is private property, Ms. Kendal, and you are trespassing. Surely you realized that before you made the jump."

"I guess I didn't think." She gave him a quick, flirtatious smile that almost softened him, until she said, "But my intentions were good."

If she'd left the last sentence out, Ed might have fallen for her half-handed apology. Now he decided that her smile had just the effect she intended and it angered him. He refused to allow anyone, beautiful or otherwise, to control his good judgement. In rebellion he growled, "Good intentions don't justify your actions, Ms. Kendal. How did you plan to get back to civilization after you landed?" Unconcerned whether the harshness in his voice provoked her or not, he decided, *Ms. Kendall deserves a good, old-fashioned spanking!*

"Surely you have telephone service back at your cabin," came her suggestion.

She gave him another flirtatious grin, but the gesture did not phase Ed. Alyssa Kendal, apparently accustomed to doing things her own way, had little regard for consequences. Regardless how attractive he found her, Ed drew his own biased conclusions now, and they weren't kind. In an authoritative tone he said, "I'll take you as far as the cabin so you can call for a ride. But after you leave, I don't want you coming back. You're a danger to my men and my property!"

"Oh?" she questioned, her voice taking on a defiant tone. "I don't recall seeing the name Sparkleman on the county recorder's plat map."

"I'm responsible for everything that happens on the Bar M."

"Who made you the boss?" she challenged.

His eyes narrowed and he gritted his teeth together. He thought about a nasty retort, but held it in reserve.

Sidekick, apparently amused by the conversation, broke into a broad grin. "Believe him, Ma'am. Ed is the boss!"

Apparently offended by Ed's sharp rebuke, she tilted her head proudly. "I shall speak with Mr. Lamont Allen about your ultimatum," she said with an air of haughtiness. "And if Luke doesn't mind, I'll let him take me back to the cabin when he goes to retrieve the climbing gear." She dismissed Ed without another glance and turned her attention to Luke. "Will that be all right with you?"

Luke looked to Ed for the answer. Ed nodded, then walked back to his horse, doing his best not to stomp away in anger. He hoped he appeared calm after their disagreement, because inside he was seething. As he mounted, he glared at both men and warned, "No special favors for Ms. Kendal. Is that clear?"

Both men nodded their agreement as Ed tugged on the reins and headed Breeze back up the far side of Porcupine Ridge. When he reached the top, he looked back and saw Alyssa Kendal riding behind Luke on his chestnut mare, while Sidekick followed next to them on the other horse. The three were involved in a steady stream of conversation.

Angered that Alyssa Kendal had such little regard for her own welfare or for the safety of others, Ed now had a knot in his belly as hard as a chunk of petrified wood. It would take the better part of three days for that knot to ease up, and that probably rankled him as much as the other issues at risk in this escapade. A stampede could have killed the men plus half a dozen head of cattle! What in blazes was Alyssa Kendal thinking? Or was she thinking at all?

Working himself into a turmoil would be counterproductive, so he attempted to shrug all thoughts of the woman from his mind. To his dismay, she wouldn't leave. In exasperation, he inhaled deeply several times, trying to focus completely on the ranch. With a great deal of effort, he finally succeeded.

The ranch, well known for its prime beef, boasted one of the largest herds in Utah. **Bar M Black Angus Beef,** used commercially at many of the finer restaurants, commanded top dollar because of its exceedingly fine flavor and fork tenderness. To his secret pleasure, Ed had almost doubled the herd that Mont Allen had raised before Ed took over.

When Mont died eighteen months ago, the Bar M Ranch went to his daughter and only descendant, Kayla Dawn Allen-Clark. She'd selected Ed as the new manager, and placed control of the entire operation in his hands. Mont and Ed's father, Sparky, had been best friends for thirty-five years. Mont and Sparky built a cabin across a small meadow from Mont's huge old lodge, where Ed and his three brothers grew up. Mont's daughter, Kayla Dawn, grew up in the lodge, her mother having died when she was a toddler.

Since Kayla and Ed, two years apart in age, grew up together, they were inseparable during childhood. When she graduated from high school, Ed hoped to marry her. But Mont had other plans. He sent

Kayla to Brigham Young University and persuaded Ed to go to Arizona State. Ed agreed only when Mont promised that he would give his blessing and allow the young couple to marry when they graduated, if they still felt the same about one another.

After graduation, Ed and Kayla had just begun to plan their wedding when Kayla changed her mind. She had received a scholarship to continue her education in California, which she apparently wanted to do more than she wanted to marry Ed. With no choice in the matter, Ed had to put his love on a back burner until Kayla came to her senses and returned home. Unfortunately, she never did. She got her doctorates, went to work for a research company in San Diego, and married Joshua Bridger Clark, a Lieutenant Commander in the United States Navy.

Somewhere along the way, Kayla had decided that she and Ed were more like brother and sister, and that was the complete end of their romantic relationship.

Ed had accepted her decision, but he didn't know if he could ever love another woman like he loved Kayla.

A good share of the time Ed just felt angry inside. He often thought that a major portion of his reasons for living had been taken away from him. In addition to losing Kayla to another man, his Pa and Kayla's father had gone back to God. Within twelve months of their deaths, none of his three brothers lived at the ranch anymore. They all had different goals and significant others in their lives.

Now the only original resident at the Bar M was Ed. In less than a year, the Bar M had shrunk in population from six down to one, and Ed was lonely . . . and not getting any younger.

In turning the ranch over to his control, Kayla had given Ed a gift he had dreamed about all his life. But he soon realized that being the ranch foreman was a full time occupation, and he'd had little time to search for another woman to love. Even if he had found her, Ed still wasn't certain he could ever love anyone as much as he loved Kayla.

As he approached the camp, thoughts of Ms. Kendal and what had just transpired flooded over him. He'd been overwhelmed to discover a woman had jumped from that plane. *A beautiful, rash, irresponsible woman with impulsiveness stamped into her forehead!*

When Ed reached the bottom of Porcupine Ridge, he directed Breeze over to the camp. The only reason the men referred to the area as the camp was because Marcus, the lead man, liked to sleep outdoors most of the time, instead of back at the cabin, like the other men.

One tent and a couple of corrals were set up almost a mile west of the lodge and cabin. They were tucked into the southeast corner of Mountain Meadow which had some of the richest pasture grass in Ashley National Forest.

Marcus, one of the best ranch hands ever hired by Bar M, came out of the tent with a package of pancake mix when Ed arrived and dismounted.

"Morning, Boss," said Marcus. "You hungry for pancakes?"

"Nah," drawled Ed. Holding the reins in one hand, he rubbed his rock-hard belly with the other hand and winked at Marcus. He wasn't about to tell Marcus why his stomach was twisted in one big knot, so he teased instead. "Pompanoosuc porridge filled me right up."

"Don't know how you can eat that stuff, Boss," Marcus made a gesture of gagging. "Now, grits would have made a fine breakfast!"

"Don't know how you can eat grits," Ed smiled. "Tastes like paste to me."

Marcus gave him a broad-toothed smile in response.

"You won't need to fix Luke any pancakes yet. He's on an errand," Ed remarked. "But Sidekick may want some."

"I noticed the woman with Luke. Was she the jumper?"

Ed nodded. "Dang fool is more like it!" he barked. "She had planned to land on this side of Porcupine Ridge to surprise us, I suppose."

"That would have stirred up the cattle!"

"My sentiments exactly," Ed growled.

"You spoke to her about it?" Marcus asked, stirring the pancake mix and some milk together in a bowl.

"She could have got herself killed!" Ed complained with a nod of his head.

"I had a pleasant night," said Marcus, obviously hoping to change the topic of conversation.

Ed smiled, grateful for the reprieve. "Didn't freeze, hmm?"

"Nope. But it was a cold one. The stars were bright as lightning bugs, and the moon was just a skinny little splinter in the black sky. It was real pleasant out here."

"You could sleep at the cabin," Ed reminded. "There's always plenty of room."

"Yep, and I could have missed the stars, too." Marcus hesitated a moment, then said, "You know, Boss, if you bring in more cattle you're gonna' need to put in a regular bunk house."

"Yea, I know," Ed agreed. "I've been thinking about that. Guess we'll have to see how it all works out."

"You're already running double the herd Mont ever ran up here," observed Marcus.

"Aw," he drawled, "Kayla doesn't mind how many cattle I run, as long as the profits stay the same or better."

"Just like a woman," Marcus grinned.

"Ain't that the truth!" agreed Ed. "Which brings me to an important subject."

"What is it?" Marcus asked as he used a stick to move a few coals away from the fire. Then he put a heavy skillet on top of them, poured some vegetable oil in the pan, and spread it around with a spatula.

"You don't need to worry any more about going to Louisiana with your wife next week. Abbot called and said he'd come for the three weeks you're gone. He's bringing a couple of friends with him. Don't know that three men can take your place, but they're gonna' try."

Marcus smiled as he poured pancake batter into the frying pan. "Thanks, Boss. I know I put you in a bind. But I ain't had no summer vacation in the fifteen years I've been working here. I've always taken it over Christmas and January. I feel much better knowing Abbot will be here to help out."

"Abbot could never take your place," Ed complimented. "You're the best dang cowpoke next to Pa and Mont I've ever seen."

Marcus smiled. "Thanks, Boss. That means a lot to me."

"And stop calling me Boss," Ed bantered. "I ain't Mont. Just call me Ed, like you always have."

"It don't seem right!" Marcus lifted the edge of the large pancake with a spatula and looked at the underside.

"Nothing seems right anymore," Ed insisted. "But humor me, will you?"

Marcus smiled without agreeing to Ed's request, and Ed knew it was a losing battle. Then Marcus flipped the pancake over in midair and let it fall neatly back in the skillet. "You sure you don't want some of these?"

Ed declined the offer with, "I'd better get on up to the cabin. Don't want to keep Ms. Kendal waiting." He swung back up into the saddle, made a clicking sound, and lightly jabbed Breeze in the flank with his spurs. "Git up!" he barked.

Immediately Breeze responded. He galloped east toward the cabin. When Ed met up with Sidekick, headed in the opposite direction, Ed slowed down long enough to say, "Better hurry on over. Marcus is cooking your favorite breakfast."

Sidekick grinned and nodded. "Git up!" he yelled, spurring his horse to a full gallop.

When Ed and Breeze passed the lodge, they turned to the right and crossed the bridge in the middle of a small meadow that separated the lodge from the Sparkleman cabin. Breeze slowed to a trot under his master's hand until they reached the three-bedroom ranch-style cabin made with hand-hewn logs.

Ed tugged on the reins. "Whoa there, Breeze!" He swung down off the saddle and tied the reins onto a hitching post, then opened the front door and went inside.

Alyssa Kendal was seated on an old rocking chair in the living room, talking on the telephone. Luke stood nearby, hanging onto every word she spoke.

Opening a closet in the hall, Ed grabbed a handful of rope, harness and other climbing gear. He handed them to Luke and said gruffly, "See if you can get that expensive parachute of hers out of the trees and back here before her ride arrives."

"Sure thing, Boss." Luke put his hat on his head, took the climbing gear and left the cabin.

Then Ed turned to face Alyssa, who was just putting the phone in its cradle. "Well?" he growled.

"My friends will be here shortly to pick me up," she said with a tilt of her head, "but I'd like to speak with your employer before I leave. I'm sure Mr. Allen won't throw me out. Where will I find him?"

Realizing she didn't even know that Mont had died, Ed decided to have some fun with her. "Well, that depends on three things," he suggested.

"And those are?"

"Where Mont is, where you're going, and when you leave!"

"I would like to speak with him before I leave," she reminded. "Where is he? Up at the lodge?"

"Unless you're related to Kayla, I doubt you'll have an opportunity to speak with him until *after* you leave."

"Riddles?" she questioned. "I'm not a child, Mr. Sparkleman!"

"Oh," he frowned. "I hadn't noticed."

Although she gritted her teeth tightly, she did not voice a complaint at his inference. They stared at one another for several long minutes, and he was somewhat surprised to find her matching his anger. Since he wasn't the one who dropped out of the sky to disrupt her life, he wondered if she even had a clue how much worry she'd caused the men on the Bar M. He was certain that she didn't have any idea how long it would take him to relax the knot in his belly that she put there.

Finally Ed shrugged, realizing there was no way he could humor her. Begrudgingly he explained, "Mont Allen died eighteen months ago. His daughter, Kayla, now owns the Bar M, but she lives in San Diego. If you'd like her address I will provide it, then you can direct your questions to her. In the meantime, I run the ranch and my word is law. Until Kayla tells me otherwise, the Bar M Ranch is off limits to people like you who have no regard for human safety and no respect for private property."

She stood slowly and turned to face the window, putting her back to him. Her shoulders drooped and for a moment he felt sorry for her. Then she straightened and turned once again, this time to face him. The anger he had expected was gone, and for a moment he thought he saw moisture in her sorrowful brown eyes.

"I apologize," she said in a soft whisper. "I guess I wasn't thinking. I have no excuse for my behavior."

Ed felt a smile forming, but held it in reserve. To his dismay, he found himself softening. When the silence became almost unbearable, he finally said, "I accept your apology."

Apparently encouraged by that, Alyssa went on, "It's just that when I heard about Mountain Meadow and studied it on a topographical map at the courthouse, I wanted to see it up close and personal. I didn't realize that I could have scared your cattle." She stopped, bit her lower lip, then looked straight at him as she whispered, "It's every bit as beautiful as I'd heard."

To his surprise, he saw no effort on her part to charm anything from him. Her apology was completely unexpected, and he felt awkward for having scolded her. But that didn't prevent him from saying, "In the future, maybe you'll contact land owners privately, before you start jumping onto their land." He gave her an uneasy smile, hoping she'd consider it a truce, of sorts.

Her response was a hopeful promise. "I will! Is there some way I can repay you for all your trouble? For rescuing me, and having Luke get my parachute for me?"

"Lady," Ed laughed, teasing her. "You haven't got enough money to repay me for all the trouble you've caused today."

Her eyes widened and he wondered for a moment if she was going to cry. Then he discerned that she didn't know him well enough to realize he had spoken in jest.

To his amazement, she held her head proudly and asked, "Then I wonder if I may inconvenience you further by asking for bathroom privileges?"

He nodded, concerned that she might misinterpret any other response he might give her. "Second door on the left."

"Thank you," she whispered and slipped down the hall.

Ed let out a long, ragged breath of frustration. Alyssa Kendal was one powerful woman! Though he doubted she realized it, she could make his world turn on end, and his life miserable until the moment he saw her drive away. *She's impetuous and irresponsible!* he reminded himself. Yet even as he did, his heart whispered, *and she's absolutely beautiful!*

Ed Sparkleman was a practical man. He made it a personal policy to think through everything he said and did. To his detriment, this habit cost him dearly in terms of friendships with others. Although he hated to admit it, Ed was actually quite shy.

It was difficult to talk to a woman and Alyssa was no exception. The ease he felt whenever he was around Kayla was one of the reasons why he loved her so much, he supposed. They'd grown up together, which made talking to Kayla completely natural. Thinking of something appropriate to say calmly to Alyssa became a major problem and Ed felt his palms sweat just thinking about her.

He walked over near the front door and studied his reflection in the mirror next to it. Ed had a lean, tall, almost gaunt look about him, like his father, Sparky. But if they had similar body structures, that's where the resemblance ended. Ed's sand-colored hair was longer on top than on the sides, but it was often hidden beneath a Stetson that was almost the same color.

His emerald eyes changed shades depending on his mood. Happy times found his eyes bright green. Somber, angry feelings changed his eyes to a deep gray-green. This feature usually made his emotions readable. Through the years he'd learned to camouflage his emotions, especially since Kayla called off their engagement years ago. He wasn't about to let another woman read anything from his expression-filled eyes, not if he could help it.

He put on a look of complete resolve, an unflinching, firm, determined look, and noticed the color in his eyes turn almost gray-green. *That's it,* he decided. *That's the look I want to give Alyssa Kendal just before she leaves.*

It was almost half an hour before Alyssa came back into the living room. The first thing he noticed was that she'd been crying, though he hadn't heard her from the living room. It surprised him, and made him feel ashamed that he'd chastised her so severely.

She had removed the parachute jump suit, brushed her hair and washed her face, apparently trying to wash away the tell-tale signs of her tears. It was to no avail for her eyes were still puffy and red. The bump on her forehead had almost faded though, and she wore a pair of navy leggings and a light blue, combed cotton shirt with a belt over it that accentuated her slender figure.

Ed's feelings of shame were quickly replaced by an almost overwhelming sensation of desire. It was all he could do not to whistle. To diminish Alyssa's tempting influence upon him, he reminded himself that he'd always preferred blondes like Kayla; though it did little good to deny that Alyssa enticed him in ways he would never admit, even to himself.

"Feeling better?" he asked somewhat awkwardly.

Alyssa nodded. "I used your hair brush. I hope you won't be mad at me for that."

A smile of tenderness and compassion escaped onto his face before he could prevent it. "Not at all."

She stepped past him and looked out the window. "My ride should be here any minute."

When she turned back to face him again, a strained silence came between them. He couldn't think of anything to say, so he went into the kitchen and put some water in a kettle. "Would you like some sassafras tea?" he asked.

Just then a car honked outside and she shook her head. "Evidently not. That's my ride," she said. "Thank you again."

"You're welcome," he said gruffly. Then, "Where shall we send your parachute?"

"The business name and address is on it," she answered. "Just send it there. When it arrives, I'll reimburse you for your trouble."

Ed nodded, put the kettle on the stove, but did not turn it on. Then he followed her like a lost puppy as she stepped out onto the porch, carrying her jump suit and helmet with her. He noticed that her warm brown hair glistened with golden highlights in the morning sun as she stepped out into the meadow. It took every ounce of control he had to prevent himself from reaching out and stroking it with his rugged hand.

The man and woman who'd come for Ms. Kendal had parked their car at the lodge, so she had to walk across the meadow and over the bridge to reach it.

Ed walked beside her, silent yet observant. A strange aching settled inside his chest and he wondered if he should say something. Anything!

Sure! You tell her to go and never come back, and now you don't want her to leave? he asked himself, completely overwhelmed by the gamut of emotions coursing through him.

Just before she reached the car, she turned and looked up at him. Her dark brown eyes glistened as she gave him a wide, flirtatious smile. Suddenly he realized that her expression wasn't intended to be coy at all, as he had originally thought. It was simply . . . Alyssa Kendal's smile! She probably gave the same expression to her parents.

An amused grin wandered across his face in response, and he was powerless to stop it. The look he had wanted to give Alyssa Kendal just before she left was certainly not the look that she got.

Ed couldn't stop thinking about Alyssa's smile the rest of the day.

Chapter Two

"Don't ever ask me to help you again!" Mike yelled as soon as the car was past the cabin and out of hearing range.

"I'm sorry," Alyssa said. "It was a poor decision."

"It wasn't a decision at all," Mike glared at her from the driver's seat. "It was your capricious nature! No wonder your grandfather refuses to let you jump Bald Mountain! I swear, Alyssa, you've got to learn to control yourself before you end up getting yourself killed! What if your parachute hadn't opened?"

"But it did."

"What if—" he began again.

She interrupted with, "I'd have used the secondary. I still had a minute or two of free-fall left."

Mike shook his head. "Alyssa, I don't know what gets into that head of yours, but if you weren't a woman, I'd turn you over my knee."

"Mike's right," said Shauna, agreeing with her husband. "I thought your accepting Abbot's marriage proposal was rash, but this! This takes the cake, Alyssa."

"I'm sorry!" Alyssa offered once again.

"If I'd known you were going to parachute out, I would never have flown the plane!" Mike growled. "You said you just wanted to get aerial photographs."

"I'm a good jumper," Alyssa insisted. "It wasn't my fault that the parachute release jammed."

Alyssa sat in the back seat, while Mike and Shauna Roberts sat in front, with Mike maneuvering the rental car down the rugged mountain road.

Mike and Alyssa had been best friends since third grade. For years Mike had tried to find someone special for Alyssa, and she'd tried to find someone for him. But neither of them cared much for the other's choices. Although both of them dated, it was always sporadic. Most men Alyssa's age thought she was Mike's girl, while the girls her age fawned so much over him that Alyssa finally refused to set them up with him anymore. She had to admit that being best buddies had put some restrictions on their dating other people. They never considered themselves sweethearts; they just liked each other's company to the exclusion of everyone else.

Until Shauna came into their lives.

The first day Shauna arrived at A & M Aviation, the paraglider pilot school that Alyssa and Mike owned together, Alyssa knew immediately that Shauna and Mike were meant for each other. There was a strong attraction between them, and when they married, Alyssa thought their match had been made in heaven.

Fortunately for Alyssa, there was no jealousy in Shauna, and she had accepted Alyssa as her best friend, too. Alyssa genuinely loved Shauna, and was thrilled that Mike had finally found someone, while Shauna seemed to care about Alyssa just as much. Whenever she wasn't working, Alyssa spent a lot of her spare time with Mike and Shauna. As a threesome, they were almost inseparable. Although Mike and Shauna were still playing cupid in Alyssa's behalf, the only one who came close, so far, was Abbot.

When they arrived at the airport, Alyssa paid for the rental car, presented their flight plan, then met Mike and Shauna out at the Cessna. They were both sitting in the back seats. "You're not flying?" she asked Mike.

"Not on your life!"

"Not even as my co-pilot?"

"No," he refused. "At least if you're flying solo I won't have to worry about you jumping out again!"

Alyssa gave him a severe frown. "Since my parachute is back at the Bar M Ranch, I don't think I'll jump anymore today."

"You'd find a way!" came his final argument.

Smiling, Alyssa climbed onto the pilot's seat. She was actually glad to take full control of the plane. Whenever Mike joined her in the Cessna, he always expected her to co-pilot for him, and she often conceded just to humor him. Perhaps her parachute stunt had gained her one advantage.

Alyssa had to admit that the episode with the parachute did not make her partner or his wife very happy. For several days after they returned to A & M Aviation near Wanship, Mike took every opportunity he could find to tell her how displeased he was with her.

&& &&

In Summit County between Coalville and Wanship, is a stretch of the greenest alfalfa fields in all of Utah. Water is obtained from nearby Rockport Reservoir through a series of irrigation canals and sprinkler systems that keep the verdant valley moist and breathtakingly beautiful.

Upon a large acreage almost in the middle of the valley, nestled between Lewis and Alexander Canyons, at the foot of the eastern slope of Porcupine Peak, there's a small, private airstrip with an older airplane hangar and a newer two-story building where Alyssa and Mike teach pilot training school for paraglider safety, use and deployment.

From April through September they maintain a tight schedule, working Tuesdays through Saturdays, and some Monday afternoons, as well. The rest of the year A & M remained busy with paraglider classes in preparation for spring, and in catalog sales of paraglider equipment.

On the foothills just above A & M Aviation, a dirt road led up to the jump site, where paraglider flights were launched. The area had three house thermals, reliable updrafts of warm air that facilitated great altitudes for paraglider pilots.

A & M Aviation was all that Alyssa had lived for the past few years, and she loved the freedom of having her own apartment, even though it was upstairs, above the flight school. It saved on auto expenses because she didn't have to drive to work, but it also made her feel shut in sometimes.

Alyssa was looking forward to the next few weeks. Regardless of Mike and Shauna's efforts in trying to find "Mr. Right" for her, she was now engaged to Abbot, and hoping, albeit half-heartedly, that she would find happiness with him. Although her partner and his wife had doubled their efforts to substantiate how wrong she was to accept Abbot's proposal, they hadn't been able to prove conclusively that the union wouldn't work.

Now Alyssa had an opportunity to find out for herself if she and Abbot had something special going or not. With some trepidation, yet also with a heart filled with hope, she packed her overnight bag early Saturday morning, before she went downstairs to work.

To her delight, Alyssa managed to slip away early from A & M Aviation, enabling her to spend time with her parents in Heber City, Utah, before Abbot would arrive. Although she lived above A & M, she usually went to her parents' home every third weekend if she could break away early enough on Saturday to do so. During winter, it was easy to close by six. But business picked up in June, so Alyssa often visited her parents just for Sunday dinner during the summer months. This weekend, however, she was expecting Abbot to arrive with his best friend from California, and her parents had generously offered them the use of their spare bedrooms.

She stopped by the photo shop and picked up the package of photographs she'd taken from the airplane just before parachuting onto the Bar M last Monday. Then she drove straight over to her parents' home and went upstairs to unpack. Afterward, she stretched out on her bed. Her mother insisted it was still Alyssa's bedroom, with just a few changes in color scheme since she'd moved out. She pushed the pillows aside, then she spread the photographs out carefully. She wanted to make certain she could identify where everything on the Bar M was located so she wouldn't be embarrassed by anything that Ed Sparkleman threw at her when she arrived with Abbot on Wednesday. Surely Ed wouldn't throw her out if Abbot was with her. After all, Abbot and Ed were brothers.

When Abbot had telephoned a few days ago, offering her a three week stay at the Bar M, she had jumped at the chance. The idea of working with Abbot and his friend as ranch hands had intrigued her, and had ultimately sent her on a photographing journey to capture the Bar M on film from the air. She'd hoped to present Abbot's brother with the photos, but since her surprise landing had antagonized Ed, she doubted she would even bring them with her.

A tear slipped down her cheek as she remembered how harshly Ed had scolded her. She had acted recklessly, but she hadn't expected him to rebuke her like she was some helpless, dim-witted child. Perhaps she should have waited for Abbot to introduce them rather than the way she'd chosen to meet Ed.

Abbot had shared so many stories about Ed Sparkleman that she felt she'd known him all her life, though he hadn't mentioned Ed's obstinate streak. The opportunity to meet the hero of Abbot's childhood had completely occupied her thoughts lately. She wanted to know Ed better and was convinced that, if he allowed himself time to get to know her, he might be surprised. He might even like her.

As she spread the photographs out on the bed, she studied them diligently. Examining each one, she recalled some of the things Abbot had told her: The Bar M Ranch, the largest piece of private property within the boundaries of Ashley National Forest, lay between Dry Fork and Black Canyon Creek in a meadow surrounded by a forest of tall pines and stands of quaking aspen trees. The lodge, built entirely of hand-hewn logs, was the largest of the buildings at the Bar M, and had a wide porch on the main level that was protected from rain storms by a deck off the second level. In front of the lodge lay an open expanse of meadow with fences around the perimeter and a corral in one corner. A small stream ran diagonally across the meadow with a wooden bridge crossing over it. A footpath led from the lodge to the cabin.

In the photograph she also saw a Jersey cow grazing in the meadow. It seemed strange that she didn't remember seeing the cow after arriving at the cabin. She'd walked across the meadow, but had no recollection of anything but her desire to get into the car and leave. At the time, she'd only been aware of Ed Sparkleman and his anger towards her and, in her desire to escape, had failed to notice anything in front of her but the rental car.

A springhouse lay almost hidden in the trees behind the lodge. Fresh watercress grew along the edges of a small creek formed by excess spring water that was diverted down the mountain to the meadow stream.

Beyond the meadow, interspersed among clumps of quaking aspens, the taller spruce and pine trees stretched toward the sky like taut, thin soldiers in lackadaisical formation. West and a little south of the meadow, a summer garden had been started, and rows of peas were already clearly in view.

Not far from the Sparkleman cabin stood a large old barn housing two rows of stables, just as Abbot had indicated. There was also a row of smaller sheds connected together. Abbot had told her these housed a jersey cow, pigs, and chickens. Behind the sheds, she could see an area that had been fenced in where the pigs and chickens could get adequate sunshine. Abbot said the Sparklemans raised, whenever possible, a good share of the food that the Bar M Ranch needed.

To the east side of the lodge was a large helipad painted with a red 'X'. A helicopter rested on it. Alyssa had to admit that she was surprised when she first saw the helicopter. Not until she'd gone across the meadow and had reached the car had she realized the helicopter had a name. Painted on the door was a sheriff's badge, and the words below it read, "Li'l Posse."

Uintah County maintained half of the long dirt road that ran along Dry Fork and led down to Highway 121 near Maeser, a tight little community meshed against the northwest edge of Vernal. From the halfway point up the mountain, where the winding road connected to the Bar M Ranch, the maintenance became the Bar M's responsibility.

Alyssa put the photographs in a row across the bed in the order they were taken. She could see that from Pine Bluff Ridge at the southeast, a clear view could be seen of the Bar M Ranch, the lodge, meadow, barns, and part of the Sparkleman cabin. Across the meadow and behind the lodge about four hundred yards up the mountainside, there was a break in the pines and a small clearing big enough for a large home or a bunkhouse perhaps. She could see the power and phone lines running parallel to the dirt road that led to the Bar M Ranch, and remembered that Abbot had told her Lamont Allen had run electricity to the property some time ago.

She took one last glance at Mountain Meadow and Porcupine Ridge west of the lodge, then gathered up the photographs and put them neatly back in the package, hoping Abbot wouldn't be too upset with her when she told him about the parachute incident last Monday. If he was, it would add one more problem to their troubled relationship.

Alyssa was still so confused about Abbot, she hardly knew what to do. Every night and every morning she would ask the Lord if she should marry Abbot, but she was beginning to think that the heavens were closed.

Mike and Shauna thought Alyssa's acceptance of Abbot's proposal was an act of total desperation, but the truth was less complicated than that! Abbot had caught her off guard, and on a capricious whim she'd said yes.

She seemed to get into a lot of trouble whenever she failed to think things through. The parachute incident and her engagement to Abbot were both good examples of that.

Impetuous Alyssa just couldn't bring herself to admit that she and Abbot were a bad match from the start. Now she worried how she could ever go through with the wedding when she wasn't sure that she loved Abbot. She liked him, that was certain, but love?

Unable to come to any conclusions, Alyssa put her thoughts away and went downstairs to help her mother prepare the noon meal. She'd wanted to let her thoughts wander another direction, to consider all the events that had transpired at the Bar M the day she dropped out of the sky to disrupt one disgruntled ranch foreman and his likeable ranch hands, but she'd promised her mother some assistance.

Mrs. Kendal smiled warmly when Alyssa came into the kitchen. "I was beginning to wonder if you'd make it."

"I try to keep my promises," said Alyssa. She gave her mother a gentle kiss on the cheek. "Shall I peel the potatoes?"

"That would be a big help," Mrs. Kendal agreed. "Oh, Alyssa, I'm so excited to finally meet your Abbot."

Alyssa put the potatoes in the sink and reached for the peeler. While she peeled the potato skins off, she said, "You'll love him, Mom. He's intelligent and handsome and . . ." she hesitated, suddenly remembering. "Did I tell you he was bringing a friend with him?"

"Yes, dear. A Mr. Clark, wasn't it?"

Alyssa nodded. "Hans Bridger Clark. He and Abbot were very close while at the University of Utah. Hans is some sort of college career man. He's got more degrees than Abbot has brothers."

"Do you suppose Abbot will get a job soon? There's not much call for an archaeologist, is there?" Her mother winked.

"You're kidding!" Alyssa exclaimed. She realized that was exactly what Mrs. Kendal was doing when she saw a sly smile form on her mother's lips. "He's had three job offers already. The only reason he hasn't accepted any of them is because he wants to work over at the dinosaur dig near Vernal. That way, he'll be near his brothers and the Bar M."

"Well, at least Vernal isn't so far away that we wouldn't get to see the grandchildren often." Mrs. Kendal grinned. "I would just die if you moved to the East coast like your sister did. I want to spend all the time I can with you and your family."

"Oh, Mom, I love the Vernal area. And the ranch! It's . . ." she hesitated. She hadn't told her mother about her escapade earlier in the week. She amended her comment to, "Abbot says it's the greatest place on earth to raise a family."

"But you won't be living on the ranch, will you?" Mrs. Kendal asked.

"I don't know yet. Abbot wanted to talk to his brother about that."

Alyssa put the peeled potatoes into a pot of salted water on the stove and turned it on. Meanwhile, her mother rolled out a batch of biscuits and cut them into rounds, then slid them onto a baking sheet. Alyssa dried her hands and took a pinch of the biscuit dough, then popped it into her mouth. "Mmm, it's delicious!"

"Alyssa!" Mrs. Kendal complained. "That can't be healthy!"

"Why not? We eat the exact same thing after it's baked."

Her mother shook her head. "You and your bread dough," she mumbled. "I may as well give up trying. You started that habit when you were two years old, and you haven't changed a bit in all these years."

"What time will Dad be home?" Alyssa asked, hoping to change the subject.

"In another half hour."

"Shall I set the table?"

"That would be lovely." Mrs. Kendal said. "Use the china, please dear."

"It's not a special occasion."

"Of course it is, Alyssa. You're home."

Alyssa smiled and gave her mother a quick hug. "Thanks!"

Within a few minutes Alyssa had placed the china on the table, arranged the silverware and napkins, and stepped to the garden to gather the first of the summer roses. The heavenly fragrance of lavender roses filled the air as she walked out to her mother's garden.

Alyssa couldn't remember a time in her life when roses didn't grace her family home, and she cherished the scent. Even her grandmother had roses such as these, only in far greater abundance, and the memories of cutting fresh roses for Sunday dinner with Grandma Mae, at times when she spent the weekend with her grandparents, almost brought tears to her eyes. If she missed Grandma Mae this much, then how much more did Granddad miss her, she wondered to herself.

As she cut a few of the most brilliant blossoms, she forced her mind away from her grandparents, and wandered it over to the Bar M Ranch. The differences between Ed and Abbot Sparkleman were evident, she thought. Abbot, usually sensitive to her feelings, had never scolded her the way his brother had. So far in their relationship, she'd never seen Abbot angry. His fuse must be much longer, and for this she felt grateful. She had to admit that both men were handsome. Ed had sparkling green eyes, very similar to Abbot's, but the resemblance ended there. Abbot's dark brown hair and his heavy beard were almost black, and came from his father, he'd said. He often shaved twice a day. Abbot was also shorter than Ed by two or three inches, a little more round somehow, but certainly not heavy. Ed was tall and lean, almost to the point of being gaunt, but he had plenty of muscle in all the right places, a fact she'd noticed almost immediately.

Alyssa shrugged. She could never love a man like Ed. She'd seen a mean streak in him, and she didn't like it. Not one bit! She remembered that Ed had softened a little after she apologized. And he had finally smiled at her before she got in the car to go home. Perhaps she shouldn't judge Ed too harshly. After all, he was soon to become her brother-in-law.

That last thought seemed to bother her more than any other.

❧ ❧

By evening, Alyssa's stomach felt like it was tied in knots. She'd been nervous all day about Abbot arriving, and the nearer it came to the expected hour, the more apprehensive she became. Resolutely, she decided to put forth her best effort at loving Abbot, regardless of the doubts in her mind. Perhaps she was making too much of the romantic notions in her head about how a relationship evolves. She had not given herself time for love to grow, and now she resolved that she would do her best to remedy that.

When a silver Accura pulled into the driveway and parked, Alyssa felt a sudden rush of adrenaline that had nothing to do with excitement: fear came to mind immediately. As Abbot got out of the car and headed up the front walk, Alyssa rushed down the front steps and into his arms, forcing her panic away. After a tender embrace, he released her and turned her around. "Alyssa, this is Hans Bridger Clark, the man I told you about."

"Pleased to meet you," she said, holding out her hand.

Hans shook it vigorously. "Well, Alyssa, I see now why Abbot has a one-track mind lately. He said you were lovely, but he didn't say just how lovely you really are."

"Thank you." She blushed under Hans' steady gaze.

Hans seemed a likeable man whose smile and easy manner dispelled any concern she may have had regarding him. He also had perfectly straight white teeth, light blue eyes, and chestnut colored hair. Taller than Abbot by at least six inches, he was also more handsome than Alyssa had thought a man with four doctorates could be. She'd expected some socially inept or unattractive type who'd spent his entire career gaining more education than one person would ever need. She was surprised, and pleased, to see that Hans was dashingly handsome.

❧ ❧

Later that night, when Abbot and Alyssa finally had some time alone together, they sat outside on a patio glider. The scent of roses from the garden wafted over them, wrapping them in nostalgia. It seemed the perfect setting for Alyssa to tell her fiancé about her visit with his brother.

"I love your hair like this," Abbot said, stroking her bobbed, brown locks.

Alyssa just had her hair cut in the style he liked. In her opinion, it looked like someone had put a bowl over her head and cut off all the hair that stuck out from beneath it. This didn't seem to matter to Abbot, and she wanted to please him, so she said nothing regarding her own preference. She even knew what his next words would be, and she was not surprised to hear him say, "You should always wear it this way for me."

He held her hand as he inhaled the cool night air. "You know," he said. "I've missed this."

"Heber City air?" she asked in surprise.

"No. Mountain air. You can almost smell it from here."

"I think it's better when you're really in the mountains. Like up at the Bar M Ranch." She hoped her statement was subtle enough to lead into her confession.

"You won't believe the air at the Bar M!" Abbot exclaimed. "It's crisp and clear! You can almost taste it."

"I know," she said simply.

"I'm sure you've been up in the mountains before," Abbot continued. "But way up, miles into the back country, it's practically unspoiled by man."

"I was at the Bar M last Monday," she admitted in a soft whisper.

"You were?" The surprise on his face indicated her statement would need some elaboration.

"Yes. I . . . have a confession to make."

He arched an eyebrow. "Then make it," he said flatly.

"Mike, Shauna and I flew over the Bar M in the Cessna to take some photographs. Then I . . . parachuted in."

"Do you think that was wise?" The sharp tone of his voice told her that he was annoyed. It was the first time she'd ever seen a hint of anger in him.

"No." She shook her head, making her brown hair swirl about her face. "It was an unwise decision," she whispered. "I'm sorry if I've disappointed you." Her brown eyes filled with fluid and slipped down her cheeks.

Abbot softened almost immediately. He took a handkerchief from his pocket and wiped her tears away. "It couldn't have been as bad as all that," he suggested.

"It was worse!" she exclaimed. "Your brother was so angry with me that I didn't have the nerve to tell him about us. He practically threw me off the Bar M and told me I was never to come back!" Suddenly the feelings Ed had evoked within her came rushing up inside and she was unable to stop the tears from spilling faster. "He still thinks I'm some irresponsible, reckless trespasser."

Abbot put his arms about her and pulled her close while she rested her head against his shoulder. "He'll get over it," he soothed. "His bark is much worse than his bite. I assure you, Alyssa. He's much nicer once you get to know him. What did you do? Stampede the herd?"

"No!" she pouted. "Though he insisted I could have."

"He's right about that," said Abbot. "He used to be kinder when I was young, but he's changed since Kayla. . . ." He left the sentence open.

"The woman who owns the Bar M?"

Abbot nodded. "Hans' sister-in-law. I told you Kayla married Hans' twin brother, Joshua."

"Yes, of course," she responded. "But what do you mean, he's changed since Kayla?"

"Nine or ten years ago, Ed and Kayla were engaged," Abbot explained. "Ed was crazy about her. He really had it bad! Anyway, Kayla came home from college the same year he did. They planned to marry, ordered the wedding invitations, even filled them all out together. A few days later, Mont told him not to mail the announcements. He said Kayla received a scholarship to get her doctorate in California, and she was going to accept it."

"Didn't she love him?" Alyssa asked.

"I suppose she did, at first. Later she decided she loved him like he was her brother, not her sweetheart."

"What a terrible thing to do to him."

"Yes, it was. But he carried that torch around with him until the day Pa died in that avalanche."

"Speaking of which, you didn't tell me that Kayla's father died, too."

"Didn't I?" he asked. "It must have slipped my mind. Lamont Allen was a great man. Everyone called him Mont. He was best buddies with Pa. They did practically everything together. Sorry I forgot to tell you."

"Your brother did," she admitted. "There I was, demanding to speak to Mr. Allen, and he'd passed away eighteen months ago."

"I'll bet that went over well," said Abbot. He sighed wearily, then added, "That was the worst Christmas we'd ever had. And Ed was right there in the thick of it. All in one swoop Pa is killed, Mont dies, and

Kayla tells him their relationship is familial. The strain nearly killed him."

"How awful," offered Alyssa. "No wonder he's such a bitter man."

"He has some pretty good reasons," Abbot confessed. "About the same time as the avalanche, he learned that our brother, Tom, was the man who'd raped Mont's housekeeper, Morning Sun. As the oldest son, Ed not only had to arrange for both funerals, be the executor of Pa's estate, and give Kayla away at her wedding, he also had to confront Tom about Morning Sun. Man, it was awful for him. I don't know how he did it."

"Then Ed never loved anyone but Kayla?"

"Never." Abbot shook his head. "He says he's accepted the fact that their relationship is familial. But I've noticed a time or two when he still struggles with it, especially when he thinks no one is watching."

"Do you think he'll ever fall in love with someone else?"

"I know he wants to, but I think he's afraid he'll get burned again."

"How terrible for him. I never realized he had so much bitterness heaped upon him. No wonder he was cross with me."

Abbot pulled her even closer and she longed for feelings that simply would not come. He didn't press for more, and she didn't offer. She resigned herself to feeling content within the security of Abbot's strong arms.

❧ ❧

Later that night, Alyssa thought about Abbot and their conversation. She felt safe with Abbot, wasn't that enough for now? Couldn't love grow between them if she allowed herself some patience?

The problem was that Alyssa wanted absolutes! And she wanted them right now!

Admitting that she was impetuous did nothing to dissuade the feelings within her. Something between Abbot and herself felt wrong, but she didn't know what it was, or what to do about it.

Before falling asleep, her thoughts wandered to Ed Sparkleman, and the glimpse Abbot had given her of what it was like in Ed's world. She didn't like what she'd seen. Ed was a man haunted by memories of a lost love from which he may never escape. The thought made her feel empty somehow, though she couldn't have explained her feelings. Something else surprised her as well. She felt a strange empathy towards Ed Sparkleman that hadn't seemed possible just a few hours earlier.

When Alyssa finally fell asleep, she found herself entrenched in visions of two faceless men with green eyes. They were both laughing at her, though neither made any sound. Startled, she awakened to find her body drenched in sweat, and terrified from the dream once again. Would these horrible nightmares never end?

Chapter Three

*E*arly Monday morning, Alyssa left her parents' home and drove directly to A & M Aviation. She was not surprised to see her grandfather, Alexander Turner, already out in the oat field near A & M, moving the water main to change directions of the massive sprinkler system. After waving to him, she parked the car on the south side of the two-story building near the office.

Alexander promptly left his work and joined Alyssa at the edge of the tarmac. His silver hair seemed to turn almost white as the morning sun peeked over the top of the eastern mountains and enveloped him. A & M Aviation and her grandfather's fields were the first in the valley to receive the morning sun.

"Good morning, Maisey. How's my favorite pilot?" His gravelly voice betrayed his age, as did his silver hair, but his frame was still rugged and sturdy as ever.

Alyssa gave him her brightest smile. She loved it when he called her by her nickname, Maisey. Her grandfather had created it for her more than two decades ago, although Maisey was just a shorter version of the original, and much longer, variation of it, which embarrassed her so much he rarely mentioned it in public. Smiling to herself, she recalled the nickname fondly: *Maisey, Daisey, Shmuckle and Roo; Maisey, Daisey, Granddad loves you!* "Granddad!" she exclaimed as she gave him a vigorous hug. "You always say I'm your favorite pilot!"

"Well, it's true. I taught you everything I know." He winked and his sparkling brown eyes smiled with him. "I missed you at church yesterday."

"I went with Mom and Dad. Sorry."

"At least you went," he grinned. "Now, if you'd said you stayed home without a good reason, I would begin to worry."

"I'll never do that!" she vowed solemnly. "At least not this week!" Then Alyssa laughed with him as he realized she was teasing him.

"Are you going to punch holes in the sky today?" he asked, changing the subject.

"Of course," she answered. "It's Monday morning. Where else would I be?"

"Where's your beau?"

"Abbot and Hans are going jet skiing at Jordanelle Reservoir today."

"Not going up in the air with you, hmm?"

"We couldn't talk Hans into it. He says he likes boats on the water or solid earth under his feet, but he doesn't care much for flying."

"I guess jet skiing has it's own pleasures," he nodded, "although I can't imagine it taking precedence over flying."

"Me, neither," she agreed. Changing the subject, Alyssa asked, "When will you take me to Bald Mountain for my parachute jump?"

Alexander Turner shook his head, but she could still see the amusement in his flashing brown eyes. "I'm not any more keen on that idea than I was twenty years ago, when you were still a toddler."

"Then you should never have told me about it, and you should never have taken Mike. It's not fair to protect me from something that you've both done safely several times."

Alexander only smiled. "Someone has to protect you, Maisey, particularly from yourself."

"It's okay," she insisted bravely, though she would never tell him how much his refusal always rankled her. "I'll wave to you, okay?"

"Do that!" he exclaimed. "I'll watch for you. And say good morning to your grandmother for me."

She gave him a kiss on the cheek. "I always do, Granddad. See you later."

The tradition she had started with Mike, and later Shauna, was to spend the first few hours every Monday in the summer, flying paragliders as a threesome for the pure pleasure of it, with no students and no concerns about inexperienced pilots.

By nine in the morning, Alyssa stood at the top of the ridge northwest of A & M Aviation ready to begin her flight. Her paraglider was the most beautiful of all of them, she decided, as she fastened her chest harness and leg straps, put on her helmet and pulled the toggles that controlled the guide lines.

She had learned to make other paraglider canopies with special patterns, rather than just the traditional rainbow panels that most companies sold. Her designs had been a major part of their catalog sales during the last year or two, and she had to admit that it was no longer just a side business. Alyssa designed the pattern for her paraglider's canopy herself, with soft silvers and varying shades of blues, and threads of silver woven into the fabric. The design was similar to a pair of elegant wings, beautiful enough for the most discriminating angel. *If angels really have wings!* she thought to herself.

Then Alyssa noticed the air pockets on the canopy were beginning to fill. The sun had reached the mountain top an hour or two earlier, and had driven the cool air down as it heated it. Then, as the warm air current moved upward, it gave Alyssa the opportunity to do what she enjoyed more than anything else: pilot her paraglider.

Within a few minutes, the warmer air created an updraft, or inverted funnel which was known as a thermal, that soon swirled upward strong enough to begin her flight. The eastern ridge below Porcupine Peak from which Alyssa and her friends always took flight had three natural house thermals, pockets of upward moving air that could nearly always be depended upon for steady, dependable canopy lifts and lengthy flights. The first house thermal was centered near a bend in the mountain between Alexander Canyon and Spring Creek, while the other two thermals were around the bend, adjacent to the exposed southeasterly ridges, directly above her grandfather's alfalfa and oat fields.

Annually, Granddad Turner rotated crops. This year, one alfalfa field came into view first after rounding the bend, then the oat field, and the second alfalfa field was beyond it.

"You go first," said Mike through his helmet radio. "I've got to help Shauna with her harness. Something's tangled."

"You want me to wait?" asked Alyssa.

"No. We'll be out there in a few minutes."

"Okay," Alyssa said. Then she stepped forward quickly, letting the warm air current lift the paraglider up in the air, and jumped off the edge of the ridge, which gave her an immediate rush of adrenaline. She squealed in delight and yelled, "Grandma, this one's for you!"

Within moments the wind was whisking past her in a strong and steady stream, and she was flying once again. The paraglider settled into the main house thermal, and seemed to come alive within the constant upward air flow.

She watched the canopy for a few minutes, making sure that it was getting enough wind, and smiled to herself at how startling blue the sky looked above it.

Immediately, she was filled with the sensation that her grandmother had joined her on the flight, and soared right next to her once again.

Shortly after Grandma Turner died, six years ago, Alyssa thought she could never have any sweeter memories than those from her childhood, spending the weekend, picking roses together, making honey candy. But now she realized she'd grown closer to the endearing woman up here in the sky. This strange sensation had come about as a direct result of flying her paraglider, with Grandma Mae's spirit at her side. Sometimes she felt Grandma's purpose in flying beside her was to watch over her and protect her. These experiences came frequently, nearly every Monday during the summer.

Alyssa wondered what would happen if she reached out and touched her grandmother. Would she be able to feel her grandmother's hand once again?

"I love you, Grandma," whispered Alyssa.

In her heart, she heard her grandmother whisper back, "*I love you, too, dear.*"

Because she was the middle child, her grandparents had done more than their fair share of spoiling Alyssa, though Grandma was always quick to point out, "She's not spoiled. She's just well-loved." Of course, Alyssa had no doubt that they doted on her siblings, Alexandria and Allin, just as much.

She rounded the bend, searching for the second thermal in order to give her friends space in the first one. As she came around the mountain, the alfalfa field below was more green than she had ever remembered seeing it before. Her grandfather, still at work, looked up and waved at her, and she reciprocated.

"You'd better hurry," Alyssa said through her helmet transmitter. "Granddad's fields are like a heavenly green carpet, and I'm an angel floating over them. The colors are so vibrant! Get out here!"

"I'm coming now!" laughed Shauna excitedly, and the sound of her enthusiasm echoed in the radio system built into Alyssa's helmet.

"I don't know why it thrills me like this every time," Alyssa said. "You'd think with the hundreds of times I've been out here, I would tire of flying."

"Same here!" Then Shauna squealed in delight as the first drop, and the accompanying surge of air that lifted her, gave her an adrenalin surge. Shauna was in flight. Her excitement, unrestrained, could be heard in her happy voice.

Alyssa pulled on the toggles, controlling the movement of the canopy until she was well away from the mountain and could see back to the bend from which she'd come. Then she watched as Shauna's rainbow colored canopy lifted and curved for a perfect flight. The rainbow colors were vibrant. *Almost alive*, thought Alyssa.

Slipping into the third house thermal, giving space for Shauna to maneuver to the second thermal, Alyssa rounded and made another complete circle. Below her, Alyssa could see her grandfather's fields and two-story white farm home, as well as his rose garden in full bloom. Various shades of roses from the palest pinks to the deepest reds, peaches, yellows and lavenders graced the garden, and Alyssa was never more astounded at how brilliant the colors seemed than that very moment. How Alyssa loved her grandparents' rose garden! Now that Grandmother was with God, it seemed that Granddad tended it with a passionate fervor unequaled during all those years when his wife was still with him. There seemed to be an innate affinity between the rose garden and his great love and loss of her grandmother. Alexander Turner's drive and dedication in tending the beautiful garden in his wife's absence had taken on some special significance to him that he'd not yet shared with Alyssa. She wondered if he ever would, or if she should ever broach the subject, but she considered it rather audacious to ask him to explain his obsession with the rose garden. Perhaps she was the only person who had even noticed.

Putting her musing aside and pulling on the toggle in her right hand, she maneuvered the paraglider in another full circle. As she did so, she saw Mike's paraglider come over the mountain ridge, and watched in delight as his canopy settled into the first house thermal.

"Wahoo!" he yelled. "It doesn't get any better than this!"

❧　❧

Later in the day, Alyssa coached a new student, then skipped lunch and headed for the office just as soon as she could break free. Although she was still doing paperwork when she wanted to be home earlier, she realized the bookkeeping would be stacked up three feet deep by the time she got back from her vacation.

Sometimes she felt the paperwork headaches of managing a business were more than she wanted to tackle. Although she'd toyed with the idea of hiring a bookkeeper, the extra salary she would have to pay would severely limit the income she and Mike were making. Just another few months of triple payments to the bank would make A & M Aviation debt free. If she could hang on a few more months, then she could afford to hire a bookkeeper.

It had been four years since she and Mike opened the doors to A & M Aviation, and it wouldn't have happened at all if her Grandfather hadn't surprised her by giving her his Cessna Skylane, complete with hanger and twelve acres of runway.

To her sister, Alexandria, Granddad had given the family jewelry, worth every bit as much as the real estate and the Cessna Skylane. As for her brother, Allin, he was to receive Granddad's farm sometime after his mission.

Granddad was scaling down his assets, as though preparing to meet his maker. He said he was getting too old to fly, though he still took the Cessna out several times in the summer. But with no one to share this passion with him, Alyssa suspected that he'd lost his reason for flying.

Alexander Turner knew, as did Alyssa, the yen for flying coursed through her veins.

She had accepted Granddad's gift graciously. After discussing her options with her parents and Mike's, she took out a small construction loan, just enough to pay for building materials.

Mike's father, a general contractor, helped Mike build the flight school, with her upstairs apartment. He was also the prime motivator in making needed improvements in the runway.

The final expenses, updating the Cessna with the finest electronics, including a new transponder and cockpit recorder, were paid for out of the same funds, but it was her grandfather who did the work on it. He didn't seem to trust anyone else to service the Skylane, and that suited Alyssa perfectly. Since Alexander had worked as an airplane technician during World War II, and several years afterward until he purchased the farm, she trusted his ability completely.

Mike and Alyssa were just now heading into their fifth season. In addition to teaching paraglider flight school, they also used the Cessna for tourist flights. A & M often had clients from all over the country who wanted to see the Wasatch and Uinta mountain ranges and Park City, including Jordanelle, Rockport and Echo reservoirs by air. Now Mike was thinking about purchasing a glider plane and expanding the business into that arena.

Returning her concentration to the projects at hand, she was glad that all she had left was filling out the bank deposit and a little filing.

Then she would be finished. Bending down, Alyssa began filing some papers into the bottom drawer of a filing cabinet.

Suddenly, she was startled by a gruff yet familiar voice behind her saying, "Pardon me, Ma'am, do you know where I could find the owner of A & M Aviation?"

The voice made her skin prickle. It could belong to no one else but Ed Sparkleman. She would have recognized the sound of his voice blindfolded.

For a full minute she debated whether to answer him or not. But even Alyssa could not be that rude. She stood up, turned around slowly and faced him, watching with secret delight as his chin dropped and his green eyes widened in surprise.

"I am one of the two owners," she said. "Mike is the other. But I suppose you came to see me, Mr. Sparkleman."

He stammered only for a moment before gaining his composure. "What the—?" Then he seemed to soften, if only for a second. When he finally spoke, his voice was stern, yet teasing. "No. Actually I came to speak with the owner about an impetuous young woman who landed at the Bar M Ranch a week ago, unexpected and uninvited."

"I can assure you," she said, "the woman has been reprimanded severely. I spoke with her personally the moment she arrived back here."

He smiled. "And how did she take this reprimand?" he questioned, a glint of amusement in his bold green eyes.

"Better than I expected," Alyssa nodded and gave him a bright smile in return. "She promised me faithfully that she would never do anything so rash again."

"My ranch hands managed to retrieve her parachute," said Ed Sparkleman. "I put it on the counter, outside your office."

"Thank you." Alyssa couldn't hold back a small giggle.

"Will I need to speak with your partner as well?" he asked seriously. "Or is he already aware that his wife acted rather foolishly?"

Alyssa held up her hand to display the diamond engagement ring on her finger. "Although the woman who parachuted onto the Bar M Ranch is engaged, I don't recall attending a wedding ceremony yet."

She suppressed her laughter when she saw a split second of disappointment on his face. Quickly, she added, "The other owner, Mike Roberts, is married, but his wife wasn't the woman that I reprimanded that day. However, you may take my word for it that Mike has been chastising Miss Kendal nearly every day since the incident."

Ed tipped his Stetson hat, gave her a knowing smile, and nodded. "Thanks for taking care of the situation before it got out of hand. I wouldn't want her jumping out of airplanes over the Bar M on a regular basis."

"I assure you, Mr. Sparkleman. She won't."

Ed gave her another nod, and turned around to leave.

"May I reimburse you for returning the parachute?" she asked, suddenly disappointed that he wanted to leave so quickly.

He turned back and shook his head. Then he winked, tipped his Stetson with his hand and said, "I was glad to do it."

When he left the office, Alyssa couldn't refrain from watching through the window as he got into a white Ford pickup and drove away. When he was gone, she sank into the chair at her desk. "Whew! That went well!" she whispered to herself. Though she would never admit just how disappointed she was to see him leave.

Had their conversation continued, she may have had time to tell him that it was his brother to whom she was engaged. Even as she thought it, a small voice inside her whispered, *You wouldn't have told him that! Not yet!*

Though he'd been playful today, she painfully remembered his anger from a week ago. No, she would tell him nothing until Abbot made the announcement himself. Perhaps Abbot could soften Ed's heart toward her.

At least they'd had this second meeting, and Ed didn't seem angry with her this time. Relief washed over her and she trembled, though she couldn't decide exactly why.

* *

As Ed Sparkleman began the drive home from A & M Aviation, a smile brightened his face. Not only had he misjudged Alyssa Kendal's character, thinking she didn't have the brains to work at anything that required careful planning, he had been overwhelmed by her ability to make him smile. Somehow she'd enabled him to see past the anger he'd felt toward her a week ago. His heart had softened when she explained how she had rebuked herself, probably worse than he could have, and it gave him a sense of admiration toward her that surprised him.

He was disappointed to learn she was engaged. For a few seconds prior to that, he'd even contemplated asking her to go to supper with him, which is why he'd baited her to learn if the 'M' owner of A & M Aviation was her spouse.

Another thing that Ed had noticed immediately was that she had cut her beautiful golden brown hair. It had been a few inches longer last week. Now she wore it in a semi-bob fashion, all one length and cropped an inch or two below her ears. Smiling, he remembered her hair in the meadow a week ago. When the sun danced off it, the brown strands had a golden edge of luminescence that he admired.

He wondered who Alyssa was engaged to, but she hadn't said. Not that it mattered. Ed would never come between a woman and the man she loved. A keen sense of chivalry dictated his character. It was this same gallantry that had determined his willingness to accept Kayla's resolution that the love between the two of them was the same as a brother and sister share, not the romantic feelings of true love as tendered between man and woman.

Giving Kayla away at her wedding, after her father died, was the only gesture Ed could think of that would prove to her that he'd accepted her decision, regardless of his personal feelings, and he knew in his heart that this was the right thing to do. He admitted, only to himself, that giving Kayla's hand in marriage eighteen months ago, as though he really was her elder brother, was the most difficult thing he had ever done in his entire life.

Ed brushed the thoughts of Kayla aside and found Alyssa floating back into his mind. It didn't matter how she wore her hair, she was beautiful beyond any woman he'd ever met.

And she's engaged! he reminded himself. *Don't even think about going there!*

He had the ranch to worry about now. By the time he turned off onto the gravel road that led to the Bar M, his mind whirled with projects and ideas for the ranch. They would start branding the new calves later in the week, once Abbot arrived. With Marcus gone to Louisiana until the middle of July, Ed would need every spare hand he could get. Marcus did the work of three men. In addition to a short-handed crew, Ed had greater demand for laborers than at any other time in the history of the Bar M. He'd recently signed a contract with the Forest Service that enabled him to utilize several thousand acres with the agreement that he would fence off those acres. That meant another ten miles of fence posts, but it also meant a better way to keep track of the herd. They had to build that fence up this summer, and he would need extra help to do it. The expenses of new fencing and more manpower was going to eat up half the year's profits, but the long term benefits would more than pay for the costs.

Driving himself harder than he'd ever had to work before had enabled Ed to see the Bar M's real potential. The tripled profits would show Kayla why she need never worry about his managing the ranch. And, he admitted only to himself, he could keep his mind so busy he wouldn't have time to think about Kayla, or about all the years he'd wasted waiting for her to come home.

Yet, as he thought about the love he'd lost, or even the work ahead of him at the Bar M Ranch, Alyssa's bright smile and sparkling brown eyes kept sky diving into his memory bank, and he found it difficult to concentrate on anyone else.

❧ ❧

Alyssa nodded off to sleep on the sofa before Abbot and Hans arrived back at her parents' home. She awakened to Abbot tickling her ear by blowing gently against it. She shivered and sat up quickly. "My," she yawned sleepily. "You're late. Are you hungry?"

"We ate at the Wagon Wheel," said Abbot, sitting next to her on the sofa. He was still wearing his swimsuit and a tee shirt. "Sorry we're late. We ran into a couple of friends from Vernal that I hadn't seen for years, and spent the better part of the afternoon baking in conversation."

"Oh," she moaned. "Look at your face! You're burned to a crisp."

Hans sat opposite them on a leather recliner. "Two weeks aboard my boat wearing sun screen and lathering his face with zinc oxide, and not a bit of sunburn. Then, when he's back in familiar territory two days, look what happens to him."

"It's no wonder," said Alyssa. "It's a mile closer to the sun at Jordanelle. Let me put something on that. Take your tee shirt off, Abbot. I'll be right back."

She went into the main bathroom and removed a bottle of aloe vera lotion from the cabinet. Returning to the living room, she spread the lotion over Abbot's back and chest.

He was wearing a silver chain with a delicate ring attached to it. "What is this?" she asked, examining the unusual jade stone set in a leaf and filigree pattern. On the inside of the ring she saw the initials:

EDS + SNT

Abbot looked at her in earnest. "It was my mother's," he explained. "Pa carried it in his wallet. He'd given it to her when they were in junior high school. She always wore it on her right hand. After she died, Pa kept it because it meant so much to him. I remember him taking it out at night and polishing it. When Pa died, my brothers thought I should have it. I've worn it around my neck ever since."

"It's beautiful," she murmured.

"You don't mind my wearing it?" he asked.

"Of course not."

He smiled, and she gave him a quick kiss on his sunburned cheek, then began putting lotion on his arms, face and chest. She hoped that touching Abbot in such a sensuous way would kindle something warm and tender inside her, but it seemed to excite her no more than putting lotion on her brother, Allin. Disappointed, she decided to focus her mind on someone else.

While she slathered Abbot, she asked Hans, "So, you have a boat?"

"I do," Hans said. "It's a Hallberg-Rassy 49 Ketch."

"A what?" she asked.

"A sailing vessel," he explained in layman's terms. "Forty-nine feet long, two masts."

"I've never sailed. Is it fun?"

"It's quite a rush in a fresh breeze."

"Were you sailing the whole time Abbot was there, or did you go fishing, too?"

"We didn't sail or fish at all," Hans admitted. "We spent most of our time at the theme parks and touring. Abbot had never been to California before this trip, you know."

"But Abbot likes to fish," Alyssa interjected.

"Trout," Abbot defended. "And like is a pretty strong word. I haven't fished much since I was a child."

"I don't care for fishing," Alyssa said. "Dad says I'm too squeamish."

Abbot grinned, "This from a woman who likes to jump out of airplanes, run off the top of mountains, and fly paragliders."

Wanting to turn the conversation away from herself, Alyssa asked, "What about you, Hans? What is your niche in life?"

Hans hesitated a moment before he said, "I don't know what my niche is, exactly. I suppose I haven't found it yet. I couldn't do the military routine like my twin brother, or follow in the footsteps of the Admiral."

"The Admiral?" asked Alyssa.

"My father," Hans explained. "Admiral Bridger Clark. We rarely refer to him as Dad, like you do yours."

"Are you an identical twin?" she asked.

"We think so, though we've never had a DNA analysis to prove it. We're both quite similar in appearance, but any resemblance ends with our personalities. I lack the drive that my brother has, and he lacks my spontaneity. I'm a 'go with the flow' man, while Josh is all 'spit and polish,' to hear the Admiral talk."

"Does it bother you?" questioned Alyssa. "To be so different, yet so much alike?"

"It used to," Hans admitted. "But one day, shortly before I received my last doctorate, I finally realized that, while Josh and I are identical in many ways, we are still two separate and distinctly different people. I finally felt comfortable with that."

Alyssa put the lid back on the lotion, and wiped her hands on a paper towel. "Then what do you do for a living?" she asked as she sat down on the floor in front of Abbot.

Both men burst out laughing. Finally Abbot explained, "Absolutely nothing at all."

Her curiosity was piqued. "I'm serious."

"So is he," Hans laughed. "I don't know what to do, exactly. The Admiral pays for everything I could ever want. I have a generous allowance and I live aboard my boat."

"Then where's your purpose? What's your reason for being?"

"Sweet Alyssa," said Hans. "That's just the point. If I knew what my purpose was, I suppose I'd make an effort at it. But I'm like a shooting star. I show up for a few seconds in a bright, flashy show of color, then I fade off into the vast horizon, untouched, and often unseen."

"I can't imagine living such a life," she said. "Do you find joy along the way?"

"Hmm," Hans stroked his chin thoughtfully. "I suppose I do, although I have to admit that I've never pondered such a question before."

Abbot rubbed the back of Alyssa's neck. "Where are all these questions coming from?" he wondered aloud.

"Oh! I'm sorry," she apologized. "I didn't mean to be rude. I was just curious, that's all."

"It's all right," Hans insisted. "It's been refreshing, Alyssa, getting a glimpse of the world in which you live."

"You're going to get a real glimpse of life beginning Wednesday," said Abbot. "Won't Ed be surprised when you two show up with me!"

Alyssa's eyes widened, but she did not voice the alarm his comment raised within her. Not only would Ed be surprised at Hans arriving with Abbot, but Alyssa would arrive as well. It would prove an interesting situation. She wondered if Ed would be able to keep his anger in check when she showed up on the Bar M . . . especially since he told her she was never to come back.

Chapter Four

After his morning prayer, Ed dressed quickly, then hurried to the kitchen where he put a large pot of pompanoosuc porridge on to cook. The men seemed to prefer this hearty breakfast during Marcus' absence, and it had become a mainstay in their diet. As soon as the porridge started to boil, he turned it off and put the lid on it.

While waiting for the porridge to thicken, he went to his bedroom and closed the door behind him. Then he picked up his scriptures from the night stand and opened them up to read.

Several minutes passed. Unable to concentrate, Ed began pondering, as he always did when he had time to reflect upon his life, about the special blessing he'd been given.

Opening his wallet, Ed pulled out a slip of paper. It was well-worn, and the folds were starting to tear from being opened up nearly every day for the last six months. His green eyes skimmed over the words he had written, although he didn't need to read it. The words from this special blessing were imbedded in his heart and in his mind from constant repetition.

Ed, now thirty-two years old, was beyond the normal marrying age for men. Having served with Sky Patrol for the Vernal and Maeser areas, and through the regional special interests group at church, he'd had the opportunity to meet nearly every single woman within driving distance.

Had he met the woman from his blessing? Surprisingly, his first thoughts went to Alyssa, but he forced himself to remember that she was engaged. *She can't be the one!* he scolded, forcing his thoughts of Alyssa into oblivion, at least for now.

His mind wandered back to the previous December 23rd. It was the first year anniversary of his father's death. Bishop Perry had called him into his office for a special visit. Both counselors were also present and Ed felt nervous. He worried that he would be called to do something stressful.

Basically a shy man, Ed was a doer, not a talker. Skittish whenever he had to speak in front of a group, or talk in church, his stomach would knot up, and he would be irritable for days before and after giving a spiritual discourse. Sometimes he'd get tongue-tied and say something completely out of line, and he nearly always regretted saying something he should have said differently. Ed preferred teaching primary children because he felt at ease being around the young ones, who weren't quite so judgmental or intimidating.

When the bishop finished with brief formalities, his countenance changed from joyful to serious about as fast as it takes to throw a lasso. "Ed, I've been praying a lot about the members of our ward lately, and your name keeps coming up. Is there something I can do for you?"

The sincerity on the bishop's face almost made Ed laugh. "No! Not that I know about, anyway."

"Well," said Bishop Perry, "would you be offended if I gave you a blessing? I've had this feeling lately that, if your father were here, he'd give you a blessing to help you over some of the rough spots in your life."

"If you think I need one," Ed had responded. "But I ain't ailing."

"Sometimes the heart is ailing when the body is fit," said the bishop. "I can't say why, but I feel that the Lord has a special blessing for you."

"Then I reckon you'd better give it to me," Ed agreed.

Bishop Perry stood, as did his counselors, and placed his hands upon Ed's head. Addressing Ed formally, he said, "Brother Edward Davis Sparkleman, the Lord is pleased with thy life and with thy willingness to assist Him in His work upon the earth. Many people benefit both spiritually and temporally because of thy diligence in living in accordance with the Savior's plan. You have carried a burden in your heart for many years, Brother Sparkleman, a burden that has been difficult for you to carry, a burden that is not in your best interest."

The bishop paused for a moment, and Ed knew in his heart what the burden was without having to think about it.

When the miracle happened, it came without fanfare. There were no angels singing overhead, no loud crashing of bells and cymbals, no rush of mighty winds. A simple, peaceful, penetrating feeling of comfort and warmth rushed through Ed as the bishop's voice changed entirely. As though he were standing in the same room with them, the gravely voice that pronounced the blessing was unmistakably the voice of Ed's deceased father, Sparky.

Ed felt his heart swell within his chest as Sparky said, "Be of good cheer, my son, for the Lord is mindful of you. He would like you to give up the burden in your heart so that He may bless you more fully. Even your children, who are waiting across the veil to join you on the earth, are concerned that you will wait too long and miss out on their special presence in your home. The Lord has prepared a woman for you who will love you with all her heart. She will be faithful to you all of her life, and will bring you joy and rejoicing as your eternal companion and as the mother of your children. Ed, my beloved son, do not let the burden in your heart stand in the way of your loving her, for she will bring joy into your life so great you will not be able to contain it."

Ed was not a man to show emotion to anyone, but that blessing worked its way into his tear ducts and caused rivulets to stream down his face unbidden. Then he heard the voice of his father change, and return once again to the voice of Bishop Perry.

"Be diligent in heeding the Lord's counsel, Brother Sparkleman. These things I pronounce upon your head in the name of Jesus Christ. Amen."

When the blessing ended, Ed stood up and wiped his eyes with a tissue from the bishop's desk. Then he shook hands with the members of the bishopric. "I don't know what to say," Ed began.

When they returned to their chairs, the bishop asked, "Do you know what burden the Lord was speaking about?"

Ed covered his eyes with one hand, until he could get his emotions under control. When he'd finally gained some composure, he said, "It's Kayla, I reckon. I have to accept her as my sister, and no longer think about her as the woman I wanted for my wife."

The bishop nodded. "Yes," he said, "that is what I was thinking also."

"Did you know Pa was here?" Ed asked.

All three men nodded, and Ed could see by their countenances that they, too, had been deeply touched by the experience.

"Sparky's been near me for several days," confided Bishop Perry. "He's the reason why I asked to see you today."

"I heard his voice," Ed admitted as a new bout of tears filled his eyes. "It was Pa speaking to me."

Bishop Perry nodded and handed Ed another tissue. "Do you think you can do as your father and the Lord have asked?"

Ed's shoulders shook as he made the confession. "I don't know. I want to think of Kayla as my sister. I've tried for months. But in my heart, I just don't know."

"If you can't," the bishop said gravely, "I fear that your children will be sent to another, and you will one day find yourself old, alone and bitter."

Ed nodded and dried his tears one last time. "I know," he said.

"Do everything you can to find this woman who will bless your life, and when you do, don't let anything stand in the way of marrying her." counseled the bishop.

As Ed pondered upon that special blessing of six months ago, he read the words he'd written upon the slip of paper in his hands:

> *Blessing given to me one year after Pa died:*
> If I remove the burden of Kayla from my heart,
> the Lord has promised me a woman
> who will love me with all her heart.
> She will be faithful to me all her life.
> She will bring me joy and rejoicing,
> both as my eternal companion,
> and as the mother of my children.

With vivid clarity he recalled the miracle of hearing his father's voice. Trembling, he whispered a heartfelt, "Thank you, Pa."

Ed put his scriptures on the night stand, folded the piece of paper and put it back into his wallet, then went out to the kitchen.

Sidekick and Luke had already eaten their porridge, rinsed their bowls and put them in the dish drainer. They were apparently out milking the cow, gathering the eggs and feeding the farm animals.

Opening the fridge, Ed got out a small pitcher of cream. He scooped what was left of the porridge into a bowl, poured in the thick cream and a little honey to sweeten it. Then he sat at the table and gulped down his breakfast in large spoonfuls.

Abbot and his two guests would arrive today. Beginning tonight, Ed had assigned Sidekick John and Luke Jennings to the bunkbeds in one bedroom. Abbot's two friends could share the bunk beds in the second bedroom. Ed's room had a king-size bed that had belonged to his parents. His brother, Abbot, would have to share with him, or sleep on the sofa.

Then he gave some serious thought to building his own home up on the hill behind the lodge. Kayla had given that piece of land to him, along with her blessing. If he built up there, he could put an extra set of bunks in both of the other bedrooms at the cabin, and two sets of bunks in the master bedroom. That would give him twelve beds, and he would have no need to build a bunkhouse. Ranch hands don't need anything more than a bed to sleep on, a kitchen to cook in and maybe a television set to watch once in a while, Ed reasoned. Two-thirds of their time they were out working the ranch, and the other third they were sleeping. A rancher's schedule was dictated by what's happening with the herd. During the summer, the men worked no less than fifteen hours a day, alternating weekend days off so they wouldn't be too short-handed. While one man worked Monday through Friday, the other worked Tuesday through Saturday. Thus, each would have a two-day weekend. All the men had Sunday off, no matter what schedule they worked. Even with this, the men earned every penny they got.

As ranch foreman, Ed worked every day, but on Sundays he only did the milking and the chores. Then he drove into Maeser to attend church, teach his primary class, and do his home teaching.

Afterward, Ed picked up Morning Sun and her eighteen-month old toddler, Matthew. He always brought Morning Sun up to the ranch Sunday afternoons, where she stayed until Friday. Morning Sun was responsible for preparing the noon and evening meals for the men, and she kept the lodge clean while living there through the week. Kayla didn't want the lodge neglected, and Morning Sun didn't care to stay alone in town now that her husband was working weekdays on an oil rig in Wyoming. She seemed to feel safe at the lodge. On Fridays, Ed drove Morning Sun back to her trailer home on the outskirts of Vernal. Her husband came home every Friday evening, stayed the weekend with her and Matthew, then left right after church on Sundays to go back to Wyoming.

Ed's younger brother, Tom, had cleaned up his act and hadn't had one drink of liquor since their father, Sparky, died eighteen months ago.

Tom and Morning Sun were on friendly terms and she easily forgave and forgot about the incident between them. Sometimes it seemed as though she really didn't believe Tom was the man who'd hurt her, and this always puzzled Ed. While Tom admitted the sin, Tom also often said he had no recollection of it, only some vague dream regarding Kayla.

Ed smiled as he thought about young Matthew. Morning Sun had Matthew to raise now, and that little tyke had stolen more hearts than his mother's.

Shaking off the reverie, Ed reminded himself that Abbot and his two friends were scheduled to arrive sometime today, and Ed was grateful for the extra man-power. With Marcus gone, he could use all the extra hands he could get. He hoped they were both capable men and not college career addicts with little ability to learn some new and difficult skills. Ed shrugged. *At least they're willing to help! That should count for something!*

A knock came at the door. Ed answered it to find Morning Sun with her toddler, Matthew, holding her hand. "Morning Sun will clean," she said, "for Abbot's guests."

"Aw, you don't need to," said Ed as he tousled Matthew's silky black hair. When Morning Sun gave him a little frown, he amended his response to, "Come on in. Clean 'til your heart's content." He swept his arm out, welcoming her into the cabin.

Matthew squealed at him and held out his hands. "Eddie!"

Ed squatted down and looked Matthew square in the face. "Did you miss me, you little rascal?"

"Miss Eddie!" said Matthew with a wide grin. He had the round, cherubic features of his Navajo mother, almost the spitting image of her. Except for his mischievous nature, there could never be any doubt who his mother was.

Ed swept the toddler into his arms, stood up and swung him over his head. Then he lowered him until their noses touched. "I missed you, too!"

"Hat!" said Matthew.

"You want your hat? It's here somewhere. Let's see!" Ed looked at the hooks behind the front door. "Hmm, which one is yours? This one?" He lifted his Stetson off a hook and put it over Matthew's head, where it sank clear down to his chin.

"My hat!" insisted Matthew, pushing Ed's Stetson off his head and pointing at a small red cowboy hat on one of the hooks.

"Oh, this one," smiled Ed. "Okay, partner, there you go."

"Pard-ers!" grinned Matthew as Ed put the red cowboy hat on Matthew's head.

"Yep, we're partners forever!" agreed Ed, putting him down. "But now I've gotta' go take care of the cattle, okay?"

"Bye!" said Matthew, dismissing Ed completely. He had his hat and that was apparently all that mattered to him right now.

Ed removed the Stetson from the floor where Matthew had dropped it, brushed it with his shirt sleeve, stuck it on his head and left the cabin.

Immediately his thoughts returned to Abbot and his guests. Perhaps Abbot would know how best to teach his friends the ropes, thought Ed, though ranching was never Abbot's strong suit. Even as a kid, Abbot had often been found in the saddle with an open book in one hand and the reins in the other. No wonder his peers always called him "Bookworm." Abbot may have inherited Sparky's dark hair and beard, but little else from their father. Abbot was more like their mother, who loved reading almost as much as she loved baking cookies for her four sons. Abbot, the baby of the family, was too young to remember their mother, since she died when he was only four; he had no idea how near in temperament the two were. Their mother was a rancher's wife from beginning to end, and she loved the meadow and wild mountain flowers as much as any woman could.

Disregarding his thoughts about Abbot, Ed spent all day roping calves and branding them. By the time evening came he was covered in a layer of mountain dust. When he saw a flash of light far off in the distance, he knew it could only mean one thing. Abbot had arrived! He nodded to Luke, "There they are."

"You go on ahead, Boss." Luke encouraged. "We'll finish up here. You haven't seen Abbot since Christmas."

Ed nodded, then tugged on the reins. "Come on, Breeze," he said. "Let's go get them settled in. Git up!" Breeze didn't need anymore encouragement than that. Within seconds he was galloping along the path that led from Mountain Meadow toward the lodge.

When Ed arrived at the cabin, he tied the reins to a hitching post and was greeted at the front door by Abbot, who pounded him on the back as he gave him a big bear hug. "Whoa!" Abbot exclaimed. "Look at you, dust from head to toe!"

"You know what it's like out there," said Ed. "Though probably not as well as I do by now."

"Come on in," said Abbot. "I have some very special people I want you to meet." He pushed the door open and stepped inside.

Ed followed him in, removing his hat in the process. When he did, two people whom he already knew greeted him with, "Surprise!"

He could not have been more astounded. Joshua stood up, but Kayla was nowhere in sight. The woman with Joshua was Alyssa Kendal, who had parachuted onto the Bar M Ranch nine days ago.

"Josh!" Ed exclaimed. "What are you doing here? And where's Kayla?"

Hans Bridger Clark gave Ed a thin smile for an answer.

"Wrong twin," Abbot said quickly. "Meet Joshua's twin brother, Hans."

"Dang if you ain't identical twins!" gasped Ed. "The resemblance is startling."

Hans reached out to shake Ed's hand. "Sorry to spring it on you like this. But there's really no easy way to meet someone who knows my brother, or vice versa, I suppose."

Ed shook his hand. "The voice is a little different," he admitted. "Maybe that will help."

Then Ed turned his attention to Alyssa. "And you?" he questioned. It sounded harsher than he wanted, but he couldn't imagine how Alyssa and his brother had connected up.

She lifted her shoulders and gave him a sweet, somewhat mischievous grin. "Surprise!" she said for the second time. "You didn't give me a chance to say that Abbot is my fiancé. . . ." Alyssa left the sentence open, and held up her left hand, displaying her engagement ring.

"You're engaged?" Ed questioned his sibling.

Abbot nodded his head up and down.

Ed gave his brother another bear hug and punched him playfully. "You sly little devil! Why didn't you tell us?"

"We just did," said Abbot. Then he asked, "But truthfully, I wanted to present her in person so you would see why I want to marry her. Isn't she a gem?"

Alyssa smiled. "Did you never wonder how I heard about Mountain Meadow when I surprised you that day?" she asked with a teasing glint in her brown eyes.

"No, I didn't," Ed admitted.

"I should have told you about Alyssa earlier," Abbot said. "But when she told me about her little escapade with the parachute and all, I figured I'd better wait and see if you were still angry with her. Are you?"

Ed shook his head. "No, I was told by her, um, boss," he smiled, "that she had been duly reprimanded."

She nodded and whispered, "Thank you."

"She doesn't have a boss," said Abbot. Then, "Oh, you mean Mike. I suppose he must have been upset with her. But then, she owns more than half the business, so . . ."

Alyssa interrupted. "Tell me about the lodge, Ed. I suppose we can graduate to first-name basis now, can't we?"

"Sure." Ed arched an eyebrow. "The lodge?"

"Yes, I noticed there were lights on over there."

"Morning Sun stays there Sundays to Fridays with her son, Matthew," Ed explained.

"Is that where I'll be staying?" she questioned. "I had thought we'd all be in tents, but Abbot was just telling me that the workers generally stay here at the cabin."

Ed smiled, finally realizing where she was going with the conversation. "The lodge would probably be best."

"You could stay here, Alyssa," Abbot offered quickly. "There's a king-size bed in Ed's room. You'd like it."

"Silly," she teased, "I'm not going to sleep in Ed's room unless I'm married to him. And how can that happen when I'm engaged to you?"

"That isn't what I meant," Abbot said with a little irritation in his voice. "You could have Ed's bedroom. Hans and I could take one of the bunk beds, and Ed could sleep on the sofa."

Ed watched her curiously, wondering how she was going to handle his brother's suggestion.

"I would," she said with a delicious smile. "But then I would have to confess to my bishop that I'd spent my vacation in a mountain cabin filled with men, none of whom I was related to. I don't think he'd appreciate that."

Ed smiled at her response and came to her rescue. "I agree," he said firmly. "It ain't proper for a woman to put herself in any situation where proprieties would be questioned. Abbot, why don't you take Alyssa over to the lodge to meet Morning Sun?"

Abbot's face fell. "But I wanted to keep her a little nearer me," he protested feebly. "Alyssa?"

She shook her head. "Oh, Abbot, you're such a dear romantic! But you'll get along fine without me."

Ed opened the front door and watched as Abbot and Alyssa walked out across the meadow toward the lodge.

Alyssa Kendal is engaged to my brother! This news came with painful disappointment; it left a knot in the pit of his stomach and a bitter taste in his mouth.

Then Ed noticed they'd forgotten her luggage. "Are these hers?" he asked Hans, while pointing at two flower-drenched suitcases.

Hans nodded. "Do you need some help with them?" he asked.

"No," said Ed. "But you might want to get settled into whichever bunk you prefer before Abbot gets back, in case you like the bottom."

A smile wandered across Hans' face. "Of course."

"First door on the left," said Ed. "I'll be back shortly."

This is gonna' be one awkward situation after another! Ed fumed. He had no claim on Alyssa, but seeing her again, and knowing she would soon become his sister-in-law, left him aching inside. *Something fierce!*

Chapter Five

*A*lyssa felt as though she had betrayed poor Abbot, but she was
frankly surprised that he hadn't thought the sleeping arrange-
ments were a bit awkward. She had no intention of staying in a cabin
filled with five men! And she had a suspicious thought that kept her
wondering if Abbot wanted her to share the king-size bed with him.

Earlier, when Abbot drove the car into the driveway by the cabin,
she noticed the lights on in the lodge, and she'd hoped that she would
be staying there. But when Abbot hedged on the topic before Ed
showed up, she was totally dismayed.

Thank goodness Ed had a little more common sense than Abbot!
Fuming inwardly, but trying to maintain a cheerful front, Alyssa slipped
her hand into Abbot's

"I hope you're not too disappointed," she whispered.

"I am," he admitted. "But I suppose I will get over it. I'd wanted
to bring you breakfast in bed, and see what you look like when you first
wake up. I had planned to surprise you."

"I look dreadful." She squeezed his hand and giggled. "And I rarely
eat breakfast, but it would have been a sweet gesture."

"Well, maybe I'll talk Morning Sun into letting me in some morning before the others wake up."

"Don't you dare!" she insisted. "Honestly, Abbot, what's gotten into you?"

"You have," he admitted. "Ever since you said you would marry me, I've had all these feelings bubbling up out of me. Will you love me enough? Will we be compatible? Will I be able to support us the way I should?"

Alyssa stopped. She turned to face him, looked deep into his green eyes and said, "Abbot, when two people love one another, they work out whatever problems they have because of that love, and they don't let anyone or anything come between them."

He gave her a brief smile, then pulled her into his arms and kissed her tenderly at first. Then his kiss changed to one of prolonged, penetrating passion, which took Alyssa completely by surprise.

This kiss knew no boundaries. It didn't stop where other kisses had in the past. It was the most possessive, selfish kiss he had ever given her, and Alyssa found herself wanting him to stop. Her eyes widened in alarm, and she soon found it difficult to breathe. Frightened, her heart started racing out of control. Fear overcame all her willingness to respond to Abbot, and she put a hand up against his chest and tried to push him away, but he was stronger than she, and evidently didn't want to release her. Panicked, Alyssa pushed again as hard as she could, but he was a strong man, and he would not release her.

The sound of someone clearing his voice interrupted them, and Alyssa looked behind Abbot to see Ed holding her suitcases. Obviously annoyed, Abbot released her.

"Sorry to interrupt you," Ed apologized. "I guess you didn't realize I was bringing up the rear."

Abbot glared at Ed for a moment. Then he said, "Guess I forgot those." He took the suitcases from Ed and complained, "What did you put in these, Alyssa? Lead?"

Before she could answer, Ed took them back. "Go on," he suggested with a twisted smile. "She probably needs you to guide her more than she needs you to carry her luggage."

Abbot nodded. "Thanks."

Relieved and grateful for Ed's interruption, Alyssa slipped her hand back into Abbot's. Then she let Abbot lead her over the bridge and across the meadow to the lodge.

When they arrived, the front door was flung open by a Native American woman with soft, rounded features, and coal black hair and eyes. Morning Sun gave Alyssa a bright smile. "Did Joshua come?"

"No," said Ed. "That's Joshua's identical twin brother, Hans. This is Alyssa Kendal, Abbot's fiancée."

Abbot let go of Alyssa's hand and gave Morning Sun a quick hug.

Alyssa gave Ed a timid smile. He couldn't possibly know how grateful she was that he had intervened.

"Good to see you, Morning Sun," Abbot said eagerly.

"You are engaged now?" she asked. "Morning Sun is pleased."

"Thank you. Is it all right if Alyssa stays over here with you for a few weeks? She's rather sensitive about staying with all us 'cowpokes' over at the O.K. Corral." He gave her a wry grin.

"This will be very nice," said Morning Sun. "Please. Come in. Morning Sun will make up a bed." Immediately she turned to go up the stairs. Ed followed her up with the suitcases.

Abbot turned to Alyssa. "I'm sorry if I offended you by not wanting you to stay up here," he said. "It's just, I'm all caught up in emotions tonight. Will you forgive me?"

"Of course," said Alyssa. She kissed him lightly on the cheek, though she could see in his eyes that he wanted more kiss from her than that. *Oh dear!* she thought. *What kind of predicament have I gotten myself into?* A little more composed, she said, "Things will look brighter in the morning. It's been a long day and we're all tired."

"Yes, I suppose that's part of it," he agreed.

Ed came whistling down the stairs, apparently so they would know he was coming, Alyssa decided. He placed a hand on Abbot's shoulder. "Shall we let Morning Sun help Alyssa get settled in? Five o'clock comes awfully early in the morning."

"Yes, well, goodnight, Alyssa," Abbot said, kissing her tenderly on the cheek.

She responded by nodding her head toward Ed Sparkleman and squeezing Abbot's hand reassuringly. Alyssa watched in dismay as the two brothers walked side by side back to the cabin. Then she closed the heavy front door and locked it. She did not want Abbot barging in with breakfast any morning during her stay there, and she prayed that he didn't have a key.

Abbot had frightened her when he'd kissed her in the meadow. Up until that moment, his kisses had always been reserved, a bit shy perhaps. But tonight, his kiss had been given with such passion, almost as though he had silently commanded her to comply. She hadn't liked it, and she decided he had probably had too much sun. *Passion is one thing,* she thought to herself, *but that kiss went way beyond passionate! It was possessive!*

Inhaling deeply, then blowing out slowly, Alyssa forced herself to calm down and take time to discover what the inside of the lodge was like. After a few moments she was able to appreciate her surroundings. The living room was enormous, with two large leather, overstuffed sofas, cream-colored with a matching chair, an oak rocking chair, very likely handmade, and a black bearskin rug on the floor. A huge rock fireplace with a lodge-pole pine mantle stood against one wall, and a hand-hewn log staircase stretched up to the second floor.

It didn't take Alyssa long to discover the spacious kitchen with sparkling counter tops and state of the art appliances with a dining area off the north end. A hall beneath the upstairs landing led to a laundry room, bathroom and den. Upstairs she found six bedrooms and two more bathrooms. Morning Sun was straightening the bedding on a huge, king-sized bed in one of them when Alyssa arrived.

"This is guest room," said Morning Sun. "Mr. Mont had four. This one is Morning Sun's favorite. Do you like?"

"It's lovely," said Alyssa. "Thank you, Morning Sun."

"Morning Sun will fix you supper?"

"We ate at the Golden Corral in Vernal before coming up. But thank you, anyway."

"What you like for breakfast?"

Alyssa smiled. The dear woman was trying so hard to please her, it made Alyssa's eyes water. "I'll eat anything you'd like to prepare," she said.

"You will marry Abbot?" asked Morning Sun.

"Well, we are engaged," hedged Alyssa.

"Then you will marry Abbot?"

"I suppose so."

"Alyssa is not sure?"

Alyssa didn't answer. She walked over to the window and touched the creamy silk draperies. "My, these are almost too elegant for a rustic old lodge like this."

"Kayla and Morning Sun chose these when she was here last summer. Kayla chose the new kitchen. Did you see?" If Morning Sun objected to Alyssa's refusal to answer her question, she did not voice it.

"I did and it's lovely," Alyssa responded.

"Kayla is not coming until August this year. She and Joshua are on holiday, sailing big boat in northwest waters. San Juan Islands."

"You miss Kayla?" asked Alyssa.

"Kayla is like Morning Sun's own daughter," explained the gentle woman. "Morning Sun helped raise her from little girl, just then walking. We love much."

"I would like to meet her sometime."

"If you come in August, you can meet."

"August is my busiest season. I'm lucky to come now."

"When you marry Abbot?" questioned persistent Morning Sun.

"That remains to be determined," Alyssa answered timidly. "We still have some issues that are unresolved."

Morning Sun patted her hand and said, "You sleep now. Rest." Then she left Alyssa with her thoughts.

Alyssa walked over to the silk draperies and opened them. A sliding glass door led to the second level deck that she had seen in the photographs. She stepped outside and looked across the meadow at the cabin.

Why had Abbot kissed her like he had? She shook her head. Love isn't supposed to be selfish or demanding. It's supposed to be spontaneous and tender. But possessive? Never!

She would have to find a way to talk to Abbot about how she'd felt tonight, about how he'd frightened her. She realized there was no other word for what she'd experienced. He had frightened her more than if she'd come upon a mountain lion in this wild and beautiful area. And she didn't want to feel like that again.

If Ed hadn't cleared his throat when he did. . . . She shuddered with the thought. What if Ed hadn't followed them? Would she have been able to stop Abbot?

Should a woman be fearful of the man she plans to marry? *Certainly not!* She placed her hands against the railing to steady herself. What happened tonight made her realize she didn't know Abbot as well as she thought she did, and this knowledge stunned her.

Alyssa trembled. If she really loved Abbot, his kiss would have been welcome. She would have enjoyed it, and responded in an amorous manner. How could she marry him when she felt no passion for him? When she finally fell asleep, it was only to dream the dream again. It awakened her several times during the night and left her weeping.

❧ ❧

Ed awakened far earlier than he usually did. Sleep had eluded him most of the night, and now he rolled off the bed, said a hurried prayer and dressed for the day. Deciding he might as well make himself useful, he slipped outside and headed toward the barns to gather the eggs and milk the cow.

These tasks were normally shared by all three men, Sidekick on Monday, Wednesday and Thursday, Luke on Tuesday, Friday and Saturday, while Ed took his turn on Sunday and on any other days when the ranch was short-handed. Since today was Thursday, it would be Sidekick's turn, and Ed could only imagine how Sidekick John would razz him when he found Ed had done the chores for him.

Thoughts of Alyssa and Abbot kissing in the meadow had disturbed Ed most of the night. She'd been surprised by Abbot's kiss, he was certain of that. Although it was dark, and he couldn't see her expression clearly, Ed saw her eyes widen and remain open during the kiss, wide open, as if she were frightened. Her hands lifted and pressed against Abbot's chest, as though she didn't want him to kiss her at all. Then his brother pulled her closer to him, as though he was unwilling to release her. Ed's first reaction was to turn his back to them and give them some privacy, but when he realized Alyssa was struggling to get free, and Abbot wouldn't let her, it angered him. With his keen sense of chivalry, Ed did the only thing he could think of to help her. He'd made his presence known.

Ed couldn't be certain how Alyssa was feeling about that kiss in the meadow. But when they'd arrived at the Lodge, while Abbot was hugging Morning Sun, Ed had noticed a pale look of relief on her face.

What kind of woman accepts a proposal of marriage from a man she doesn't want to kiss? Or had she merely known Ed was behind them and didn't want an open display of affection? If that were true, then why had she paled? Why had she kept her eyes open? Why had he sensed fear in her? And why had her expression at the lodge made him feel like she wanted to say much more than, "Thank you for carrying the luggage."

Alyssa Kendal perturbed him, probably more than any woman had ever done. Although Ed thought he preferred blondes (since Kayla was blonde, and she was the only woman he'd ever loved), he was surprised that he found Alyssa's brown hair so attractive, with golden highlights in it that glowed, almost like an angel's halo, whenever a light shone on it. And her brown eyes had a sparkle to them that even Kayla's couldn't match. When Alyssa smiled, somehow her eyes glistened and smiled with her. *And her mouth!* He dwelled for a moment in deep thought about how tempting her mouth was— then, *No! I ain't going there!*

He heard a disgruntled moo and blinked. Then he noticed he had already drained Bessie's udder, and she was now protesting.

"You want to keep her, too, I see," said Sidekick John from behind Ed. He was leaning against the open barn door, watching him curiously.

Ed looked over at him, but didn't respond. *How long has he been there?* he wondered. Nodding toward a basket filled with eggs, he said,

"I gathered, but the nests need new straw. I'll take the milk and eggs up to the lodge and check on Abbot's guest." He hoped Sidekick would dismiss his notion regarding Ed's feelings towards Alyssa, but he was disappointed.

"Yep! You want to keep her, too!" Sidekick grinned. Before Ed could respond to the accusation, he slipped out through the open barn door and headed toward the hen house.

"Dang green-horn!" Ed muttered under his breath. He spread fresh salve over Bessie's udder and teats, then grabbed the basket of eggs in one hand and the bucket of milk in the other. Within minutes he was at the back door of the lodge, relieved that Morning Sun had seen him coming and had opened the door for him. He carried the milk and eggs in and set them down on the counter, next to Abbot's fiancée, who was eating breakfast.

"Morning," he said softly.

Alyssa nodded and took a bite of golden pancake.

Silently, Ed poured the milk through a strainer into a stainless steel container, and put the freshly strained milk into the refrigerator. Then he removed another container from a previous morning's milking and carefully skimmed the cream off it. When he was satisfied that all the cream was separated, he poured the skim milk into two pitchers, capped them, and put them back in the refrigerator. Afterwards, he wiped the eggs off with a dry cloth and put them into an egg crate in the fridge.

"That should hold us for a few days," said Ed. "Where's Matthew?"

"Sleeping," said Morning Sun from the kitchen sink.

Alyssa, sitting at the kitchen counter, was dressed in levis and a plaid green shirt. She wore cowboy boots and a leather belt. And she was eating whole wheat pancakes with homemade blackberry syrup, eggs, and bacon.

Ed gave her a smile and a wink. "I heard you didn't care much for breakfast," he teased.

She glared at him as though furious he would say such a thing, so he backed off. "Guess you were hungry."

"It must be all this mountain air," she suggested. She arched an eyebrow in his direction, then nodded toward Morning Sun, who had returned to washing a skillet at the kitchen sink.

He didn't understand whatever message Alyssa was trying to give him, but he knew it had something to do with Morning Sun. "You feel like working hard today?" he asked.

"Yes," she agreed. "Just show me what to do, and I'll try my best."

"You know how to ride, I hope."

"Of course. Airplanes aren't the only things I fall out of; saddles come to mind, as well."

"I see," he grinned. "Well, Abbot and Hans are still sleeping. I suppose it'll be up to me to teach you."

She wiped her mouth with a napkin. "Thank you, Morning Sun. You're a very good cook!"

Morning Sun turned and gave her a grateful smile. "Alyssa come back with saddle sores. Morning Sun have salve for that!"

"And believe me, she does!" said Ed, opening the back door and holding it for Alyssa to pass through.

She grabbed her jacket off the back of the chair and followed him to the barn. On the way he said, "What was that back in the kitchen? I didn't quite understand your . . . unspoken message."

"I didn't want to offend Morning Sun," she explained. "Although it's true that I rarely eat breakfast, she offered supper last night and we'd just eaten. Then she offered to prepare breakfast in the morning. I didn't have the heart to tell her no. And I was worried you would say something more to give me away."

"Ah," he sighed in relief. "So that was it." He was glad it wasn't something worse. And he was surprised at Alyssa's eagerness to refrain from hurting Morning Sun's feelings. It pleased him to know she could be empathic as well as impetuous.

Alyssa nodded. By this time they'd reached the barn and Ed swung the big doors wide open. In one of the horse stalls, he slipped a bridle over a chestnut mare, slid the bit between her teeth, and fastened the bridle with leather straps. Then he pulled the reins up to the mare's long auburn mane and said, "Her name is Daylight. She's not in the prime of life, but she's gentle and obedient."

"Well, hello Daylight," said Alyssa, rubbing the mare's neck. "You and I are going to become fast friends, I hope."

Ed couldn't help smiling when he noticed Alyssa take a big gulp of air when she'd said, "I hope."

They soon had both horses, Daylight and Breeze, saddled. "Do you need help getting up?" he asked.

"No." She grinned. "Getting on a horse isn't when I have problems. It's getting off that's been a little bumpy." She put her left boot into the stirrup. Then, grabbing the saddle horn with both hands, she swung her right leg up and over the saddle.

"Dang slick," Ed drawled. "I can tell you've been in a saddle before."

"My granddad taught me," she explained. "The fields you saw around A & M are his, and he used to have horses, though it's been a while."

Ed nodded, swung a lean leg up and sat in the saddle atop Breeze. He made a clicking sound with his mouth as he gently dug a spur into Breeze's flank and pulled the reins to the right. Breeze turned and trotted out of the barn ahead of Alyssa and Daylight. "Just follow my lead," Ed called back to her. "We'll go down into Mountain Meadow first and see if Luke and Sidekick have a branding fire ready."

Ed looked back occasionally, and noticed that Alyssa had no trouble getting Daylight to follow him. Daylight, who was more familiar with the routine than he was, knew exactly where to take Alyssa. By the time they arrived at camp, Daylight was primed and ready for a good days work.

Was Alyssa also ready? That question would soon be answered.

❧ ❧

Luke waved the moment he saw Alyssa. "Hello, Ms. Kendal! Glad you could join us."

Sidekick sauntered over playfully and gave her a wide grin. "Does this mean we get to keep you?" he teased.

This time Alyssa didn't take offense. "For a little while," she said, "provided you mind your manners."

"I've got manners?" he asked as though stricken with fear. He tugged at his shirt. "Where? I didn't see any manners when I got dressed this morning."

Alyssa laughed. "Well, perhaps I was mistaken."

"Whew!" he said, wiping his brow. "You scared the dickens out of me."

"You do like to tease, don't you?" she asked. "I'll have to think of some way to get even."

"Dang right," said Ed. "The green-horn needs someone to keep him in line, if only for the next few weeks."

Before the first hour was up, Ed taught Alyssa how to use a whip, ride right next to a calf, and without actually striking the calf, make the tip of the whip crack. This sound would spook the calf into going in a direction away from it, toward one of the men riding with lassoes. They wouldn't let her lasso a calf just yet, but she had the full day to work on her whip cracking. Riding came easy for her, and she was amazed at how comfortable the saddle felt beneath her.

She also discovered that Ed had many strengths she hadn't expected. In addition to being a thoughtful teacher, he was patient and persistent. He never yelled at the men, but if they didn't perform to his expectation, he'd give a brief comment that seemed to inspire, rather than belittle.

Ed could rope and brand a calf quicker than John or Luke. To their one calf each, Ed could always get three calves ready for the branding iron.

Sometimes Luke would lasso while Sidekick wielded the branding iron; sometimes they switched.

Alyssa did not mind roping calves, but she firmly refused to brand any calf at all. She just didn't have the heart.

Amazed at how quickly time passed when working with the cattle, Alyssa felt like they'd just started when Hans and Abbot arrived with two big baskets of food Morning Sun had prepared for their lunch. She glanced at her watch. Surprisingly, it was already past noon.

Soon she was biting hungrily into a piece of fried chicken. As she forked a mouthful of potato salad, Abbot sat down beside her. He'd apparently eaten before coming out to the meadow.

"You must have gotten up early," he said sheepishly.

"Mmm," she mumbled, her mouth still full. After she swallowed, she said, "About five, I guess. I remembered you telling me that ranching is an early riser's job."

"Well, Hans and I may have blown it today, but we'll be awake on time tomorrow." Abbot stood up and slid his fingers into the pockets of his jeans. He looked rather dashing in western clothing, she decided. And he was behaving quite well after last night.

It seemed that all the men had a certain charm about them today. She wasn't sure if it was for her benefit, or if they were always this well-mannered.

The rest of the day, Alyssa helped Hans and Abbot move steel fence posts from a delivery truck to two wagons. Her arms ached by the time dusk arrived. Wearily, she dismounted Daylight, allowing Abbot to take the mare back to the stables for her, while she went back to the lodge. She was so tired she didn't know if she'd have the strength to reach the landing.

However, Abbot had invited her to join him and the other men for some hot chocolate and roasted marshmallows out in the meadow. She felt obligated to go.

Dragging her aching limbs up the stairs, she forced herself to take a shower. The water poured over her for quite a while before she finally felt refreshed enough to face anything other than a soft pillow. After she dried herself with a towel, she slipped into a pair of sweat pants, tee shirt and a zip-up fleece jacket. She had learned last night how quickly it cools down once the sun sets in the Uinta mountains. Finally, she joined the men in the middle of the meadow, not too far from the stream. They had built a large bonfire, and put logs around it for everyone to sit upon.

Morning Sun remained at the lodge, unwilling to leave Matthew to sleep unattended. The toddler had already won Alyssa's heart while doing nothing more than sleeping in his bed. However, Morning Sun promised to wake him up early tomorrow, since she would be going back to Vernal for the weekend.

Alyssa was a little nervous about that. Morning Sun's absence would leave her alone in the lodge by herself, with five men just across the meadow. She made a mental note to speak with Ed about the safety of her staying there by herself. After all, the lodge was the place where Morning Sun had been assaulted a few years ago.

She pulled a marshmallow from a plastic bag and stuck it onto the end of a whittled branch, then held it over some coals at the rim of the campfire until it turned golden brown. Ed offered her an enamel cup filled with steaming, hot cocoa. Alyssa thanked him and sank down onto a large log stump.

Ed sat next to her while the other men started a boisterous game of Dare, cowboy style. It wasn't long before Sidekick had been dared to stand on his head in the stream. She didn't know how he had the energy, but he dashed over, walked straight into the stream, boots and all, then found a spot where it would be the least hazardous, and performed the feat. With water swirling past Sidekick's head and the men chanting to count how many seconds he lasted, Alyssa was amazed when forty-three seconds passed before he came up for air. She shivered, and worried how Sidekick had endured all the cold water rushing into his nose while he was upside down.

Then Hans said, "Who'll dare to go longer than Sidekick?" Alyssa was surprised to see Hans come out of his self-absorbed shell and participate.

Soon all the participants were drenched and laughing so hard they could scarcely stand up, with exception of Ed and herself.

"Dang fools!" Ed muttered loud enough that Alyssa heard it.

"I agree," she said, watching the others with a bit of amusement. "Are they always like this?"

"Oh, they're mellow tonight," he said. "You should see how they unwind when a woman's not around."

"Would I really want to?"

He seemed to consider her question, then said sheepishly, "No."

"I'm a little nervous about Morning Sun going home tomorrow." Alyssa hinted while the men were preoccupied with their games.

"She's not," said Ed. "I called her husband tonight and asked him to spend the next few weekends up here at the lodge."

Although Alyssa was surprised at his thoughtfulness, she managed to say, "Thank you." She felt a little light-headed and assumed it was tiredness, though she had noticed feeling the same way earlier in the day when Ed was teaching her how to round up the calves.

"I figured you'd be worrying about it." He touched the brim of his Stetson and nodded to her.

"That's very considerate."

"I doubt the men would ever bother you up there alone. But Pa taught me what an ounce of prevention is worth . . . long ago."

Alyssa didn't know how to respond to Ed's thoughtfulness, so she just gave him a smile and sipped on her cup of hot chocolate. When she finally realized the men's games could go on for hours, she said to Ed, "I'll never make it up in the morning if I don't go to bed. Will you tell Abbot goodnight for me?"

"Sure." Ed nodded and gazed into the fire, his eyelids puffy with sleepiness.

"Thanks." Alyssa stood and walked over to the bridge, across the meadow and back to the lodge. She doubted the other men even knew she'd gone. But she felt that Ed had watched her walk every step of the way. She couldn't decide whether this pleased her or not.

When she opened the door, she found Morning Sun on the sofa making a pair of soft moccasin-like slippers. "How interesting," she said, sitting beside her to watch as she carefully sewed tiny little beads into an intricate design above the toe.

"Elijah will like. Do you think so?"

"Yes," said Alyssa. "I think he'll like them very much."

"Elijah is coming home tomorrow."

"Ed wants him to come up here tomorrow. He wants you both to stay at the lodge over the weekend."

"My husband will do that. He is kind that way."

"Ed said he'd telephoned him already and asked him," Alyssa said. "Is that all right with you?"

"It is all right with Alyssa," observed the older woman. "That is enough."

"Thank you." She gave Morning Sun a quick hug. "It means a lot to me."

"You're welcome."

Alyssa stood. "Well, if I don't go to bed, I'll end up asleep on the sofa in another few minutes. Goodnight, Morning Sun."

The older woman nodded, then returned to her beadwork with a satisfied smile.

Alyssa climbed the stairs slowly, forcing her legs to move. She ached everywhere and could easily tell she was out of shape. There were so many places on her body that hurt she didn't dare count them. When she saw that Morning Sun had turned down her bedding, she nearly wept with joy. Almost unaware, she kicked off her shoes and collapsed on the bed face first. *One day down, twenty to go.* Within seconds she was fast asleep.

Chapter Six

When the alarm went off at five in the morning, Alyssa found her body in the exact position in which she fell asleep, but the blankets had been pulled over her. Morning Sun had taken the role of a protective and tender mother, and for this, Alyssa felt extremely blessed.

She rolled off the bed, said her morning prayers, then changed clothes quickly and went downstairs.

Morning Sun was stirring something in a pot on the stove. "You like?" she asked.

"Smells good," said Alyssa. "What is it?"

"Old recipe, called pompanoosuc porridge."

"What's it made with?"

The older woman smiled. "Cracked oats, wheat, flax seed and corn. Very good."

"I'll try some," said Alyssa. Although she wasn't really hungry, she didn't want to appear ungrateful.

Morning Sun smiled. "Tastes good with cream and honey." She dished Alyssa a healthy portion, then slid a small pitcher of cream and a bottle of honey over to her. "Mr. Mont used to eat porridge every morning. He liked."

"You were fond of Mont Allen, weren't you?" Alyssa questioned, surprised at the affection she heard in Morning Sun's voice whenever she mentioned him.

"Like family. Like kind, wise father."

"Are your parents living?" she asked as she poured some cream and honey on the porridge, stirred it and put a spoonful in her mouth.

"No. Parents died before Morning Sun work at ranch. Mr. Mont and Kayla became family." A tear slipped down her cheek. She wiped it away quickly and gave Alyssa a smile. "Morning Sun miss both sometimes."

"Mmm, this is really good," complimented Alyssa. To change the subject further, she asked, "When will Matthew wake up?"

"Morning Sun will bring him today, during lunch. You like?"

"That would be wonderful," said Alyssa. "Thank you."

Within a few minutes, Alyssa was out at the barn, where she found Luke just finishing up with the milking. "Is it all right if I get Daylight ready?"

"No need," said Luke. "The boss did."

"Oh?" she asked, surprised that Ed was already up and about. She glanced at her watch. It was only five-thirty. The sky was just barely beginning to lighten; the early dawn held hidden promises of what the day would bring.

"Yep. He and the others are out at Mountain Meadow. Do you remember how to get there?" Luke asked, lifting the bucket up and putting it on a stool.

"Past the lodge and follow the trail," she said.

"Yep. That'll do it. I'll be along shortly."

"I meant to thank you for rescuing my parachute," she said.

"Just following orders," said Luke. "Sorry I didn't get back with it before you left."

"Oh, that's all right. It arrived safely enough." She gave him a wide smile and went to find Daylight.

The chestnut mare was saddled and waiting for her in one of the stables. Alyssa quickly mounted the horse and found her backside a little saddle sore in the process. It was a good thing she'd only spent the morning in the saddle yesterday, she decided. Hopefully, today wouldn't be too painful for her. She made a clicking sound, and gently nudged Daylight with the heel of her boot as she tugged the reins. Within minutes she and Daylight were on their way along the trail that led to Mountain Meadow nearly a mile away.

The wind whisked her hair back from her face, and she was disappointed that she'd cut it again, but it seemed to be the style that Abbot preferred. She hoped she would find time to speak with Abbot in private. There were several things about their relationship that were not right, beginning with her hair and ending with his kiss the other night. When it came down to the real reason for her concerns about Abbot, Alyssa knew what was bothering her. Somehow she'd been sucked in by all of Abbot's attention and had finally caved in to his proposal. What kind of engagement was that? She wasn't certain they should be talking about marriage at all.

By the time Alyssa reached the camp, the men were well into their work of branding the cattle. She spent the rest of the morning chasing calves, whipping the air about them and leading them to the man and horse nearest her with a lasso, which was not as much fun as the men were having. Today, she decided, she would learn to use a lasso herself.

At noon, Morning Sun arrived in a small wagon pulled by a gray mare named Shadow. Little Matthew, dressed in farmer pants and a red plaid shirt, sat beside her on the buckboard. She reined the horse to a halt and set the brake. Then she put Matthew down and pointed toward Ed. "Go get Eddie," she told him. The toddler looked around until he spotted Ed, then headed toward him as fast as his little legs could carry him.

Ed dismounted Breeze and tied the reins in a clove hitch to a hitching post next to the corral. He walked toward Matthew as the toddler sought him, arms outstretched. "Hi there, partner!" said Ed as he swooped the boy up into his strong arms. "Did you miss me?"

"Miss Eddie!" said Matthew, clapping his hands in delight.

Morning Sun went to the rear of the wagon and lowered the tailboard that formed a handy platform for serving lunch. She pulled a box out onto the platform and unloaded it. Inside was a large pot of baked beans and a tray filled with ham sandwiches, potato chips, peanut butter cookies and cold, raw milk.

Alyssa walked over by Ed, who was holding Matthew now, to introduce herself to the young boy. The toddler looked curiously at her. His dark brown eyes seemed to ask, *Who are you?*

"Matthew, this is Alyssa," Ed said to the boy. "Can you say hello?"

"Hewo," said Matthew.

"Hello, Matthew," Alyssa smiled. She reached out and placed a hand against his cheek. "Do you know what this means?"

Matthew shook his head shyly.

"It means I love you," she whispered softly.

His brown eyes sparkled almost as much as her own. He reached a chubby little hand out and touched her cheek in response. Then he looked at Ed and squealed in delight, "Issa uv me!"

"I guess she does, partner," agreed Ed.

"Issa uv Eddie?" questioned little Matthew audaciously.

Alyssa smiled at his precocious inquiry. She also noticed that Ed was waiting for an answer almost as eagerly as Matthew. She gave them both a wide smile and said, "He's a good partner, isn't he?"

"Pard-er!" squealed Matthew. He wrapped his arms around Ed's neck and squeezed with all his strength.

Afterward, Ed held Matthew out to Alyssa.

"Do you want to come to me?" she asked.

The toddler hesitated, uncertainty evident in his eyes. Then he snuggled against Ed's shoulder. "Miss Eddie," he said.

"Maybe tomorrow," suggested Ed. "Are you hungry?" he asked Alyssa as he started toward the wagon.

The men had gathered around Morning Sun, each waiting their turn to receive a large plate with several sandwiches and a huge scoop of baked beans. Ed and Alyssa held back until the ranch hands had been served.

While waiting, Alyssa stepped behind Ed and played peek-a-boo with Matthew, poking her head out from behind Ed's back on either side. Each time she did, Matthew would giggle and squeal in delight. Soon the three of them were laughing contagiously.

After the others had been served and found places to sit, Alyssa took the plate with the smallest portion of food on it, then smiled at Ed shyly as she looked around for her fiancé.

Hans was sitting with Luke and Sidekick, but Abbot was sitting alone, across from the corrals on a big boulder, and well out of hearing range of the others. Realizing this might be the perfect time for her and Abbot to talk privately together, she turned back to Matthew and said, "I'm going to sit by Abbot. But I'll play with you some more later, okay?"

Matthew snuggled against Ed's shoulder in response. Ed nodded to her and tipped his hat with his free hand. Then he handed Matthew to Morning Sun and picked up his plate.

Alyssa carried her lunch plate across the meadow toward Abbot. "Hi," she said when she reached him. "Remember me?"

He smiled. "Vaguely."

"Mind if I sit by you?"

"I'd be disappointed if you didn't."

She sat down beside him on a huge rock. A light breeze fluttered the quaking aspen leaves and danced with her golden brown hair. The scent of spruce and pine mingled with the crisp mountain air.

"Enjoying yourself?" he asked as she took a bite of her sandwich.

"I am. It's hard work, but very rewarding."

"Not much of a vacation," he admitted. "Do you mind spending your time working this hard?"

"Not at all," she said as she nudged him gently with her shoulder.

He gave her a weak smile. "You do like it here, don't you?"

"I love it," she agreed. "Of course, I am a bit stiff and sore in a few places." She rubbed her backside. "I suppose I'll have to ask Morning Sun to let me use some of her salve tonight."

"It'll do the trick," said Abbot. "It always has."

"I didn't notice it so much last night," she admitted. "I think I was too tired to notice anything except how worn out I was."

"You didn't say goodnight," he pouted momentarily.

"You were having fun," she remembered. "Besides, if I'd gone near that stream, I'm sure you would have found a way to toss me in, and I was already too cold for that."

"You're probably right," he agreed. "I would have."

They ate in silence for a few more minutes until his plate was empty.

"I really need to talk to you, Abbot," she began. "There are some things bothering me that I think we should discuss."

"I think so, too," he said. "But you go first."

Alyssa hesitated. This wasn't going to be easy for her, but she had to voice her concerns before their relationship went any further. "I've been having second thoughts."

His green eyes widened in surprise. A gentle breeze whisked his dark brown hair off his forehead. "Oh?"

"Remember the other night when you kissed me in the meadow?"

"How could I forget?" he questioned. "It was all I could do not to lash out at Ed for interrupting us."

"I felt the opposite," she confessed. "I was glad he did."

"Why?" he asked, obviously dismayed at this admission.

"I hadn't wanted you to kiss me like that. It was too much, too soon. And when I'd tried to push you away, you wouldn't let me."

Abbot remained silent, searching her face as though puzzled by her feelings. Finally he said, "I hadn't realized."

"I felt frightened," she admitted. She noticed a flash of irritation in his eyes, but he didn't say anything, so she continued. "When two people love each other, their first thoughts should be directed toward how the other one is feeling. You say you hadn't realized, and I believe you. But I also believe that if you really loved me, you would have known how frightened I was. You would have felt me trying to push you away, and you wouldn't have been blinded by your own passion. Do you understand what I'm trying to say?"

He hesitated for several long moments. "I guess you don't realize what you do to me. Ever since you agreed to marry me, I've been counting down the hours. I admit that I let myself get a little out of control that night, but it's far more difficult for men to suppress passion than it is for women."

Alyssa shook her head. "Some men use that as an excuse to lure women into bed with them, but I don't believe it." She waited for his response, but he looked off at the forest beyond the meadow as though he hadn't heard. When he finally looked back at her, she saw moisture in his eyes, filling the rims, but not spilling over.

"Do you love me?" he whispered, a hint of uncertainty in his voice.

His question brought up all the feelings she feared to discuss with him, and she knew she couldn't answer it with any amount of certainty. "I think love is something that you grow into," she whispered, studying his expression. "Up to this point in my life, I've found that love isn't something that I automatically feel, or that I have any control over." Reluctantly she shook her head. "I can't say that I love you beyond all measure." She hesitated, and for a moment she saw a bit of sadness in Abbot's green eyes. Hastily she added, "But I do love you, Abbot. It's just that my love for you isn't as fully developed as you may want it to be. You'll need to be patient with me. I'm willing to bend for you, but I'm not willing to break. Do you understand?"

He studied her face for a moment, then nodded. "I'm trying to understand. I want this to work for both of us, but I have to ask you something first."

"What is it?" she asked timidly.

He put their plates upon the ground and turned to her, then ran his fingers through her thick brown hair and gazed lovingly into her dark, brown eyes. "When will it be time to meet some of my needs?"

She admired his tenderness with her. "If you're speaking of intimacy, you know as well as I that it will come on our wedding night."

He seemed annoyed with her answer. "Don't you think we should find out if we're compatible in that arena before we get married?" he suggested.

Alyssa's mouth dropped open and she inhaled sharply. "Abbot!" Completely astounded by his question, she felt her heart tighten within her chest.

He rolled his eyes and pouted, but after a moment, he said, "Sex isn't the only thing that troubles me, Alyssa. I think you're expecting a temple wedding, though you haven't said, but I'm not sure that's where I want to marry. Wouldn't the meadow be an ideal place, or if it rains, the lodge?"

Alyssa shook her head. "Abbot, you know how important a temple wedding is to me."

He let out a long, ragged breath. "Alyssa, I'm not sure I believe the church is true anymore. Hans and I have had some pretty serious discussions about it, and I'm not sure I even have a testimony."

Alyssa bristled. "Hans doesn't believe in anything!" she protested. She amended her response to, "Unless it's living on the dole system and becoming a professional student."

"That was an unkind thing to say!" he scolded. "Hans is a decent man, and he does believe in God. He's just not sure God can be found at any one church. People say they're Christians, but their actions scream out to the world that they're not! Look in the mirror, Alyssa! You believe in Jesus Christ, and say that you follow Him. But Jesus taught us not to judge people, and look what you've done to Hans. You've judged him and you've only known him for a few days."

A lump formed in her throat and her eyes filled with tears. "I'm sorry," she apologized. "I didn't realize that's what I was doing."

Her tears seemed to soften him, and he put his arms around her, pulling her close to him. "A lot of Christians are hypocrites, Alyssa. They profess one thing but their actions say another."

She pulled back just far enough to look into his green eyes, and was surprised to see so much passion in his feelings.

He let go of her and said with conviction, "At least when I tell you I want to be intimate with you, I'm honest. I'm not on a pedestal, looking down at the world and condemning it. And I'm not pious on Sundays while living the life of a sinner through the week."

Hesitating a moment, he finally confessed, "There are things about God that bother me, Alyssa. I don't understand how God can take my parents away without considering how I would feel about it. I hardly remember my mother, and when Pa died, I hadn't finished college. He didn't even get to come to my graduation."

"God's ways are not man's ways, Abbot."

"There's one other thing," he finally admitted. "I don't like the idea that God considers man as less than the dust of the earth. What kind of a Father tells his children that?"

"You've never given any indication in all the time I've known you that you felt this way." Alyssa dabbed at her eyes with the cuff of her shirt sleeve. "You've attended church with me several times. When did you start feeling like this?"

He hesitated before answering her. "About six months now. During the two weeks that I spent with Hans on his boat, we had some very interesting conversations. Do you know he's read all the standard works?"

She shook her head. Frankly she was surprised to hear it. Then she realized she was judging Hans again, and she knew that was unfair to him.

"His brother gave him a complete set for Christmas last year. Joshua gave everyone in his family a set. The man's possessed, I suppose."

He gave her a crooked grin and somehow it made her smile. "Hmm," she teased. "Guess Kayla married an all right guy, after all."

Abbot shrugged. "Alyssa, I do love you. With all my heart, I do. I'm just not sure about all the other things in my life."

"What do you suggest we do?" she asked, but her heart felt heavy with the seriousness of their conversation. "Do you want me to give the engagement ring back?"

"No!" he exclaimed. Then he pulled her against him once again, and whispered so no one could possibly hear but her. "I love you, Alyssa. I want to marry you. You said the other night that when two people love one another, they should work out whatever problems they have, and not let anyone or anything come between them. I agree with that. But I also think that there has to be some bending. Maybe I can't be exactly who you were expecting. But isn't there some room for a compromise?"

Alyssa hesitated. She hadn't realized she would be asked to give up a temple wedding for the cause of love. That was something she simply could not do. Finally, she faced him with all the resolve she could muster. "Abbot, I will not marry outside the temple. If that means I have to wait until you're ready, I will. But the longer I have to wait, the longer you will have to wait for the intimacy that you want."

Abbot took in a deep breath, and she could see that he was struggling with her ultimatum. Finally he said, "All right. I'll do my best to find the spark that I used to have for the gospel, if you'll do the same to spark up the flame I want to find in you on our wedding night."

His willingness to abide by her wishes touched Alyssa in a way that surprised her. Suddenly Alyssa realized how she could help him. "Oh, Abbot, something just occurred to me. When my sister got engaged, she and her fiancé read scriptures every morning and evening together, and prayed together every day. Perhaps we should try the same thing. It may bring us closer together and help us both in areas where we're lacking."

He smiled. "Except that you're going home in a few weeks and I'm staying here at the ranch until we get married."

"Silly," she punched him playfully in the arm. "Adam was living in Boston at the time and Alexandria was still in Heber. They read scriptures by telephone morning and night."

"Sounds expensive." He gave her a little frown.

"Then put it on my phone bill until we get married. I'll pay for it."

"No, I think I can pay the phone bills."

"Then you'll do it?" she asked eagerly.

He nodded. "What have I got to lose?"

She considered answering verbally, but in a surge of spontaneity, she kissed him in lieu of an answer. The kiss was gentle and exquisitely tender. This time, however, Abbot knew the boundaries of their intimacy. To her delight, he respected them.

When she let him up for air, he smiled. "I get the point."

Chapter Seven

The rest of the afternoon Ed taught Alyssa how to lasso a calf and restrain it for branding. She had asked Abbot to teach her, but he'd reluctantly turned her over to Ed's tutorial skills, saying he couldn't do it as well as Ed could. Although Abbot and the other men helped, Ed was the main instructor.

Alyssa wouldn't have minded Ed being her teacher, but every time he stood behind her, helping her twirl the lasso opening over her head, she felt giddy and light-headed. It took all of her stamina to keep these physical sensations under control. She also wondered if she was not eating enough. Sometimes if she skipped a meal or two, her blood sugar plummeted, making her feel something vaguely similar, yet different somehow.

It took the entire afternoon, but by dusk she finally managed to lasso a small calf, jump from the saddle, lay the calf on the ground and bind its hooves. All the men cheered, whistled and shouted their praise.

However, Alyssa still cringed as the branding iron was placed against the animals left hind quarter. Subjecting a calf to that hot poker was something she couldn't force herself to do.

"Tomorrow we start using the post driver," Ed informed the five workers as they headed back to the stables at dusk. "We'll work in shifts. Four hour rotations and three teams. Decide who your partner is and get your system set in your minds. Rotate duties every hour so you don't get worn out."

"How long will it take?" she questioned.

"With fifty-three hundred posts, we should be able to get them placed and driven in eight weeks, maybe nine, and then the wire crimping begins."

"Perhaps I should be glad I'm only staying three weeks," Alyssa teased.

"I'd like to stay longer," Hans said unexpectedly. "See the fencing through, if that's okay. If you agree, I'd like to work until after the cattle drive this fall."

"I'd be glad for the extra help," Ed nodded in agreement.

"I thought you were heading out in July," reminded Abbot.

"Then what would I do?" Hans asked. "Sit around on my boat the rest of the summer? No, this is a challenge and I'm up to it. I want to see the job done."

A look of amazement crossed over Abbot's face, but he didn't say anything. Alyssa was sure her expression was similar. Rich, pampered Hans was buckling down to the ranching lifestyle better than she'd thought he would. *Will miracles never cease!!* she mused to herself.

Then an expression wandered across Hans' face that puzzled her. His demeanor seemed to indicate that he had an ulterior motive in mind, some personal agenda that he had no intention of sharing with them. *There you go again!* she scolded herself silently. *Judging Hans unfairly!* She tried to dismiss the idea entirely. Still, she had an unsettling feeling that Hans had more on his docket than ranching cattle.

By nine that evening, Alyssa had showered and lathered her backside with Morning Sun's relieving salve. She had just climbed into bed when she heard Morning Sun calling her name.

Groaning silently, she got out of bed and opened the door.

Morning Sun was holding a set of scriptures. "Alyssa will read scriptures tonight with Abbot. Morning Sun will read with you?"

Alyssa's mouth dropped open in amazement. Abbot had remembered when Alyssa hadn't. *Bless his pointed head!* she thought, realizing he had other motives behind his diligence in keeping their agreement.

"I'll be right down," she told Morning Sun.

The older woman smiled broadly and turned away.

Alyssa put on a pair of jeans and a tee shirt, then grabbed her scriptures and headed downstairs. She was surprised to see all five men, clean shaven and neatly dressed, waiting for her.

"My word!" she exclaimed. "I come downstairs expecting one man and find five of them waiting in the living room!"

Abbot spoke up first. "Um, actually Alyssa, we call this the gathering room."

"Why?" she asked curiously.

"Mont's wife said it was big enough that a crowd could gather here," he explained. "It's been called the gathering room ever since."

"I like that," she said, "and that's exactly what we have here tonight, a crowd."

Ed was seated on the big overstuffed chair, his scriptures on his lap, studying her. *Like a panther studies moving prey,* Alyssa thought. Luke and Sidekick were on one sofa, Hans was seated on the big old rocker, and Morning Sun brought in a chair from the kitchen. Abbot had saved a place on the sofa for Alyssa, right next to him.

When she sank down beside him, she realized that all eyes were looking to her to lead them. "Well," she said, "since this is a patriarchal gathering, may I defer to Ed to select someone to offer an invocation?"

Ed's head came up with her suggestion. His eyes narrowed, but he didn't voice a complaint. "I guess I'll say it tonight," he offered.

Everyone bowed their heads and Ed began with a direct, yet humble prayer that thrilled Alyssa more than she'd ever admit. Although his words were simple, she doubted that any others would have suited the occasion better.

> "Our Father in Heaven,
> Thank thee for thy holy words which we're about to read.
> Thank thee for these good people gathered here.
> Bless that we will understand not only what we read,
> but what thou would have us do for those around us.
> And bless the woman who got us all together. . . ."

All the men echoed a subdued "Amen," and Alyssa opened her Bible to Matthew. "Thank you, Ed," she whispered. Then to the others, she said, "I thought we could start with the New Testament. Perhaps we can each read a couple verses and go around the circle until we get the first two chapters read. Does that sound agreeable?"

All the men nodded in agreement, some with a fairly gruff, "Yep!" in accompaniment.

"Very well. Perhaps the person who sits in the rocking chair each time should be the person who starts. Tonight that would be Hans."

"My pleasure," Hans said, opening his Bible.

As they read together, Luke had a difficult time reading and this worried Alyssa. Hoping he wouldn't give up without making his best effort, she noticed that most of the men seemed to pretend they were unaware of Luke's stumbling over the words. However, Hans studied

Luke closely, and she hoped he wouldn't say anything to make Luke feel uncomfortable. To her relief, Hans said nothing.

By the time the first two chapters were read, and all had participated, Alyssa felt divine inspiration settle upon her in the gathering room. It filled her with such sweetness that she found herself silently praying that everyone had experienced the sensation as well.

Before they stood up to leave, she asked if Ed would call on someone to offer a benediction. He suggested Abbot, who complied willingly. After the prayer, Alyssa said, "Thank you all for coming. If you'd like to join us for scriptures in the morning, Abbot and I will be reading again at four thirty."

Sidekick arched an eyebrow in dismay, then gave her a mischievous grin and moaned, "Does this mean we HAVE to keep you?"

To his remark everyone laughed, including Alyssa. After the men said goodnight, they started to leave. Abbot held back while Ed followed Morning Sun into the kitchen, leaving Alyssa and Abbot alone.

"Why did you invite all the men to read scriptures with us?" she asked him. "Not that I'm disappointed. It was a sweet gesture. I was just surprised."

"I didn't invite them," he smirked. "They followed me."

Alyssa burst out laughing.

"It's not funny," he said dryly. "I picked up my scriptures and headed for the door when Hans asked where I was going. I told him you wanted to read scriptures together, but he said that was a likely excuse as any for me coming over here."

"They actually followed you?"

"Yes. Luke said I would try any excuse to spend time with you, and I said if they didn't believe me they could join us. Five minutes later, here we were!"

She gave him a quick hug. "You can invite them over anytime," she suggested. "It was much more enjoyable than their creek bath last night."

"I've got to get back over there, or they'll pester me the rest of the night," he said, giving her a quick kiss on the cheek. "I guess I'll see you first thing in the morning."

"Okay. Goodnight, Abbot."

After watching him leave, Alyssa turned to go upstairs, but she had only reached the second step when she heard Ed's voice behind her.

"What was all that about?" he asked, twisting his hat around in his hands nervously.

"What?" she questioned, turning around to face him.

"All that, 'Ed, choose someone to offer the prayer' routine. I didn't call this meeting together!" he snapped.

"I didn't mean to offend you," she apologized. "In my home, my mother always deferred to the oldest male in the room, or the patriarch of the group, to call upon people to pray. I meant no disrespect. Quite the opposite, actually."

He glared at her for a moment. "So you meant to honor me as the oldest man here?" he huffed.

"No." Alyssa smiled. "You're taking offense when none was given, I assure you."

"Hans is older than me by at least a year," he pointed out.

"I know that," she affirmed. "But you are the oldest priesthood bearer, and this was a gathering created for a religious purpose. Doesn't that make you the most qualified to preside?"

"Oh!" Then he slapped his Stetson back on his head, turned on his heel and stomped away.

When he had closed the door, Alyssa sank down onto the stairs, put her elbows on her knees and her head in her hands. *It seems I can't please either brother!* she agonized silently.

⁂

At four in the morning Ed turned off the alarm, rolled out of bed and onto his knees. He stayed there for a while, talking things over with the Lord. When he finished, he got up and slipped into a pair of wranglers and a cotton shirt.

He'd been cross with Alyssa last night and he knew he should apologize, but she'd caught him off guard and he'd responded before he thought his actions through, which wasn't like him at all. Unable to understand how he could have reacted without considering consequences, he shook his head, silently chiding himself for it. Perhaps Alyssa's bad habit was contagious, though he certainly hoped not.

She'd put him in his place, that's for sure. As patriarch of the Sparkleman family, and in Joshua's absence, Ed was also patriarch of the Bar M Ranch. He had never considered that before. Up until that moment, he considered himself as "just Ed, the ever present cowpoke," or "Boss," as his men liked to call him. He had to admit that Alyssa's calling him a patriarch, and her expectation that he should act accordingly, scared him.

Ed hadn't gone on a mission for more than one reason: He didn't know how to talk about his faith; he felt awkward and inhibited in any group of his peers; and when he was nineteen, he wasn't converted enough to the gospel to even consider sharing it with others.

He'd wondered over the years why he felt so shy around people, especially women. While growing up, his whole life had been centered around "the ranch." He didn't know any other way of life until Mont insisted he go to college, though attending Arizona State University hadn't changed him much. He'd received his degrees in criminal law and animal husbandry. Still, Ed was anything but refined. And missionaries were supposed to be refined.

A mountain man with every fibre of his being, Ed knew he could never be a sailor or an archaeologist; he wasn't even the best pilot in the world. His backside belonged on a saddle, his Stetson belonged on his head, and his boots belonged in the stirrups. Ranching wasn't just something he did to earn a living, ranching was who he was; it defined Ed and gave his life purpose.

For a moment, bittersweet memories flooded over him; he recalled that Kayla had wondered if he could ever like sailing. *Hmpf!* Water was for three things only, in his opinion: Drinking, bathing, and fishing! He hated the theater, and he thought ballroom dances were for city folk who had nothing better to do.

Ed pulled on his boots, finished buttoning up the shirt, and grabbed his Stetson. When he heard the men stirring about, he hurried out of the cabin and across the meadow because he wanted to speak to Alyssa without an audience. Within a few minutes he arrived at the back door of the lodge with his scriptures in his hand, hoping Alyssa would give him a moment to apologize.

Morning Sun was preparing pompanoosuc porridge in the kitchen. Ed tapped on the window pane and saw her turn and smile at him. Then she scurried over and unlocked the door.

"Morning," he said. "Is she up?"

Morning Sun nodded. "Alyssa makes her bed."

Ed savored the smell of the porridge. "Mind if I have some?"

"Porridge must set first," she told him. "When Alyssa comes, porridge is ready."

"I'll go check on her." He squeezed Morning Sun's hand affectionately, then went into the gathering room and up the stairs.

"Alyssa!" he called out.

He only had to wait a moment until she opened a door and peeked out at him.

"Oh," she said dryly. "It's you!"

"That bad, hmm?" he asked, giving her a wide smile.

Carrying a pair of boots, she opened the door all the way and stepped into the hall. She was dressed smartly in jeans and a western shirt made of a plaid material in aqua, white and light gray. She looked sharp and lean, with feminine curves in all the right places.

Ed wasn't able to refrain from whistling. "Whoa, girl!" he remarked. "No wonder my men are falling all over themselves to spend time with you."

"You're just trying to make up for being so rude last night," she said smugly.

"Not exactly," he denied. "But I did come to apologize."

She went down the stairs in front of him, as though she hadn't heard, so he followed her.

"Dang it, Alyssa Mae! Do I have to grovel?"

Alyssa turned quickly. Her mouth dropped open and her eyes widened. "What did you call me?" she asked, looking up at him harshly.

He arched an eyebrow. "Oops!" Then he stammered, "Well, er, that is, um . . ."

She crossed her arms and gave him a determined glare.

"Abbot mentioned what your middle name is," he confessed sheepishly. "I sort of like the sound of the two together."

"And that's all?" she questioned.

"Of course that's all," he defended himself. "What else?"

She squared her shoulders to inform him, "The only person who ever called me by my first and middle name together is my father, and only when he was very, very angry with me." She arched an eyebrow as though asking if that had been his intent.

"I ain't angry," he insisted, as a surprised smile wandered across his rugged face.

"Then what are you doing here?" She glanced at her watch. "Twenty minutes early."

"I told you. I felt bad about last night and I came over early to apologize. I didn't want to be in the hot seat all day."

"I don't know if I want to forgive you," she said stiffly. "Because you were angry with me, I didn't sleep well, and now I'm just plain irritable."

"I'm sorry," he admitted, this time with as much tenderness as he could find inside him. "If it's any consolation, I didn't sleep well either."

Alyssa seemed to soften a little and he gave her a soulful expression, one that he hoped would show her just how sorry he really was.

"And if you're irritable, I know these will help," he suggested, holding up his scriptures.

"I certainly hope so," she said.

"Does that mean I'm forgiven?" he questioned.

She exhaled, but he also heard a little tenderness in it, and he was pleased to see the corners of her mouth curl, as though she was trying to suppress a smile.

"I suppose," she agreed. "But honestly Ed, don't do that to me again. I have nightmares when I'm upset, and I don't handle them well."

"Would it help to share them with someone?"

"It hasn't so far."

"Then I'm doubly sorry that I upset you. I'll try not to anymore."

When she nodded, he could tell that she was still a little irritable, and he decided to use a different approach. "Dang it, Alyssa Mae, you're even pretty when you're angry! Now is that fair to all my men?" He was hoping to make her smile just a little before the others arrived.

It apparently worked. Her brown eyes glistened as the corners of her mouth curled into a wide, brilliant smile.

Ed took off his Stetson and hit his knee with it as he exclaimed, "Dang! That smile would knock the meanness right out of a polecat! Alyssa Mae, I may have to fire you, if you keep this up!"

As though she suddenly realized what he was trying to do, she burst out laughing, and the sound was music to his ears.

But like all good campfire stories, this one came to an end when Abbot came knocking at the front door, with the rest of the men at his side. Ed didn't know whether to be disappointed or relieved.

🕊 🕊

By eleven-thirty that morning, the sun had warmed the meadow, and outer shirts had been removed and tied at their waists. Tee shirts were all they needed by this time of day. During her childhood Alyssa had learned to dress in layers, especially when visiting her grandfather. That habit had been good practice for the Bar M Ranch. As the day heated up, some layers could be taken off, but if a squall rushed in, a layer or two could be put back on.

Alyssa and Abbot had driven twenty steel posts into the mountainside.

Her arms and hands ached from hauling the heavy posts and inserting them into the post driver. The heavy work gloves she wore prevented scrapes and blisters, but did nothing to prevent fatigue. Alyssa shook her hands inside the gloves, trying to restore the circulation in them. Then she walked back to the wagon and grabbed another bundle of posts while Abbot prepared the post driver for another beating.

Suddenly, Abbot stopped and held his hand out to prevent Alyssa passing him. "Shhh," he whispered. "Look."

Just below them, dancing around the tall pine trees, two young bear cubs nipped at one another playfully.

"Back up," whispered Abbot. "Where there are cubs, there's a mother nearby."

Alyssa put the posts down immediately and did as she was told. They reached the wagon, walking backwards, looking toward the cubs and around them for any sign of the bear cubs' mother, but they did not see her.

"I'll check the area out," said Abbot bravely.

"Why don't we take a break for now?" suggested Alyssa, a bit fearful for both of them.

Abbot paused a moment, then reluctantly agreed. "To the horses?"

She nodded. "Now!"

They raced across an open space toward the horses and mounted them with a swiftness unexcelled in previous days.

Almost before she planted herself in the saddle, Alyssa yelled "Go!" and dug her heels into Daylight's flanks.

Abbot did the same with his horse and they began a hasty gallop up the trail toward Mountain Meadow, a half mile away. When they came riding into camp, Sidekick and Luke both brought their horses alongside them.

"Where's the fire?" asked Sidekick, his long red hair curling out from beneath his hat.

"Bear cubs!" Alyssa exclaimed. "We didn't wait around for the mother to show up."

"Get the gun, Sidekick," Abbot said. "We'll go spook them off."

Luke nodded toward the west. "Here comes the boss. Let's see what he wants us to do."

Alyssa was relieved to see Ed riding his white stallion toward them across the lower end of the meadow. Hans rode alongside on a chestnut stallion.

When they reached the group, Ed drawled, "What's this, a hen's party?"

"No," Alyssa said with a chuckle. "There are two bear cubs down by the fence line."

"Go on up to the lodge for lunch," he said directly to her. "I hope you can get there before Morning Sun starts out with Matthew. I'll go check it out. Sidekick, get your gun and come with me."

"I want to go with you," Abbot complained.

"Take care of your fiancée first!" Ed growled. "When she's safe, then think about what you want to do!" He looked at Alyssa. "Now, go!"

Alyssa didn't have to be told twice. She coaxed Daylight into a steady gallop, with Abbot, Hans and Luke at her heels. Morning Sun was ready to start loading the wagon when they arrived. They gathered around the kitchen counter and ate steaming spaghetti while they waited for Ed and Sidekick John to join them. But Abbot took his plate and went off into the meadow to sulk.

Fifteen minutes later, Ed walked through the kitchen door with Sidekick right behind him. All eyes turned to Ed's.

"The mother wasn't far from the cubs," Ed explained. "I'm glad you got away without attracting her attention. I think we'll skip fencing for the rest of the day." To Alyssa he said, "In the future, you should keep your horse nearby. Your horse can run faster than any bear can. Those of us who have them will start packing rifles with our saddle-bags."

"Perhaps you should speak with Abbot," suggested Alyssa.

"I spoke with him!" Ed growled. "He ain't got the sense God gave a mule!"

Sidekick held up a handful of small bells, almost the size of golf balls, with bright, tinkling tones. "But I got bear bells," he said, apparently hoping to change the conversation.

Alyssa noticed a look of relief on Ed's face when he said, "You should each wear one of these on your belt whenever you go out. If a bear hears you coming, normally it'll leave long before you arrive. We ain't seen too many bear up here, but there are plenty of tracks. Stay within visual range of a partner at all times because the mountains don't give up secrets."

When Ed and Sidekick sat down to eat, the conversation became a little more light-hearted. By the time lunch was over, Alyssa had calmed down considerably. But her concern was for Abbot. She slipped away from the others and went out to the meadow where Abbot was sitting on a log near the burned out campfire from the other night.

"Are you okay?" she asked as she moved a log over to sit beside him.

"This isn't any of your business!" Abbot snapped.

"Abbot, I only—"

"Better get back in the lodge where you'll be safe," he growled. Then he stomped off toward the cabin.

Alyssa shook her head. Both brothers had tempers, it seemed. She couldn't decide which of them was in the right this time, Ed, for thinking of Alyssa's safety first, or Abbot, who'd been humiliated in front of the other men.

Chapter Eight

*E*d insisted Alyssa stay indoors the rest of Saturday, and she spent that time helping Morning Sun make berry pies for Sunday dinner. Morning Sun's husband, Elijah, had taken Matthew into Vernal for supplies, and the rest of the men had gone back out to work.

Alyssa wasn't disappointed. She had rounded up more calves and hauled more steel posts than she ever wanted to see again. Her arms and legs ached worse than her backside. But it didn't seem that she was as sore as the first two days. She hoped she was getting used to such hard physical labor.

Saturday night everyone joined her for scripture study. Everyone except Abbot.

When she finally went to bed, she spent several hours tossing and turning, trying to drive the nightmare away. Alyssa no longer thought of it as merely a dream; it had become an important reason why she almost didn't want to go to sleep at all. When she awoke the next morning, she knew the issue of her engagement to Abbot would have to be resolved soon, or she may never be able to sleep peacefully again. Her body was wearing down with nightmares.

Abbot didn't attend scripture study with her and the men on Sunday morning, either. But he did agree to attend church with her, perhaps only because he knew she would go with Ed if he refused to take her. Alyssa sat beside Abbot in the car as he drove to church, feeling dismayed that he was still unwilling to talk about his problems.

Her mind wandered as they traveled down the winding dirt road toward Maeser. She wished Abbot would start attending scripture study again because it was going rather well. Luke seemed to be reading a little better, and she could tell he'd been touched a time or two by the spirit when she saw moisture in his eyes. The men usually had some interesting gem to toss out at the group after each session, as though they'd been thinking of something to say that would please Alyssa.

There were times when Alyssa noticed Ed watching her as she read along. *But all the ranch hands do that!* She decided it must be difficult for men to live their lives in the lap of a cattle herd, without a woman around. Of course, Morning Sun was at the Bar M most of the time, but she was at least fifteen years older than Ed, and a happily married mother.

As she pondered her relationship with Abbot, Alyssa found, to her dismay, that she had been comparing Abbot to his brother since the very first day they arrived. Considering, she was not surprised that Abbot came in with lower scores than Ed in nearly everything Alyssa noticed.

Abbot wasn't especially fond of Matthew, or at least he didn't go out of his way to play with the precocious child. It didn't matter what Ed was doing, if Matthew arrived, it could wait until Ed and his little partner had spent some time together.

Ed always appreciated what anyone did for him, or for the ranch, and he always said "Thanks," or "Good job," to his men. Abbot, on the other hand, rarely thanked anyone for anything. Ed would look for ways to help each of them with a job, a skill or a problem. But

Abbot usually looked the other way, and this annoyed Alyssa. And of course, it was Ed who had taught her how to lasso a calf.

Alyssa looked over at Abbot and a tear slipped down her cheek as she realized she may never break through the barrier Abbot had built for himself. What troubled her more was that she wasn't sure she wanted to.

In silence, she watched the road ahead of them. Hans was riding with Ed in the white pickup, but there was no dust kicked up by the tires today. It had rained all night and the air was damp and cool. The welcome moisture had even subdued the dust storm that normally followed any vehicle traveling this rugged mountain road.

After straightening her skirt, she pulled down the visor and looked in the mirror to make sure her mascara hadn't run. When she was satisfied, she pushed the visor back in place.

Finally Abbot broke into her thoughts. "Are you still mad at me?" he asked.

She looked over at him and studied his expression. "I wasn't mad at you to start with."

"Yes you were. I saw that expression on your face when Ed scolded me like a school boy."

"I was frightened because he seemed concerned about my safety," she admitted, "but I was never angry."

He remained thoughtful for a moment. Then he said, "Ed was right, you know. He's always right."

Determined not to be baited by his remark, Alyssa remained quiet. Finally Abbot said, "I guess you've got Hans swayed."

"Oh?" she asked, surprised at his statement.

"After they came back to the cabin from reading scriptures with you last night, Hans said he'd never felt such a calming influence."

"And that means I've swayed him?" she questioned, a little irritated at the insinuation.

"You know what I mean. You've got all the men thinking about God, and what God would want them to do."

"And you?" she asked. When he didn't answer, she asked it once again. "And you?"

There was a long silence. Then he said, "I just can't get the spiritual high you want from me, Alyssa."

"Skipping scripture study won't make it any easier," she observed quietly.

"I know that!" he snapped. His tone was sharp, almost angry. Finally he shrugged and explained, "It's just that there are too many unanswered questions in my mind, Alyssa. Every time I think I've found the answer to one question, two more bubble up in its place."

"You need to keep trying," she suggested. She waited a minute or two, and when he didn't respond, she asked, "You do believe in God, don't you, Abbot?"

"Of course I do. That hasn't changed." His voice sounded a little irritated by her question. Then, as though he wanted to prove that he still believed in God, he said, "Just because I'm a scientist, it doesn't mean that I don't believe. I know there has to be more to this world than soil and water and air. What about all the intricate patterns of leaves and plants, and how man uses oxygen from them while they use carbon dioxide from us? Everything in nature is too well organized to have happened all by accident."

"That's good," she commended, relieved that he still recognized a supreme creator.

However, when Abbot's next remark came, she knew that he was no closer to longing for the things of God than he'd been a few days ago. "Except that we're no better than the dust of the earth, remember?" he questioned, and his voice was almost sarcastic. "In scripture, the Lord says, '. . . how great is the nothingness of the children of men; yea, even they are less than the dust of the earth.' How could God say that, Alyssa? We're His children!"

It was easy to see how upset Abbot was by this verse. Alyssa quietly opened her scriptures and found the right chapter. Silently she read the verses with a prayer in her heart, asking the Lord to help her resolve the problems that were causing Abbot to stumble. When she was finished reading, she prayed once again. Then, with the page open on her lap, she asked, "What does the dust do, Abbot?"

He looked over at her as though he was humoring a small child. "The dust doesn't do anything!" he snapped in frustration.

"Yes," she insisted. "Even the dust has a specific purpose. What does it do?"

He appeared to be deep in thought for a few moments, then he said, "It is pushed around by the wind and settles on everything it can. What kind of purpose is that?"

"Does it lift heavy objects?"

"No."

"Does it swim mighty rivers?"

"No. It only moves when something, or someone, moves it."

"So it doesn't think?"

"No."

"It doesn't calculate or reason?"

"No." He arched an eyebrow as if to ask where she was going with this line of questioning.

"Does it obey?" she asked.

"No."

"Are you sure?"

"No. Yes. Whatever."

"Think about it Abbot. Does the dust do what it is supposed to do?"

"Of course it does," he exploded. "It's dust!"

"If dust does what it is supposed to do, then would it be appropriate to say that the dust obeys God?" she asked.

He inhaled sharply, then he nodded. "I suppose it does," he answered.

"Do you obey God?" she questioned.

He opened his mouth as though he'd intended to answer, then he closed it again. "No," he said finally. "You know I don't."

"Maybe before you condemn God entirely, you should read the six verses that precede his observation about the dust. They speak almost entirely about how disobedient man is in the eternal realm of God's plan."

"You're saying that, because I'm disobedient, I am less than the dust of the earth?"

"I'm saying that, when you take a scripture out of context, it often changes the way God intended you to understand His word."

"You just don't get it!" he complained. "We're talking about something that doesn't breathe or smell or see or eat. It doesn't think or talk or build bridges. It just sits there!" he barked.

Alyssa remained silent for a moment before she made her final observation: "Yet with all these limitations, dust still finds it necessary to obey."

&s ɛ&

While they were waiting after church for Ed to arrive from teaching his primary class, Abbot linked fingers with Alyssa and said, "You know, we don't have to wait for Ed. We could just leave a note on the truck and tell him we've gone ahead without him. I'm sure he would understand."

"No," she insisted. "That would be rude."

"I've done it before," Abbot coaxed. "He won't be the least surprised."

"I would never do that to my brother," she said, "and since Ed is soon to become my brother, I feel that I should treat him like that now."

Hans turned to face Abbot and said, "If we don't leave now, they'll have closed by the time we get there."

Abbot's expression fell and he heaved a sigh of regret.

Alyssa, realizing her fiancé had deceived her, made no effort to control her temper as it rose proportionately to his dismay. "Where were you planning on taking me?" she questioned.

Abbot almost choked on his words before he got them out of his mouth. "I promised to take Hans up to Dutch John before the marina closes. He wants to run the Green River while he's up here."

"Did you explain to Hans that the Lord expects us to keep the Sabbath day holy, and that this is something you could do any other day?" she asked.

An eyebrow lifted on Hans' face as he watched Alyssa cautiously, but firmly, stand her ground with Abbot. When she saw Hans' expression, she realized that he had no idea he was infringing upon their obligation to the Lord.

"Do you intend to keep up this charade after we're married?" asked Abbot.

"It's no charade, Abbot. I intend to do as our Father in Heaven has asked us."

"Regardless of my feelings?" His voice was pitched with anger now.

Alyssa turned her back to him, refusing to answer.

Abbot put his hand on her shoulder. "Alyssa?"

Stubbornly she said, "You should have told Hans he can call Dutch John in the morning. Don't your brother and his wife manage the river rafts?"

"I suppose we could phone," said Hans, apparently dismayed that he had overstepped his bounds. He nodded in favor of Alyssa's suggestion.

"No!" Abbot growled. "Alyssa, remember what you said about working out our differences? You're not even trying!"

"I am trying," she protested. "It's the Sabbath and I'm trying to keep the day holy, as the scriptures teach us."

"Fine!" he barked. "Stay here and ride home with Ed! We'll see you back at the ranch later on."

"You have your free agency, Abbot," came her defeated response.

Hans intervened. "We don't have to go up there today. We can telephone and go another time."

"No!" Abbot almost yelled at him. "I'm not going to live my life scheduled around her sense of priorities. Maybe it's time she realized that!" He got in the car, slammed the door shut, and turned on the ignition.

"I'll talk to him," said Hans to Alyssa. As he got in the car with Abbot, he said, "You're going to regret this before the day's over. Why don't we just stay here?"

But Abbot was apparently too angry. He put the car in drive and pressed the gas pedal, squealing the tires on the pavement as he left.

Alyssa couldn't prevent the tears from welling up in her eyes. She pulled a handkerchief from her handbag and dabbed at them. Feeling completely alone, she sat down on the grass near Ed's white truck and waited. Fortunately, nearly all the congregation had gone home, and she was, for the most part, unnoticed. Thankful that she'd worn her calf-length skirt, she pulled her knees up to her chest and rested her head against them. After a few minutes she heard the church door swing shut and she tensed, thinking it was another member.

Then Ed sat beside her on the grass. "So," he said, "Abbot and Hans took off without you?"

She nodded. He removed the handkerchief from her hand and wiped her tears away. "Dang, Alyssa Mae, I could have told you this would happen sooner or later."

"Then why didn't you?" she asked.

"I was hoping Abbot had grown up by now." Ed gave a long and weary sigh. "He used to ditch church all the time when we were younger and go joy riding with his friends."

"Well, at least he waited until after church," she admitted. "He wanted to take Hans up to Dutch John and go river rafting. I didn't think that was an appropriate Sabbath activity, so he yelled at me and left when I refused to go."

"Did he tell you that our brother, Will, lives up there with his wife? Maybe he just wanted to introduce you."

"There's no need to champion his cause," she complained. "They wanted to rent river rafts."

"They could have telephoned Will and reserved ahead," he admitted.

"That's what I suggested."

Ed helped her up on her feet. "Then he'll hear about how foolish he is the minute he gets back, from both of us."

"No," she whispered as her bottom lip quivered. "You can talk to him if you want, but I'm through talking." She removed the engagement ring from her finger and gave it to Ed. "Just give this to him," she said sadly. "I think he'll understand."

Inhaling sharply, Ed asked, "Are you sure you want to do something this rash? You may regret it later on."

"No," she confessed. "I won't. It's been coming for a while now, and I just haven't had the courage to admit it."

"But he loves you," Ed protested. "You're gonna' throw that away?"

"He loves himself," she pouted. "I don't think he ever really loved me." Tears filled her eyes and spilled down her cheeks.

"Do you want me to take you home?" he asked.

She looked up into Ed's gray-green eyes and said, "To the lodge, yes. I was promised three weeks up there, and I'm not giving that up for Abbot or anyone else. If he's uncomfortable with me there, then he can choose Hans as his partner, and I'll choose someone else."

"You are a stubborn one, Alyssa Mae!" he said, but his voice was teasing her again, like he had yesterday morning.

"Then don't you ever forget it," she said with determination. "Shall we go?"

He opened the truck door and helped her in, then came around to the driver's side. When he had fastened his seat belt and turned on the ignition he said, "If we hurry, we might find Matthew still awake. We could play peek-a-boo with him. That would cheer you up."

"Isn't he a doll?!" she asked with a wide smile.

"One look at him on the day he was born and my heart melted," admitted Ed. "We've been partners ever since."

"He's pretty attached to you," she said. "I'm surprised you haven't married, Ed. You'd make a great father."

"Maybe one day I will," he said. "I never thought so until lately, but now I'm beginning to change my mind."

"Oh?" she asked.

"A little nudge from the man upstairs," he admitted.

"I see," she said. "Well, after today, I'm going to refuse all offers of marriage that come along until the 'man upstairs' tells me straight out that I've found the right one."

She noticed a grimness about Ed's expression as he drove the truck toward the Bar M Ranch. "I thought you already had," he said hoarsely.

"I guess not," she admitted, but didn't comment further.

After a moment of silence, Ed counseled, "Rash decisions can destroy lives. You know that, don't you?"

"Not this time."

"Alyssa, I know Abbot loves you," Ed insisted. "He told me how he feels about you. If you break up now, you could ruin him for life. Believe me, I know."

"He doesn't know what love is. I may not even know what love is, but I certainly know what it's not. Love is not all sex, and it's not all romance. It's not controlling one another, or playing mind games. It's not yelling or belittling or humiliating, and it's certainly not abandoning. Yet all the things that I believe love is not, Abbot believes love is."

"He doesn't feel that way at all," Ed persisted.

"Boy!" she exclaimed. "He doesn't need a cheering squad with you around."

"I'm serious," said Ed. "Abbot's a good man. He can be a little irresponsible at times, but he—"

She interrupted him. "Abbot has no respect for God or for womanhood. He wants intimacy outside the marriage covenant, and he doesn't want a temple marriage! How can I possibly marry him under those conditions?"

"He told you this?" Ed asked, obviously surprised at her outburst.

She nodded and tried to keep the tears from tumbling. "He told me that it's more difficult for men to control passion than it is for women."

"Do you believe that?"

"Of course not. I told him it was just an excuse men use to convince women to go to bed with them."

Ed laughed. "Good for you!"

Alyssa suddenly felt embarrassed by their conversation. She blushed. "Oh, Ed, I'm sorry. I hadn't intended to rant like this."

"I'm glad you did," he confessed. "I didn't realize my brother had wandered that far away from the straight and narrow."

"I'm sure he'll make someone a great husband," she said with a sigh. "But it's not going to be me. The man I marry will have to believe like I do, that family and God come before everything else."

"That's not such a tall order," he teased. "Why, even I could pass on an order like that."

Alyssa blushed, then smiled to herself. *Yes*, she agreed silently, *I believe you could.*

❧ ❧

Ed stomped back and forth across the living room floor until Sidekick came out of the bedroom and threw a pillow at him.

"If you have to pace, at least remove your boots, Boss. We're trying to sleep."

The men were as irritable as Ed, and he knew exactly what was bothering them. They were just as eager to strangle Abbot as he was.

Ed tossed the pillow back. "Sorry," he growled. Glancing at his watch, he saw that it was nearly midnight. He stepped outside and away from the house to do his pacing in the meadow.

The lights in the lodge had been off for more than two hours. A sick feeling in his gut told him that this was not going to be a night he would remember fondly. He'd told Alyssa he would give Abbot the ring back, regardless of his protests that she was making a rash decision. As their conversation had continued in the truck on the way back to the ranch, he realized her decision wasn't unwise at all. She had already given the engagement a great deal of thought. She wanted a man who could take her to the temple, and she would settle for no one less. He admired her willingness to bend to the Lord's will. If she followed her own counsel, he was certain she would find someone new.

For that matter, she could have me!

Stopping himself in mid-stride, he leaned his head back to gaze at the stars and ask himself, *What am I thinking? Considering Alyssa for myself, without giving Abbot a second thought? Dang fool, that's what I am!* he decided. He'd let his special blessing go to his head! Now he vowed that there would be no improprieties between himself and Alyssa while she stayed at the Bar M Ranch. None! Ed didn't want to be accused of taking Alyssa away from Abbot.

Ed would give the ring back, tell his brother what a dang fool he was, and that would be the end of it. That would be the entire extent of his involvement in this sorry mess.

He paced a while longer, but he'd been pacing for almost three hours. Finally his legs tuckered out on him, and he sank wearily onto a log in the middle of the meadow, his hat in his hand.

How long he sat there, he didn't know. Perhaps he'd even dozed off a little. But his head jerked up quickly when he heard the wheels of a car crunching on rocks as it turned into the driveway. The headlights illuminated him brightly, so Ed knew Abbot had seen him.

He stood up, stuck his Stetson back on his head, and walked toward the car. Abbot and Hans got out and came toward him.

"What is it?" Abbot asked immediately. "Is something wrong?"

"It's private," Ed said gruffly.

"That's my cue," Hans interjected. "I'll see you in the morning." He turned and went into the cabin.

Ed waited until he saw the bedroom light switch on. Then he faced Abbot. Although he tried to keep the edge of anger out of his voice, he failed miserably at it. "What the blazes were you thinking, Abbot? Or were you thinking at all?"

His brother hedged, "What do you mean?"

"Alyssa!" Ed growled. "How could you abandon Alyssa?"

"I knew you would take her home."

"Well, you evidently did something to change her mind about you," said Ed, careful not to reveal everything that he knew about his brother's relationship. "She cried half the evening away. And she told me to give you this." He held out the engagement ring.

Abbot looked at the beautiful diamond sparkling in the moonlight as it lay in his brother's hand. He took a step backward and the color blanched from his face. "What did she say?" His voice squeaked.

Ed felt torn between Alyssa's wishes and Abbot's anguish. He didn't know how much to tell Abbot, or how little. "She said she wouldn't marry a man who didn't love her."

"She thinks I don't love her?" he demanded hotly. "One little disagreement and she thinks I don't love her?"

"I don't know," Ed said. "I told her what you said the other night about loving her. But she's not convinced, and nothing I said seemed to sway her convictions."

"Did you take her back to Heber?" he asked. "I'll go right now, I'll talk to her. I'll apologize."

"She's still at the lodge," Ed told him.

"She is?" Abbot's eyes darted back and forth as though he was thinking the situation through. "She stayed! That means there's still hope. Otherwise, she'd have gone home."

Ed shook his head. "I don't think that's why she stayed," he explained. "She said she was promised three weeks up here, and she wanted to stay. But she plans on choosing a different working partner."

"Who?" he asked. "Is someone else making a move on her? Who is it?" His voice had taken on a dangerous tone.

"Whoa!" Ed encouraged. "You're barking up the wrong tree, Abbot. No one's making a move on anyone."

"I'll go talk to her," he said, his tone deflating some. "We can work this out. It wasn't that much of a quarrel."

"I don't think it was just today," Ed tried to explain. "I think today was the last straw."

"What makes you think that?" Abbot asked sharply. "Did you make a play for my girl?"

"I don't think she ever was your girl!" Ed snapped. "She's not chattel, Abbot. She's a woman with feelings and needs and wants. And you ignored all that for your own petty selfishness."

"Oh, I see how it is!" Abbot yelled. "The man who's been trying to take her away from me is my own brother!"

Abbot took a swing, but Ed stopped it with one hand, grasping Abbot's fist like it was a pesky fly.

"I'll admit I've wanted to, you dang fool!" Ed hissed. "But the truth is, I love you too much to do that to you! You think I don't know what it's like to be rejected? You think I want my own brother to go through what I've been through? Not now! Not ever!" He hesitated only a moment, then choked out, "The only difference between you and me is that you asked for this!" When Ed felt the tears stinging his eyes he forced them back, refusing to let anyone, even his own brother, see him cry. "Maybe your loss will teach you a lesson or two about how to treat a woman. What's happened between the two of you is your own doing, and if you were half a man you'd admit it!"

Ed knew his words cut his brother to the core, but it was the only way he could force Abbot to see what his actions had cost him.

Abbot sank to his knees, a broken man who'd just lost the woman he loved. "Help me keep her," he wept in his brother's arms. "You could always help me out when I messed up before."

Ed rubbed Abbot's shoulder. "I can't," he rasped. "I tried, but I failed you this time, partner. I'm sorry."

Chapter Nine

*A*lyssa heard most of the conversation between Ed and Abbot as they quarreled out in the meadow. Waiting in her bedroom at the lodge, behind the curtain with the sliding glass door wide open, she'd been pacing just like Ed had earlier. She was amazed at how well sound traveled across the meadow, especially when someone was yelling.

Her heart ached inside. She should have told Abbot herself. But if he had wept in her arms, as he was now doing in Ed's, she didn't know if she could have kept her resolve. Her empathic nature wouldn't have permitted it. Now she rocked back and forth, her arms folded, her hands clutching at her sides, as if she could somehow assuage the pain she'd caused.

Ever since she and Ed returned to the Bar M earlier in the day, she'd had a negative effect on everyone there. Although she tried to put on a brave front, every time she thought about the argument with Abbot at the church and her feelings the past few weeks, she knew she'd made the right decision, no matter how much it saddened her. And when the truth glared out at her from deep within, her eyes would sting and she would find herself crying, regardless how hard she tried not to. During scripture reading last night, she had been unable to concentrate, and soon found tears slipping down her cheeks. Not wanting to have a complete breakdown in front of the men and Morning Sun, she had rushed from the gathering room without finishing and without saying goodnight to anyone.

"Oh, Abbot," she whispered in the quiet of the bedroom, "I'm sorry, but I just can't marry you."

She wished it could have been different between them, for she certainly hadn't set out to deliberately ruin Abbot's life. With more resolve than she realized she had, Alyssa knew that she did not love Abbot enough to change her decision now. She'd accepted his proposal on the spur of the moment, without thinking through the consequences. Yet ever since then, she'd regretted being so impulsive. She loved Abbot as a dear friend, but she did not have the other feelings that should accompany someone deeply in love.

Kneeling at the side of her bed, she sought the comfort and peace that only the Lord could render. She had emotionally wounded a man she cared about. Asking for the Lord's forgiveness, she prayed that He would forgive her. Deep sadness was soon replaced with calm and gratitude. The Lord had other plans for her, but until He revealed to her what those plans were, she would marry no one.

For several hours Alyssa stayed on her knees, pleading with the Lord to show her, beyond any shadow of doubt, who the right man was when she finally met him. Petitioning with her might, she asked the Lord to let her knees go weak when the right man kissed her for the first time. Even if she fainted completely, at least she would know. She also wanted to receive a burning in her bosom that lingered after all the other physical sensations had passed, so she would know for certain that her feelings were not generated out of lust. She wanted no confusion as she'd had in the past. When the man whom the Lord had chosen for her finally kissed her, she wanted to receive every conceivable confirmation possible. Although she didn't have a clue what the Lord intended to do, she wanted Him to convince her once and for all that she had met the right man, whenever that day arrived.

After she closed her prayer, she waited on her knees until she received a warm and comfortable feeling that began in her chest and spread outward, attesting to her by the spirit that the Lord had heard her prayer. Intuitively, she sensed that God would make Mr. Right known to her in such a way that she would not be able to deny it, and a still, small voice whispered to her saying, "You will know him the moment he kisses you."

"Thank you, Father. Thank you," she cried, tears streaming down her cheeks. When she'd closed this prayer of gratitude properly, she climbed into bed, but she did not sleep for quite a while. Watching the chill night breeze dance against the curtains, she wondered who the Lord had in mind for her, and how God would tell her when she found him. How would she feel when he kissed her? It would have to be something earth-shaking, otherwise Alyssa worried she would be insensitive to a simple, soft whisper. She also wondered if she would have to kiss a lot of men before that mountain top feeling came to her.

Around three-thirty in the morning she finally fell asleep, and for the first time in months, she slept peacefully, deep and sound, with no dreams of any kind. It wasn't surprising, when the alarm clock rang half an hour later, that she had difficulty waking up. Alyssa rolled over and turned off the alarm. Her pajama clad legs sank off the bed until she was on her knees once again, ready to offer her morning prayer.

To her amazement, she felt someone lifting her up, unaware that she'd fallen asleep in a praying position by the side of her bed. When she opened her eyes, she found Hans soft baby blues peering down at her as he tenderly placed her back on the bed.

"Did you have a rough night?" he asked as he pulled the blanket up over her.

Alyssa nodded.

"Perhaps you should sleep a little longer."

"Mmm," she agreed. "I'm so tired."

"I see that." He grinned. "It would be awfully easy to take advantage of you while you're in this condition," he teased.

She studied Hans' face for a few moments. Handsome was probably an understatement when describing Hans, she decided sleepily. "But you won't," she whispered. "That's not your style." Fleetingly, she wondered if Hans was the man the Lord wanted her to marry. Should she kiss him and find out?

"Oh?" he asked as though she'd given him a personal challenge.

"No," she yawned. "You accept things from silver platters when they're offered freely, and this bed is too soft to be a silver platter."

"Does that mean you're offering freely?" he quizzed.

She smiled at him, wondering once again if Hans was the one with whom she should fall in love. When he kissed her, she was not surprised, nor did she protest. It was an experiment for her. She tasted his lips and enjoyed the kiss, but when he released her, she felt a voice inside her say, *No, he's not the one.*

Then her eyes closed and she fell blissfully asleep, a smile of relief lingering upon her lovely face. This time her dreams were filled with angels and light, as though the Lord himself were preparing her for someone special.

◆§ §◆

Having just witnessed Hans kissing Alyssa, Ed turned away from the open bedroom door and walked quietly back down the hall. Descending the stairs into the gathering room, he saw that all the ranch hands' eyes were upon him. "It doesn't look like she's gonna' join us this morning," he told them.

"She's still mad at me?" Abbot questioned, his eyes puffy and red.

"I didn't ask her," came the answer. "She was too sleepy."

"Are we going to read scriptures anyway?" asked Luke.

"I am," said Ed as he sank into the overstuffed chair.

"Well, I'm not!" Abbot declared.

"Me, neither," said Sidekick John. He glared at Luke until the younger man closed his scriptures. "Let's go milk the cow and gather the eggs," Sidekick suggested.

Just before the two went out the front door, Sidekick said to Abbot, "It's a good thing for us that you broke her heart. Now she's fair game!"

Abbot jumped up from the sofa. "You come near her and I'll—"

Ed stood and grabbed Abbot's arm before he could take a swing. "Simmer down! Sidekick was only joking."

Sidekick and Luke retreated through the front door. *Rather quickly*, thought Ed.

"I'm going to find Hans!" Abbot said when Ed released him. Then he stomped out of the lodge.

Fat chance! Ed thought with grave irritation. *He's upstairs kissing Alyssa Mae!* Unsuccessfully, he tried to subdue a ball of anger growing in the pit of his stomach. He couldn't decide if he was more angry that Hans would attempt to wedge Abbot and Alyssa further apart than they already were, or if the knotted mass in his belly came from intense, unadulterated jealousy.

He stepped out onto the front porch and sat down in the rocker, noting the pre-dawn light beginning to illuminate the meadow. A minute or two after he saw Abbot go back in the cabin across the meadow, he heard the creaking of the kitchen door and knew Hans was trying to sneak out of the lodge undetected. Ed stood up and walked quietly to the end of the porch, then leaned his lank body up against the front wall where he waited breathlessly. When Hans was nearly beneath him, he startled him by asking gruffly, "How in blazes do you expect Abbot to win Alyssa's affection back if you're pursuing her yourself?"

Hans stopped as still as an ice sculpture melting under the refiner's fire. "It's over between them and you know it," Hans said with a hint of assurance in his deep voice.

"Give the man a fighting chance," Ed pleaded. "You've got no business kissing the woman Abbot loves."

"It's over," Hans said stubbornly. "If you saw me kiss her, you also saw that she offered no resistance. In fact, I think she rather enjoyed it!" He gave a wide, hopeful smile that Ed could just detect in the pre-dawn light.

Ed jumped off the porch and landed right in front of Hans, startling him. "I'll tell you this one time and one time only, Hans," he warned dangerously. "No one's gonna' come between Abbot and Alyssa, not on the Bar M. If they don't reconcile, it's between the two of them. But that ain't gonna' be hindered by one of us!"

"One of us?" challenged Hans. "That sounds like you're interested in Alyssa, as well."

"Don't even go there!" Ed warned dangerously. "You won't come out in one piece if you do!"

❧ ❧

As Hans walked across the meadow in search of Abbot, he felt uneasy. He hadn't realized until that moment that Ed Sparkleman had an undeniable interest in Alyssa Kendal! Disappointment flooded his emotions momentarily, and Hans found himself wishing he hadn't made any promises to Kayla and Josh.

How had Kayla known? he wondered. Hans never believed in miracles before meeting Kayla, but after a few short hours with her, she'd thrown his entire system of beliefs into an abys so deep he couldn't fathom it. Doubting he'd ever be able to dredge up his former creeds without serious pondering, his heart was touched with the truth of her simple words, "Man is often the tool Heavenly Father utilizes in His desire to bless His children."

When Kayla had voiced her concern about Ed Sparkleman, the rancher she'd forsaken in order to marry Hans' twin brother, Josh, she set off a chain reaction none of them could have foreseen. Josh and Kayla, unitedly engaged in an effort to find a woman who could fill Ed's life with joy, offered every prayer they could think of in his behalf. Cupid never worried more than Kayla and Josh did about Ed.

Hans recalled the incident that occurred months ago, as though it was just yesterday: While dining aboard Hans' sailing vessel, *Bridge*, Kayla had offered the blessing on their evening meal. She asked the Lord, "Where is Ed's soul mate? How can we be instrumental in helping Ed find her?" When she closed her prayer, Hans noticed that she waited, as though listening to some secret answer directly from God Himself.

Hans' instincts told him that he was in serious trouble when she finally lifted her head and looked straight at him. The unexpected tears in her eyes surprised him.

"Hans," she said with absolute conviction. "Somehow, God will send you to help rescue Ed Sparkleman."

Her statement had caught him off guard and he almost choked on a piece of salmon. He'd laughed to regain some composure, then exclaimed, "You've got a wild imagination, Kayla! I've never even met the man! And I have no intention of going back to Utah. Ever!" But he saw no leniency in her deep brown eyes, nor in her determined expression.

"Hans," she persisted. "If God presented you with an opportunity to be His instrument in doing His work, would you tell Him no?"

Hans recalled that he had fidgeted with his dinner fork, debating whether or not to stab the pineapple-stuffed salmon with it and completely ignore Kayla's question at the same time, or say what was really on his mind: that he found Kayla to be a sweet, but visionary woman, who had a tendency to want to interfere in other people's lives, a place where she wasn't really wanted. When she asked the question, he found his fingers stiff and unyielding; his hand, poised around the utensil, refused to respond to his silent bidding.

Kayla had issued a challenge to him, and Hans knew he could not pass it by without serious effort. He thrived on challenges, and she knew it!

The memories from that night faded, and here he was in Utah, in the one place to which he swore he would never return. How was Hans to know that he, too, would have feelings for Abbot's ex-fiancée? Painfully, he walked across the meadow at the Bar M ranch, holding his own heart in one hand, and Ed's in the other, asking himself, *Am I willing to become the sacrificial lamb in Ed's behalf?*

A sweeping sensation akin to goose bumps, but somehow more internal than exposed upon his flesh, came over him. Was Hans being guided by a power greater than his own?

When Kayla heard about Abbot's offer, to bring Hans with him to help out on the Bar M ranch, she had insisted that the Lord was sending him there for a reason. *But at what cost?*

Would Hans lose his soul if he failed God now?

"Are you there, Lord?" he whispered in the pre-dawn light. "Can you hear me?" Then he waited until he felt a strange warmth growing inside his chest.

& &

Alyssa rolled off the bed, said her prayers quickly, then changed from pajamas into a pair of jeans and a shirt. The sun was streaming through the curtains as they fluttered in the breeze, and she was dismayed to see that it was almost noon. Although she'd slept peacefully all morning, without a hint of dream anxiety, she chided herself for sleeping so long.

Quickly she went downstairs. Morning Sun was not in the house, and the wagon was gone. She'd apparently already left to bring the men their lunch out at the camp.

Dashing back upstairs, Alyssa brushed her teeth and her hair, put on her clothes and a splash of makeup, grabbed her boots and headed back downstairs.

When she reached the bottom step she heard the kitchen door close, so she called out, "Morning Sun, is that you?"

"Nope," came Sidekick's familiar voice. "Just your neighborhood pests, keeping an eye out for you."

"For me?" she asked, giving him a quick grin as he walked into the kitchen. Luke came in behind him, acting nervous, yet determined somehow. "Am I in danger?"

"No, Ma'am," said Sidekick. "But me and Luke were worried about you after what happened yesterday."

"It was a stressful day, wasn't it?" she quizzed. "But you don't need to worry about me. I'll be fine. I'm sorry if I upset you both last night."

"Will Abbot be all right?" Luke asked.

"I'm afraid Abbot will have to find someone else who can love him the way he wants," she suggested.

"Then your engagement is honestly over?" Sidekick asked.

Almost hopefully, she thought.

"Yes," she insisted. "Why? Are you volunteering to take Abbot's place?"

Sidekick paled. "No, Ma'am."

"Yes, Ma'am," said Luke with a determined look on his face.

Sidekick gulped and amended his answer, "We mean, yes, Ma'am, if you want. . . ." He left the sentence open.

"We've been talking it over," Luke added hastily. "You can have either one of us. We may not be the perfect match for you. But you know we're both reliable."

"We won't hurt you like Abbot has, neither!" Sidekick growled.

Alyssa needed to diffuse the situation, but she hadn't a clue how. Then a thought occurred to her. She gave them both what she hoped was a serious expression. "You're too kind to me," she admitted. "Perhaps I should marry you both!"

Their eyes widened and their mouths dropped open simultaneously. With deflated egos, they exclaimed, "Both of us?!!"

She gave them a mischievous grin and teased, "Gotcha!"

Sidekick's eyes changed from surprise to pleasure, and she noticed a hint of admiration in them.

But Luke would not give up. "I know I'm younger than you are, Alyssa, but I'd never treat you like Abbot has. He deserves to get dumped, I think."

"Luke—" she began, but he cut her off.

"I'm a dependable Navajo, and I'm sincere and a hard worker."

Tears stung at the back of Alyssa's eyes. Had she enchanted the entire camp? "You're a sweet boy, Luke."

"I'm eighteen!" he complained.

"I know," she said. "But I have a strong feeling that there's someone really special out there for you. Wait and see."

"You're someone special," he whispered. "You know all about God, and you like reading His words. When we read together, I'm slow at it. But you never say anything to discourage me. I always have a good feeling in my heart when you're around."

"That's the sweetest thing anyone has ever said to me," she confessed. Standing on tiptoe, she kissed his cheek affectionately. "If the Lord doesn't send someone special for me in the next few years," she said with a wink, "I'll seriously consider your offer, Luke."

The young man fairly beamed. "I'll wait for you," he told her, "unless that special someone you were talking about comes along first."

"I think you'll find her before you know it!"

She noticed Sidekick fidgeting, but before he could add his qualifications to the conversation, she said, "I'm sorry, Sidekick. You're a sweet man, too. And your offer is more than generous."

He nodded, his red hair bouncing against the collar of his shirt.

"What can I do to make it up to you?" she asked. "I really didn't mean to—"

"Could you kiss me, too?" he asked, a playful tone in his voice again.

"You're kidding, right?" she bantered back.

"No, Ma'am." Sidekick grinned mischievously. "I ain't!"

Alyssa shook her head and smiled. She gave him a tiny little kiss on his cheek and was delighted to see his skin blush as crimson as his shoulder-length hair.

"Now," she said, as though she hadn't kissed either one of them, "aren't you two supposed to be somewhere else? Morning Sun is out at the camp with your lunch by now."

She gave them a nod toward the door and almost giggled when they both sauntered out of the house like men who had just tasted a bit of heaven. However, she couldn't dismiss the soft whisperings of the spirit as she'd kissed each man. The words were imprinted upon her heart, like tender footprints leading her along a different path. The Holy Ghost had comforted her after she'd kissed Luke and again after she'd kissed Sidekick with, "No, he's not the one."

When the two ranch hands left, Alyssa sat down on the sofa and put her boots on, then she went out to the stable to saddle up Daylight. Within a few minutes she was riding the chestnut mare along the trail to the meadow at a hasty trot.

The affection of Ed's employees surprised her and almost brought her to tears. The only one who hadn't made some sort of pass at her, so far, had been Ed.

Smiling to herself, she wondered if Ed had been contemplating a similar idea. It was just last night that she heard Abbot yelling at Ed, "Oh, I see how it is. The man who's been trying to take her away from me is my own brother!"

Then Abbot had tried to hit him, but Ed had stopped the attempt with very little effort. "I'll admit I've wanted to, you dang fool!" Ed had barked in return.

What is it with the men in this camp? she worried. *Now that I'm not engaged to Abbot, am I fair game to all of them?* The more she thought about it, the angrier she became. The fact that she and Abbot were no longer engaged did not mean that she was up for grabs, and all the men needed to know it. What could she do to convince them, once and for all, that she had no real interest in any of them?

Impetuously, Alyssa wondered how the men would react if she walked straight over to Ed and kissed him in front of everyone. Then she could announce, "I'm sorry, men, but it's not fair to exclude Ed from your little contest." Perhaps that would stop all of them, including Abbot, from pursuing a relationship with her any further. Her anger turned to laughter as she thought about it. Not only would her actions surprise all the men, it might even be fun.

With the same reckless impulsiveness inherent within her that had given her courage to drop out of the sky uninvited upon the Bar M Ranch, Alyssa made her decision. She knew she would carry it through, regardless of the consequences.

She laughed aloud, unable to control her giggling as she contemplated what she was about to do. Then she said to Daylight, "Go!" as she dug her heels against the mare's rear flanks.

It only took a few more minutes to reach the camp. She dismounted Daylight and tied the reins to the hitching post. Hans and Abbot were visiting nearby while Sidekick and Luke were still eating lunch. Morning Sun was putting the remaining food in the back of the wagon.

Alyssa looked toward Ed. He had evidently finished eating, and he stood about forty feet away from the other men. Bent over, he was watching Matthew examine something on the ground.

When he saw her walking toward him, Ed straightened and gave her a quizzical look, as if he intended to ask her how she was feeling.

Unable to suppress a smile, she thought how surprised all the men were going to be as she quickly crossed the distance between herself and Ed before she lost her nerve. When she reached him, she turned around to ascertain that all four ranch hands were watching her; she was not disappointed. Then she turned back to Ed Sparkleman.

"Morning," he said. "Are you—?"

Before he could get another word in, she reached her hand up, removed his Stetson hat, then wrapped both arms around his neck, and pulled him close to her. The look of surprise on his face was worth her effort. Giving him no warning whatsoever, she lifted her face nearer his and planted a long and serious kiss upon his lips.

His arms came around her and he pressed her to him, prolonging their embrace. She was surprised at his reaction, but she allowed the kiss to continue longer than she had intended, longer than it should have.

Amazingly, she wasn't afraid in the least, yet his kiss was no less passionate than Abbot's had been several nights ago. Unexpectedly, she realized she was not the only one actively involved in their embrace. And to her utter dismay, she found that she didn't want the kiss to end at all.

When he finally released her, she stepped back and turned around to begin her bold declaration to the men. But she couldn't remember what she wanted to say. She felt like she was standing at the top of a mountain looking down, and she was so dizzy she could hardly stand. Her heart started pounding strangely and a warm feeling in her bosom spread from deep inside until the warmth made her tingle from the top of her head to the tips of her toes.

Alyssa looked down at her knees and realized they were starting to buckle. A distinct, soft and powerful voice whispered inside her with vivid clarity, a voice she would never be able to deny. It said, *"Yes, he's the one!"*

Completely caught off guard by these unforeseen emotions, Alyssa found the only words she could speak, and raggedly at that, were, "Oh! Oh. . . ."

Then she fainted completely.

Chapter Ten

$\mathcal{E}$d caught Alyssa a split second before she hit the ground. His Stetson hat dropped out of her limp hand and rolled away. The men stood and rushed over to him as he lifted her up into his arms. He could tell by their grim expressions that all four were furious with him.

"What?" he asked. Although his head was spinning, he forced his voice to remain steady. "What did I do? I'm just the victim," he insisted.

When he saw that no one was convinced, he exclaimed, "*She* kissed me!" Yet, even before the words left his mouth, he knew they weren't completely true.

Abbot's face was pale as a full moon, his eyes somber and almost gray. He glared at Ed like a hungry cougar.

Hans started the barrage when he said in an accusing tone, "She didn't faint when she kissed me!"

"Not when she kissed me, either," said Sidekick.

"Me, neither," squeaked Luke.

Abbot's color changed from ghostly pale to reddened flames of anger. "She kissed all four of you?!!" he shrieked.

Three of them nodded, but Ed held his ground. Abbot already knew Alyssa had kissed him!

"I've seen enough!" Abbot yelled. "My best friend *and* my brother? You two are despicable!" Then his eyes raked over Luke and Sidekick John as though they were nothing more than a sleazy irritation. "She must really be desperate!" he growled as he spun away from them and headed toward the horses.

"Abbot! Wait!" Ed called after him, but he couldn't put Alyssa down. He didn't know what was wrong with her, and he looked at his men for a solution.

"Give her to me and go after him," Hans suggested, reaching out to take Alyssa from him.

Ed hesitated. Hans was the last man he wanted to take Alyssa from him. "You go!" he insisted. "At least he didn't see you kiss her!"

Hans glared for only a moment, then reluctantly agreed. He turned and followed after Abbot, yelling, "Wait up! Abbot, can't we talk about this?"

Before Ed could think straight, Abbot and Hans were both riding their horses in a mad race back toward the cabin.

Ed carried Alyssa to the wagon, while Sidekick and Luke followed side by side, bringing Matthew with them.

"So she kissed you two as well?" Ed asked them both, unable to keep the irritation out of his voice.

"Not like she kissed you!" Sidekick exclaimed. "It was just a peck on the cheek!"

"That's all it was," insisted Luke. "She said she thought we were sweet."

Ed nodded just as they arrived at the wagon. Morning Sun had moved the serving dishes to one side and spread a blanket out in the bottom. He lifted Alyssa over the side rail and lowered her gently onto the wagon bed. "Grab something for a pillow!" he barked at the men.

Within a few seconds they returned with their jackets. Luke rolled his up in a soft ball and handed it to Ed. Sidekick covered Alyssa's shoulders with his.

"Get back to work," Ed growled as he placed Luke's jacket carefully under Alyssa's head. "And don't let her kiss you again!" he warned. Both men, duly chastened, nodded and resumed other duties.

Then Ed checked Alyssa's pulse and watched the steady rising of her chest as she breathed. He gave a sigh of relief. "Alyssa Mae. Can you hear me, honey?" he asked tenderly, unaware he had used the endearing term. He stroked her cheek, but she did not respond. "We'll need the smelling salts from the house," he said to Morning Sun.

She nodded, picked up Matthew and handed him to Ed. "Issa seeping," said Matthew as Ed put him in the wagon beside Alyssa.

"Yes, partner," Ed exhaled, feeling some of the anger softening in him at Matthew's remark. "Can you drive?" he asked Morning Sun. "I'll sit in back with her, to prevent her from bouncing around too much."

Morning Sun nodded, and Ed helped her atop the buckboard. Then he jumped into the back of the wagon bed, and lifted Alyssa up as he sat down next to her, to cradle her head on his thigh.

Matthew put his head on Alyssa's arm. "Issa seeping," he whispered softly. "Shhh."

Ed nodded and stroked Matthew's hair.

"Issa uv me," said Matthew sleepily, then he placed his chubby little hand on Alyssa's cheek exactly as she had done to him last week. He gave Ed an endearing smile, then snuggled up against Alyssa and closed his eyes. Within a few minutes Morning Sun had coaxed Shadow to turn the wagon around and they were headed along the trail toward the lodge, which was about how long it took young Matthew to fall asleep.

Ed felt his anger melt away as he watched Matthew sleeping, curled up in a fetal position against Alyssa.

He looked upon Alyssa's face, noticing how long her dark eyelashes were, and how they curled on the ends. She was a beautiful woman, a fact he had realized the day he removed the helmet from a parachute jumper and found Alyssa in his arms.

As well as a dang fool! he reminded himself. *What in blazes was she thinking, kissing me in front of Abbot? In front of everyone!* This was the second time she'd done something completely reckless and irresponsible, as though she hadn't considered there could ever be consequences. Surely she had to know that everything she did would affect someone.

He had to admit that she was angry with Abbot and hurt by him as well. But surely she knew that Abbot was hurting just as much as she. Did she have to rub salt in fresh wounds?

Bewildered, he offered a brief prayer, asking the Lord to help Abbot forgive Alyssa's reckless behavior and to forgive Ed's equally reckless response to her as well.

Then Ed pondered about the kiss she had initiated in the meadow. It happened so unexpectedly he'd completely forgotten anyone was watching them. He'd been caught up in that kiss, and he had responded to it as though it were the most natural thing in the world. She'd kindled a flame within him that made him tremble.

Why didn't I push her away? Agonizing over those few moments until his heart ached inside him, he realized he hadn't pushed her away because he'd enjoyed the kiss. Reluctantly, he admitted to himself that he'd longed to kiss her!

Ed had responded to Alyssa's kiss the way a man does when he's fallen in love with a woman. The thought made him shake all over and he broke out in a cold sweat. He couldn't have fallen in love with Alyssa in such a short time. Abbot would never forgive him! Ed would never forgive himself! Forcing his mind to focus on Kayla, in an effort to eradicate the memory of Alyssa's kiss, Ed recalled a whirlwind of memories of him and Kayla together, of their kisses, of his passion for her. When he did this in the past, it always left an angry sadness inside him that he expected to replace whatever feelings he had for Alyssa. To his dismay, the haunting melancholy failed to settle upon him. He began to doubt that anything could diminish his desire for Alyssa Mae Kendal.

By the time they reached the lodge, Ed's emotions had turned from anger to fear. Why had Alyssa fainted? What was wrong with her? Would he be able to revive her? "Get the first aid kit," he said to Morning Sun as she set the brake and climbed down from the wagon. Within minutes she returned with a red emergency pack and handed it up to Ed.

"Morning Sun will take Matthew inside," she suggested.

After Ed laid Alyssa back down on the rolled up jacket, to protect bumping her head, he handed Matthew to Morning Sun and nodded. While Morning Sun took Matthew inside, Ed opened the first aid kit and searched for the smelling salts. When he found the small cylinder, he broke it in half and moved it back and forth below Alyssa's nose. She didn't respond at first and he worried that something was seriously wrong with her.

Suddenly she gasped, cringed and shook her head. When her eyes opened, he gazed down at her for several long minutes, giving her time to remember what had happened. He was surprised when her eyes filled with tears and she rolled over, away from him. When she started to shake, he realized she was struggling to prevent herself from crying in front of him.

"Alyssa?" Gently he put his hand on her shoulder.

She moved her shoulder forward, as though she didn't want him to touch her. "Go away," she moaned as suppressed sobs seeped out of her, making her tremble.

"Do you remember what happened?" he asked.

"Yes!" she cried. "Now leave me alone!"

"Since I'm the only one who seems to worry about consequences around here," he scolded, "I ain't leaving until I know you're gonna' be all right!"

"I'm fine," she sobbed. "Please, Ed."

Tugging at her shoulder, Ed forced her to roll back over, but she kept her face covered with her hands.

"Alyssa?" he asked, totally bewildered by her tears. "Don't cry," he coaxed.

He hadn't intended to anger her, but apparently he had, for she sat up, scooted off the blanket and jumped out of the wagon, almost in one smooth motion. Without saying another word to him, she ran up the front steps, across the wide porch and into the lodge, slamming the door behind her.

Exhaling deeply, Ed worried that he'd committed a terrible injustice against her by responding to her kiss the way he had. He waited a few moments, then he heard the slamming of a door upstairs. Evidently the sliding glass door was open in the guest room, for he could still hear her crying. Alyssa's wrenching sobs were so horrible, they nearly ripped his heart out as he waited for her to stop. But she didn't stop crying, and this completely unnerved him.

He stuffed the first aid supplies back into the red pack and zipped it shut. Then he took it into the lodge and stepped quietly to the hall closet to put it away.

Morning Sun came tiptoeing from the den where she had placed Matthew in the playpen to nap. "Alyssa cries," whispered Morning Sun with a sorrowful expression.

Ed noticed a few tears in her eyes as well.

"Why?" Ed questioned. "What caused her to act like this?"

Morning Sun turned away from him. "Men are not very wise," she said as she left him alone and went out to the wagon to bring in the lunch dishes.

Ed waited downstairs for what seemed like hours, listening to Alyssa sob. When she finally stopped, he waited another fifteen minutes, then stepped noiselessly upstairs and eavesdropped outside the bedroom door.

Hearing nothing, he realized Alyssa was driving him mad with anguish. He had to talk to her or he would never be able to face himself in the mirror again. Timidly he knocked at the door.

"Who is it?" she asked.

"It's Ed. May I come in?"

"No! Go away!"

"Alyssa Mae," he insisted, trying to keep his voice calm, which was quite a feat with his heart pounding like a jackhammer inside his chest.

"Don't call me that," she said. "Now, go away!"

"I need to talk to you," he persisted gently.

"I have nothing to say," she whimpered. Then he heard her throw herself upon the bed, and the crying started all over again.

Turning the doorknob, he opened the door a crack to peek inside. Alyssa was face down on the bed, and she had a small, framed photograph of Abbot in her right hand. Just seeing the picture sent a lump up into his throat, and he thought he was going to choke.

"Alyssa," he whispered in utter futility.

She rolled over and glared at him. "What is wrong with you?" she demanded. "I don't want you here!" Then she threw the photograph at him.

Fortunately, he pulled the door closed before it could strike him. Hitting the door, it shattered, and he heard the tinkling of broken glass as it landed on the floor with the frame. "Oh, no!" he heard her moan. Then her sobbing began once again.

He waited a while, trying to decide whether to stay until he convinced her to talk to him, or to go back to work until she calmed down. He finally decided on the latter.

&s ?&

By the time Hans arrived back at the Bar M, it was nearly eight in the evening. His horse was still tethered to a hitching post by the cabin, as was Abbot's. He led Abbot's stallion over to the barn, removed the saddle and blanket, then led the horse into one of the stables where he brushed him down good and gave him a bucket of oats. Then he went back out to the chestnut stallion he'd been riding earlier and easily mounted the horse. As he headed down the trail toward Mountain Meadow at a gentle trot, he was dismayed at how his mind wouldn't let go of the events that had occurred earlier that day.

He hoped Alyssa was all right. But he had his own suspicions for why she fainted, and the thought depressed him. Of course, if his hunch was correct, it would make his sister-in-law happy, as well as his twin. And wasn't that their main desire for Hans staying at the ranch?

How could Hans see the assignment through to the bitter end since his own heart had been unwittingly captured by Alyssa?

Earlier in the day, Abbot insisted that Alyssa had kissed Ed to get even with him, but Hans knew that couldn't be farther from the truth. If Alyssa was in love with Abbot, she wouldn't have responded to Hans' kiss that morning. She had no audience when Hans kissed her, yet she had responded to him. *Though not with the same passion as she had with Ed!* he reminded himself. Alyssa kissing Ed was completely unexpected, but it wasn't a revenge tactic, not at all.

Hans had noticed the surprised look on Ed's face when Alyssa removed his Stetson, which indicated that Ed had no idea what she intended to do. During the kiss, Hans had to admit that all the men were in absolute agony, including himself. Yet he couldn't blame Ed for responding to her. What normal male wouldn't have?

After that passionate kiss between Alyssa and Ed, when she had turned around with such triumph and then surprise on her face, Hans had the distinct impression that she'd just learned something miraculous and appalling, both at the same time. Hans believed it was that startling discovery that had led to Alyssa's complete collapse. At thirty-three, Hans had been around enough women to know what the look on Alyssa's face meant. He was not blind to a woman's passion for the man she loved.

Knowing that Alyssa had fallen in love with Ed did more than dismay Hans. It broke his heart. *Alyssa is easy to fall in love with!* he reasoned.

After that kiss in the meadow, Hans' first concern was for Abbot. Alyssa's reaction to kissing Ed had been witnessed by Abbot and had hurt him terribly. Indeed, she had hurt all the men.

Hans shook his head, perplexed. If he could discern Alyssa's intentions, he could make some sense out of the day. But learning that Alyssa had kissed every single man in the camp absolutely baffled him. *And disappointed me!* he admitted silently.

When he arrived at Mountain Meadow, Hans waved to Sidekick and Luke, who were just heading back toward the cabin. They pointed in the direction of the fence line. Realizing Ed would still be putting in fence, Hans headed toward the last row of posts nearly a quarter mile down the mountain through a dense, dark forest. Dusky shadows made it difficult to see, but he followed the loud *ka-thunk, ka-thunk* sound that reverberated through the trees, indicating that the post driver was still running. Soon he noticed a lantern hanging in a tree not too far away.

Heading for the light, he found Ed nearby finishing another post. Ed looked up when Hans dismounted and tethered the reins to a nearby quaking aspen tree.

"Evening," said Ed. "How's Abbot?"

Hans sighed. "He's on his way back to San Diego."

Ed nodded and grumbled, "Dang fool!"

"I told him that," said Hans. "But after the incident in the meadow, he wasn't interested in listening. I finally gave him the key to my boat and told him he could stay there as long as he wanted."

Hans put on a pair of gloves and lifted up a steel post to be put in the post driver.

They pounded fence posts without speaking for almost an hour. When they were done for the night, Ed hung the battery-powered lantern on the saddle horn and climbed atop Breeze. Hans mounted his horse, and they headed back through the meadow, riding toward the ranch at a leisurely pace.

After a long silence, Ed finally asked, "You're staying here, then?"

"I told you I would. I may not know what I want out of life yet, but I am reliable."

"What about Abbot?" Ed asked, his voice gruff.

"He doesn't need a babysitter," Hans observed quietly.

"No, he needs a good hog-tying!"

Hans nodded. Deciding it might be wise to change the focus of their conversation away from Abbot, Hans asked, "How's Alyssa?"

"Crying her heart out," said Ed. "She's still in love with Abbot, and I ruined it for both of them."

Hans shook his head, wondering how Ed could even believe that when he was on the receiving end of Alyssa's kiss. "If she does love Abbot," said Hans, choosing his words carefully, "then your responding the way you did would have caused some fairly serious problems, but—"

"Why the blazes did she kiss me?" Ed asked, interrupting him.

"More importantly," said Hans. "Why did you respond as though she were the only woman in the world for you?"

"The only thing I can figure out," Ed pondered aloud, disregarding Hans' question completely, "is that she kissed me to make Abbot jealous. That's the only answer that makes any sense."

"If she still loves him," Hans insisted. "But I don't think she does."

"What makes you think that?"

"I kissed her this morning, too. I hadn't intended to, but she issued a challenge. Everyone knows I thrive on challenges, so I accepted it." He shrugged. "She didn't seem to mind."

"No," Ed agreed, "but she fell asleep within seconds afterward, so I wouldn't say it was too earth-shaking for her."

"Don't be petty, Ed," Hans complained. "I'm only bringing this up to show you why I don't believe she's in love with Abbot."

"You'd think so if you'd stayed," Ed hissed. "I was able to revive her with some smelling salts, but she cried practically the whole day. Later on I went upstairs to talk to her, but she threw a picture of Abbot at me!"

"Bewitching woman!" said Hans, surprised to hear what had happened in his absence.

"Dang right," said Ed. "But she's also reckless and impulsive. She has no regard for consequences."

Hans considered what Ed had told him for a while as they ambled along, riding their horses on the trail back to the ranch. Regardless of Ed's conclusions, Hans' instincts told him Ed was way off base.

Finally Hans shook his head. "No," he insisted. "I think you're wrong about Alyssa. I don't think she was trying to make Abbot jealous. When I kissed her this morning, I got the sense that she wasn't in love with anyone, that she was 'testing the waters', so to speak."

"Then what about the photograph?" Ed demanded. "She was crying with these gut-wrenching sobs that nearly tore my heart out! And there's that dang photograph clutched tight in her hand!"

Hans remained thoughtful, but he was unconvinced. He couldn't get Alyssa's expression out of his mind. "Then tell me," he finally said, "what kind of reaction did you sense from her when she kissed you?"

"I—" Ed clamped his mouth shut. "That's none of your business."

"I see," said Hans. "Then maybe I should explain the reason why I believe Alyssa isn't in love with Abbot. After you responded to her kiss, I saw something you didn't."

"I was right there," Ed began.

"Yes," Hans interrupted, "but she turned her back to you right after you let her go, and she looked at us. You didn't see her face. I did."

"What did you see?" Ed demanded.

Hans thought about it for a while before he answered. He hoped he could explain it to Ed in such a way that Ed would believe him. "I saw a woman who'd just kissed the man she loved, only she didn't know she loved him until that very moment, and she was so astounded, she fainted. That's what I saw."

Ed remained silent, as if trying to digest Hans' theory. Finally he grumbled, "How would you be able to tell all that from one short-lived expression?"

"Come on, Ed!" Hans retorted. "Even you know that look! Have you never met up with a woman in love before?"

"I'm not saying that," Ed persisted. "I'm saying, you can't tell from one expression what a woman is thinking. No one can!"

Hans hesitated. He searched through his memory, trying to locate some feedback with which to drive his point home. When he finally extracted it, he smiled. "You know that video Mont and Kayla made together the night before the avalanche?"

"What of it?" Ed asked, apparently irritated by Hans' stubbornness.

"Kayla let me watch it a while ago," he explained. "Remember when Mont asked Kayla how she knew the difference between the love she felt for you and for Josh?"

"Where are you going with this?" Ed demanded.

"Just hear me out," Hans insisted.

Ed exhaled slowly and his nod was barely perceptible.

Hans took the expression to mean he could continue. "Do you remember her expression when she spoke about how she loved Joshua?"

Although Ed glared at him, Hans plunged on. "The look on Kayla's face as she expressed her feelings for Joshua was the exact same look that I saw on Alyssa's face this morning, right after she kissed you!"

"She didn't act like a woman in love when she came to!" Ed snapped. "You have no idea how her crying sent out mixed signals!"

"Give her a break," Hans complained. "I don't think she knew she was in love with you until she kissed you."

"Then why was she crying?" Ed growled. "If she suddenly found out she loved me, why did she spend the whole day crying about it? Is falling in love with me such a terrible thing?"

Hans weighed his final comment carefully before he suggested, "It's common knowledge that you're still pining over Kayla. Maybe she realized she didn't stand a chance."

They rode in silence then, and Hans could not decide if Ed believed him or not. By the time they reached the cabin, the lights were out and the other two men were asleep. While Ed heated up some beef stew, Hans took a quick shower.

Hans chastised himself for telling Ed as much as he had, especially since he had nothing more concrete as evidence than the look on Alyssa's face. Then he rationalized his actions by reminding himself that he liked Ed, and he felt a little sorry for him. When Kayla married Josh, she destroyed any hope Ed may have had that they would get back together. He wanted to give Ed a little bit of hope, and he believed that is what he'd done.

Of course, it also dashed all hope for Hans to make any moves on Alyssa himself. Hans always felt attracted to women who were already engaged, or in love with someone else, and he resigned himself to this fate.

After a quick shower, Hans came out of the bathroom wearing a bathrobe and rubbing his hair dry with a towel. "Well?" he asked with a smile when he saw that Ed was still looking out the kitchen window toward the lodge.

"Her bedroom light went on," said Ed.

"Good. She's still awake. Maybe she'd like some company."

"She won't even talk to me," Ed admitted.

Hans heard the defeat in Ed's voice. The man was hurting worse than Abbot, he decided. He wondered how Alyssa must be feeling. "You don't suppose she's packing up, getting ready to leave us, do you?" asked Hans.

"I wouldn't blame her," said Ed. "After all that crying today, I wouldn't be surprised, either."

Hans would have to do something to stop her or he would never see any romance unfold between Alyssa and Ed. "She can't leave!" said Hans. "I won't stand for it!"

"It's obvious whose heart you're trying to protect!" Ed growled.

"If you only knew!" Hans snapped in disgust as he went back into the bathroom. When he returned, he'd combed his hair and dressed in casual clothing.

"You're not going over there?" Ed asked.

"I am!" said Hans. "Which is something you should have done a long time ago."

Chapter Eleven

How long Alyssa cried before she fell asleep she didn't know, but it was dark outside when she awakened, and she was surprised that she still had her jeans, western shirt, and boots on. She hadn't eaten all day, though she wasn't hungry. Her throat was parched, and she felt chilled and thirsty.

After turning on the bedroom light, she opened the closet door and took out a soft fleece robe. Putting it on over her clothing, she went into the hall, leaving the light on and the bedroom door ajar. Quietly, she slipped downstairs and into the kitchen where she poured herself a glass of cold water, drank it quickly, then went out on the front porch and sat in a comfy, hand-hewn rocking chair. The crisp mountain air refreshed her, and she inhaled it deeply, hoping it would jar her memory awake.

As she remembered the circumstances that had brought her back to the lodge and into the guest bedroom, she shuddered. Alyssa wanted to cry, but she couldn't find any tears left inside her. It seemed as though every teardrop she would ever shed had already been wrenched from her.

She looked at her watch, pressed a button on the side of it, and saw the digital display light up. It was ten-fifty. The night sky was cloudless, and a million, dazzling stars winked at her from a velvet canopy overhead. Once again she wondered how she had ever come to this point in her life. Perhaps it would be easier on everyone if she just packed up and went back to Heber.

Mixed emotions coursed through her as her mind darted off in several directions at once. *Focus!* she demanded.

Clearing her thoughts completely, she finally allowed one man's face to enter, and as he did, she remembered the look of surprise Ed had given her a split second before she'd kissed him. She closed her eyes and took herself back to that moment. She could still feel his Stetson hat in her right hand, his shoulder muscles beneath her forearms, his arms wrapped tightly around her, pressing her against him. She could smell his skin, dusty from branding calves, yet with a masculine scent that was all his own, a scent she loved, a man she loved. Ed Sparkleman.

Alyssa had asked the Lord to show her who she was supposed to love, and He had. He had given her every sign she'd asked for in her search for love. She'd felt that mountain top feeling for which she had waited. She'd felt dizzy, warm, tingly, weak-kneed, and she'd fainted. Yet the burning in her bosom had remained with her through her tears that day and even as she sat in the rocker at that very moment.

Ed hadn't understood why she cried, nor was he ever likely to know, she admitted to herself. Her brow knitted in a frown. The answer was a simple one, but it was also one that left Alyssa with no options. Ed wasn't the man with whom she had expected to fall in love. A man obsessed with lost love, Ed's dreams were haunted by another woman who'd married someone else. His hopes were unfulfilled and his passion would always belong to Kayla Clark, owner of the Bar M Ranch.

What hope did Alyssa have of ever turning Ed's heart from Kayla?

She'd heard the agony he felt in his voice when he said to Abbot the night before, "You think I don't know what it's like to be rejected? You think I want my own flesh and blood to go through what I've been through? Not now and not ever!" Ed's words came storming into her memory with such vehemence it took Alyssa's breath away.

Why had the Lord chosen Ed as the man she should love when He knew Ed couldn't love her back? And marriage? Could that ever happen between them? According to Abbot, Ed was unreachable, and had been all of his life. Ever since Ed was a young child he had loved Kayla. Though she'd forsaken him and wed another, still he loved her. What hope was there for Alyssa to find even the tiniest particle of room in Ed's heart?

"Are you all right?" came a familiar male voice, interrupting her thoughts.

She opened her eyes and saw Hans standing on the bottom step of the porch. "Yes," she answered, relieved it was Hans and not Ed.

"Would you like some company?" Hans asked.

Although she really didn't want company, she said, "Why not?"

Hans sat on the top porch step. "Thank you. I'm glad to see you're feeling better."

"Are you?"

"Yes, we all are. Sidekick and Luke went to bed early, but I guess they've been moping about like they've just lost their first puppy. And Ed is worse than a Kodiak in heat!"

"That bad, hmm?" she asked, surprised at his analogies.

Hans nodded. "And I'm bewildered and frustrated just as much as they are," he confessed.

"Why?" she asked. "Hans, you're a drifter. You don't seem to want permanency or commitment in your life. Why has all this bothered you?"

"You don't know me well," he admitted. "On the surface, I seem like the kind of man who 'takes things from silver platters when they're offered freely,' to use your own phraseology. But it's only because I haven't found my niche yet. Just because I don't know where I belong, that doesn't mean I'll always be like this. I'm sure once I find what I'm looking for, I'll settle down, marry someone who loves me regardless of all my faults, and live happily ever after."

"I'm sorry," she apologized. "It was a bit rude of me to say that to you. I hadn't meant to hurt you."

"I wasn't hurt," he admitted. "But I was surprised. No one ever put it to me quite that way before."

"I have the nasty habit of sometimes acting, or speaking, without thinking it through," she admitted. "I suppose I'm somewhat impulsive."

"I believe Ed says you're reckless, with no regard for consequences."

"Yes, I'm sure that's how he'd describe me."

Hans laughed. "I like your impetuous ways," he decided aloud. "And you have a tender spirit about you, as well."

"Spirit?" she questioned with a short laugh. "What do you know about spirit, Hans?"

"Very little," he confessed. "But I do know that I have felt something in my heart when I've joined you and the others for scripture study. You don't plan on giving that up, do you?"

"I think I'll go back to Heber City," she decided aloud. "There's nothing here for me now, except heartache and disappointment."

"That's not true!" he exclaimed. "You have no idea the inspiration you are to all of us. Luke adores you and loves our scripture sessions together. I've been coaching him before we come over each time, so he won't stumble over his words so much."

"You surprise me," she said. "I didn't know that."

"Then you haven't noticed that he's always been the first one to sit in the rocking chair."

Alyssa had noticed, but she assumed it was because no one wanted to be first, and all the others beat him to the safer seats before Luke arrived. "Really?" she asked.

Hans nodded. "I've been reading the first two verses in the chapter with him. Then we've been counting out how many more verses until he reads again. We read them together several times before he comes over, so he doesn't stumble and feel awkward."

"What a sweet thing to do," she commended.

"Don't tell him I told you. He's rather sensitive about it."

"I know," she admitted. "I'm learning that you have qualities I may have overlooked."

"Then you'll stay for two more weeks?" he asked, a hint of anxiety in his voice. "You owe it to yourself to do that much."

"I don't know," she hedged. "I'm sure Ed doesn't want me to stay after today. I treated him terribly."

"I don't think you realize what a big chink you've put in his armor," Hans suggested.

"Oh?"

"Alyssa, if you go home now, you'll disappoint all of us, and you'll let the Bar M Ranch down. Abbot's already left, and now Ed's short handed."

"Abbot's gone?" she asked quietly, relieved that her voice didn't quiver.

"You surely didn't expect him to stay after what you did in the meadow?" he asked, a bit of surprise in his voice.

"I didn't think about it," she admitted. "It was irresponsible! I exhibited a total disregard for consequences, just as Ed told you."

"I think it was the best thing to happen to Abbot," Hans disagreed with a wink. "He's treated you poorly more than once, and Sunday was inexcusable."

"It wasn't just Sunday," she admitted. Then she asked, "Where did he go?"

"I took him to the airport and gave him the key to my boat. He's going to stay there for a while."

"And you?" she asked, dismissing the topic with little concern. "Will you leave the Bar M soon?"

"I don't plan on leaving until the season ends. I gave my word I would stay, and I am a man who keeps his word."

"Well, I guess if you can tough it out for one whole summer, I can tough it out for two more weeks."

"That's the spirit," he encouraged. "Alyssa, you're not terribly hurt about Abbot going away, are you?"

"No. I don't know why I accepted his proposal in the first place," she confided. "To tell you the truth, when he proposed, I was more shocked than surprised."

"Then you're not going to be moping around, nursing a broken heart?" he questioned.

"No." She hesitated. Should she be sharing all her secrets with Hans, knowing he would go back to San Diego and mete out every morsel to his best friend? Deciding to be selective in the information she gave him, she said, "I do love Abbot, but I've come to realize that it isn't romantic love. I feel no passion toward him, like a man and woman would share, though I'll always think of him as a very dear friend."

"And when you let me kiss you this morning, how did you feel about that?"

She blushed, and was grateful for night shadows that hid the fact. "I hope I didn't lead you on, Hans," she said quickly. "But I just didn't feel anything particularly special between us."

"So there's no reason for me to pursue a relationship with you?"

"I'm sorry," she said, shaking her head firmly.

Hans sighed, but she hoped it was entirely pretentious. "Then there's just two more problems to solve."

"And those are?"

"You don't have a working partner now that Abbot's gone. Will you be mine?"

"What about Ed?" she asked.

"He does the work of all four of us," he said. "Besides, he's so uptight over this Abbot thing he's going to be a bear to work with for a while."

"And the other thing?" she questioned, without answering whether or not she would become his working partner.

"When you do go back home, would you mind if I came down on Sundays to visit? I won't expect any romantic involvement from you. It's just that you've given me some insights into this gospel angle, and I want to know more from your point of view. Abbot wasn't much help in that area, I'm afraid. I could go to church with you, and you could continue teaching me why it is that your faith sustains you so."

She hesitated. He wanted answers and she wasn't sure how to let him down gently. Finally she said, "I think I'll trade off partners every day for a while, not get too involved with one worker at a time." She reached down and took his hand, then gave it a gentle squeeze. "But my parents and I would be pleased to share the gospel with you on Sundays."

"Great," he said with a light-hearted lilt to his voice. "Well, if we're going to be up by four in the morning for scriptures, we'd better go to bed, don't you think?"

Alyssa stood. "Yes, I do."

"Goodnight, Alyssa."

She watched him walk across the meadow and over the bridge. Soon he was opening the cabin door. With a heavy heart, she snugged the robe around her and went inside.

❧   ❧

"Well?" Ed demanded the minute Hans walked in the door. He was dressed in jeans and a wrangler shirt, and his boots.

"I think you'll be disappointed if you don't show up for scriptures in the morning," suggested Hans with a mischievous look about him.

"She's not leaving?" Ed asked, and was dismayed to hear the words come out with such relief in them.

Hans smiled at him for a moment, then said, "No. She still wants to stay the full three weeks."

"Did she say why?" Ed asked.

"Something about her stubborn streak."

"What did she say about Abbot?"

"Not much," admitted Hans.

"Was she heart broken when you told her he was gone?"

"No," Hans said. "Not at all. Guess I'll turn in."

"Goodnight," said Ed, still uncertain what to think.

While Hans went down the hall to the bedroom, Ed put a Levi jacket on and stepped outside. He looked up at the lodge and noticed the light was off in Alyssa's bedroom now. With quick, decisive steps Ed walked toward the barns and then beyond them. He didn't stop until he was four hundred yards northeast of the lodge in a little clearing in the forest about a hundred feet square.

The moon, waxed into its second quarter, illuminated the area enough to suit him. Ed took a tape measure from one back pocket, and four small stakes from the other. He measured carefully, marking off the approximate corners for the house he planned to build. When he was finished, he walked to the center of the clearing and slowly whirled around, deciding if the view was good from all angles. From where he stood, he could see Pine Bluff and part of the road that led up to the Bar M Ranch.

This would be the perfect spot to build a house for that special woman the Lord had promised him, he decided. From the front porch she would be the first to see him coming home.

Ed didn't have enough courage to believe that the special woman in his life would ever be Alyssa, but for the first time since he met her, he had hope. Realizing that Hans was the man responsible for the aspirations that now grew inside him, Ed was surprised and humbled by Hans' eagerness to play cupid for him.

When he finished contemplating all that he would need to do to build the house, and any relationship he might have with Alyssa, he got down on his knees, and offered up a prayer unlike any he'd ever given before.

❧ ❧

At four in the morning, Ed's alarm clock buzzed. He turned it off and rolled off the bed. He was still dressed in the jeans and wranglers he'd worn last night, having returned just before dawn to the cabin. Hurriedly, he stepped into the bathroom, washed his face, brushed his teeth and combed his hair.

On the way out the front door, he grabbed his Stetson hat, but he didn't put it on. He walked straight across the meadow, jumped the mountain stream in the narrowest part in one big leap, then hurried across the meadow and up to the back door of the lodge, where he tapped on a window pane.

Morning Sun opened the door to him and smiled. "Alyssa is much better," the woman blurted out the minute he walked in. "Much better."

Her observation gave Ed more hope than he knew what to do with. *Temper yourself!* he silently scolded. *Everything isn't set in gold yet!* He still didn't know why Alyssa had held the photograph of Abbot in her hand. Or why she'd cried. But if he was patient with her, perhaps in time she would tell him so he could understand.

"You got a spare bowl of porridge for me?" he asked.

Morning Sun nodded. If she'd noticed he hadn't put his hat on yet, she didn't mention it. But he could almost see the wheels in her mind working round and round. She dished him up a large bowl of porridge while he got out the cream and honey.

He was about to bless the food, but he noticed Morning Sun smiling at him shyly, which gave him no indication that would help him understand what she was thinking.

"Some men learn faster than others, Eddie," she said wisely.

He thought on her words for a moment. Then she nodded her head toward the upstairs bedroom and Alyssa. Suddenly he realized she was telling him that Alyssa cared about him and he'd better be ready for her. "I hope so," he responded, giving her a wink.

When Morning Sun went back to the stove, Ed bowed his head. *Heavenly Father, help me be calm, assured, confident. Put to rest my fears about Abbot, and if she does still love him, help me to know it. Don't let me get tongue-tied around her and—"*

When he heard Alyssa coming down the stairs, he closed his prayer quickly, then looked up at her as she came into the kitchen. What he saw nearly made him fall off the stool!

She'd taken great pains to look her best, but he guessed right away that she wasn't going to be working that day because of the cream-colored dress that she wore, with high heeled shoes and a dainty necklace that draped delicately around her slender neck. He gave her a low whistle before he could stop himself. Then he took a spoonful of porridge, evading the surprised look she gave him.

She smiled in response and said timidly, "Good morning, Ed."

"Morning," he said, choking on the porridge in his mouth. Somehow his throat had closed up on him and he found he couldn't swallow. He coughed and sputtered until Alyssa patted him on the back and Morning Sun handed him a glass of water.

"Are you all right?" Alyssa asked.

"Sure," he drawled, then coughed again. "Dang it all, Alyssa Mae! You should warn a fella' before you show up dressed like that! You could give someone a heart attack!"

She ignored his compliment and said, "I'm sorry about yesterday, Ed. I'm afraid I wasn't myself at all."

Her words sounded like an angel's voice, all tinkly and pure. He shook his head, trying to get these images out of his mind.

"Does that mean you won't forgive me?" she asked and he noticed a little pout forming on her lips.

Her lips! he thought as if in a fog. *She's got some mighty fine lips!* Then he stopped himself. *Whoa!* "Of course I forgive you," he managed to choke out. "I was just trying to get my windpipe clear."

"Oh."

She sat down on the bar stool beside him and his heart started thumping like a steam engine inside his chest. Beads of perspiration formed on his forehead and a knot rounded up in his belly. *I think I'm a goner!* he worried.

"I hope you won't mind if I don't go out to the camp today," she said. "I need to spend some time in the temple."

"Sure," he said. "I was gonna' run into town for a while this morning anyway. I can take you there, if you'd like."

"Thank you," she said. "I hope it's not too much trouble."

"N–no, it's no trouble at all." He scooped another spoonful of porridge into his mouth and gave a silent prayer that he wouldn't choke on it. To his great relief, he didn't.

"No porridge for me," said Alyssa to Morning Sun. "I'm not hungry yet."

Morning Sun nodded. "You're very pretty," she said.

"Thank you. It's one of my favorite dresses."

Ed heard the front door close and realized the men had arrived. He felt more disappointed than relieved, but he followed Alyssa into the gathering room, hoping she hadn't noticed he could hardly walk. He hurried to the overstuffed chair before his knees buckled completely.

The expressions on the men's faces was quite a sight, Ed thought, as they saw how Alyssa looked this morning. Sidekick stumbled over the bear skin rug and Luke caught him just before he went down. Hans whistled appreciatively and Ed gave him a sidelong glance to discourage him.

"Good morning," she said sweetly. "Come on in. Are you ready to read?"

Luke nodded and sat in the big rocking chair. "You look beautiful!" he said.

"Thank you, Luke. You look pretty good yourself."

"Somebody pinch me," said Sidekick, almost drooling, as he sank onto the sofa. "I think I'm still dreaming."

"You said you were going to stay," reminded Hans with a puzzled expression.

"I am," she reaffirmed. "But I need to go into Vernal this morning. I hope you can get along without me for one day."

Hans smiled. "Then you're not going back home?"

"Not for two more weeks," she promised.

Morning Sun brought a chair from the kitchen and sat upon it, while Alyssa sat down on the sofa next to Sidekick and opened her scriptures.

"Ed?" she asked.

"Hmm?" He looked at her in a daze, wondering what she had asked him.

"Would you like to be our Patriarch?"

"Sure! Um . . . Why don't you offer the prayer, Alyssa?"

"Thank you," she said, and bowed her head. The others followed her example. After the prayer, Alyssa said, "Luke, you've got the hot seat. Would you like to start?"

Ed couldn't tell what they read that morning. He couldn't even say what Alyssa had prayed for. His heart kept wandering from the scriptures in his lap to the woman on the sofa who had captured his heart with amazingly little effort on her part.

Chapter Twelve

After the men left that morning, Ed waited a few moments. Alyssa came away from the door and walked towards him. "Alyssa," he began, "about yesterday."

"We can talk in the truck," she suggested, touching his arm. "It will give us a little more privacy."

"Sure." He offered no protest.

"I'll be ready to go by six. Will that work for you as well?"

"Seven would be better," he hedged. "I need to go out to the meadow and make sure everything's running smoothly. Then I'll come back and clean up."

"Okay," she agreed. "Seven it is."

"Would you mind if I go to the temple with you?" he asked. "I reckon it couldn't hurt me."

Alyssa hesitated. She had wanted to spend the day praying and fasting about him, and his presence wouldn't make that very easy.

He seemed to sense her hesitation and amended his request. "Or not. I have a lot of business to attend to in town."

"I'm going to several sessions today. Perhaps you'd like to attend the first one with me, then take care of your business afterward."

"Sounds good."

Alyssa turned away. "I'd better not keep you," she said over her shoulder. "You probably have a lot to do before we can go."

"Seven o'clock then." He walked toward the door.

"Ed, you forgot your hat."

He turned back around. "Where did I put it?"

"In the kitchen on the counter."

"I knew that," he grinned sheepishly.

She smiled as he went into the kitchen, picked up the hat, slid it onto his head and walked out through the kitchen doorway.

Ed was in a curious mood this morning, she decided. Although he'd been amenable to her wishes, he'd seemed distracted somehow. She didn't know quite what to think of him.

After helping Morning Sun with what few breakfast dishes there were, Alyssa went upstairs and spent some quiet time in the bedroom, reading scriptures and praying in preparation for the day's activities.

How could I have fallen in love with a man like Ed? Alyssa wondered. More important than that, how could she ever hope that he would return her feelings? She had already determined that, if Ed was unable to give up his fantasies about Kayla, then she would be unable to give him her heart.

One thing was certain in Alyssa's mind. She must tell Ed once and for all about Abbot. As she'd prayed most of the night and morning about her feelings for Ed, she felt led by the Spirit that Ed was still uncertain where Abbot fit into her life. She also realized that Ed would want to know why she had spent the entire day crying yesterday, but she might never be able to share that information with him.

By seven in the morning, Alyssa had read several sections in the Doctrine and Covenants. As she thumbed through them, she was led by the Spirit to section seventy-five, verse sixteen, where the words seemed to jump off the page at her. She read it aloud several times:

"And he who is faithful shall overcome all things. . . ."

Her heart filled with joy as she read it, and she immediately dropped to her knees and prayed, asking the Lord to help her be faithful. The thing she wanted to overcome more than anything else was Ed's broken heart. When she had closed her prayer properly, she waited for the sweetness of the Spirit to fill her soul, beginning in her heart and spreading outward, until it left no doubt that she could accomplish what the Lord had assigned her.

When Ed arrived wearing a dark suit, white shirt and tie, and no Stetson, she was surprised at how handsome he looked. She couldn't remember a time when he'd looked so good to her. But she forced her feelings into submission. She hadn't known she was in love with him before yesterday, and she would have to find a way to guard her tender feelings until she was certain that she had replaced his memories of Kayla.

"Are you ready?" he asked.

"I am."

He opened the front door for her as she waved goodbye to Morning Sun and Matthew. Then he offered his arm like a true gentleman as they walked out to the truck.

When she was safely secured with the seat belt, he closed her door and walked around to the driver's seat. Within a few minutes they were on their way down the dusty, winding road that led to Hwy 121 near Maeser.

Ed began the conversation by saying, "I suppose you're gonna' tell me what all the fuss was yesterday."

"Fuss?" she asked, perplexed by his question. "You mean my crying, or something else?"

"I ain't talking about anything else, Alyssa Mae," he said, giving her a hopeful smile.

"I'd like to talk about Abbot for a while, if that's all right," she said, changing the subject.

He paled a little and gave her a gruff, "Sure!"

For a moment she wondered if that was the right tactic, but she felt in her heart that it was, so she continued. "Abbot and I met when he brought Shauna to the A & M for paraglider lessons. She and Mike hit it off right away, which left Abbot out in the cold."

"I don't need to hear all this," he said, loosening his tie as though he was uncomfortable.

"Yes, Ed, I think you do," she insisted. Then, ignoring his protest she said, "I felt sorry for Abbot. We started talking and he asked me out a few times. By the end of summer we were good friends, while Mike and Shauna were getting married. Through that winter, while Abbot was at the university, we talked on the telephone a lot and he managed to break away for a short visit on Thanksgiving and Easter. The next summer we flew paragliders together several times. He's quite good at it, and I enjoyed his company. Although he worked at the ranch those two summers, I was never invited over. I honestly thought I was just Abbot's friend, someone he could hang with, talk to, that kind of thing.

"I was busy getting the A & M going, working sixteen-hour days in the summer quite a bit, and all through the winter building up sales from our catalog and equipment lists, selling paragliders, teaching jump classes. I enjoyed my work, and I didn't have much time for dating. I wanted to get the business solvent and successful, and I was driven to accomplish my goals.

"When Thanksgiving came last year, along came Abbot. He seemed a lot more attentive than usual, brought me flowers and boxes of chocolate. I don't eat chocolate, by the way, but I was too polite to tell him."

"I ain't gonna' get you any chocolates, then," he chuckled. "I only need to be warned once."

Alyssa laughed with Ed, and she realized he was loosening up, perhaps even getting into the story. She continued, "Christmas arrived, and so did Abbot. After the ward party, he took me over to Jordanelle and we looked out over the reservoir together. It hadn't frozen over yet, and when a car passed across from us, the lights danced off the water. It was a lovely evening."

She studied his face carefully, hoping to see some slight glimmer of understanding about Abbot, but she didn't. Reluctantly, she decided to continue, regardless of the outcome. "He told me that night that he loved me, that he wanted to marry me, and he presented me with the engagement ring. I was flattered, but I didn't know if I loved him, and if I did, I didn't know if I loved him enough to marry him."

A muscle along Ed's jaw tightened. She reached out and touched Ed's hand, which was taut on the steering wheel. After she rubbed his fingers for a minute, he seemed to soften. He traded hands to steer with, and released his right hand to slide her fingers into his palm. She liked the sensation immensely, and gave his hand a gentle squeeze in response.

When she finally felt him relax again, she said, "I told Abbot I would have to pray about it. I asked him to be patient with me. He agreed, and when he left, he insisted that I keep the engagement ring. At night, I would often bring it out and admire it. I wanted to marry. I love the concept of marriage, but I wanted to be certain. I felt that Abbot had a place in my life, and as I prayed, I realized that I liked him a lot, but it wasn't right. It just didn't feel like we were right together."

By this time, Ed had turned the truck east, onto Highway 121, and headed toward Vernal and the temple. "You don't have to tell me all this," he said softly, his voice a hoarse whisper.

"I do," she insisted. "Ed, I've prayed about it so many times, and I just feel in my heart that you need to hear the whole story."

He nodded and gulped, "Then I reckon you better continue."

She bit her lip in anxiety and said, "Abbot called nearly every night after Christmas to ask if I had decided. He told me over and over that he loved me, and he begged me to become his wife. Although I knew in my heart that the love I felt for him was more like the way I love Mike and Shauna, like I love a dear friend, I finally caved in. On Valentine's Day he showed up on my doorstep with three boxes of chocolates and a dozen roses. I was so surprised, and pleased that he was so persistent, that I told him I would marry him. I knew there was going to be trouble earlier on in our relationship when he kept telling me how much he liked my hair bobbed. I'd had it done this way the first summer we met, on a whim, I suppose."

"You do have a habit of doing things impulsively," he admitted, giving her a quick smile that almost made her heart turn over.

"I like my hair longer," she said, "but I tried to please him. If my hair got too long he'd complain that he didn't like it. Finally, I got it trimmed whenever I knew he was coming, just so he would compliment, rather than the opposite. I know it seems like a little thing, but to me it felt like a control issue."

"I guess I ain't gonna' complain about your hair, either," he remarked, giving her another wink.

Alyssa laughed at his comment, and he gave her a wide smile.

When they arrived at the temple, Ed pulled into the parking lot, and turned off the ignition. He turned to face her, to listen to her, and this pleased Alyssa.

She continued, "Abbot started making comments about church when I wanted to go on Sundays. He said he felt it was time wasted. I felt it was time spent together, but he didn't see it that way. I began to have doubts about marrying him at all. Then he invited me to come spend three weeks at the Bar M. I thought we would finally get some practical time together. He could see how irritable I get on a day-to-day basis, and vice versa. Although I hoped being together every day would put us *both* off this marriage issue, I hadn't expected Abbot to be hurt so badly."

"You really didn't want to marry him at all, did you?" he asked, a twinkle in his green eyes.

"No," she admitted. "I didn't. And when Abbot kissed me the night we arrived at the ranch, when you interrupted us, it was too much!"

He arched an eyebrow as though he was surprised she would mention it to him.

Alyssa explained. "Abbot pressured me beyond limits I had set for myself. I didn't like it, but when I tried to push him away he didn't seem to notice, or to care. He frightened me."

Ed nodded thoughtfully, but she was relieved when Ed didn't say he wasn't going to kiss her then.

"I talked to Abbot about it, like I told you the other day. And the rest you pretty much know, except for this. I have prayed every morning and every night for six months for the Lord to tell me that Abbot was the one. And I've never really gotten an answer until yesterday."

"Yesterday?" he asked.

"Yes," she admitted. "I'd been having confused feelings for six months, and you would think that would have told me something, but I wanted a definitive answer."

He turned her hand over and drew little circles on the palm, as though unaware that he was even doing it. Alyssa found that she enjoyed the sensation it stirred within her, and it seemed as though this was a part of him that he was giving to her.

"When you came upstairs yesterday, I had been praying about Abbot. I told the Lord I had decided not to marry him, and asked the Lord to confirm to me that I had made the right decision."

"And did He?" Ed asked tenderly.

"Yes," she nodded. "I felt the answer with every fiber of my being, and I was crying because I was so relieved. I had made the right choice, regardless how painful it was for Abbot. I had done what the Lord wanted me to do."

"I'm glad you got your answer."

"I had been asking the question all wrong," she explained. "For six months, I had asked the Lord, 'Should I marry Abbot?' But I should have said, 'I've decided to marry Abbot. Please tell me if I've made the right decision.' If I had done that, I wouldn't have spent so much time agonizing over him, and he wouldn't have been so wounded. I had forgotten that the Lord wants us to reason things out for ourselves, make our decisions, then ask Him if those decisions are correct."

He stopped drawing circles on her palm, and lifted his hand up to rub her shoulder. "You had a pretty rough time, yesterday," he said. "Let's go recharge your spiritual batteries, shall we?"

"Yes," she agreed. "I'd like that very much."

When they met in the chapel, ready for the first session, Alyssa picked up the Doctrine and Covenants and placed it on her lap. Unexpectedly, it fell open to section seventy-five, verse sixteen, where the words again jumped off the page at her. *He who is faithful shall overcome all things . . . Oh, thank you Lord. Thank you!*

By the time Alyssa had finished three sessions in the temple, she was comforted. In her heart, she felt that she and the Lord had come to an agreement. Yes, Alyssa loved Ed beyond all earthly reason. He was the man whom God had prepared for her. But if he couldn't give up Kayla completely, Alyssa would not pursue a relationship with him. She may have strength in many areas, but getting her heart broken was just not one of them.

Alyssa had explained to God that she had tender feelings, that she was laying her life open to heartbreak from which she might never recover. If she had any reason to believe that Ed would be unable to find a place in his heart for her, she would go straight back to Wanship and try to forget about the handsome ranch foreman who had stolen hers.

When she asked if this decision was agreeable, she felt in her heart that the Lord would not require her to endure more than her heart could bear.

Sweetness and warmth filled her soul from the top of her head to the tips of her toes. As long as the Lord was guiding her footsteps, she would not fear.

❧ ❧

After he left Alyssa at the Vernal temple, Ed drove over to the city and county building to start the preliminary steps for building his new house. He'd agreed to pick Alyssa up at four o'clock, and it took just about that amount of time to pick up forms, check out contractors, hire a surveyor, an architect, and a building engineer. Fortunately for him, Vernal is a fairly small town, and he knew most of the people who'd been in the community for any length of time. It wasn't a matter of checking credentials for Ed. It was a matter of deciding which ones would be least likely to take offense if he hired the other guy.

He stopped by *Kentucky Fried Chicken* and picked up a couple of two-piece meals, then drove back to the temple. When he arrived, he only had to wait a few minutes for Alyssa to come out, but that gave him the time he needed to sift through his thoughts and organize all that she had told him that morning. He'd been too busy before then to sit back and ponder anything.

His first thoughts went to Abbot. He determined to write him a long letter and try to apologize for letting Alyssa kiss him, or for responding to her kiss, or whatever he had to say to ease his brother's anguish over the situation. His heart ached and he felt keenly his role in the betrayal of Abbot. Because Abbot was his brother, he wanted Alyssa to be in love with Abbot, to rush out to San Diego, to beg him to forgive her, to make up and marry him.

However, from a purely personal standpoint, Ed wanted Alyssa to love him. He finally admitted to himself that Alyssa may be the woman promised to him in his special blessing.

Gratefulness flooded over him as he realized Alyssa had never really loved Abbot at all, not the way that a man and woman love when they want to marry, make babies and grow old together. Regardless of the desire and the longing that he felt for Alyssa, if there was any hope at all that Abbot still had a chance for happiness with her, Ed would not come between them. But knowing that Alyssa's heart never belonged to Abbot from the very beginning made it easier for Ed to hope she might eventually love him.

Hans had asked him an interesting question the night before, Ed remembered, one that he'd not answered: What kind of reaction did Ed have when Alyssa kissed him?

He thought on the moment long and hard, recalling the feel of her against him, the taste of her lips on his, the eagerness in her to respond to him, the surprise on her face when he finally let her go. If that wasn't an intimate moment between them, he didn't know what one was! It seemed as though something tangible had passed between them, like she'd given him something no other woman had, and accepted something from him in return. He couldn't explain it, and until he knew for sure why she'd kissed him yesterday in the meadow, he didn't know if he should try.

Although he was relieved that she had not kissed him to make Abbot jealous, he was still puzzled why she'd kissed him at all. That bothered him a great deal and he wanted to nudge some kind of reason out of her.

Also, she hadn't explained why she'd been devastated when he finally revived her in the back of the wagon. She'd wept so hard he thought her heart would break, or his would. He didn't understand why she refused to talk to him at all after that.

Ed didn't know if he was supposed to apologize to Alyssa for responding to her kiss in the meadow, or to pretend it hadn't happened or didn't matter. She had his mind so messed up he didn't know if he could ever sort it all out.

He'd felt keenly at the clearing early this morning that Alyssa was the woman whom the Lord had prepared for him. He'd told the Lord he felt drawn to Alyssa in a way he'd never been drawn to Kayla before, and he had asked for the Lord's guiding influence regarding her.

Ed pulled the slip of paper out of his wallet and read it over once again, though he had no need to read it. His father's blessing was burned into his heart and mind for all eternity. *She will love me with all her heart, she will be faithful to me all her life, she will. . . .*

"Were you waiting long?" came Alyssa's cheerful voice, breaking into his thoughts.

He gave her a broad smile. "No," he said, folding the paper. He slid it back into his wallet and put the wallet back in his pocket. Then he held the door open for her.

As he slid onto the driver's seat, he asked, "How was it?"

"Enlightening," she said, but she didn't elaborate.

Chapter Thirteen

"Mmm," Alyssa nearly drooled as she looked at the two boxes of chicken on the seat of Ed's white pickup. "Supper?"

Ed nodded and gave her a wide smile. "Sure. Are you hungry?"

"Starving," she admitted.

"Well," he drawled, "I figured since you skipped breakfast, and that was almost twelve hours ago, you might be hankering for something to eat. I thought we could have a picnic at a special place I like to visit sometimes."

"Is it far?" she asked.

Realizing she may be too hungry to wait, Ed suggested. "About ten minutes away, but you can eat now if you'd like."

"I think I can wait ten more minutes," she said.

He drove east on Highway 40 toward the tiny community of Jensen. Soon he came to a meeting house belonging to the Church of Jesus Christ of Latter-day Saints. The brick building seemed to be situated in the middle of nowhere, surrounded by scattered farms to the east and north. On the south side of the highway there were fields that seemed to stretch on forever. Ed parked in the east parking lot and helped Alyssa out of the truck, then brought the boxes of chicken and a blanket over to the shade of a large shade tree that grew on the southeast corner of the church property. While Alyssa held the boxes, he spread the blanket on the grass, then took the boxes of chicken from her while she folded her legs beneath her and spread out the full skirt of her cream-colored dress to prevent any wrinkling of the fine fabric. Ed sat down beside her and gave her one of the boxes.

"Would you bless the food?" he asked.

Alyssa smiled. "Thank you," she agreed.

After her prayer, Alyssa opened the box Ed had given her and started eating a drumstick right away, before he managed to get his box open. "I guess you were hungry!" he exclaimed.

Alyssa laughed. "I told you I was starving!" she admitted, taking another bite. "I haven't eaten since Sunday night."

"No wonder!" he exclaimed. "I didn't realize, I'm sorry."

"You must have had some inkling," she suggested. "Otherwise, why bother with a picnic?"

He smiled. "Perhaps I had ulterior motives."

She gave him a quizzical expression, but he didn't elaborate. Instead, Ed took his time eating so he could study Alyssa. She was evidently too hungry for conversation anyway. When she had eaten all of her chicken and cole slaw, she traded her baked beans for his cole slaw and ate that as well. Then she stretched out on the blanket, tucking her skirt smoothly beneath her legs.

"This was a lovely idea," she said, using her hands as a pillow for her head. "And a beautiful place."

"I wanted you to see it," he explained, looking down into her brown eyes, loving the tiny freckles that sparsely dotted the bridge of her nose. "This is where my ancestors, the Timothy clan, settled when they came to America from Wales. My third great grandmother's maiden name was Davis, which is my middle name. Being a namesake to an ancestor always made me feel special somehow. The Timothys are a strong, devoted family, and I'm proud to belong to them. They owned a big chunk of property here in Jensen. Some say right across the highway from this church."

"Do they still own any of this land?"

"No," he replied. "It was sold at least two generations ago. Now the church owns this piece, and the rest is divided up with several different owners. I'm not sure who owns the pasture on the other side, but I heard a distant cousin owns that blue house you can see across this field." He pointed east and just a little bit north of the church.

"My mother's middle name is Mae," Alyssa confided. "I never cared for it much until. . . ." She hesitated.

"Until?" he encouraged.

Alyssa blushed. "Until you started calling me Alyssa Mae."

Ed couldn't prevent a smile from wandering across his face. He was pleased to hear her confession.

"Mae was my grandmother's name. Granddad always called me Maisey, because I am her namesake."

"I like nicknames," he admitted. "My father was always called Sparky, which suited and defined his character."

Changing the subject, Alyssa said, "Abbot told me that you move the herd from the Bar M before winter sets in. Where to?"

"The winter range is about sixty miles south of Lapoint. We have two families that live down there. Manuel's family raises hay and oats for us during the summer and helps Marcus through the winter. Except for vacations, Marcus stays with the herd wherever it goes. In the winter, he and his wife make up the second family, but she doesn't care to spend her summers up on the ranch, so he drives down to the range on weekends."

"I've enjoyed trying to fill in for Marcus," she said. "But in my real life, I'd rather stick to flying."

"At least that's something we have in common," he offered. "I have a helicopter and you have a Cessna. Perhaps we could teach each other a thing or two."

"I'd like that," she admitted. Have you ever flown a paraglider?"

"No. They worry me a little. No engine, you know."

"Oh, but it's beautiful," she insisted. "It's so quiet up there without a motor. It's just you and the canopy and the wind. It's like you step off the world and put your hand into God's."

"I guess you'd need to," he teased. "Put your hand into God's, that is."

She punched him playfully in the arm. "Seriously!" she bantered. "Sometimes you can catch a thermal that will take you up a mile or more. It's how I envision the angels must feel, flying above in a world that we can only dream about."

"If you promise not to scare the dickens out of me, maybe I'll sign up for a class or two," he conceded. "I get a rush out of flying Li'l Posse around."

"Believe me, flying an engine driven aircraft is far more scary than flying a paraglider."

"You like your work, then?" he questioned.

She nodded. "Most of the time. A few more payments and A & M will be debt free, then I can hire a bookkeeper. I hate that part."

"But the teaching and the flying?"

"There's no better way to get that close to heaven," she said, "except at the temple."

"And you like to parachute out of airplanes as well?" he teased.

"Believe me, that was an unusual day. I'd been disappointed for quite a while that Abbot hadn't invited me to the Bar M. Then when he did, I was too excited to wait. And I'm a firm believer that the best way to see a place for the very first time is from the air. So I talked

Mike into piloting the Cessna. We got some great photos, by the way, while we were circling up there that day. I'll send you copies when I get back, if you'd like."

"I would," he agreed. "But what made you decide to jump that day?"

"I don't know. It wasn't the brightest idea I'd ever had, and I realized that about two seconds into the jump. I'd miscalculated the wind gusting off the top of Porcupine Ridge. When my chute didn't open, I was too busy trying to figure out what was wrong to worry about which side of the ridge I was going to land on. About the same time I went out of your line of vision, it opened up full and I had almost six minutes of float time before I hit the trees."

"Then you really enjoy parachuting out of airplanes?"

Alyssa nodded. "Granddad taught me when I was only twelve. I've loved it ever since. My biggest goal, jumping Bald Mountain, has yet to be reached."

"Why would you want to jump there? I've heard it's one of the most dangerous jumps in Utah."

She smiled. "You don't need to worry. Granddad would never permit it, even if the plane is mine now. And Mike says I need to learn more about rough terrain jumping before he'll take me up."

"I'm relieved to hear it," he teased. "Judging by what happened the day you parachuted onto the Bar M, I'd say rough terrain jumping isn't your strong suit."

"Well," she conceded, "that wasn't the best idea I ever had."

Ed nodded. "Ain't that the truth!" he teased.

Wondering if he could lead into a conversation regarding her other impetuous act, he took a deep breath and decided to go for it. "Why did you decide to kiss me yesterday?"

Alyssa sat up and turned her back to him without answering.

"Don't be upset," he coaxed as he reached out with both hands and rubbed her shoulders. "I just haven't figured that move out yet, and it's bothered me. I thought at first that you were trying to make Abbot jealous, but when you explained about your relationship with him, I knew that couldn't have been the reason."

She brought her knees up to her chest, letting the full-skirted dress float around her ankles. Leaning forward, she wrapped her arms around her knees and said, "Mmm, that feels good. You'd make an excellent masseuse."

In response, he rubbed her neck and shoulder blades as long as she let him. But he didn't ask anything more. He decided to give her time to reconsider whether or not she wanted to answer his question.

After a few minutes, she said, "Does there have to be a reason for everything?"

He considered her response before he said, "In my mind, there does."

"Hmm," she reflected. "Have you ever done anything for which you had absolutely no reason at all?"

"Not very often. Once, I think," he admitted, remembering his reaction to Alyssa calling him the patriarch of the Bar M Ranch.

"Well, I suppose I'll have to give you a reason, won't I?"

"I hope so."

"Does it need to be true? Or can I make something up?" She grinned mischievously.

Not deterred by her question, Ed answered with total sobriety. "What purpose would it serve to lie to me?"

He waited once again for her response. After a while his hands grew tired, and he finally stopped massaging her neck.

He watched her shoulders lift and fall in a little shrug. With her back still to him, she said, "I guess the only thing I can tell you is that it began as a whim after a little bit of a temper tantrum."

"You kissed me because you were angry with me?"

"No, I was angry with Abbot, and men in general. Hans, Luke and Sidekick had all offered themselves as replacements for Abbot yesterday morning. At first I thought their attention was harmless, but the more I thought about it, the angrier I became. None of them had considered what I wanted! They may have meant well, but it offended me."

"So why, exactly, did you kiss *me?*" he asked, still uncertain of her reasoning.

Alyssa blushed.

"Please," he coaxed.

She lowered her eyes and her lip quivered when she finally confessed, "On a whim, I suppose. I thought 'Ed's the only one who hasn't kissed me yet. He might as well get his chance.' After the notion popped into my mind, I acted upon it without thinking it through."

"I see," he said, though it was disconcerting to consider. She'd kissed him on a whim during a temper tantrum! It was not a comforting thought, and he almost wished she hadn't told him.

It angered him to learn that the other three men had sought her out, offering to compensate Alyssa in her agony. Their behavior disgusted him!

He didn't say anything for several long minutes, but there were many questions he still wanted to ask her. Finally he gathered courage and proceeded. "Did you consider whether or not I wanted you to kiss me?" he asked, hoping she could answer that question to his satisfaction.

She frowned. "No."

"It seems to me," he suggested as he laid back upon the blanket behind her, cradling the back of his head with his hands, "that the whims you've foolishly jumped into, when you hadn't considered the consequences, have had disastrous, or near disastrous results. Do you suppose your actions are trying to teach you something?"

"Are you scolding me?" she asked, turning to face him.

"No," he answered with absolute sincerity. "I'm just trying to figure you out."

Alyssa laughed. "Well, if that's what you're trying to do, you're fighting a losing battle. My parents have been doing the same thing for twenty-five years, and they still haven't managed it." After a brief pause, she admitted, "I guess I'm hopeless."

"I wouldn't go so far as to say that," he consoled.

"Well, maybe not *completely* hopeless."

"Did you like it?" he asked, hoping to catch her off guard. When her eyes widened, he knew he'd succeeded.

"What?"

"Did you like kissing me?"

She turned around again, putting her back to him. But she answered quicker than he had expected. "I don't think I want to answer."

"Oh?" he questioned, wondering if he'd angered her somehow.

When Alyssa turned back to look at him, he saw a mischievous glint in her eyes. "I don't think I can answer," she teased. "It's hard to tell with just one kiss."

He grinned as he realized what she was suggesting. But their first kiss, and the reasons behind it, still worried him. He waited a few minutes, hoping she'd give him a more definitive hint that she wanted to kiss him again. Her next question answered his completely.

"Did you like it?" she asked timidly, still refusing to answer his question.

He shrugged. "I definitely think it will take a little more kissing to be sure."

Alyssa grinned and her smile lit up the sparkle in her brown eyes like glistening diamonds. She bent over him, looking into his eyes as well. Then her gaze traveled across his face and concentrated upon his lips.

Ed wanted to bring his hand up, place it gently on the back of Alyssa's head and bring her lips against his, but he also wanted their second kiss to be completely initiated by her. He didn't want to force her, and he didn't want to frighten her, as Abbot did once before. The waiting seemed to stretch on for hours, although it could only have been moments. When at last she brushed his lips with hers, the agony of waiting was more than fully compensated.

Ecstacy flowed through him like nothing he had ever experienced. He found the courage to bring his hand up to her head, to wind his fingers in her silky brown hair, to taste her lips with such passion that he doubted his life could ever be the same as it was before that moment.

Then she withdrew and the disappointment he felt was immediate.

"Maybe," she said, licking her lips, then giving him a delicious smile. "What do you think?"

Pleased with her answer, he sat up and scooted nearer. "Maybe," he teased. "But I couldn't quite tell for sure."

Alyssa planted her lips against his one more time, wrapped her fingers around his neck and kissed him with such fervor that he could only respond by pulling her closer to him, and savoring the moment. Unwilling to let her go, he was pleased that she had no desire to push away from him.

A car honked as it went by on the highway next to the church. They'd been spotted. He withdrew and watched with pleasure as Alyssa blushed. "I hope you've decided," she giggled, "because this is not a very private place to be kissing."

"Hmm," he teased. "Maybe I do like it when you kiss me." He stood up and helped her to her feet. "Come on, Alyssa Mae. We need to start back."

They folded the blanket together, gathered the trash, and headed for the truck. After he had her safely inside, he started the engine. Before the truck pulled away, she slid her hand across the seat and placed it in his.

Although Ed was grateful they were now in the truck, where it was a little more private, his heart pounded so fiercely he didn't know if he could even drive. Holding Alyssa's hand seemed to calm him somehow. She didn't say anything for a few minutes, and he hoped she was recalling the past few moments with as much awe and wonder as he was.

When she finally spoke, she said. "Maybe I do, too."

He looked over at her and noticed that mischievous look that he was learning to love more all the time. He couldn't get over how her eyes seemed to light up his whole world as they sparkled whenever she smiled. He'd never seen such beautiful eyes before, and he silently prayed she would save most of those sparkles for him.

By the time he'd turned off Highway 121 and onto the long dirt road that ran along Dry Fork and led to the Bar M Ranch road, Ed's heart slowed a little and he felt a sense of contentment that he could not explain.

"Do you suppose we should take you to see a doctor?" he finally gathered enough courage to ask her.

"Whatever for?" she questioned, surprise evident in her voice.

"Well," he drawled. "You didn't faint today when you kissed me, but you did yesterday. Perhaps you should have a doctor check you over."

"I know why I fainted yesterday," she said. "And I'm just fine, thank you very much."

"Do you plan on telling me why?"

"Don't count on it," she teased.

He was disappointed, but he said nothing. He had to pay attention so he could turn off Dry Creek road and up onto the old, almost abandoned, Pine Bluff trail. Within moments the truck was bouncing up the steep incline.

"Where are we going?" Alyssa asked.

"I want to show you something," he explained. Within a few minutes the truck was parked on a bluff that overlooked the Bar M Ranch. "The view from Pine Bluff is probably the best view from any angle."

"It's lovely," she agreed. "You can see all the way to Porcupine Ridge from here."

He turned off the engine. "Alyssa," he began, "I have one more question for you, one that I've been thinking about all day. I need to ask it, but I guess there ain't no easy way."

Her eyes widened and her mouth dropped. Then she held her head up stubbornly. "If it's what I think it is, I won't answer," she declared.

"Dang it, Alyssa Mae! You are the most stubborn woman I've ever met!" he complained.

"I know," she agreed. "And I'm impulsive, reckless, and I have no regard for consequences."

"That, too!" he declared. "But I can be just as stubborn as you can, and I'm not going to be denied this one."

"What is it?" she questioned, though her voice clearly held denial in it.

Ed swallowed hard. "I don't understand why, when you finally revived in the wagon yesterday, your eyes filled with tears and you were suddenly so distraught. What caused that terrible outburst?"

"I'm not going to answer you," she said stubbornly.

"Why?"

"I don't know that I'll ever answer it," she insisted. "There are some things that you simply have no right to know."

"Perhaps if you knew how I felt then, or what I've since tried to figure out about your tears, you'd change your mind." He studied her expression, but he didn't see any softening on the subject.

"A woman is entitled to a little privacy, and I insist you respect mine."

He let out a ragged breath. "Will you ever tell me?"

"I don't know," she admitted. "But right now, if I told you why I was crying in the wagon, and nearly all day, you would wish that I hadn't told you at all."

He arched an eyebrow and gave her a quizzical look. "That bad?" he asked.

"I'm simply not going to discuss it any further." She closed her mouth defiantly and looked off into the distance.

Ed could see that the topic was still too tender for her when he noticed the liquid increasing in her eyes. "Look!" he exclaimed, trying to change the subject so she wouldn't cry again. "See that clearing over there?"

"Yes, I do."

"I'm building a house right there. Then I'm gonna' convert the cabin to a bunk house. By next summer I'll be able to triple the herd and have twelve ranch hands helping me run this place. I've got big plans for the Bar M Ranch."

"Do you own that clearing?" Alyssa asked.

"Yep. Kayla deeded me a hundred-acre spread up beyond the lodge. She said she expects me to build a house on it, marry some sassy woman, and raise a meadow full of children."

"Do you plan on doing all that Kayla expects?"

"I hope so," he said. "I certainly hope so."

"Tell me about Kayla," she suggested.

Her request caught him off guard and Ed cringed. How could he possibly talk about Kayla in a way that Alyssa would understand? Finally he asked, "What do you want to know?"

"What's she like?"

"Blonde hair, brown eyes, cute dimples."

"That doesn't tell me what she's like," Alyssa said.

"She's a marine scientist and a sailor who's married and hoping to have her own meadow full of children someday." Ed's answer sounded lame, even to himself, and it seemed she was still waiting for a better description. "I don't know what you expect me to say," he finally whispered.

"Do you still love her?" she asked.

Ed hesitated. Alyssa had to have heard all the stories about himself and Kayla. As Hans had suggested, she may feel that he could never love anyone but Kayla. After the past two days, he wasn't certain that was true anymore. But she hadn't asked him for a lengthy discussion. She'd asked a yes or no question, and Ed would not lie to her. Finally he nodded his head. "Yes," he confessed, unable to keep the melancholy from his voice. "I do."

"What kind of house do you want to build over there?" she asked, as though his answer had not disturbed her in the least.

Disappointed that she had changed the subject so quickly, he replied, "A log home, timbered off the Bar M Ranch, of course." He had hoped he could tell her about Kayla, about their relationship. Perhaps if he discussed it with her, she could understand why he still loved Kayla.

"Like the lodge?" she asked, interrupting his thoughts.

"Similar, but different."

"How long do you think it will take?"

"If I can get the exterior done by fall, I could work on the interior this winter. Perhaps by May or June, I suppose, next year."

"I hope you build a big home," she said, though he noticed she was very near crying again.

"I will," he promised.

&s &a

Later that night, after scriptures, Ed walked up to the clearing to ponder the time he'd spent with Alyssa. He regretted telling her that he loved Kayla without further elaboration. He wanted to explain why he still loved Kayla, and he'd been disappointed when Alyssa had changed the subject. He supposed the only reason he still loved Kayla was because he didn't know how not to love her.

But did he love Kayla the way he once had? Did he still love her deeply, passionately, and with all his heart? He thought seriously about Kayla, and for the first time in his adult life, he couldn't remember how it felt to hold her. He no longer had any intimate longing for her, and he couldn't recall what he'd felt like when he had. This new insight pleased him, and he knew he was closer to getting rid of the burden as he had been asked to do by the Lord and his pa in his special blessing.

Now all Ed could think about was how much he longed for Alyssa, and there was no doubt in his heart about his feelings for her. He loved her beyond all reason. He wanted to build the house on that very property with Alyssa in mind. He wanted to know she would walk the floors with their babies in her arms, and they would gaze at the stars together on warm summer nights from the deck he wanted to build off the master bedroom. He wanted to sit on the front porch of the house he built and hold Alyssa's hand, and watch their children grow up there. He wanted to kiss her over and over again in their house, every morning and noon and night. He wanted to caress her silky brown hair until it turned silver with time, and watch their great-grandchildren play at their knees.

All the things he wanted to do with Alyssa, he realized for the first time, were things he'd never dreamed so intensely of doing with Kayla. Even when they were teenagers, and would come up here to kiss, he realized it was always just a dream. With Alyssa it was no dream at all; it felt like a reality.

Finally Ed realized the truth regarding his relationship with both women. Kayla didn't belong with Ed; she never had. Although Alyssa didn't belong with Ed, either, at least not yet, he now had hope that someday she would. If Alyssa asked him about Kayla again, next time he would have a better answer.

꧁ ꧂

Alyssa reflected on the conversation between herself and Ed before retiring to bed that night. Ed wanted to know why she fainted and why she cried. She couldn't answer either question until she knew whether or not she could remove all traces of Kayla from his heart and plant herself there instead. She had hoped that was beginning to happen earlier this evening, when he'd responded passionately to her kisses.

However, when he admitted that he loved Kayla, he hadn't qualified it like she had when she'd told him about Abbot, and Mike and Shauna. That omission was the greatest hurdle for Alyssa, and apparently for Ed, to overcome. He hadn't said he loved Kayla like a dear and treasured friend. When asked if he loved Kayla, Ed had answered simply enough. He'd hesitated, as though weighing whether or not to tell Alyssa the truth, but he had finally confessed, "Yes, I do."

The moment he'd said it, Alyssa felt a resounding thud in her heart that actually hurt. A hollowness settled in her chest that seemed both terrifying and painful. And it had not gone away. Though she loved Ed with all her heart, she wondered how she could remain at the Bar M Ranch, knowing that he may never be able to reciprocate her feelings because he still loved Kayla Clark.

Alyssa had just two weeks left at the Bar M Ranch. Would that be enough time to win his heart, to eradicate what had been growing inside him for more than twenty years? She shook her head sadly, realizing that even two years may not be enough time.

There was no redeeming factor in their love triangle, and Alyssa resolved that she would go back to Wanship immediately, without pursuing a relationship with Ed if she found that he could not let Kayla go.

She remembered the scripture the Lord had given her and tried to focus on being faithful, but she still had doubts. Would her love be strong enough to endure a wedge called Kayla? Ed would have to slay his own dragons, and Alyssa hoped she would be a strong enough reason for him to want to.

She thought about their kisses tonight, and how he'd made her feel inside. Alyssa had never known real love until the past two days. The feelings and emotions he evoked inside her were undeniable. Yet she had kissed him; it wasn't the reverse. All three kisses they'd shared had been initiated by her. Of course, Ed had responded eagerly all three times, but what single man wouldn't?

Alyssa licked her lips with the memories, and found them still warm and tingly, as though he'd just finished kissing her. It amazed her and she found herself wondering why he hadn't kissed her goodnight after they'd arrived back at the Bar M Ranch.

With grave resolve, Alyssa decided that if they should kiss again, Ed would have to be the one to kiss her. Then, and only then, would she have hope that Kayla was losing her hold on his heart.

When she fell asleep that night, she dreamed the dream, but this time, she saw her husband's face. To her great relief, he looked exactly like Ed Sparkleman. The peace it gave her to say those words to him was indescribable, and Alyssa whispered, "I love you with all my heart."

Chapter Fourteen

*E*d was in a much better mood when he awoke Wednesday morning. Having eliminated the burden of Kayla from his heart the night before, he felt it was time to get to know Alyssa better, and give her some time to know him. Perhaps he would get a chance to explain to her how he was feeling toward her.

After scriptures, he'd given Hans the assignment to take Morning Sun into town for groceries and supplies. Then he set off for Mountain Meadow where he arrived shortly after Alyssa and the men did. Since they'd already greeted one another just before scripture reading that morning, there was no need for formalities.

"Who's Alyssa going to partner up with?" Luke asked, a hopeful look in his eyes.

"I say we draw straws," suggested Sidekick playfully.

"I'd like her to come with me today," Ed asserted, knowing the men would not question his authority. Then he touched the brim of his Stetson and nodded his head at Alyssa. "If that's all right with you?"

"Fine," she said, giving him a bright smile.

"Luke and Sidekick, you start the branding. We've only got another day or two left of that. We have a cow missing, so Alyssa and I will do some scouting for her."

"Luke mentioned that he hadn't seen her yesterday," said Sidekick, "but it plumb slipped through my mind. Sorry, boss."

"She's bound to turn up," said Ed, though he was worried about the calves. He was certain this cow was carrying twins, and her disappearance was cause for concern.

The two men both nodded, though not as eagerly as he had hoped, and set off toward the camp to build a fire and get started.

"Shall we go?" Ed tugged on the reins, lightly bumped Breeze in the flanks and headed off toward the far end of Mountain Meadow.

Alyssa followed him on Daylight. Once they reached the area called the meadow basin, they slowed the horses to a walking pace.

"The missing cow is due to calve any day," he said as they ambled along.

"How do you keep track of them?" she asked.

"Not only do I count a lot, but when you've been around them as long as I have, you learn to pay attention to bone structure, eyes, shapes of faces, any odd protrusions or blemishes. And you do a lot of calculating. I have a spreadsheet on my computer with every single black Angus we've got or had for the last five years."

"I could never keep track of them all," she admitted.

"Keeping track of the individuals isn't all there is to ranching. The Bar M has always been a ranch-to-restaurant program. We raise all our own hay and feed on the winter range, and these mountains provide an awful lot of grass. The rain we get here in the summer is phenomenal when compared with Utah as a whole."

"Believe me, I know about Uinta rain squalls," she said. "In girl scouts one year we went camping up at Butterfly Lake. It rained the whole time we were there, with exception of a two-hour break right before we were supposed to leave."

He smiled. "Up here you keep a rain slicker in your saddle bag because you never know what's gonna' happen with the weather, though I have to admit it's been drier this summer than I've seen in quite a while."

They reached a mountain basin, the lowest piece of land on the Bar M Ranch, where a crystal blue lake was fed by a small spring and by seasonal streams still full this time of year. Usually by September the stream beds decreased to a small trickle and the lake shrank to half its summer size until winter snows melted once again. "Here's where we do some of our best fishing," Ed told her. "All native rainbows, and delicious."

"It's beautiful, Ed." Then she asked, "What will happen if the cow we're looking for delivers before we find her?"

"Hopefully, nothing. Most of our calves are born before we bring the herd up here. Down on the winter range we have birthing barns we can put them in. Occasionally, a few will surprise us and conceive later than we calculated. Birthing up here isn't dangerous, it's just not as convenient, since the herd is spread out over so many forested sections. Usually calves are born with little help from us, but once in a while complications arise. One of the prime indicators that something is wrong is when a cow wanders off for a couple days without returning."

"I don't see her anywhere." Alyssa said, searching the area carefully for any sign of movement.

"Let's go up across Porcupine Ridge. It'll give us a better view. Maybe we'll see something from up there."

Approaching from the south end of the ridge, they made their way up a steep, winding trail single file.

Ed cringed from the nervous knot inside his belly. Now that he and Alyssa were alone together, he felt awkward and tongue-tied. His palms were sweaty, and beads of perspiration formed on his forehead.

He hoped Alyssa wouldn't mind working with Hans tomorrow. However, Ed had no intention of letting her work with Luke or Sidekick. Although he felt they could both be trusted, he worried, after her remarks yesterday, that she may feel uncomfortable with them. Hans seemed to have a fairly level head on his shoulders. Alyssa was able to talk with Hans easily and they had a good rapport together. Since Hans evidently enjoyed playing cupid where Ed and Alyssa were concerned, and Hans claimed he had no serious interest in Alyssa, Ed wouldn't have to worry about him. He shrugged. Besides, Hans already knew how crazy Ed felt about her.

What troubled Ed the most was how he, himself, would ever be able to work with Alyssa around. Just being near her this morning sent him over the edge emotionally. He couldn't concentrate on anything but her; his heart pounded so loud he couldn't think clearly. He felt his answers to her questions were inept and restrained.

His reaction to her nearness put them both at risk. A rancher who managed cattle in these mountains had to be focused. There was danger around every corner from rock slides to avalanches, from rattle snakes to mountain lions and bears. If Ed was swooning over Alyssa, he could put his men, his cattle, himself, or even Alyssa in danger. Perhaps it would be safer for everyone if he kept his relationship with Alyssa strictly on a business basis while working the ranch. *However,* he thought with a silent smile, *there's always the mornings, evenings and Sundays!*

When they reached the top of Porcupine Ridge, they stopped and surveyed the meadow far below them.

"It looks different from this end than it does from way over there where I crash-landed that day." She looked to the north end of the ridge, nearly a quarter mile away.

Ed pointed toward an area on the far side of Porcupine Ridge where trees, long dead, had been snapped in two like matchsticks, and huge boulders lay strewn about as though they were the play toys of a giant's child. "Do you see that wide path of broken trees and rocky rubble?"

"Was there a rock slide?" she asked.

"Avalanche," he explained. "That's where my Pa died while saving Kayla's life."

She hesitated for a moment, then said, "It must have been awful for you."

Ed nodded, "I'm proud that Pa was willing to give his life for Kayla. The Lord says there ain't no greater love a man can have than to lay his life down for another. I reckon Pa earned a special place in heaven for his sacrifice."

He had hoped that by bringing Kayla into the conversation, Alyssa would be more inquisitive about her, but she didn't seem interested in asking anything more. Ed felt disappointed. He worried that Alyssa misunderstood his statement from yesterday, and he wanted to tell her that although he still loved Kayla, he had finally realized his feelings lingered because she was a treasured friend and a part of his family.

However, Ed didn't want to force Alyssa's heart. A simple reference to Kayla once in a while, just enough to nudge Alyssa's curiosity, would help Ed determine if she was ready to learn more. That would have to suffice for a while.

He remembered that Alyssa didn't like to be forced into anything. Abbot's forceful kissing and his demand that her hairstyle be a particular length were both control issues for her. Ed would say and do nothing that would make her feel he wanted to dominate her.

After a few moments of silence, Alyssa said, "I can't quite see the camp from here."

"There's a knoll with a stand of pines hiding it from our line of vision," he explained. "When we get to the eastern end of the ridge, it'll pop into view."

She coaxed Daylight ahead of him, and they started across the top of Porcupine Ridge. About halfway across, where the ridge bent in at almost a ninety-degree angle, she tugged on the reins and said, "Whoa, Daylight." Turning back to look at Ed, she gave him a happy expression. "Do you feel that?" she asked, stretching out her arms, letting her hair lift from a warm thermal coming up the face of the ridge.

"I do," he said, enjoying far more than just the swirling air as it wrapped around Alyssa playfully.

"You've got a great thermal here," she said. "It would be perfect for flying my paraglider."

Nodding, he smiled at the thought. With the exception of her free-fall the day he met her, he'd never seen her fly. He hoped to get the opportunity sometime.

Alyssa looked down and pointed toward the trail that led to the camp. "There's Morning Sun bringing lunch."

Ed looked far below them and a little to the east. He could see the lunch wagon on it's way.

❧ ❧

It started to rain around six that evening, so Ed gave everyone the rest of the night off. Sidekick and Luke went into town to "check out the chicks," they said. No sooner had they left when the clouds blew themselves away, leaving the sky crystal clear and the air chilly.

Hans and Morning Sun had returned from town with a truckload filled with supplies. While he and Ed carried in boxes and put things away, Alyssa sank into a bathtub filled with bubbles and soaked for a long time, savoring the way it made her backside feel after so many hours in the saddle.

Afterward she dressed in a mid-length broomstick skirt filled with bright fuchsias, aquamarines and purples and an aqua-colored blouse that matched. Ed, Hans and Alyssa played with Matthew in the gathering room, while Morning Sun prepared a plateful of tacos.

Ed and Hans excused themselves right after supper. Alyssa watched them walk toward the barns, knowing there was still a cow to milk and animals to tend. She volunteered to wash the dishes while Morning Sun got Matthew ready for bed.

After she was done, Alyssa went out onto the porch and sat down on the top step. The sun had already set in the western sky and dusk had settled upon the millions of meadow flowers, changing their hues from brilliant colors to soft, muted shades.

The air was crisp, and with the night came the stars, appearing across the sky one by one as the darkness pushed the sunlight away. Alyssa started counting the stars as they first appeared, but after a short time, there were too many to count. The Milky Way was closer and brighter than she'd ever seen before, and she finally understood how it came by its name. It seemed that someone had dipped a giant paint brush in a bottle of thick, rich milk, and painted a wide swath of it across the night sky.

Morning Sun propped the front door open, leaving the screen closed. She often sat in the rocking chair nearby and embroidered pillow slips next to a driftwood lamp so she could feel the cool night air waft into the lodge. "Morning Sun will sew tonight," she said. "Will you like?"

"You're fine," said Alyssa. "The light from that small lamp doesn't even shine out here, and I can still see the stars."

Nodding, Morning Sun sat in the rocker near the door and began her handiwork.

Alyssa looked over at the barn and saw Ed walking toward her as she sat on the porch step. Smiling to herself, she had hoped he would spend some time with her. When he reached the steps, he took them by twos.

"Saving me a spot?" he asked.

"If you'd like," she whispered.

When he sat down beside her, he whispered back, "Don't want anyone to hear us?"

She shook her head and answered, "It's just so peaceful, don't you think?"

"Alyssa," he hedged, and she heard a sense of hesitancy in his voice. "About yesterday. . . ." He let it trail off, as though he didn't really want to question her.

"What about yesterday?" she asked, her guard coming up.

"When I asked you about your fainting spell and crying afterward."

"I'm not talking with you about that," she reminded, unable to keep an edge of impatience out of her voice. They were no longer whispering due to the sensitive topic of conversation.

"I ain't asking you to," he said. "I've been giving it a lot of thought, and I'm gonna' trust your judgement."

"Oh?" Her eyes widened in surprise.

"You said that if you told me why you were crying in the wagon, I would wish you hadn't. Well," he drawled. "That's good enough for me. I ain't gonna' ask you about it again."

The sense of relief she felt at his statement made her sigh audibly. "Thank you, Ed. I appreciate that."

"You're welcome." He was silent for a few minutes, then said, "I've been watching you closely this past week. Most of the time you seem to think things through quite well. Like with those bear cubs, for instance. You didn't panic, but took every precaution to stay safe."

"I wasn't just thinking of my safety," she admitted. "I was thinking about everyone else's, too."

"That shows a real sense of good judgement," he admitted. "I'm impressed."

She punched him playfully in the arm. "I'm not always impulsive," she said. "In fact, I'm often quite the opposite."

"I'm beginning to realize that," he said. "I'm sorry that I upset you that first day you were here. I didn't realize, when you dropped right out of that Cessna in the sky, that you were more than just a spoiled, beautiful woman who was used to getting her own way. Now I'm beginning to think that you're an angel's gift, disguised in a parachute jumpsuit."

"Thank you," she said as she smiled at his analogy. "When I fly my paraglider I often feel like I'm flying with angels."

"I'd like to see you fly sometime," he suggested.

"Perhaps you'll get that opportunity. Wanship is only a few hours from the Bar M."

"It takes a person of strong character to fly paragliders and jump out of airplanes," he complimented.

Giving him a mischievous grin, she teased, "I've found a few redeeming qualities in you as well."

Then she spread her arms wide and looked up at the night sky. "Have you ever seen so many stars in all your life?"

"Nearly every clear night," he laughed. "But I grew up here, remember?"

"You certainly had it good," she said, a hint of envy in her voice. "In Heber, the street light just outside my bedroom window always took precedence over the stars when I was a child."

His eyes brightened as a thought seemed to form in his mind. "Alyssa Mae," he said, his voice tinged with excitement. "There's a daybed in the lodge somewhere that we could move onto the deck outside your bedroom. Mosquito season won't be in full swing for another few weeks, and you may enjoy looking at the stars to fall asleep at night. It will be chilly, but Morning Sun can round up a pile of quilts for you."

"I would love that," she agreed.

"Come on, let's go find it."

He took her by the hand and led her to the door, opened it for her, then followed her inside.

Within a few minutes he had carried the daybed from the farthest bedroom, through the guest room she was staying in, and out onto the deck. Morning Sun brought fresh linens, pillows, and a stack of quilts. Then Ed helped her make it up properly.

When they were done, Ed stretched out on the bed and pulled Alyssa down beside him. She snuggled into his arms, enjoying the position immensely. Feelings of tenderness nestled in her chest and she wished, if only for a moment, that they were married, and that this was their deck off the master bedroom.

"The stars don't get any better than this," he whispered.

"Oh," she sighed. "It's probably one of the most heavenly views I've ever had."

"I always liked to look at the sky when I was a boy," Ed admitted, "but I guess I'd gotten used to it over the years. Dang! What a sight!"

They heard the sound of a door closing, and footsteps coming across the meadow. Alyssa slid from the bed and went to the railing. Hans was on his way up to the lodge.

"It's Hans," she said. "We'd better go downstairs."

Ed stood up and took her hand, his green eyes caressing her with a poignant longing that equaled her own. "I reckon so," he reluctantly agreed.

Feelings that had once been dormant, were kindled inside her, and a sudden disappointment came over her at the realization that the private time she'd enjoyed for such a brief moment was over now.

They arrived on the porch about the same time Hans did.

"Good Evening," said Hans.

"Evening," Ed nodded, though his voice held a touch of irritability.

"Sorry to bother you," Hans explained, "but Kayla called. She said to ask you to call her back on her cell phone as soon as you can."

Ed squeezed Alyssa's hand. "It must be important. She's on vacation up in the San Juan's. I hadn't expected to hear from her until August."

She gave him a smile. "Go call her, then."

"Goodnight, Alyssa." Ed stepped quickly down the porch steps and out across the meadow, nearly stumbling over a small rock along the edge of the path.

Alyssa frowned as she watched Ed go, then sank upon the top porch step and sighed deeply.

Hans sat down beside her. "Trouble?" he questioned.

"No," she answered quickly. Seeing his eyebrows raise as though he didn't believe her, she responded more truthfully, "And yes."

"Need a shoulder?"

"Can I trust you?" she asked.

She studied Hans' face as he seemed to search his mind for the appropriate answer. His blue eyes were even bluer in the moonlight, and his chestnut brown hair waved in all the right places. He was really quite handsome and Alyssa found herself wishing she knew someone who was available for him.

"Have I done something that makes you feel like you can't?" he finally asked.

She smiled. "No, you haven't."

"Well, then . . . ?"

Alyssa considered his offer, then nodded her head. "How can I be sure you will keep what I share with you confidential?"

He sealed his lips with an imaginary key and gave it to her. Then he said, "Now no one can take this information unless they get the key from you," he promised.

She put the imaginary key in her mouth and swallowed it.

He laughed. "I get the message!"

Alyssa nodded, satisfied that he would keep his promise. "Do you ever think Ed will get over his romantic feelings for Kayla?" she asked, grateful for Hans' friendship and loyalty.

"Did you want to talk about Kayla or Ed?" he asked.

Looking at his sensitive expression, her intuition suggested that he already knew her feelings toward Ed. She marveled at what a dear, sweet friend Hans had become in such a very short time. Trusting the look he gave her, Alyssa simply said, "I've fallen in love with Ed, but I suspect you already know that."

"I do," he answered. "All of us do."

"Who knows?" she questioned, a little panic stricken at his confession.

"Morning Sun, Sidekick, Luke and I."

She arched an eyebrow. "How? I haven't said anything."

"We saw it on your face that day in the meadow, right before you fainted."

"Does Ed know?" she asked, unable to restrain the concern in her voice.

"No. I don't think he does," Hans answered thoughtfully, almost guardedly Alyssa thought. "Am I to understand that you don't want Ed to know you're in love with him?"

"That's correct," she said with a sigh.

"Why?"

"Surely you know the story about Ed and Kayla."

He nodded, but the expression he gave her seemed somewhat perplexed. "Kayla and Ed were engaged once," he admitted. "She broke it off, moved to California, met and married Joshua. Does that about cover everything?"

"No," she answered. "You forgot to mention that Ed still loves Kayla."

"Who told you that?"

"Ed did."

Hans' eyes widened in surprise. "What did he say, exactly?"

"I asked him if he loved Kayla, and he said, 'Yes, I do.' He didn't qualify the statement, either."

"Then he's a bigger fool than Abbot," he complained.

"That wasn't very kind."

"I'm not in a charitable mood," he said. "I thought Ed was over Kayla by now."

"I don't think so. But even if Ed hadn't told me himself, there's still all that Abbot said when we were together."

"What did Abbot say exactly?"

"That Ed is still haunted by lost love, and that Kayla is the only woman Ed may ever love."

"Nonsense!" said Hans. "I don't believe that!"

"What is the truth regarding their relationship?"

"As near as I understand it," Hans explained. "And mind you, this is only from Kayla's side of the story . . . they were childhood sweethearts. After college she wanted to further her education, and she knew that Ed wanted to be a rancher, which is a lifestyle that she didn't want. She learned that her feelings for him were like the love a brother and sister share with each other. According to Kayla, Ed told her that he understood that and accepted it. She said that he rarely calls her Kayla anymore; he calls her 'Sis.' That should say something about how he feels."

"But haven't you seen his face light up when he hears her name?"

"I haven't," Hans admitted. "I'm sorry."

"Just tonight, when you told him Kayla wanted him to call her, his eyes lit up and so did his pace. He just couldn't wait to leave me with you, and race off to call his precious Kayla. He was in such a hurry he couldn't even concentrate on where he was going."

"I'm sure you're mistaken," he said thoughtfully.

"Well, bring her up in your conversation sometime and watch Ed's reaction. I'm afraid he'll never find room in his heart for me. And I won't share his heart with Kayla."

"That's too bad," he said, "because you'd like Kayla if you had the opportunity to meet her."

"Maybe if I knew a little more about her," Alyssa suggested.

Hans smiled. "Knowing Kayla is like opening your life up to a fresh ocean breeze. She's always got a positive attitude, she's quite brilliant, and she treats my brother like he's a king. It's really too bad that she fell in love with my twin. If he hadn't married her first, and I had found her before he did, I may have married her myself."

"I'm learning to resent her," Alyssa admitted. "Every time I hear her name, I cringe. Imagine feeling that unkind toward someone I've never even met!"

"It seems to me," Hans observed dryly, "that you're the one with the hang-up about Kayla."

❧   ❧

When Ed dialed Kayla's cell phone number, he found his hand shaking. Offering a quick prayer before he pressed the send button, he whispered, "Please, Lord, let Kayla and Josh be all right." Then he sank onto the king-size bed in the master bedroom where he would have some privacy, in case Hans came back early.

The phone rang three times before Kayla answered, "Hello."

"Sis," Ed said. "Remember me?"

"Oh, Ed!" Kayla exclaimed. "I'm so glad you called."

"What's wrong?"

"Nothing with Josh or me, but what's going on between you and Abbot?"

"You've talked with Abbot?" He knew his voice had more than indicated how distressed he was over this topic.

"He called earlier this evening and cried for nearly an hour. Ed, I don't know what to do for him."

He could hear the tears hidden behind her words, so he defended himself. "Dang fool!" he grumbled. "If he'd waited until we could explain to him."

"He says you stole his fiancée from him. Is that true?"

"No. Alyssa Mae was having second thoughts about marrying him and had already given his ring back before I got involved with her."

Kayla laughed. "So, you *did* get involved with her?"

He heard the hopefulness in Kayla's voice, but until Ed knew where Alyssa's heart was headed, he wasn't sure he wanted hope dangled around like a carrot just out of his reach. "We shared one morning at the temple, one picnic lunch and three kisses," he growled. "If that means I'm involved with her, then so be it."

"Don't get angry, Ed," Kayla soothed. "Just tell me everything that's happened. Maybe we can figure a way to make it all work out."

Ed spent the next few minutes bringing Kayla up to date about Abbot. When he was finished, he said, "So what's your plan?"

"We've invited him up to sail with us for a few weeks. He shouldn't be alone at a time like this."

"When he gets there, will you do me a favor?"

"What?"

"Feed him to the sharks!"

"Ed!"

"You know I was only joking, Sis."

After they said their goodbyes, Ed lay back on the bed. Why did the problems in his life keep growing faster than he could keep up with them? He'd just gotten his brother, Tom, straightened out, and now it was Abbot's turn. Thank goodness for Kayla in their family. She may be able to work a miracle with Abbot that Ed and Alyssa could not.

He wandered out to the living room, wondering if Hans had come back yet, but he hadn't. Ed looked from the kitchen window across the meadow to the lodge. Hans and Alyssa were sitting side by side on the porch, and he could hear their laughter across the meadow.

He was surprised, and a little dismayed, that they had so much to talk about. Ed had spent most of the day with Alyssa, though he had talked very little, and she had carried most of the conversation.

Hans had seemed perfectly at ease with her, and Ed found himself wondering if he would ever be able to make her laugh like Hans could.

Finally, in an attempt to console himself, he thought, *At least I was able to give her the stars!*

Chapter Fifteen

*L*ater that night, Alyssa stared up at the sky above her as she stretched out on the daybed on the deck, soaking in the beauty of the velvet backdrop with its myriad of brilliant diamonds above her. Snuggling under a stack of quilts, she felt warm and content. The thoughtfulness Ed had for her comfort and enjoyment touched her deeply.

Hans had stayed to visit until almost midnight, and she was exhausted from riding in the saddle all morning. But now the calf lassoing seemed more like fun than work to her, and she didn't mind that part of it, except the branding, of course. Her backside wasn't quite as sore as those first two days, either. She seemed to be a little more toned and firm, as well, and she liked the feeling. When she got back to A & M she would start a running program, to keep her in the same kind of shape ranching had started.

No wonder ranchers can eat like lions and stay slim and well-muscled, she decided. *They exercise from sunrise to sunset!*

When she fell asleep, Alyssa had the most delicious dreams of Ed and her together. They were so pleasant, she didn't want to come out of them at all. When the alarm clock rang, she turned it off, unaware that she was still asleep, and continued reveling in the beauty of her dreams.

The next thing Alyssa knew, it was late morning. The sun, streaming from the east over Pine Bluff, made patterns upon her face as it filtered through the leaves overhead. She could hear the meadow larks singing as a summer breeze danced with the quaking aspen.

To her dismay, she realized that the men were already out at camp. Alyssa jumped out of bed, made it up quickly, threw some work clothes on, and dashed downstairs.

Morning Sun was playing with Matthew on the living room floor. The two were surrounded by a dozen or more tiny toy people and farm animals, as well as a miniature barn and stables.

"Issa!" the child squealed in delight when he saw her. He stood up on his pudgy legs and toddled over to her.

After picking him up, she gave him a big squeeze and said, "Alyssa loves you." She put her hand on his cheek, still trying to teach him.

His brown-black eyes glittered as he held out a stubby little hand and put it on her cheek. "Issa uv oo," he said.

Alyssa laughed and tousled his black hair. "You're almost there, pal. But Alyssa has to go. Okay?"

"Mafew uv Issa!" he said, this time patting her cheeks with both his hands.

She looked in surprise at Morning Sun! "He learned it!"

Morning Sun nodded. "He says it all the time."

Alyssa gave Matthew a big kiss on the cheek. "Way to go, Matt!"

He squealed with laughter, then hugged her fiercely.

Finally, she put him down. "Bye," she said as she left the lodge and headed out to the barn.

Within a few minutes, she was sitting atop Daylight, headed toward the camp. When she arrived, no one was in sight. Knowing the branding was almost finished, she concluded that all the men must be laying up fence today. Deciding to go look for them, Alyssa tugged the reins and pointed Daylight toward the fence line, half a mile downhill, past a quaking aspen and pine tree forest. When she got past the trees and into a little clearing, she first heard, then saw Hans using the post driver to pound another steel fence post deep into the mountainside. To her surprise, he was by himself.

Alyssa felt very selfish, sleeping in while he was out here slaving away by himself. She made a clicking sound with her mouth, and gently nudged Daylight in the flank. The chestnut mare started a quick trot toward Hans.

Then, without any warning, Daylight reared up on her hind legs and whinnied pitifully. Alyssa tried to hang on, but the saddle slipped sideways, frightening Daylight all the more. The mare reared up again, throwing Alyssa off in the thick grass. Alyssa screamed as she landed with a dull thud. Then Daylight whirled around and took off in the direction from which they had come.

For a minute or two she could only lie there with the wind knocked out of her. Then Alyssa sat up, shook her head and shoulders, and felt her backside for any serious injuries, but she was all in one piece. She started to stand up when Hans appeared.

"No," he said. "Stay still. You might have broken something."

Alyssa pushed his hand away. "I didn't damage anything," she insisted, "except my ego." She stood up and dusted off the back of her jeans. "Whoa," she said. "I may have a nasty bruise or two, but I'm not broken."

"You're lucky Daylight reared up when she did," Hans told her. "Why?"

"Look," he said. "I managed to kill it before it got to you."

Across the path she would have taken, a dead rattlesnake lay upon the ground, its skull crushed by a rock.

She closed her eyes and looked away. "Ooh!" She shuddered. "Will you please get rid of it?"

Using a stick, Hans draped the dead snake over it, then carried it some distance away down the mountainside. Alyssa couldn't watch him take it away. The sight of it was too gruesome. She kept her eyes toward the quaking aspens higher up and wondered if they would ever find Daylight. The frightened mare was nowhere to be seen.

Then she heard a horrible shriek, along with vicious growling sounds, coming from the direction Hans had gone. Without thinking, Alyssa ran toward the sound with all her might. What she saw made her scream out in terror. Hans was unconscious on the ground and a large black bear was mauling him. She grabbed one of the steel posts and ran forward with it. Without stopping, she ran straight toward the bear's face where the steel jammed into the bear's eye.

"Get!" she screamed. "Get out of here!" She hit the bear again, but it turned toward her, angered. Glancing down at Hans she could see a big gash across his right shoulder, all the way down to the shoulder blade. Blood was soaking through his shirt, and he was lifeless, lying face down in the deep mountain grass. The sight of his wounds made her so angry she didn't know what she was doing. She screamed and swung the post with all her might again and again at the bear, hitting it over and over in the head, until the bear finally turned around and ran away.

Alyssa dropped the post and knelt beside her injured friend, praying that he was still alive. "Hans," she cried. "Hans!"

She heard him whisper, but his voice was ragged, "Is she gone?"

"Yes," she answered. "Oh, Hans, you're still alive!"

He rolled over. "Of course," he said. "I'd heard that if you were attacked by a bear you should pretend you're dead, but I must say, your technique worked a little better than mine." He sat up, then hunched over, obviously in pain.

"You're bleeding badly, Hans. We've got to get you to a hospital," she said. "Do you think you can walk?"

"I don't know. She bit into my calf pretty good."

Alyssa looked at his left leg. His jeans had been shredded, and blood was seeping through the pant leg. She removed her outer shirt and wrapped it around Hans leg, putting steady pressure on it as she tied it in place. Then she removed his outer shirt and tied it around his shoulder, saying, "We need to keep pressure on these wounds."

"We need to do something more than that," he whispered, but the look in his blue eyes was one of pure terror. "She's back!"

Alyssa spun around, grabbed the post with one hand, and Hans' good arm with the other. "You've got to get up!" she commanded. "No matter how painful it is!"

"Play dead!" he insisted, shaking his head.

"No! She's mad now, and she won't stop with mauling. Get up!"

She yanked on Hans' good arm and helped him as he managed to stand. "Get to your horse!" she said, backing up towards him. "Go!"

He held onto her elbow. "You're coming with me!"

She pulled her arm free and backed up with him. "Don't worry about me, just get on that horse! I'm right behind you!"

They backed up together until they reached the horse, but the black bear was angry. She kept pawing the ground like a bull, evidently getting ready to rush them.

Alyssa helped Hans as much as she could, but she was also holding onto the post and facing off against the bear. Every muscle in her body screamed with adrenaline.

Hans tried to get up on the horse, but he fell back down twice and couldn't make it. While still watching the bear, Alyssa put the post down and pushed Hans up with all her strength. Finally, he was able to get up on the saddle, but he was in shock and bleeding profusely. He leaned over the saddle horn, taking the reins limply in his left hand.

Alyssa lifted her foot to put it in the stirrup, but a ferocious growling sound made her stop, boot in mid-air. She turned back to look at the bear. To her horror, the hostile animal had started a mad rush towards her, apparently determined that she wouldn't get away. Without thinking of the consequences, she slapped the horse as hard as she could in the backside and yelled, "Go!"

The horse leaped forward, and Alyssa grabbed the post once again, preparing for the charge. Just seconds before the bear reached her, she realized she wouldn't even be able to slow it down. She dropped the post and ran as fast as her legs could carry her. In her mind she uttered feverish prayers about running and not being weary, and about giving her feet wings of lightning.

A rifle shot echoed from her left, and she heard the bear stumble. Alyssa kept running. She wasn't going to wait and see if the bear was still coming. Then she saw Ed off to the side of her on his palomino stallion. He had a rifle in his hand. In mid-gallop, he took aim and fired another shot. Evidently the bear was still chasing her. Alyssa screamed as she tripped over a fallen branch.

"Get up!" she heard Ed's voice yelling at her.

She didn't have to be told twice. She pulled herself up and started forward, running with all her strength. She could hear the bear huffing and growling not two yards behind her. Then Breeze came between her and the bear. She heard a great cracking sound as Ed shot the bear at point blank range. Alyssa kept right on running.

Then Breeze was by her side, and Ed was yelling, "Stop! Alyssa, stop!"

Feeling her feet slowing down beneath her, Alyssa finally dared to look back. A black furry ball lay in a bloody heap a hundred yards behind her. She bent over and put her face against her knees to keep herself from fainting.

Ed jumped off Breeze and swept her into his arms. "Are you all right?"

"Hans!" she cried, allowing herself to lean against him. "Hans was mauled! He's bleeding terribly! We have to find him!"

"Sidekick's gone after him."

"We have to help him," she insisted, but her knees wobbled and began to buckle beneath her.

Ed picked her up and carried her over to Breeze. He helped her into the saddle, then swung up behind her.

Alyssa felt the strength draining from her. She trembled and leaned back against Ed, completely exhausted.

He wrapped his arms around her and took the reins in his hands in front of her. "Git up!" he barked.

Breeze leaped into a gallop and carried them all the way back to the lodge. When they arrived, Sidekick had Hans stretched out on the porch. Morning Sun was holding pressure on Hans' calf, while Sidekick was pressing against Hans' shoulder.

Ed helped her down off the palomino stallion and made her sit on the step. "I'll fire up Li'l Posse," he said to Morning Sun. "Alyssa's liable to go into shock. Watch her a moment."

Morning Sun lifted her hands from Hans' calf. "It's stopping," she exclaimed. The relief in her voice was clearly evident.

"Good," Hans moaned. "Bleeding to death wasn't on my summer itinerary."

Alyssa started to shake uncontrollably. Morning Sun brought a fleece blanket and wrapped it around her.

Within minutes they were in the helicopter, headed toward Ashley Valley Medical Center. Sidekick was still maintaining pressure on Hans' shoulder. Ed was piloting, and Alyssa was trembling on the seat beside him.

When they arrived, Hans was rushed immediately into surgery.

Alyssa was put on a gurney and given an intravenous line with some medication in it. Several warmed blankets were piled on top of her. Finally her teeth stopped chattering so she could talk.

Sidekick John had gone to get a bite to eat at the snack bar. Ed stayed and held her hand.

Still numb with shock, Alyssa said, "Thank you, Ed. You saved my life."

"You saved Hans' life," he responded.

"I nearly cost him his life," she admitted.

"How do you figure that?"

"I forgot to wear my bear bell," she admitted. A tear slipped from her eye and he wiped it away with his fingertip.

"The post driver was running," he comforted. "With that thing pounding away, you shouldn't have needed a bear bell."

Alyssa persisted. "I was late getting up. If I'd been there earlier, none of this would have happened."

"Where do you think that bear was, Alyssa Mae? It was waiting for anyone who got too close."

She interrupted him. "That doesn't matter. I should have disregarded the snake. If I hadn't insisted Hans remove it far from me, he wouldn't have been attacked. If he had died, I wouldn't be able to live with myself."

Ed shook his head, his gray-green eyes dark and stormy. "I left Hans alone while I went to search for our lost cow. I should have checked the area more thoroughly. Had I done so, I would have moved Hans to safety before the bear could attack. If anyone's to blame, it's me. The bear had evidently claimed it's territory, and we were intruders."

"But . . . ," she began.

He put his fingers against her lip. "The bear was only protecting its offspring."

"Or," said Sidekick John from the door, a sandwich in his hand, "it could have just wanted to keep you, like I do," he grinned.

Ed shook his head, but Alyssa smiled. "Always trying to cheer us up, aren't you, Sidekick?"

"That's what I do best," Sidekick said with a wink.

❧ ❧

By six in the evening, Hans was out of surgery, and sleeping in a room at Ashley Valley Medical Center. Although his wounds were deep, they were not life-threatening. He'd lost a lot of blood and the doctors wanted him to stay overnight for observation.

Alyssa felt like she was in a catatonic state where she was not asleep, but not really awake, either. She rested her head on the side of Hans' bed, as she waited for him to awaken from the anesthesia and talk to her. Ed had gone to get her something to eat, for Alyssa would not leave Hans. She felt responsible for him, and she was going to stay by his side until he was safely back at the lodge.

Someone stroking her hair startled her. She lifted her head and looked at Hans smiling at her. He was positioned on his left side, and was running his fingers through her hair.

"Sleepy, hmm?" he asked.

"Numb would be a better word," she admitted.

"Me, too."

"How do your wounds feel?"

"Not too bad, considering I almost became the main course at a bear's banquet."

"Oh, Hans, I'm so sorry. Will you ever be able to forgive me?"

"For what?" he asked. "You didn't bite me."

She smiled. "For making you take the rattlesnake away. For sleeping in and leaving you alone."

"You saved my life. I don't think that bear was done with me when you got there. I think she was just getting started."

"I feel terrible about what happened to you."

"Risk of the job," he said. "I knew bears were out there. I took the risk. That's all life is, really, one risk after another." He gave her a crooked grin.

"You're impossible," she said. "What am I to do with you?"

"You could kiss me better," he suggested.

Her eyes widened in surprise. "Will that help?" She gave him an impish smile.

"It couldn't hurt."

She stood up and looked down at him, then put her hand on his cheek. "You've become a dear and treasured friend," she said. Then she placed her lips on his cheek and gave him a quick kiss.

"Well?" she asked.

"Much better," he replied, though his voice sounded like he was still half asleep.

Just then Ed sauntered into the hospital room. "All they had was tuna fish or egg salad. Which would you like?"

"Tuna," she said. "Thank you."

Ed handed her a tuna sandwich and some potato chips on a plate and he kept the other one. Alyssa sat back down and took a small bite. Although she wasn't hungry, she knew the food may restore some of her strength.

"Don't I get any?" Hans asked.

"Not without permission," said Ed. "You can't even go to the bathroom in here without asking."

❧ ❧

By the following evening, life at the Bar M Ranch started to return to normal, and Ed was glad to be home again.

Although Hans was heavily bandaged and using a crutch, he was in good spirits. He was stretched out on one of the cream-colored sofas at the lodge where Alyssa had insisted he stay so she could take care of him.

For the fifteenth time, Hans told the story of his attack to news crew and magazine reporters. The story seemed to get bigger and bolder with each telling, but at least Hans always credited Alyssa for saving him. When the last reporter left, Hans turned to Ed and pleaded, "No more, please. I'm not on display any longer."

Ed was relieved. He thought there had been enough publicity at the hospital this morning, and Alyssa had been by Hans' side nearly every step of the way. She had insisted they stay at the medical center in Vernal the night before. Fortunately, he was able to telephone Josh and Kayla, and the Admiral's family before the news broke on the West Coast.

Luke came down from the Bar M Ranch and picked up Sidekick so they could take care of the animals and round up Daylight. They found the chestnut mare pacing at the back door of the barn, skittish, but otherwise unharmed. And they'd found the lost cow that Ed had been searching for at the time of the attack. Somehow she'd managed to give birth to twin calves completely on her own, and all three animals were well.

When they arrived home on Friday, Ed made phone calls to get some extra help at the Ranch. He hired six temporary workers to come in and lay up the rest of the fence, and assigned Sidekick as foreman over them until Marcus returned. Then he ordered two sets of bunkbeds that Sidekick and Luke brought into the cabin that same day, putting one set in each of the two smaller bedrooms. The extra expenses would cut into the profits, but he wasn't going to allow Alyssa or Hans back out at the camp again. If they didn't like it, then they'd have to go home. He'd made his decision and that was final. Now all he had left to do was tell Alyssa and Hans about the change in plans.

He walked from the kitchen into the gathering room where Alyssa had made a comfortable bed for Hans on the sofa. Hans didn't want to be moved upstairs because that took him away from all the ranch's activity, so they'd compromised.

If Alyssa hadn't kissed Hans yesterday at the hospital, Ed wouldn't feel so miserable. But she had, and he'd seen it. With all the crazy, mixed up feelings inside him, he wondered how Alyssa could be the woman the Lord had promised him. He didn't think his heart could go through another lost love. Not a second time. And not from Alyssa. But there was no denying what he saw. And when he'd rescued her from the bear, her only thought was for Hans. Alyssa had evidently fallen in love with Hans Bridger Clark.

Hans had been wrong about where Alyssa's affections lay, and so had Ed. It was the second time Ed had lost a woman to one of the Admiral's sons and he was beginning to think how grateful he was that there were only two of them!

Ed sighed as he watched Alyssa fluff the pillow up for Hans. The injured man was lapping up every ounce of attention he could get. Not that Ed blamed him. If Alyssa doted on him like that, he'd welcome it just as eagerly.

Still trembling inside when he contemplated how close he came to losing her completely yesterday in the meadow, Ed shivered. If he'd been one second later getting there, she would have been killed by that bear. *Killed!* He shook his head. *No, I couldn't have lived with that!* Had Alyssa died it would have been far worse than her falling in love with someone else. *But not by much!* his heart shuddered. *Not by much!*

❧ ❧

Alyssa felt numb, as though her whole body had been caught in a vacuum, but no one seemed to notice. Her day had been spent caring for Hans, letting reporters in, getting pillows, bringing food, holding Hans' hand, doing all those things she felt she owed him. At least a hundred times since the attack yesterday she had thanked the Lord for sparing Hans' life, knowing she could never survive emotionally if she'd been responsible for his death.

Regardless of everyone's protests, she still felt accountable for Hans' condition. If she hadn't slept in, if she hadn't insisted he remove the snake, if she hadn't turned her head away when he did remove the snake, she may have been able to warn him in time to prevent his injuries.

Alyssa tried to render whatever comfort she could to Hans and prayed that it would be enough. At the same time, she felt numb inside, and she kept wondering who was going to comfort her?

Slipping into the bathroom, she ran some cold water over her face and blotted it with a towel. Her skin was pale, cold and clammy, and she realized she might still be in shock. Forcing herself to drink a glass of water and then another, she hoped the extra fluids would help her function better.

What was bothering her the most was Ed. Since the attack he'd been withdrawn and had hardly even spoken to her. It felt like that horrible bear had somehow ripped their fragile relationship in half. She realized that her feelings didn't make much sense, but she had nothing else to go on. Ed certainly hadn't made any attempt to comfort her, or to help her get through the emotional upheaval of the experience.

Although he'd tried to accept responsibility himself, in her heart she hadn't let him.

As she came downstairs, the telephone rang. Ed was playing with Matthew on the living room floor, so Alyssa stepped into the kitchen and removed the cordless phone from the counter. "Bar M Ranch," she answered.

A woman's voice said, "May I speak with Ed Sparkleman?"

Curious, Alyssa asked, "May I ask who's calling?"

"It's Kayla Clark."

"Just a minute. I'll get him."

Irritated, Alyssa took the cordless phone to Ed. "It's Kayla," she said. Then she sat beside Hans and held his hand.

Ed stood up with the phone, speaking quietly with Kayla, as though he really didn't want Alyssa to hear what he had to say. He stepped across the living room and headed toward the kitchen.

Hans looked up at her. "You're pale," he observed. "You probably need to retire early tonight."

"I'll be all right," she insisted.

In the background, she could hear Ed talking to Kayla about Hans' injuries, assuring her that she had nothing to worry about. Then she heard Ed say, "I'll get him. I love you, too."

Alyssa's hand tightened on Hans' hand, and he almost winced with the pressure. He looked at her as though realizing why she was upset, but he said nothing.

Ed stepped back across the gathering room and handed the phone over to Hans. "Your sister-in-law wants to get it straight from you."

Hans nodded and took the phone. "Hi, Kayla."

Ed stood up and gave Matthew a piggy back ride up to his bed. When he came back down, Hans was still telling Kayla all the little details about the attack, but Alyssa hadn't heard a word Hans said.

Three little words were rolling around in her head and her heart, three little words she had hoped Ed would say to her, yet she'd heard him say them to Kayla.

Alyssa looked up at Ed as he held out his hand to her.

"Want to get some fresh air?" he asked.

"Okay," she nodded, placing her hand in his.

Ed led her outside onto the porch and down the steps.

It was already dusk, one of her favorite times of day in the meadow, yet she could not see any of the colors because the gray in her heart was so heavy. As they strolled across the meadow, Ed released her hand and stuck both of his in his jeans pockets.

Here it comes! she agonized. *He's going to tell me that he doesn't want me here. I'm interfering in the affairs of his heart.* She steeled herself for the inevitable, but even when it came, she was still shocked.

"Alyssa, I don't want you out at the camp again," he said. "It's too dangerous. I should have realized that sooner."

"What are you saying?" she asked.

He looked down at her, but she didn't see the bright green eyes of a few days ago. She saw gray-green eyes with an unbending stiffness in them. "You can stay here at the lodge for the rest of your vacation time, but you won't be working with the men any longer."

"You don't think I have anything to say about that?" she asked briskly.

"It doesn't matter if you do. I'm the ranch foreman and my word is law. If you want it changed, you'll have to get Kayla to overrule me."

"And if I don't want to stay at the lodge without earning my keep?" she questioned.

"Then you're welcome to go, no questions asked."

Alyssa's mouth dropped open and she closed it quickly, hoping he hadn't noticed. Ed was asking her to leave!

"Fine!" she snapped, then turned and headed toward the lodge.

"Alyssa—" he said, taking her by the elbow.

She pulled it out of his grasp and said, "You've made yourself perfectly clear, Mr. Sparkleman!"

"Alyssa Mae!" he protested.

"Don't call me that!" she hissed. "Only the people who care about me have that privilege!" Then she spun around once more, raced up the steps, across the wide porch, and through the heavy front door.

When she had closed it, Alyssa felt like crumbling to the floor, but there was still Hans to consider. She walked behind the sofa, gave his good shoulder a gentle squeeze and said, "I believe I will retire early."

"Is something wrong?" he asked quickly.

"No," she lied. "Suddenly I'm just very tired."

On her way past Hans, she grabbed the cordless phone from the end table and went upstairs. Once inside the guest bedroom, she pulled the heavy door shut and made certain that the sliding glass door was closed as well. Then she sank to the floor in the middle of the room and dialed a memorized number.

After two rings, she heard a familiar male voice answer, "A & M Aviation. Mike speaking."

It was so good to hear Mike's voice that she started crying. "Oh, Mike, you're still there! Can you please come and get me?"

"Alyssa, what's wrong?" he asked.

"I can't tell you on the phone, but please, Mike, please come get me."

"I'll leave right now. Where exactly are you?"

"At the Bar M Ranch. Do you remember the way?"

"Yes, will you be all right until I can get there? It's at least a two hour drive."

"I'll be fine."

When she hung up, Alyssa threw all her clothes into her two suitcases and neatly straightened the bedroom. Then she waited, sitting in the middle of the floor in the darkness of her room, numb and still very much in shock, though she couldn't decide if it was from the trauma of being chased down by a bear, or from being emotionally mauled by Ed Sparkleman.

When an hour passed, she tiptoed through the hall, suitcases in hand, and down the stairs. Hans was snoring gently as he slept on the sofa. Alyssa went out the kitchen door and made her way in the dark until she was well out of sight of the cabin and the lodge. Fortunately, there were no lights on in either structure. Then she continued walking down the dusty mountain road, using a flashlight to guide her along for almost an hour, until she saw the headlights ahead of her.

After she climbed in Mike's Trail Blazer and he had turned it around and headed back toward Heber City, Alyssa broke down and sobbed almost uncontrollably. Mike was patient enough to wait until she was done. Then he listened attentively while she bared her soul to him, grateful that she had a friend like Mike to lean upon.

He took her back to A & M Aviation, to her apartment on the second floor over the offices, and carried her luggage up the stairs for her. Shauna was already there when they arrived.

Alyssa sank into Shauna's open arms and wept again, unable to stop the tears from falling. While Alyssa cried, Mike explained all the sad details to his wife. Her two best friends stayed with her until three in the morning when she finally fell into a deep and troubled sleep.

Chapter Sixteen

*W*hen the men arrived at the lodge for scriptures the next morning, Alyssa did not come downstairs.

Ed was still irritated that she hadn't stayed to talk with him last night. She'd been so angry at his decision, she hadn't given him a chance to explain all his reasons. Besides, he'd wanted to do the right thing by telling her that if she was interested in Hans, he understood. And he'd wanted her to explain what she meant when she told him that only the people who cared about her could call her Alyssa Mae. Why hadn't she included him in that category? But she'd gone back into the lodge angry. From past experience, he didn't know how long it would take before she'd cool down this time.

Morning Sun came downstairs just as Sidekick, the last one to arrive, came in and sat on the sofa opposite from where Hans was recuperating.

"Is she sleeping in again?" Ed asked Morning Sun from the overstuffed chair.

The older woman walked past him without answering. Ed followed her to the kitchen. "Didn't you hear me?" he asked.

"I hear," said Morning Sun.

"Is she sleeping or not?"

Morning Sun turned and glared at him, not unlike she had done when he was a bothersome ten-year old. "You are not wise as Morning Sun once thought."

"What?" he asked, completely perplexed.

Morning Sun shook her head. "God sends an angel's gift to you, but you send her away."

"She's gone?" he asked, unwilling to believe her. "She can't be gone! I'd have heard a car come in!"

"She was quiet. Only Morning Sun heard."

"Why didn't you wake me?" he demanded.

"You send Alyssa away. Why should Morning Sun tell you that she obeys?"

Ed cursed and raced up the stairs. "Alyssa! Alyssa!"

He flung the door to the guest room open. The bed had not been slept in. Opening the dresser drawers and the closets, he found them all empty. Pulling the curtains aside, he looked out the sliding glass door to see that the daybed was neatly made. The only evidence that Alyssa had ever been in the guest room was the cordless telephone sitting in the middle of the floor.

Ed grabbed the phone in his hands and pressed the redial button. He waited through two rings. Then a recording with Alyssa's voice said, "You have reached A & M Aviation. Our business hours are Tuesday through Saturday, 8 A.M. to 5 P.M. Please leave a message at the tone and we will return your call as soon as possible. If this is an emergency, please call 435-654-3135." Ed hung up and dialed the emergency number. A sleepy male voice answered. "Hello."

"Is Alyssa there?" asked Ed.

"No, who is this?"

"Where is she?"

"Who is this?"

"It's Ed Sparkleman. She isn't here at the Bar M Ranch, and I'm worried about her. Do you know where she is?"

"All I can tell you, sir, is that she's safe and she's not taking any calls. I'm sorry." Then the man hung up.

Ed dropped the phone and turned toward the door. Alyssa had left the ranch. She'd left Ed and Hans and all of them. Confused and heartsick, Ed didn't understand her motive. Why would she leave Hans when he needed her? Could Ed have misread her signals? A sinking feeling formed in the pit of his stomach. Winded, he staggered down the stairs. The first thing he saw was the startled faces of the three men who'd also grown to care about the beautiful Alyssa.

Hans began the interrogation when he asked, "What did you tell her last night?"

"She left us?" Sidekick's voice quivered.

Luke said, "I'll go find her, Boss. She'll listen to me—"

Ed cut him off. "No! She's gone and that's all there is to it!"

"I don't feel like reading today, Boss," said Luke. He headed dejectedly toward the door. Sidekick followed him out like a newborn calf after its mother.

When the front door closed behind them, Hans asked Ed once again, "What did you say to her?"

"The same thing I'm gonna' tell you!" snapped Ed. "I've decided it's too dangerous to have you working at the camp. If you want to spend the rest of your vacation here, you're welcome to stay."

"That's what you told her?" Hans asked incredulously.

Ed nodded. "Then she asked me what she should do if she didn't want to stay without earning her keep."

"And?"

"I told her she was welcome to leave, no questions asked."

"You idiot!" Hans exploded. "Do you know what you've done?!"

"It figures you'd be this upset," Ed replied sarcastically. "You're the only one of us who stood a chance with her!"

"I had no chance with her at all!" Hans declared.

"You saw how she was since the attack," defended Ed. "Kissing you, pampering you, attending to your every need."

"If you saw her kiss me, then you saw it at the hospital, with her back towards the door. She kissed me on the cheek, and only because I asked for it. But she hesitated long and hard before she gave me that one little peck."

"Why would you ask her to kiss you when you know how I feel about her?" Ed growled.

"I was just coming out of anesthesia," Hans explained, his voice filled with rage. "Give me a break! You're the one Alyssa loves!"

"You didn't see her when she realized the bear was dead!" Ed growled. "Her only concern was for you!"

"I was bleeding out! And she felt responsible for that!"

"I told her if anyone was to blame, it was me!"

"She was in shock, man! Do you think she even heard you?"

"Of course!"

"In shock?" Hans yelled. "She may have heard, but it couldn't have registered. She told me at least a dozen times yesterday how sorry she was for sleeping in late, for not being at the fence line sooner, for making me take the rattlesnake away. She was convinced she could have prevented the attack somehow."

Hans ran his fingers through his hair as though he felt as haggard as Ed did. Then Hans said, "I can't believe you asked her to leave! You were so close to winning her heart."

Ed was astounded by Hans' rage. If a Brahma bull had rammed his gut with all it's strength, he wouldn't have felt more winded. But he wasn't going to collapse in front of Hans. The sinking feeling in his stomach was the only sensation motivating him now. He grabbed his Stetson from a hook by the door, but he didn't bother to put it on.

Then he staggered outdoors, across the meadow and into the Sparkleman cabin. When he was finally in the privacy of the master bedroom, he fell across the king-size bed, his strength completely drained from him. His Stetson slipped from his hand and rolled onto the floor.

"She's gone," he whispered raggedly. "Pa, what have I done? Alyssa Mae is gone."

Alyssa stayed in bed most of Saturday, sleeping fitfully off and on. When she finally ventured downstairs just before closing, Mike was ready to lock up. She still had eleven days vacation time left, and she knew exactly what she wanted to do with them.

Mike smiled when she came down the stairs from her apartment and picked up her paraglider. "That's the spirit, Alyssa," he said. "Get ready for Monday's flight early. You need to get back up in the sky, where you belong!"

"I'm going up in the morning," she said flatly.

"On the Sabbath?" he asked as he arched an eyebrow in surprise.

"I have to!" she retaliated sharply. "So lay off!"

"I won't come over and help you," he warned. "You'll be on your own."

"I've been on my own before!"

"Alyssa, going against the Lord isn't going to mend your broken heart."

"I'm past feeling," she snapped. "And it's my life!"

Mike backed off, and Alyssa got her gear ready for Sunday, then went out to the airplane hangar and opened the big doors. Within fifteen minutes she had clearance from Heber Air Traffic to make a short run over the Uinta mountains, and she had the Cessna in the air.

"Where are you headed?" came Mike's voice over the radio.

"None of your business," she told him and turned the radio off.

Piloting the plane until nearly dark, Alyssa flew within ten miles of the Bar M Ranch, but she couldn't persuade herself to fly any closer. She didn't want Ed to see her plane in the sky. Impetuous as she was, she wanted nothing more than to parachute out and land in the meadow in front of Ed's cabin, to tell him she loved him, regardless of his affection for Kayla, and to kiss him again. But after what he'd said to her in the meadow last night, she doubted she would ever set foot in it again.

Normally Alyssa loved flying the Cessna. But for some reason, tonight the magic of flying was gone. There was no thrill, no surge of adrenalin. On the way back to Wanship, she flew a few aeronautical stunt maneuvers but the rush she sought could not be found. Resignedly, she landed the plane on the airstrip in front of A & M Aviation and taxied the plane back into the hangar.

Mike had finished and was gone for the night. Alyssa sighed with relief. She wanted no more confrontations with her partner.

After closing up the hangar and locking it securely, she sought the privacy of her apartment. Something inside her aching heart begged her to get down on her knees and pray. But she refused to do it, feeling betrayed by the one person she had trusted most: the Lord had let her down. God had given her that mountain top feeling, and had told her that Ed was the man she should love. When Ed shook her off like so much dust on his shirt sleeve, she felt that God knew this would happen, but He had allowed it anyway. God's betrayal was not something Alyssa was likely to forget . . . or forgive.

On Sunday morning, as she opened the door to her Toyota, Alyssa was amazed at how much dust it had collected in the ten days she'd been at the ranch. Her whole world seemed dusty to her, as though it had completely changed in the time she'd been gone. Driving up to the ridge just below Porcupine Peak, she felt numb and completely blind to the beauty of the mountains and meadows around her.

After harnessing into her paraglider, she stepped off into the sky that Sunday morning and said, "You told me that the faithful will overcome all things. Well, here I am God. I was faithful and I overcame nothing. Ed won't give up Kayla, but he will give up me. Thanks for nothing!"

She did not enjoy her flight, for everything in the world seemed dull and faded, mirroring the feelings in her heart.

❧ ❧

Monday morning Mike arrived early and was busy at the front counter when Alyssa came downstairs. He gave her a sheepish, somewhat timid smile.

"Shauna's not going up with us?" she asked.

"Neither am I," he admitted. "Shauna has a doctor's appointment this morning, and wants me to go with her."

"Is she sick?"

"No. It's her . . . annual physical."

Alyssa noticed his hesitation, but she shrugged. "You're not missing much," she informed him, and found her voice cold and brittle.

As she went around the counter to get her helmet off a shelf behind it, Mike blocked her way. She looked up into his stormy, dark eyes and felt tears stinging hers. Without warning, Mike pulled her into his arms and held her like a father would comfort a wayward child.

"I'm sorry for not being here for you yesterday," he said softly. "You needed a friend and I let you down."

"It's okay," she whispered. "I wasn't in the right mood for friendship."

"How about today?" He released her, then tilted her head up with a strong hand on her chin. When she didn't answer, he asked, "Friends?"

Alyssa nodded, but she couldn't smile at him like she knew he wanted. His apology touched her, yet her heart ached so badly she doubted she would ever be able to smile again.

Something felt broken inside her. In the past, flying the paraglider had always helped her when life got ugly, but yesterday it hadn't helped at all. She hoped today would be different.

"Do you want me to drive you up?" Mike asked, picking her paraglider bag up from a lower shelf.

Nodding, she silently slipped into her blue jumpsuit, grabbed the matching helmet, and climbed into Mike's Trail Blazer. He started the engine and drove up the winding dirt road that led to the ridge just below Porcupine Peak.

When they arrived at the launch site, Alyssa realized immediately that her truck was missing.

Noticing her distress, Mike said, "Shauna and I picked up the Toyota yesterday. It's at our house. We were going to clean it up for you and bring it back later today."

"Thanks," Alyssa said, "It was pretty dusty." But she still couldn't find a smile inside herself to give him.

At the top of the ridge Mike helped her lay out the canopy and straighten all the tethered lines. "Wind conditions are perfect," he said. "You can probably stay up all day if you want."

Lifting the control lines, Alyssa let the canopy fill up with air. When it was full, she pulled the toggles and the paraglider rose above her head. She stepped quickly forward, rushing off the top of the ridge and leaping into the air as she had done hundreds of times before, then waited for the rush of adrenalin that normally accompanied that first lunge. But she felt no surge of excitement.

Looking up at the canopy, Alyssa could not see the threads of silver woven into the blue material. In fact, the fabric looked more gray than blue, and she was surprised to see that the cloudless sky was almost as gray as the canopy itself.

Alyssa looked down at the earth, hoping to see the vibrant greens of the alfalfa fields, the shining golds of the oat fields, but they were no longer vibrant. They were drab and lifeless, just like the feeling inside her heart.

Pulling on a toggle, Alyssa sought for the house thermal to her right, and was not surprised to find it. This thermal was always the strongest. She swooped around through the sky in a figure eight formation, climbing higher and higher into the thermal until she could loop those loose three-sixties that took her in an upward spiral. Soon she was nearly a mile above the once verdant earth.

She closed her eyes and waited for the feeling that she was flying with angels to thrill her as it had hundreds of times before. But no matter how long she waited, nor how hard she tried, the angels were gone, and there was only Alyssa, alone beneath the gray canopy.

When the realization that something was truly broken inside her finally sank in, silent tears spilled from her dark eyes and she maneuvered the paraglider into lazy circles to begin a slow descent. Passing high above her grandfather's home, she looked at the rose garden, but all she saw was an assortment of bleak and dreary blossoms, varying in shades from pale gray to charcoal.

Her grandfather was pulling weeds among them and he looked up to wave when Alyssa's shadow passed over him, but she didn't return the gesture. "I can't, Granddad," she whispered. "I just can't."

Alyssa maneuvered the paraglider into loose figure eights and climbed higher once again, but the beauty all around her failed to ignite that spark of joy she used to know. The world was no longer beautiful. In Alyssa's eyes, it was colorless and drab.

When she was less than a hundred yards from the ridge, she panicked. She hadn't seen or felt any of the beauty or joy she had hoped for, almost prayed for. Would she never thrill to the rush of paragliding again? *The beauty of flying a paraglider has to be up in the sky somewhere!* she thought, and she determined to try once more. Alyssa began the figure eight series of maneuvers again, then climbed higher, ever higher in loose ascending circles.

However, it didn't matter how high she climbed or how hard she tried, she couldn't find that angelic feeling she'd had in times past. Not even her beloved grandmother was there to say, "Good morning, Maisey." There were no angels flying with her anymore and she felt the tears slip down her cheeks. Whatever it was inside her that had made her love flying had broken when Ed invited her to leave the Bar M Ranch, and she didn't know how to fix it. With unshakeable determination, Alyssa made up her mind that she would find her love for flying again, or she would die trying.

For the remaining days of her vacation, she spent her time up in the sky, flying her paraglider every day from sunrise to sunset. She always returned feeling empty inside and unable to capture the joy that she had once known beneath the canopy. Several times her granddad waved to her, but she didn't bother to return the gesture; she was too distraught to care.

When she returned each evening, the message box at the office would be full of pink slips. As she read them, she felt nothing but emptiness:

"Ed called."

"Call Ed."

"Hans called."

"Ed called X 3."

"Fourth call from Ed."

Alyssa even got a few messages from Sidekick and Luke, but she shredded every one of them. For eleven days straight, including Sundays, she flew her paraglider every day, all day. When she arrived each evening at her apartment she often found notes taped to the door:

"Ed called for you. Call him, Love Dad."

"Ed called here all day for you. He said he wasn't giving up. Maybe you should call him. Love, Shauna."

"Who's this Ed that everyone is upset about? Please talk to me. Love, Granddad."

"If I get one more call from Ed I'm changing my number. Love, Mike."

"My number has been changed to 435-654-7877. Don't put it down as the emergency num-

ber at the school. Use your own number for
that. Thanks. Love, Mike."

Unfortunately, when Alyssa knew she had to show up for work
on Thursday, she still didn't want to face anyone. She called in sick,
crawled back into bed, and that was where Mike and Shauna found
her two days later, but she'd locked the bedroom door from the inside
and wouldn't let them in.

About an hour later she heard someone outside her bedroom, but
she ignored the noises, buried her head under the comforter and curled
up in a fetal position. Mike was evidently trying to get the door open.

When she felt someone sit on the side of her bed, she yelled,
"Mike, I don't want to talk to you!" When he didn't respond, she
threw the comforter off to yell, "Mike! I don't—"

To her utter surprise, it wasn't Mike or Shauna. Her visitor was
her grandfather, Alexander Turner.

"First off," he said, "it's Granddad. And second, I don't care
whether or not you want to talk to me. I want to talk to you."

Just looking into his dark brown eyes, and seeing the sadness from
her own reflected there, Alyssa threw her arms around his neck and
wept a thousand tears.

All the time she cried, Granddad rubbed her back, stroked her
hair and comforted. "I'm here for you, Maisey. Granddad's here for
you."

Finally the tears stopped flowing and Alyssa was able to gain some
composure.

Granddad handed her a box of tissue and waited patiently for her
to blow her nose and wipe her eyes. When she was done, he said,
"Now, tell me how you managed to let one man put you into such a
hysterical state."

"Is that how you see me?" she asked, dismayed at his description of her.

Alexander Turner nodded. "You haven't been out of bed in two days, and you haven't been eating. You look as though you've lost twenty pounds when you didn't have enough fat on you to lose three. And all this crying, Maisey . . . is it helping?"

"Nothing's helping," she complained. "I think my heart died, and I'm just waiting for my body to join it."

"I think your ego is a little bruised, that's all," he said. "I also think that your refusing to return Ed's phone calls is immature and downright ridiculous."

"Well," she sniffed, "I think it's ridiculous for him to even bother. He's the one who told me to leave. I've only done what he expected of me."

"Then why do you suppose he keeps calling?" Granddad asked.

"Maybe to ease his conscience, I don't know," she said, "but I'm not going to talk to him on the phone."

"Why not?"

"Because I can't see his face if we talk on the phone. He's got very readable eyes, Granddad. Trust me. I can almost see what he's thinking when he looks at me, and I don't trust what I can only hear. You know how much I have to see things for myself."

"Yes, but how can he arrange to see you again if you don't speak to him on the phone?"

"I'm not ready to see him," she whispered. "I don't know if I'll ever want to see him again."

Granddad shook his head. "You don't really feel like that, do you?" he asked.

Alyssa sighed wearily. "I don't know how I feel," she finally admitted. "Except that I don't want to hurt anymore. And I want to fix what Ed broke inside me, but I don't know how to do that, either."

"Let me make you a bowl of soup, Maisey, and while I do, I want you to tell me everything you're feeling inside."

"Oh, Granddad, I don't want to burden you with all that."

"I'm not leaving until you do," he said. "So unless you want your grandfather to become a permanent shadow around you, I expect you'll do your best to accommodate me."

"I never could keep anything from you, could I?" she asked.

He grinned. "It's kept us close all these years. Now, where are your potatoes?"

"I don't have any."

"That's okay because I think I have a couple in my pockets." He rummaged through his farmer pants and brought out two potatoes and a small onion. "Now all I need is some milk," he said with a wink.

By the time Granddad had a steaming pot of creamy potato soup ready for her, and insisted she eat most of it, Alyssa had shared the past three weeks with him, reliving in vivid detail all the feelings in her tender heart. She even told him how she felt her love for flying had been shattered by Ed when he'd asked her to leave the Bar M.

They shared a quart of strawberry ice cream for dessert, and Alexander Turner told her about the rocky road he'd traveled during his engagement to her grandmother. Granddad licked the spoon clean and said, "We had a quarrel shortly after we got engaged. Your grandma was so upset, she threw the ring at me, and refused to speak to me for three months afterward."

"What was the fight about?"

"I don't know. By the time those three months were up, neither of us could remember why we'd quarreled, and we made up."

"How did you finally get her to talk to you?"

"I didn't give up. I took out a loan on my car and spent money on flowers every day for a while. Thought I'd have to get a second mortgage on my farm, too. But your grandma loved roses, and I knew that if she got enough roses from me, she'd eventually soften."

"So what happened?"

"Well," he drawled as his mind filled with memories, "I finally decided that I was going to go broke if I kept buying fresh roses, so I went down into Heber to the nursery. I picked out a dozen rose bushes and sent those to her with the message that if she still loved me, she'd bring them back and plant them just where she wanted them in our yard, the one that would also be hers when we said 'I do' at our wedding. That way she would have roses all summer long, for the rest of her life. I also warned her that If she planted them anywhere else, that would be my last and final effort at trying to win her back. Then I waited to see what would happen."

To her surprise, Alyssa was a lot more like Mae Campbell-Turner than she'd realized. New tears filled Alyssa's eyes. "Those are the same rose bushes in front of the house?" she asked. "The ones you're always fussing over?"

Granddad nodded. "She called them our love roses. We tended them side by side for all the years we spent together, and now I carry on our tradition."

"I thought you fussed over them because that's where she died."

"That, too," he said. A great sadness came over him as he remembered that day. "I saw her sink down by them as I was on my way in from the field. She'd gone out to pick roses for the supper table. I knew she was in trouble, and I offered to call the ambulance, but she said no, she had waited just long enough for me to get there, and now she could go home. I remember telling her that I wouldn't like it if she died just then, but she said that as long as she had me by her side and our love roses surrounding her, she didn't mind dying so much."

"No one told me this part before."

"I never told anyone until now. It was a private, spiritual moment that we shared together, and I always felt it was something not everyone should be privy to."

"How long—?" she began.

He interrupted her. "If I'd gone into the house to call the ambulance, she would have died before I got back. All alone," he added as his eyes moistened from the memories. "The last words she ever spoke to me were, 'When you're ready to die, Alex, just sit down here by the roses, and I'll come for you. I'll take you home with me.' I promised her that I would. Then I kissed her." A single tear ran down Granddad's cheek and he wiped it away. "When her spirit left her, I started crying like I was still a little boy. After a while the tears stopped, and I held her body in my arms and rocked her back and forth for a long time, wishing I could have gone with her."

Alyssa went around the table and hugged him. "They're the same roses that Mom got her starts from, aren't they? The ones growing in front of her house?"

"Yep. And the same ones that you'll get starts off of for your house. Those roses were planted because of her love for me. I figure she'd want all her grandchildren to have some."

"If we all get married," Alyssa interjected, though she couldn't keep the sadness out of her voice.

"Even if you don't," said Granddad.

When Alyssa could not possibly force another bite down, they washed the dishes together and tidied her apartment. Then Granddad said, "How long are you going to keep refusing Ed's calls, Maisey?"

"Until August," came her reply.

"That's only a few weeks away. He'll be relieved to hear that."

"You're not going to tell him that," Alyssa insisted.

"How's he supposed to know that you'll start responding by August? He needs to have some hope, you know."

"Granddad," she said, putting an arm around her grandfather's shoulder and staring straight into his eyes. "I say August because that's when Ed will stop calling or leaving messages for me."

"What makes you think so?"

She cringed. "Because that's when his beloved Kayla will be at the ranch. After she arrives, he'll be too enamored to even remember that I exist."

"I'll wager his calls won't stop coming in August," her grandfather baited. "And if I'm right, then you'll owe me a flight over the Bar M ranch in the Cessna."

Alyssa smiled at his suggestion. He'd finally given her a sharp bargaining tool. "If Ed does stop calling in August, you'll owe me a jump flight over Bald Mountain."

Alexander Turner frowned belligerently, but she only glared back at him, more determined than ever. "That's the only way I'll agree," she added evenly.

Finally he concurred. "All right."

"Promise," she insisted, knowing that Alexander Turner would never go back on his word. "A man's word is his bond!" she reminded him. It was a quote he'd taught and practiced his entire life.

Alexander hesitated for a moment, apparently sensing that she'd trapped him. His eyes narrowed and he glared at her for a moment.

Alyssa did not back down. She lifted her head slightly and stuck out her chin in her most defiant stance.

Finally, Granddad nodded. "I promise," he agreed, "because if he stops calling you in August, he doesn't deserve you."

"I couldn't agree with you more."

"That brings us to just one more problem," Granddad hedged.

"What is it?"

"I miss my companion at our church meetings. I have no one to sit beside when you're not there."

"I can't trust God right now, Granddad. You know that."

"He still trusts you."

Alyssa glared at her grandfather for only a moment because all she got in response was a defiant, challenging expression from him.

"He told me that the faithful would overcome all things. I thought he meant that if I was faithful I would be able to help Ed overcome his feelings for Kayla. But God let me down completely. How can I trust Him again?"

"Perhaps," Granddad suggested slyly, "God only meant that you would be able to overcome yourself."

"What's that supposed to mean?"

"It means that you are your grandmother's grandchild . . . and your three months will soon be up."

✺ ✺

After a whirlwind of compromises, Granddad agreed to be her liaison, and was able to enforce Alyssa's decisions upon those closest to her: Mike agreed to screen all the telephone calls that came into A & M. Granddad extracted her parents' promises that they would drop the subject of Ed entirely. And anyone who received messages from Ed were to turn them over to Granddad, not to Alyssa.

Then she changed her telephone number at the apartment. And last, Alyssa demanded that everyone stop trying to convince her to return Ed's phone calls. She wasn't going to return them until after she found out what August brought her way. If he gave up calling her in August, she would know that she never had a place in his heart at all. And if he continued to call through August, it would mean that even Kayla couldn't take Ed's mind off Alyssa. She would begin to have hope once again.

In exchange for everyone's consideration, she would try to get back into her normal routine. She even agreed to give up flying on Sunday, though she wasn't certain about going back to church; fortunately, her family and friends agreed to give her time and space.

In July, Ed's phone calls started to slow down. Instead of eight a week, he was down to four a week. His last call came on the thirtieth of July. As Alyssa predicted, Ed didn't call at all the first week in August, and then his calls stopped coming altogether.

Granddad, furious that he had trusted Ed to keep on trying, made sure that the entire family knew why Ed's messages stopped coming in August: Ed's true love had returned to the Bar M ranch.

Alexander Turner now had little reason to consider Ed a suitable candidate for his granddaughter's affection, and he became cantankerous whenever Ed's name was brought into any conversation. And that was when Alyssa finally understood that she never had a remote chance of winning Ed's heart from the very beginning.

Chapter Seventeen

"You're not yourself, Ed," Kayla observed quietly at dinner the last Sunday evening in August.

Ed looked up at her curiously, as though trying to decide how to respond. "I think I inherited your father's gut," he said finally. "Even sassafras tea doesn't help much."

"I've read that chamomile might work better."

Ed gave her a stubborn glance. "No, thanks anyway."

"Have you seen a doctor?" she asked.

"Sweetheart, I'm sure Ed's fine," said Joshua, coming to his rescue. "No," she said, shaking her head so her blonde curls bounced against her shoulders. "I know you too well, Ed. You've been despondent for weeks now. You're not just brooding over Abbot, are you? It's still Alyssa, isn't it?"

Ed bent his head down, apparently so he wouldn't have to look up at her. "What if it is?" he grumbled.

Hans caught Kayla's attention and shook his head, trying to warn her off the topic, but there was no stopping Kayla. If Hans knew her at all, he knew that she would not back down, especially where Ed was concerned.

Hans had no choice but to sit at the same table with Kayla and watch her fall all over herself trying to pry out of Ed what he plainly did not want to reveal. Had she no idea how Ed was feeling? Or how sensitive the topic of Alyssa would be to him? The ranch foreman had been torturing himself ever since the day Alyssa left more than six weeks ago, and Hans wasn't the only one who'd noticed.

"Ed, what can we do to help?" Kayla persisted. "Should we go see her? Would she talk to us?"

With these questions, Ed's head came up. He glared at Kayla for only a moment. Then he softened enough to say, "No. Leave her alone."

"Are you still calling her?" she asked.

He shook his head, and Hans was surprised to learn that Ed had given up. He'd expected Ed to continue trying to call Alyssa.

"You can't just quit," Kayla persisted.

"That's what she wants from me," Ed responded. "Whatever we had before she left isn't there anymore, at least not for her." Then he put down his fork and placed his napkin on top of the plate of food. "I'm not hungry. I think I'll go for a walk."

"Oh, Ed, I'm . . . sorry," Kayla offered tenderly.

With his hand on the door knob, he did not turn around, but his voice carried easily back to them. "You've done nothing wrong, Sis. Don't apologize for caring. That's what being part of our family is all about."

Hans could tell she wanted to say more, but Joshua put his hand on her arm. "Not now," he said firmly. "Let it rest."

Ed turned long enough to nod to Joshua, as though thanking him for his intervention. Then he slipped out through the back door, leaving a somber mood behind at the dining room table.

Finally Kayla broke the silence. "Hans, why didn't you tell us he was so distraught over Alyssa? All this time I've thought it was over Abbot."

Mulling her question over in his mind a moment, Hans debated how to respond to her question. Reluctantly, he opted for the truth. "If he'd wanted me to tell you, I would have."

"We've got to do something," Kayla insisted.

Joshua rolled his eyes and looked at Hans in bewilderment. "I think you and I are caught between a rock and a hard place," he observed dryly.

Nodding, Hans could only agree. Kayla would not back down. He and his twin were lodged between a woman with cupid thoughts and a man who was impervious to her arrows.

Kayla glared at both of them. "We're not going to sit idly by and watch Ed disintegrate. If nothing else, I'll go speak with Alyssa."

Hans cringed. "I think you're the last person she would ever agree to see," he observed.

"Why?" Kayla asked, apparently confused by his statement.

"You're ninety percent of the reason why she left," he confessed.

"But I thought Ed asked her to go."

Wearily, Hans explained, "Right before he made that ignominious error, he told you he loved you on the telephone. Alyssa heard it. She thinks he sent her away because he's still in love with you."

"But he's not!" Kayla complained. "Somebody has to tell her that."

"I tried," Hans confessed. "The night before the bear attack we talked for hours on the front porch, but I couldn't convince her that Ed's heart didn't belong to you. Two days later she heard him talking to you on the phone, and right afterward, he told her she was welcome to leave."

"Then you have to keep trying to see her again," Kayla insisted. "If she told you that much, she must trust you. Hans, please. I can't bear seeing Ed this miserable."

Hans shook his head. "Not on your life. If she happens to show up sometime, I'll be happy to see her, but I'm through meddling in this mess. If I'd followed my first instincts I would have ignored Ed's needs and filled a few of my own. At least I would have had enough common sense not to send her away."

"But you promised," she insisted. "Last April on your boat, remember?"

"I said I'd try," he reminded. "And I have tried. But it's apparently out of my hands."

"No," Kayla persisted. "The Lord answered my prayer that day and I'm not going to start doubting Him now. He said you'd be instrumental in helping Ed, and you will. We just have to figure out how."

Joshua threw back his head and laughed. "Hans!" he exclaimed. "You'll never win in a battle of wits with Kayla! You should know that by now."

Hans could only respond with a long, weary sigh.

&s è&

By the last silent week in August, with no contact from Ed whatsoever, Granddad finally conceded that he would have to fly the Cessna over Bald Mountain in the high Uintas, and watch Alyssa parachute down, knowing that it was rough and dangerous terrain for a man, let alone for a woman. But it would also be the thrill of a parachutist's lifetime, she argued, as well as the ultimate challenge. And besides, he had promised, and to anyone who knew him, a gentleman's word is his bond.

Fortunately, Mike and Shauna agreed to drive up to Bald Mountain in order to bring Alyssa back after she landed, and film the entire experience for her with Mike's high-powered zoom cam. They'd left A & M early in the morning and would be on site within another half hour.

Alyssa checked and rechecked her parachute, making certain that neither release would jam this time. She had replaced the main chute release shortly after Ed brought the parachute back to her last June, and it was working well. The secondary release also worked properly.

Anxious anticipation welled up inside her as she contemplated what she was about to do. Perhaps this new experience would help her recapture some of her love for flying, for nothing had changed with the paraglider, and she still hadn't found any angels among her. The vibrant colors that she used to love had not been evident in any of her flights since she left the Bar M ranch.

When Granddad was satisfied with the running condition of the Cessna, he gave her a wink and a nod. "Are you ready for this?"

She was already sitting in the co-pilot's seat. "I am," she agreed.

Her grandfather climbed aboard and sat in the pilot's position. "You may not find what you're looking for, you know. You may not be able to fix what you think is broken inside you by jumping Bald Mountain, and you'll have to keep your wits about you to make it down in one piece."

"I have to try," she insisted, wondering if he was trying to back out on his promise.

"Do you remember everything that I told you?"

"It's all imbedded in my memory banks," she assured him.

"Then let's go put you on the jump of your life."

Thank you, Lord! she thought to herself, relieved that her grandfather intended to keep his promise. *Finally you're on my side.*

"The Lord's always on your side," Granddad observed quietly as he fastened his seat belt and manned the controls.

For a moment his comment unnerved her. She hadn't spoken aloud, yet somehow he had understood her thoughts. The closeness they'd shared together the last six weeks took her breath away. Her granddad had become even closer to her than Mike or Shauna, and it was a time she would always treasure. The love and compassion her grandfather had for her made her feel special, and he was a great comfort to her during July and August. He'd even opened up about Grandma Mae, for whom Alyssa Mae had been named.

Her grandfather flew a paraglider with Alyssa on Mondays, putting his farm chores aside to spend time with her. How could she ever tell him how much all his concern and caring meant? The bond between them grew stronger with each passing day.

By the time Alyssa had notified Heber Airport of their flight plan, and received their clearance, the Cessna was rolling down the runway and into the air. Her grandfather gave her a brief smile just before she commented, "Pushing the envelope again, Granddad?"

"They were going to clear us anyway," he explained. "But by the time I wait around for it, I could be punching holes in the sky."

As the plane banked and came into a sharp climb, Alyssa felt her excitement mount. Excluding the challenge of Ed Sparkleman, she'd wanted this opportunity more than any other she'd encountered for as long as she could remember. Her grandfather held the community title in his youth for having parachuted over Bald Mountain seven times in one summer. He'd been twenty-two at the time, but the thrill he'd felt could always be seen in the sparkle of his dark brown eyes.

Because Alyssa had inherited those sparkling eyes of his, she often felt it was one of the reasons why they had connected so tenaciously through the years. While little girls idolize their fathers, Alyssa had put her grandfather on a pedestal far above her dad, where he'd stayed with loving adoration, now much more vividly than in years past.

That he was willing to fly over Bald Mountain and watch her parachute from above amazed her. It was something he'd sworn for years that he would never do. It thrilled her to know that he loved her enough to keep such a rash promise.

Now, as she mentally prepared for what lay ahead, she realized how much it cost her grandfather to keep his word. The mountain itself was not the challenge to a parachute jumper. The thrill came in the voracious thermals that resided around it, some swirling gently, others with such fury it was a difficult and dangerous task to land safely. Bald was an understatement when describing the mountain, which only had forest at its base on two sides, and several crystal clear lakes on the north. The face of the mountain, and all around it, was little more than jagged, wind-swept rock. With nothing to impede the wind's progress, the air around Baldy swirled in vortex formations of varying degrees of strength. It was, beyond any doubt, one the greatest challenges to parachute jumpers around the entire state.

However, Granddad taught Alyssa to seek for the thermal that swirled at ninety degrees from the mountaintop, for this was the only area that would allow her to use the parachute as a paraglider, and actually climb with it, rather than descend alone. Not every parachute jumper had this information, and many were tumbled about while trying to safely land at the mountain base in a little clearing by a crystal-blue lake.

Her main purpose in wanting to jump Bald Mountain was not in the exciting thrills of such an adventure. Though no one knew it but Granddad, she wanted to see if she could once again feel the presence of angels much higher up than her paraglider allowed. Perhaps she would recapture what she'd lost when Ed broke her heart. Hopefully, the forest green and the jagged mountains would finally become crisp in her vision, and the true colors would fill her with a sense of awe and wonder as they used to do. Although she was excited, there was still a sense of concern because she hadn't yet repaired what was broken inside her.

Alexander Turner was silent for the first fifteen minutes, and this worried Alyssa. He normally came alive when piloting the Cessna, and she'd expected today would be no different. While he was quiet, she tried to take in the beauty of the High Uintas, but she couldn't see the verdant forest nor the crystal blue lakes that dotted the rugged mountain-scape. Her vision had a gray veil over it, a veil that had fallen upon her the night she left the Bar M.

As they headed toward Bald Mountain, almost seventy miles east of Wanship, they cruised at an altitude of 15,000 feet. They planned to go between Mount Lovinia and Tokewanna Peak in order to pass Baldy and come in from the North, the best advantage point for parachute jumping.

When they were within a few miles of Mount Lovinia, Granddad cleared his throat, as though he had something important to say. Finally he began, "Alyssa, I've had a change of heart about Ed Sparkleman. I believe now that I was wrong."

"About what?"

"About his feelings for you," he confessed. "I was wrong about him, and so are you."

"Really?" she asked. "Is that why you conceded that I won the bet, and we're on our way to jump Bald Mountain?"

"Maybe the reason he quit calling is because you wouldn't return his calls," he suggested, refusing to answer her question.

"No," Alyssa said, irritated that her grandfather would bring Ed up at a time like this, knowing that she was jumping today to help rid herself of the damaging effects Ed had on her tender heart. "You know the real reason why he quit calling me."

"You're wrong," he insisted. "I think he quit because it wasn't doing any good."

"September is only two days away, Granddad. It doesn't matter anymore, does it?" she asked.

Then her grandfather said, "When your grandmother broke our engagement, and wouldn't answer my calls, I finally quit, too. I wrote and told your grandmother that this was my last effort, and if she didn't respond to it, I wasn't going to try anymore."

"He won't write."

"Maybe he will."

"He won't."

"How can you be so stubborn?" he asked.

"I'm related to you."

Granddad nodded and didn't say anymore.

For the next few moments of silence, Alyssa was grateful. She wanted to think of the pending parachute jump and everything Granddad had taught her about it. She tried to ignore his remarks, and to picture Bald Mountain clearly in her mind, recalling her descent strategy instead.

Suddenly, the engine started to make a strange chugging sound, almost like a car engine that wasn't getting enough gas. Granddad pulled out on the choke and pushed it back in for a moment. She let out a sigh of relief when the engine responded quickly by restarting.

"Get your parachute on!" Granddad yelled. "Now!"

Alyssa nodded, though she didn't tell him she would never jump from the plane while he was on board and in trouble. Rather than worry him about that, she strapped herself into the parachute harness, then waited breathlessly, hoping the engine would stay running.

"Maybe we should turn back, Granddad. I can jump another time. I don't know that I can do it now, anyway. I'll worry too much about you getting back safely."

Her grandfather didn't say anything, but he complied with her wishes, banking to the right to come about and head back. This action told her he was worried it could happen again.

Suddenly the engine sputtered a second time. "Open your door!" her grandfather yelled. "And latch it! We may have to jump!"

"But you don't have a parachute!"

"I can piggy-back, if it comes to that, Maisey. Now do as I said."

The engine turned over and chugged a little, but it didn't start again. While he was busy trying to start the engine, Alyssa latched her door open, saying a fervent, silent prayer for the first time since she'd left the Bar M. Now she could hardly hear whether or not the engine was running because the wind screamed through the cockpit like a wild banshee.

Granddad yelled into the radio, "Mayday! Mayday! Mayday! This is Charlie Tango 473, calling Sky Patrol. Over!"

Alyssa couldn't hear whether or not someone had responded because the wind was too boisterous to hear it. Then her grandfather yelled even louder. "Mayday! Mayday! Mayday! This is Charlie Tango 473. We are two miles south of Tokewanna Peak, headed toward Mount Lovinia. Our engine has failed and we are going down. I say again. Charlie Tango 473 is going down!"

By now the plane had dropped in altitude and the engine had completely quit. They were coasting in a Cessna that was incapable of landing like a glider, and even if it were, there was no clearing in which to do so. Thick forest lay between them and Mount Lovinia, and there would be no place to land. Even if there were a clearing, they would run out of runway before the plane hit the mountain.

When Granddad removed his earphones, she followed his example and removed hers. "When I tell you to jump, Maisey, you jump!" barked her grandfather.

"Not without you!"

"Don't worry about me!" he yelled.

"I'm not jumping without you!" she screamed.

"Yes, you are!" As he said those words, he banked the Cessna sharply to the right, rolling Alyssa out of the seat and out the open door, into the blue sky with nothing to impede her descent but her wit and her willingness to pull the chute release.

"No!" she screamed. "Granddad! No!" For several long moments she tumbled, unable to right herself enough to grab the parachute release. Finally, when she was catapulted into a forward thrust by the wind, she quickly yanked on the strap that released the blue parachute high above her, slowing her descent considerably. The wind swept her backwards and toward the east.

This position gave her the opportunity to watch the Cessna, but when she saw it roll and spin, nose-first, toward a mountain of rock and forest, she stared at it in horror. By banking the plane to put her out of danger, her grandfather had caused the Cessna to roll out of control, sealing his own fate. Spinning as it was doing, he would be unable to right it, which might have given him a chance to survive. Now there was no hope at all that he would live through the crash.

"Granddad! Granddad!" she screamed over and over again.

The Cessna nose-dived straight into a massive rock formation on the side of Mount Lovinia, where it exploded in a ball of flames and debris.

For seven long minutes she watched flames bursting southwest of her. Seven long minutes to remind herself how Granddad wanted to die among his rose bushes, where he had promised Grandma he would wait for her to come and get him. Seven agonizing minutes to tell herself that if she hadn't accepted his wager, he would be alive. His death was on her head, and she would never be able to deal with that fact. Never.

In her heart she knew that Alyssa Mae Kendal had succeeded in killing her own grandfather.

In shock, Alyssa was completely unaware how rapidly she was approaching the ground until she saw pine boughs rushing past her face. Then her parachute tangled in some tall pine trees, bringing her to a violent jolt in mid-air. The impact compressed the harness strap against her chest, giving her a moment of concern as to how much damage it had done. Had it cracked her ribs or deflated her lungs?

It really didn't matter, for Alyssa was in no condition to unbuckle herself and land safely on the ground. Even if she'd cleared the trees, her mind was still on the mountainside with her grandfather.

With the wind knocked out of her and a stabbing pain in her chest, Alyssa felt a dark weariness come over her, and she slipped into unconsciousness while she was still dangling from the parachute harness.

ᔑ ᔒ

Ed was just sitting down on a large boulder to eat a plate of burritos that Morning Sun had prepared for the men when he saw Kayla riding swiftly toward them on Daylight. It seemed as though she were racing with the wind. Standing up, Ed walked quickly over to the wagon, put his plate on the tailboard and looked up as Kayla arrived.

"It's sky patrol!" she exclaimed before he could ask her what was wrong. "A plane went down west of Baldy and they need you right away." Kayla slung down from Daylight and gave him the reins.

"I'll bring Breeze back. Go!"

Nodding his appreciation, Ed turned the horse's head, then spurred her on with a quick jab in the flanks. "Git up!" he yelled.

It didn't take Daylight long to reach the lodge. Joshua was waiting by the helicopter.

"We'll see you when we see you," Josh said, taking the reins in exchange for the keys and a sky patrol flight jacket he held in his hands.

"Thanks," said Ed, grabbing the jacket and keys. He opened the helicopter door and climbed in. "Better get Daylight over by the cabin. This thing still spooks her."

While Joshua led Daylight away at a quick pace, Hans stepped down off the porch and hurried over to the helicopter. "What is it?" he asked.

"Don't know yet."

Ed turned on the VHS radio as Hans stood by the helicopter, listening to the conversation.

"Sky patrol, this is Li'l Posse, over."

"This is sky patrol. Glad you could make it, Ed."

"What have we got?"

"A Cessna Skylane went down between Lovinia and Tokewanna. The transponder gave us a good position, and we've got three planes starting a grid from that point."

"Who's going with me?"

"We're trying to round someone up. The problem is, several men are on vacation."

"It's daylight. The wind's favorable. We should see something down with the clarity we have."

"Heber City is trying to round up a couple of their planes, to make it go quicker."

"Was it a local?"

"One of theirs, I guess. Belongs to A & M Aviation."

"Say again?" Ed asked as the name stuck in his heart, causing his chest to constrict tightly.

"A & M Aviation. They cleared their flight plan with Heber City at 1030 this morning, headed for Baldy for a parachute jump."

"Did they say who was flying the plane?" Ed asked, though he was amazed that he sounded so calm. Inside he was shaking violently and he worried if he would even be able to fly the helicopter in his emotionally shattered condition. Alyssa had once told him she wanted to jump Bald Mountain. Now he prayed that she was not on board that plane.

"That's a negative, Ed, but there had to be at least two people on board."

"These are friends of mine," Ed admitted. "Any chance I can go on ahead. I'll take a man from here."

"That's affirmative," came the response.

"I'll let you know when I'm on site. Li'l Posse out."

Ed looked at Hans. "It's Alyssa's plane," he said. "You going?"

Hans didn't answer. He just stepped up into the helicopter, grabbed the binoculars from the back seat, and put on a set of head phones.

Nodding, Ed fired the chopper up. As soon he had liftoff, he headed the nose due west toward Tokewanna Peak.

"Was she in the plane?" Hans finally asked when he'd recovered from the shock of learning it was Alyssa's.

"I don't know," Ed responded. "But grab my satellite phone and call her family. We can try to find out."

"Do you know all their numbers?" Hans asked.

Ed gave him an arched eyebrow in response. "Blindfolded."

Since it was Monday, Ed knew A & M wouldn't be open, but on the chance that she might have left a message, he asked Hans to call there first.

After completing the call, Hans shook his head. "Just a recording. They're closed today."

"Try Mike's number," he said. "435-654-7877."

"I thought it was unlisted," Hans observed.

"This is Vernal," Ed responded. "It depends on who you know."

Nodding, Hans dialed, but soon said, "No answer."

"Try his cell phone," he said, giving him another number.

Hans complied and waited for a few moments. "Is this Mike with A & M Aviation?" he asked. "This is Hans Clark. I'm riding with sky patrol in search of one of your planes. It apparently went down west of Bald Mountain."

There was a pause. Then, "You're breaking up, Mike. Go to a signal area and return my call. I say again, you're breaking up."

Hans looked at Ed, but he didn't say anything.

"Alyssa was flying the plane for a parachute jump," Ed reasoned, feeling a sick numbness growing inside him. "If Mike's on the ground, it had to be Alyssa."

"It could have been someone else," Hans offered, but the look on his face told Ed that even Hans didn't believe that.

After a few minutes, the satellite phone rang. "Yes," said Hans after pushing the button. "Yes, Mike, I hear you fine now." There was a long pause. Then Hans handed the phone to Ed. "I can't do this," was all he said. His eyes filled with fluid and he put his head in his hands.

Ed took the phone from him. "This is Ed Sparkleman," he said. "Mike?"

"What is this?" Mike asked. "Some kind of sick joke, Ed?"

"No," Ed responded. "You were at the ranch. You saw my helicopter. I'm sure Alyssa told you I fly for sky patrol. Heber City called us in on the search."

"I'm calling Heber," said Mike. "If you're lying. . . ."

"If I'm lying, you can have my helicopter," said Ed. "And my share of the ranch." There was a long gasp, a strangled moan, then silence. "Was Alyssa on the plane?" Ed asked, though he knew the answer before it came.

Finally Mike said, "Yes, with her grandfather. We'd been waiting for her for over two hours. She was going to jump Bald Mountain, and we were supposed to pick her up."

"Why?" Ed asked. "That's crazy!"

"That's Alyssa," said Mike. "But then you know that already. I'll drive on over to Heber. Maybe they need a spotter in one of their search planes."

"Then I'll see you in the sky," said Ed. He pressed the off button and handed the satellite phone back to Hans.

After he put it in the back seat, he filled in the details for Hans.

"You don't suppose she got the jump in before the plane went down?" Hans asked.

"She'd have been with Mike by now if that were the case," Ed responded. "Alyssa and her grandfather went down with the plane."

"Maybe they were able to parachute out before the crash," Hans suggested.

Ed shook his head. "I doubt there would have been more than her parachute on board."

As they neared Mount Lovinia, the area where the plane went down, they could see a trail of black smoke that still wafted skyward from the crash. A plane was circling and they listened for a minute to the radio chatter regarding the sighting. Then Ed broke in with, "This is Li'l Posse with sky patrol, over."

"Is that you, Ed?" came a familiar voice.

"Red Bill?" Ed questioned.

"One and the same."

"Any sign of life?"

"We haven't seen any, but you might be able to get a better look."

"I'll go see."

Ed nosed the helicopter down toward the wreckage, but all he could see was a twisted pile of burned out metal, debris scattered in a half mile radius, and one burning tire. Unable to see body parts anywhere, they circled the area for a quarter hour, with Hans searching outward in grid formation until they'd covered a mile radius all around the plane. All the time, Ed kept thinking, *She's alive. She has to be alive.* But the longer they searched, the more futile the feeling. Finally, he had no choice but to face the facts. Alyssa and her grandfather had remained with the plane and were incinerated.

Hans and Ed both looked for footprints leading away from the wreckage, but there were none, and the ground appeared soft enough in places to have shown some evidence of escape.

Ed sucked in a deep breath and blew it out again. A tightness seized his heart and he thought for a minute that he was going to lose control completely. If Hans hadn't been on board with him, he would have lost all sense of propriety. With Alyssa gone, what did Ed have left to live for?

Finally, more out of duty than anything else, he made his report. "Looks like it exploded upon impact. I doubt anyone inside survived. And I see no evidence of escape. However, there's no sign of body parts anywhere and there was at least one parachute on board. Let's broaden the perimeter and see if we can spot anything."

"Will do," said Red Bill.

"I'll work my way north, low, just over the trees. You fellas come in a little higher. The woman on board had a blue parachute. Holler if you see anything."

"Blue?" asked Red Bill. "We saw some blue about five miles northeast of here. We thought it was a new lake formation, because it isn't on the chart."

"Let's check it out," said Ed, a surge of adrenalin rushing through him as he headed forty-five degrees northwest of the crash site. Within a few minutes he had the blue 'lake' in sight. But it wasn't a reflection of the sky off water; it was a silvery blue fabric tangled in some very tall pine trees.

"There she is!!" Hans yelled, looking through the binoculars. Then he handed them to Ed. "She's not moving."

Ed put them up to his eyes for only a moment. Keeping his hand on the stick seemed just as important right now. His will to live increased within him the moment he saw her parachute.

No, Alyssa wasn't moving, but that didn't mean she was dead. He'd seen her landing skills in action, and it was quite likely that she had fainted, or had the wind knocked out of her.

He gave the binoculars back to Hans and looked for a place to land. About a hundred yards farther west he saw a small clearing. It would have to do. On the radio he said, "This is Li'l Posse, over."

"Red Bill here."

"I've got Alyssa in sight. We're going to set down and render assistance. Over."

"You're about fifteen miles from any road in. Looks like you'll have to bring her out by chopper. Will you need more workers? Over."

"I'll let you know when we reach her. Li'l posse out."

As soon as he had the helicopter on the ground, Ed grabbed a couple of duffle bags from the back and handed one to Hans. Then he released the patient basket and slid one end of it to him. "Hurry!" he said. "Every second we save might keep her alive that much longer."

But he didn't have to waste his breath. Hans was in remarkably good condition, regardless of the weeks he spent lying around under doctor's orders. For the last three weeks, Hans had been back to work on the ranch. Grabbing the end of the basket and slinging the bag over a shoulder, Hans was on his way almost before Ed could respond.

When they reached the tree where Alyssa hung, still strapped in her harness and tethered to the parachute, Ed called out to her, but she gave no response. Since she was about thirty feet off the ground, he wasn't exactly sure how he was going to get her down without further injury.

"I think she's breathing," said Hans. "If you watch long enough, you can see her chest move."

Ed paused long enough to ascertain that Hans had spoken correctly. Relief flooded over him when he realized Alyssa was still alive.

Rummaging through one of the bags, Ed tossed a VHS to Hans. "Keep Red Bill up to date on the details," he instructed as he put on a vest filled with assorted climbing gear. Then he stepped into a harness, threw a lasso over the stub of a broken branch, and latched it onto a carabiner. Pulling his way up to the first branch, which was nearly twenty feet above him, he only stopped long enough to decide how next to proceed. He tossed a second rope up a little higher, looped and latched onto it, and pulled himself up onto the first branch. From that point on, climbing was much easier. He simply used the interior branches like a ladder until he was about level with Alyssa. Then he secured both lines on two branches above him and scooted out onto another branch nearby to examine her more closely.

Just seeing her again brought moisture to his eyes and made his breath catch in his throat unevenly. But this was not how he'd wanted to see Alyssa again. Shaking visibly, Ed worried that he would make some critical error trying to save her.

Her hair was a bit disheveled and she had bruises on her cheeks, apparently where her face hit the tethers or branches when she fell into the trees. Alyssa was extremely pale and cold to the touch. After checking her pulse and finding it thready and weak, he made a decision he knew she would be mad about when she finally woke up, but he had no choice. He would have to damage her expensive parachute without her knowledge or permission. But his biggest worry, that she was going into shock, became an afterthought. She was already in shock, and spiraling downward.

Calling down to Hans, Ed yelled, "I'm going to fasten a couple of pulleys with the rope over these two branches, attach the rope to her harness, cut the parachute tethers, and lower her down. It's the fastest way. Do you think you can catch her if my plan falls apart?"

"Aren't you supposed to use some sort of safety protocol?" Hans yelled back. "What if you fall out of the tree before she does?"

Ed moaned. "Now I see the difference between you and your brother. You're frightened by your own shadow, Hans."

"Only in the mountains where the bears are," Hans retorted.

Nodding in understanding, Ed removed the rope from him and fastened it in three places onto Alyssa's harness, then made a tripod with the remaining rope that came together and attached to a loop slung over the first pulley. Then he repeated the process with the second rope and pulley.

Just before slashing the tethers loose, he pulled on one of the ropes and made certain that he could support her weight and lower her down at the same time. Satisfied that he could manage that much, he tossed the rope with the longest end down to Hans and cut the parachute tethers.

"Get the basket ready below her. The less we have to traumatize her, the better. And use this line as the secondary. If mine fails, she'll have a backup."

Hans nodded, slid the basket into position, and braced the rope around his waist for leverage. "I'm ready," he called up.

The second he was ready, Ed began lowering Alyssa down. Her breathing seemed labored and he was concerned that they would not be able to reverse the direction her body was spiraling if they did not hurry.

"Quickly," he said. "I think we're losing her."

Chapter Eighteen

$\mathscr{A}$lyssa didn't want to open her eyes. The voices she kept hearing worried her. For some strange reason, she thought she heard Hans and Ed whispering nearby. And she didn't understand why. The last thing she remembered was calling out her grandfather's name as she fell from the plane.

The plane. The Cessna crashed and her grandfather . . . *no, it can't be! He can't be gone. He can't be!*

A beeping sound went off near her head and she heard a woman say, "Doctor, she's racing again. We still haven't got it under control."

A man's voice said, "Increase the digoxin to five milligrams and let me know if she wakes up."

"What is it?" she heard Ed ask.

"Will she be all right?" questioned Hans.

Alyssa moaned and moved her head from side to side. "No!" she cried, surprised to hear her voice sound so far away. "Granddad! Granddad!" Then she felt something pounding in her chest, like a squirrel trying to claw its way out. It frightened her, which only seemed to make her chest pound more fiercely.

As quickly as the pounding started, a calm, peaceful quiet came over her, and she felt herself drifting away.

"Doctor!" said the woman. "She's crashing."

❧ ❧

Watching Alyssa sleep peacefully for the first time since she arrived at the hospital five hours ago, Ed was thrilled to notice some color returning to her cheeks. Her heart rate was steady, between seventy and eighty beats per minute, and her blood pressure had not elevated in almost an hour. Yet still she slept. A few times he'd seen her eyes flutter, but she couldn't seem to focus on him, and she always slipped back into her dream world before he could say anything to her.

He looked over at Hans, who was also asleep in a recliner set up in the same hospital room. It was nearly nine at night, and he had finally telephoned Mike, telling him he thought she was going to make it. Mike, in turn, had then contacted Alyssa's parents, who were still in shock regarding her grandfather's death. Mike told Ed that Alyssa's mother was taking the news of her father's passing gravely.

There was still no word on Alyssa's grandfather, except that they hadn't found any evidence of a body at the crash sight. He could have incinerated, but now he doubted that was likely. He'd learned that the Cessna didn't carry enough fuel to completely incinerate a body. Sky patrol had asked for some clothing from her grandfather's home, so they could send in the dogs. Perhaps Alexander Turner had gotten out of the plane before it crashed, or he may have been thrown out on impact, which would have explained the lack of footprints outside the wreckage.

"Where is he?" came an anxious voice from the hall.

Ed recognized Kayla's tone immediately and he looked up just in time to see her walking past the nurse's station. He stood to greet her as she came in the door.

Unexpectedly, Kayla threw herself into his arms. "Thank heavens!" she exclaimed. "You're all right!"

"Of course I am," he comforted, hugging her in response. Then, fearing she would awaken Alyssa, he led her out into the hall. "What made you think I wasn't?"

"On the news," she whimpered. "They said a helicopter may have gone down in the search." Sighing, she leaned against him for support.

"Of course we went down," he explained. "We flew down, landed, rescued Alyssa, then brought her here. I don't know why the media can't seem to get it straight."

Kayla shook her head, "And Hans?" she asked.

"He's fine, too. He's just resting." Hoping to change the subject, he asked, "Where's Josh?"

"Parking the car. I made him drop me off at the front door. I've been in tears all the way down the mountain."

"Over an ornery polecat like me?" he asked, giving her a crooked grin.

Kayla burst out laughing, then hugged him fiercely. "You're my family!" she exclaimed. "You and the boys are the only family I have now."

"Next to me, of course," said Josh as he joined them. "I suppose if you're unharmed, it's safe to assume Hans is all right, as well?"

"See for yourself," Ed responded, nodding toward Alyssa's room.

"I trust you," Josh admitted. "Although I certainly think the news channel owes us a big apology."

❧ ❧

"Is it still August?" Alyssa asked the nurse who came in to take her vital signs. She opened her eyes and looked up at her.

The older woman smiled and said, "For two more days. Are you going to stay awake for me now?"

"That depends," said Alyssa, "on who's in my room at the time."

"There's someone you don't want to visit you?" she asked.

Alyssa nodded to Ed, Kayla, Josh and Hans as they visited outside the hospital room. "Them," she said.

"Are you sure?" the nurse asked. "They've all been very worried about you."

"I don't want anyone here but Mike or Shauna Roberts. That's all."

"Did you know that two of those men rescued you? They told us they were close friends of yours."

"Did they?" Alyssa asked. "But isn't that Ed's job? Doesn't he work for sky patrol?"

"Well, yes, but a little gratitude could go a long way. If it weren't for them, you would have died in those mountains. You were in shock when they found you."

"They should have let me die," said Alyssa, turning her head to the wall when she noticed Ed looking her way. "Don't let them come in," Alyssa whispered. "Please."

"No, of course not," said the nurse.

Alyssa closed her eyes, exhausted, wishing she had died rather than face life knowing she was responsible for her grandfather's death. She heard footsteps come into her room and Ed's voice ask, "Is she waking up?"

"She's still very tired," said the nurse. "And she doesn't want any visitors right now."

"She spoke to you?" Ed asked.

"She said she didn't want any of the four of you to visit her. I have to respect her wishes."

"Why?" asked Ed.

"She's distraught over her grandfather," said the nurse. "And she'd rather not be disturbed right now."

"Alyssa, don't do this," Ed pleaded. "Alyssa, please, I need to talk to you."

"Mr. Sparkleman, that will be quite enough. She doesn't want to see you right now. Perhaps she'll change her mind later, when she's feeling better."

"Alyssa," he began once again.

But Alyssa was beyond reason. She rolled onto her side and wept softly, praying Ed would give up and leave her alone.

When next she awakened, Mike and Shauna had replaced Ed and Hans and it was still dark outside.

"Hi," whispered Mike. "I hope we didn't wake you."

"No, I didn't know anyone was here, it's been so quiet." She pressed a button on the side bar of the bed and raised the head a little so she could see them better. "Have you been crying, Shauna?" she asked, noticing her friend's puffy eyes.

Shauna nodded. "What else did you expect?"

"Did they find Granddad?" she asked as tears filled her own eyes.

"They told you about him, then?" Mike gave her a perplexed expression.

"I watched the plane go down," Alyssa said. "He was still in it when it crashed."

"But—" he began.

Shauna interrupted him. "But you're going to be okay," she said. "And all we want you to do right now is get better."

"That's right," said Mike, taking her hand. "That's all you need to worry about."

"Do my parents know?"

"They were here earlier. They said they'd be back tomorrow."

"I don't want to see them," insisted Alyssa.

"But why?" Shauna asked. "They're your parents."

"And I am responsible for Mom's father dying. How can I ever face them again?"

"But—" Mike began to protest.

This time Alyssa interrupted. "I just want to go home."

"In a few days, when the doctor says you're strong enough," said Shauna.

"What's wrong with me?"

"No one's told you yet?" asked Mike.

"No one's told me anything," she complained.

"Your parachute harness compressed your chest somehow when you landed in the trees, causing some cardiac arrhythmia. It's probably nothing. They think it'll mellow out with time and bed rest."

"That's it?"

Shauna nodded. "When you were first brought in, you were in shock. Ed told us you nearly died in the emergency room, but they were able to jump start you."

"You spoke to Ed?"

"He's down in the foyer. The nurses won't let him come in here."

"He's worried sick about you, Alyssa," said Mike. "Don't you think it's time you talk with him?"

"Why?" she asked.

"Because he saved your life!" Mike exclaimed, clearly exasperated with her. "And because he loves you."

"He loves Kayla," she whispered.

"How do you know that?" Shauna asked. "He seems so distraught about you, so . . . haggard."

"Don't let that fool you," warned Alyssa. "He's always a little rough around the edges." *But he cleans up nicely.* The thought came into her mind unbidden, and she pushed it aside, chiding herself for thinking it.

She couldn't win where Ed was concerned. Now, he'd evidently convinced Mike and Shauna that he was not a threat to Alyssa.

Wearily, she closed her eyes, wondering when the nightmare would be over. *But when you're still in the middle of the tunnel, and there is no light at either end, it's a little difficult to tell if you're making progress!*

⁂

The dreams had returned and Alyssa could see Ed Sparkleman, his emerald green eyes laughing at her. Though she tried to tell him, "I love you with all my heart," she could not do so. Her voice didn't work, and all she could do was move her lips in a vain attempt to tell him how she felt. She tossed and turned and awakened with a start several times. But every time she drifted back to sleep, she could see Ed's eyes, and hear his laughter, as though he thought it was amusing that she had fallen in love with him.

"Maisey," came a gruff voice, awakening Alyssa from another nightmare. It was the wee hours of morning on her fourth day at the hospital, and it was September. She listened for a minute, thinking that her grandfather's voice was only in her dreams.

Then he spoke again. "Maisey, wake up. It's me, Granddad."

Opening her eyes immediately, Alyssa saw her grandfather standing near the bed beside her. "Granddad?" she asked, uncertainty threatening to claim her consciousness.

"Lie still, Maisey. Don't exert yourself," he said, and his voice was the most beloved sound she'd heard in a long time.

"You're alive?" she asked. "But how did you make it out of the plane?" Although she was thrilled to see him, she was still confused, and in her weakened state, she didn't know what to think.

"You know your grandmother . . . always has to have the last word. She wanted me to keep my promise, so she just grabbed my hand and pulled me out before the plane ever hit the ground."

"But how?" asked Alyssa, totally confused now. "I didn't see you get out of the plane, Granddad. I didn't see you."

"Well, here I am. You see me now, don't you?" he asked tenderly.

Filled with joy, she looked into his deep brown eyes, thrilled to know that she had inherited those dark sparklers from him. "I thought you died in the crash," she said, "and it was all my fault. If only I hadn't made that stupid bet!"

"I didn't die in the plane, Alyssa," he reaffirmed. Then, changing the subject, he said, "I can't stay long, but I had to see you. I wanted to tell you about Ed. He really does love you, Maisey. He does!"

"Not like he loves Kayla," she argued. "They were both here, Granddad, and they were hugging and very familiar with each other. It's not an image that's easy to erase from my mind."

"If he contacts you again, you have to listen to him. Will you do it?"

"Only if I don't have to face him."

"First you won't speak to him by phone. Now you refuse to see him face to face. How can he prove himself to you when you leave him no options?"

"Granddad!" Alyssa exclaimed in bewilderment. "Ed's behavior here at the hospital was a painful reminder to me: Ed doesn't love me like he loves Kayla."

"Have you never hugged Mike?" he asked. "In front of Shauna?"

"Of course. I hug them both all the time."

"Kayla is just a treasured friend, a sister to Ed."

"How would you know that?" she asked. "When did you meet them?"

Her grandfather only shook his head. "When are you going to start listening to me?"

"When I agree with you."

"All right," he conceded. "You win. But at least trust me on this other issue."

"What is it?" she asked, growing weary of his persistence.

He paused for only a moment, and his voice changed from somber to mysterious. "Today your world and how you perceive it is going to change drastically. Please don't be frightened or troubled by what transpires. God had His hand in preserving your life for His eternal reasons."

Alyssa was confused by his request, but she didn't voice it.

"And remember, Maisey, with God, nothing is impossible."

"I know that now," she said. "God brought you out of that plane and back to me."

Her grandfather leaned over and kissed her on the forehead, though she did not realize it. Her eyes closed sleepily and she whispered, "Goodnight, Granddad."

"Goodbye, my little Maisey."

❧ ❧

After breakfast, Alyssa was feeling much better. She took a shower, shampooed her hair, and brushed it out until it glistened.

The doctor arrived shortly afterward and he seemed very serious as he sat down in a chair next to the bed with her chart in his hands. "Tell me about your grandfather, Ms. Kendal."

She almost laughed, but decided against it. "He's a wonderful man," she responded. "He loves to fly, though he doesn't do it as much now that Grandma is gone."

"Have you always been close to him?"

"Of course." Without thinking her answer through, she added, "He's my grandfather."

"When did you last speak with him?"

"A few hours ago."

"He was here?" came the doctor's startled response.

"Sure. He came to see me early this morning. Didn't you know that he made it out of the plane before it crashed?"

The doctor gave her an impassive look, wrote a few things down in her chart, then turned his attention back to her. "The first night you were here you told the nurse that you wished the rescuers had let you die. Why was that?"

She wanted to give him something lame and childish in response, but she held the retort in check. "Because I thought I was responsible for his death," she answered evenly.

"Why did you think that?"

"Because I won the bet. He wouldn't have gone if I hadn't won."

"You thought since you'd wagered and won, that you were responsible for his death."

"That's what I just said."

"Because he died when the plane crashed?"

"No, because at the time I *thought* he had died in the plane crash."

"But now it's immaterial, because he's still alive, and he visited you here early this morning?"

"Now you've got it," she answered smartly.

"Do you still wish your rescuers had let you die?"

"Obviously not," she retorted. "My grandfather is still alive."

The doctor wrote a few more notes. When he was finished, he looked at her and smiled oddly.

"When may I go home?" she asked.

"I'd intended to release you this morning," he said. "Your heart has stabilized and your vital signs are excellent."

"But?" she questioned.

"Frankly, I'm a little concerned about your state of mind. Would you tell me what happened in the plane, when the engine failed?"

"I don't know," she confessed. "It started chugging funny. Granddad restarted it, and we thought that it would run all right. Then it sputtered a second time and he never could get it running again. After that, everything happened so fast it's not completely clear. I remember the plane rolling and I fell out. Somehow I managed to pull my parachute release. I watched the plane fall out of the sky and crash, but after that, I don't remember anything until I woke up here."

"Have you ever had suicidal tendencies before the accident?"

"I don't have them now," she complained. "I said that the other night because I was horrified by the thought that I'd been responsible for my granddad's death."

He nodded, then stood up. "I see. Well, I suppose I could let you go today. But I'd like you to see a crisis management worker a few times after you're home. Anytime someone is subjected to trauma of this magnitude, it tends to make one's thought processes a little erratic."

"All right," she agreed. "I'm sure I can manage that."

"There's just one more thing," the doctor said.

"What is it?"

"Your grandfather couldn't possibly have been here this morning."

She almost smiled, but decided against it. Perhaps she should humor him. "Why not?" she asked.

"It's my understanding that Alexander Turner's body was found the day of the accident."

That's impossible! she wanted to scream, but she kept herself deliberately in check. If she fainted or showed the least bit of anxiety, they might keep her, or lock her up for good.

"May I go?" she asked quietly.

"It's called denial, Ms. Kendal. It sometimes happens after such a terrible trauma."

Alyssa grit her teeth together to prevent herself from crying out in pain. "May I go?" she repeated the question tersely.

"Certainly," he said. "I'll prepare your release forms."

When the doctor left, she picked up the telephone and dialed Mike's number. It went directly into his voice mail, so she left a short message and tried A & M's number. To her dismay, she heard Mike's voice answer, "I'm sorry, but A & M is closed due to a family emergency. We will reopen on Tuesday, September 5th. Please leave a message at the tone and we will call you then."

Unfortunately, she had no money with her to take a cab or a bus, and she didn't want to call her mother. How could she speak to Mrs. Kendal, even by telephone, knowing she was responsible for her grandfather's death? How could she ever face her parents again?

If her grandfather hadn't been in to see her this morning, if he was dead, then it had to have been his spirit that visited her. He'd told her not to worry about what transpired today, that with God, nothing was impossible. Now she had no choice but to believe him, for she could not deny that he'd been there just a few hours ago. Of that fact she was certain.

Finally Alyssa dialed Mike's cellular phone. Shauna answered on the second ring.

"Where are you?" Alyssa asked.

"About ten miles from the hospital," said Shauna.

"The doctor released me. I'll wait out front for you."

"All right. Are you feeling better?"

"Just tell me the truth," Alyssa insisted. "Did Granddad die?"

There was only a moment's hesitation before Shauna said, "Yes. He did."

"Did they find his body?"

Another pause, then, "Yes."

"I'll see you in a few."

Hanging up, Alyssa quickly dressed in the same clothing, jeans and tee shirt, that she'd worn the day of the accident. Her parachute jumpsuit was also hanging in the closet but she left it there, determined she would never fly again.

Feeling much stronger, Alyssa didn't wait for anyone to push her out of the hospital in a wheel chair. Instead, she walked right past the nurse's station without even glancing at it.

When she reached the foyer, she stepped swiftly past the automatic doors and out into the sunshine. To her dismay, she also found she was back in Vernal. How that had happened, she didn't know. She could only assume that it was the closest medical facility in proximity to where they'd found her after the Cessna went down. But why hadn't she known where she was for the past four days? Her hospital room had a window, but she didn't recall looking out through it.

Alyssa walked over to the curb, determined to put as much distance between herself and the hospital as she could. Unfortunately, a diligent nurse had a different agenda. Hearing someone calling her name, Alyssa turned around to meet her.

"Miss Kendal, I'm glad I caught you," said the nurse, a little winded from having to chase Alyssa down. "Doctor signed you out, but he wanted you to get this prescription filled. When you've taken all of it, he would like you to be evaluated by a cardiologist as a follow up. I need your signature, stating that you understand these instructions."

Alyssa sighed. "Anything for the good doctor," she said, signing a paper on a clip board and receiving the prescription order.

"I hope you have a pleasant journey home, Miss Kendal, and that your flying days will be much safer in the future."

"I have no intention of ever flying again . . . in the future or anytime."

The nurse smiled wanly. "Take care of yourself," she said. Then she turned around and went back into the hospital.

"That would be a real shame," came a familiar voice behind her.

Alyssa cringed, refusing to turn around and look at Ed, or even respond to his comment. For one brief moment, she blamed Ed for all that had happened the past week. But knowing he would never have agreed to her jumping Bald Mountain, she knew it wasn't fair to him, and she could only blame herself. If she hadn't accepted her grandfather's wager that Ed's phone calls would keep coming through August, Granddad would still be alive.

Ed stepped around in front of her giving her no choice but to look at him. Just seeing him again, with her eyes open this time, made her heart act strangely inside her. How she wished she already had the prescription filled, for she surely needed something to slow down her racing heart.

"Are you never gonna' speak to me again?" Ed asked quietly.

At first Alyssa refused to respond, but the longer she waited, the worse she felt, and she wasn't sure it was physical suffering at all. Finally she stiffened her back and glared at him. "I have nothing to say."

"That's a start," he admitted. "How do you feel?"

A car honked behind her and she turned quickly, grateful to see Mike and Shauna pulling up to the curb in the Trail Blazer.

Reaching out, she put her hand on the door handle, but Ed put his on her elbow. "Alyssa Mae," he whispered, his voice ragged and filled with pain.

"I feel like going home," she said. "Please let me go."

He released her, stepped back while she opened the door, then looked searchingly into her eyes as she sat down on the back seat. Lowering his body until he was eye level with her, he said, "You're gonna' have to talk to me sometime."

"As long as it's not in August, right?" she asked, and was surprised that her voice sounded so flat and uncaring when her heart was screaming how much she loved this man.

"What's wrong with August?" he asked, an eyebrow arched in puzzlement.

"Look," she said candidly, "I've had a really bad summer, my granddad is dead, my flying days are over, and you just managed to wreck my homecoming. I'm sorry if you don't understand why I have nothing to say to you right now, but I don't know what you're expecting from me."

"I've been worried about you," he whispered.

"You don't need to worry anymore. You saved my life and the doctor says I'll be fine now." As an afterthought, she added, "I'm not sure I was worth your effort, but maybe someday I'll understand why you did that. Now, may I please go home?"

"May I call you? Will you allow me to do that much?"

"Why?" she asked, trying to keep all emotion out of her voice. "What purpose will it serve when I can only say that I have nothing to say to you?"

She saw his mouth tighten and a muscle twinge along his jaw. Then he nodded with obvious resignation, stood up and closed her door.

As Mike drove away, she watched Ed staring after her, and the expression of lost love was written plainly in the contours of his face and in the sadness in his gray-green eyes, though she refused to acknowledge it.

·ఄ   ఄ·

If Alyssa thought seeing Ed again was such a terrible strain on her, she had no idea what she was in for when she picked up her prescription and finally arrived back at her apartment. Her grandfather had forewarned her that life as she knew it would change drastically, but she had no idea how much.

Mike and Shauna came upstairs to her apartment with her and stayed for a while, helping her sort through legal documents until they'd located the title and insurance papers on the Cessna. For some reason they seemed to find an excuse for not leaving her alone, and Alyssa was beginning to wonder why.

Finally, she could live on the edge no longer. She sat down at the kitchen table and asked pointedly, "Will you both stop dancing around the issues and tell me what's bothering you?"

Mike sat across from her and took both her hands in his. "How's your ticker?" he asked, and his expression became grave and unbending.

"I took my medicine when we got home, just like the doctor told me," she reminded. "I'm a little tired, but I'm all right. Now what is it?"

Shauna shook her head and gave Mike a soulful look that plainly said, *Not yet,* but Mike ignored his wife and looked straight into Alyssa's dark eyes. "She's stronger than you give her credit for, hon. Trust me on this."

Biting her lip, Shauna relented and sat beside Mike at the table. When she nodded her consent, Mike said, "What happened after we left here last Monday?"

"What do you mean?" she asked.

"What happened?" he repeated. "Did you quarrel with your grandfather? Did you take the plane out while you were angry with him? Or do you even remember? Think about it, Alyssa. What happened?"

She shrugged, wondering why Mike would question her like this. "We didn't quarrel at all. Granddad tinkered with the engine for a bit. You know, checking the oil, the brakes, the battery cables. All that stuff. Then we left around 10:30 that morning. After that, it's a matter of record."

Staring into her very soul, Mike said, "It's not a matter of any record, Alyssa. Your granddad wasn't on the plane. His body was found in his yard, after the plane crashed."

"That's impossible!" she cried, a sick feeling welling up from deep within her at this revelation. Denying what she'd been told, she demanded hotly, "Why are you saying that, Mike? Why?"

"Think it through, Alyssa. You may be suffering from post traumatic stress syndrome. Do you honestly remember your grandfather in the plane with you?"

"Of course he was in the plane!" she snapped. Intense anger replaced the shock of Mike's revelation. "I wouldn't be here otherwise.

He yelled at me to jump and I refused to leave without him, so he rolled the Cessna in order to get me out. He put the plane into a sharp right bank unexpectedly and I was grasping blue air in less than a second. He saved my life by doing that."

"Are you sure?" Mike questioned.

"Mike!" she cried. "You don't believe me?"

Shauna reached out and touched her arm. "We don't know what to believe anymore."

Remembering that very morning, Alyssa confided, "Granddad was in my room this morning. He came to see me at the hospital."

"Not unless it was from beyond the grave," Mike responded.

"Then it was," she insisted. "He said that God had his hand in preserving my life for an eternal purpose."

"First he flies the plane with you and now he visits your bedside, after he's been dead for four days?" Mike released her hands and shook his head. "Think about what you're saying, Alyssa. You're not making any sense."

"My grandfather was in the plane with me!" she yelled.

"Then how did his body manage to end up in his yard, right next to the rose garden? He was at his place when the plane hit the ground!" Mike demanded.

"You think I hallucinated his going with me?" Alyssa asked, feeling nauseous from the shock and accusation in Mike's eyes.

"It's the only explanation," he gasped.

The telephone rang, interrupting them for a moment. Shauna answered it while Alyssa made a run to the bathroom. Everything she'd eaten for breakfast she expelled. When she returned, pale and shaking, she sank down upon the chair.

"That was your father," Shauna said. "He wanted to remind you that the funeral is tomorrow at one o'clock."

An Angel's Gift 299

Alyssa nodded. "Will you both go with me?" she asked.

Mike shook his head, then put his face in his hands and started weeping like a little child. "I can't," he said. "Not until I know what happened."

"I'm not lying, Mike!" Alyssa insisted. "Granddad was with me in that airplane. Why would I lie?"

"Why would you take the plane out alone?" Mike asked. "Did Alex refuse to go with you? Was it like that first Saturday night when you came home from the ranch? An impetuous, reckless act that you didn't bother to think about? When will you learn that every action has a consequence attached to it?"

"I didn't take the plane out alone!" Alyssa cried. "And I have learned all I care to about consequences! Your inability to believe me indicates how you really feel about me, Mike. I thought we were best friends. And I have done nothing to make you distrust me. But since you do anyway, I think it's best if you leave."

"Alyssa, he's just distraught," Shauna apologized for her husband. "Ever since they found your grandfather, he's been wracking his brain trying to figure out how this all happened."

"When Granddad was at the hospital this morning, he told me that things would get a little strange today. I didn't know what he was talking about, but I'm willing to bet this was it. He also reminded me that with God nothing is impossible. Now, I'm weary. I'd like you both to go away and leave me alone."

Chapter Nineteen

t the time of Alexander Turner's funeral, Alyssa stood beside the rose garden in his yard. She'd gone to the funeral home earlier to pay her respects and sign the guest book so that her family would know she had been there. She didn't want them to think she didn't care, but she couldn't face anyone just yet, and so she'd refused to stay for the services. Instead, she drove straight to Granddad's farm and sat down on a porch step next to her grandparents' love roses.

"Granddad," she whispered, hoping somehow he could hear her. "You were right about things being strange around here. Everyone thinks I lied about your being on the plane. I don't pretend to understand how all this happened, but I expect you're just as stubborn at keeping your promises as I am about Ed. This wasn't the way I wanted it to happen. You were supposed to live another twenty years, at least. You weren't supposed to die now. Not in a plane crash and not surrounded by some great mystery. I don't understand it all, but I'm glad the Lord saw fit to let you die here instead of on the face of Mount Lovinia. I'm especially glad you were able to keep your word to Grandma. God must have known you didn't want to die without fulfilling that special promise you made to her."

Tears slipped down her cheeks. "I've thought about what you said in the plane," she continued, "about Ed. If he contacts me again, I'll listen to what he has to say, but only because I feel like it was your dying wish. It's already September, and except for our visit at the hospital, I haven't heard from Ed since July thirtieth. And after what's happened, with everyone thinking I'm totally nuts now, I suppose he'll be glad to be rid of me.

"And one other thing," she sighed and forced the tears away. "I've decided to start going back to Church. If God can do what He did for you, letting you keep your promise to Grandma, then maybe I should trust Him more. Thank you for reminding me, I needed it."

❧ ❧

The following week was a blur. Mike and Alyssa resumed working at A & M, but their communications were strained and clipped. Alyssa didn't broach the subject of her grandfather and neither did Mike.

Whenever the aviation authority or the sheriff questioned her about the crash, and whether or not her grandfather had been with her, Alyssa would only say, "I thought so at the time."

Alyssa learned that the tape recording that had automatically recorded the Mayday call from her grandfather was garbled, and the wind screeching in the background made it almost impossible to hear whether it was really his voice or not. To make matters worse, the cockpit voice recorder from the plane could not be found, so there was nothing tangible to make anyone believe Alyssa's version of what happened.

Mike seemed to soften a little, no doubt in part because his wife wouldn't put up with his stubborn rejection of Alyssa. Although he kept a safe distance, he didn't seem to mind that Shauna tried to maintain a close relationship with her.

Alyssa's plan to give up flying was thwarted by Shauna, who had retrieved Alyssa's jumpsuit, helmet and boots, and finally persuaded her that piloting the paraglider was nothing like flying the Cessna. With her encouragement, she ventured out the first Monday in September, and though she found she still enjoyed flying, it was never with the same sense of enthusiasm as it had been before Ed came into her life.

Having reconciled herself to her grandfather's death, she was relieved that he had apparently not suffered. The autopsy stated that Alexander Turner's death was attributed to "causes unknown." But Alyssa knew. Somehow God took her grandfather out of the plane and brought him back to the roses, allowing him to keep his promise. Granddad would never have broken his word to his beloved Mae, not if he could help it. God had His hand in Alexander's death, Alyssa was certain of that much, and this knowledge softened the edges around the unusual circumstances regarding it. And it encouraged her in spiritual matters. She started to believe that God was still concerned about her, and that He would, ultimately, help her along her journey in life.

Since Ed made no effort to contact her after the day she left the hospital, she concluded that he had given up trying to reach her. Though this saddened her, it also gave her a sense of freedom that she'd not had before the accident.

Alyssa finally felt that she could venture outside the cocoon she had built for herself, though she had yet to contact her parents. She still wasn't certain what they thought of their daughter who had inadvertently caused the death of their father, and who seemed to be a little crazy right now.

Grateful that her hair grew quickly, almost two inches since she left the Bar M the last week of June, she decided she would first visit a beautician. Her hair was layered and loosely permed so that, as it grew longer, she could style it more easily. The new look gave Alyssa a little confidence, and this pleased her.

❧ ❧

By mid-September, business started to slow down, giving Alyssa time to work on the catalog that would be mailed for holiday sales. Fridays and Saturdays were still very busy, and would be until the weather got nasty, but they were no longer up in the air five or six days a week with novice pilots flying their paragliders.

Mike had mellowed considerably. He and Alyssa were almost back to the friendship they'd shared before the Cessna crashed. But there were still doubts floating in Mike's mind, Alyssa knew, for she could still feel a trickle of anxiety between them that had not yet been settled.

Alyssa had several interviews with her bishop, repented of her Sabbath day irreverence, and started to feast upon the spirit once again. He was the only other male, besides Mike and the doctor at the hospital, with whom she shared those last few moments during the plane crash. Her experiences with her grandfather had turned her heart back to God, and she prayed that her faith would never be shaken again. Just knowing that Mae had led Granddad home to die in a more peaceful way, had touched Alyssa's heart, and she had finally forgiven herself for being the impetus that led Alexander Turner into the Cessna in the first place.

In the most perilous of times in her life, the Lord had been mindful of her, and had preserved her for an eternal purpose. Although these thoughts comforted her, she still could not put aside her doubts and concerns for Ed. If the man she loved had a role to play in her future, as the Lord told her, she could not envision it.

Then, on Wednesday morning she received a package in the mail. As Mike handed it to her he said, "It's time, Alyssa."

"What time is that?" she asked.

"Time to give a sinking ship one last chance."

Alyssa looked at the package and noticed the return address. It was from Ed Sparkleman at the Bar M Ranch. She sighed wearily and opened it with resignation. August was long over and Kayla had probably gone back to San Diego. Apparently Ed was feeling lonely once again, though she couldn't imagine what he had sent her. Inside the package she found a cassette tape and a short note that read:

> Dear Alyssa;
>
> My faith in miracles began almost two years ago, when I was a witness to one. I've heard that you are a witness, also (rumors travel fast in rural areas). When sky patrol failed to retrieve the black box at the Cessna crash sight, I spent a few days going over the area myself. After I finally located it, I asked for permission to send you a copy.
>
> Your grandfather was a wise man. I'm sorry for your loss, but encouraged to know that he will always watch over you.
>
> Hope you're feeling better.
>
> Love, Ed.

Completely surprised, Alyssa found a smile forming slowly on her lips that she could suppress no longer. Tears filled her eyes and she looked up at Mike, who was still watching her closely. "It's the cockpit flight recording," she whispered. "It's proof that Granddad was with me on the plane."

Mike reached up on a shelf behind them and grabbed the cassette player. He took the tape from her and inserted it. Then he pressed the play button.

For the first ten minutes of the tape, there was nothing but silence. But when her grandfather's voice came over the recorder loud and clear, as did her responses to him, she almost wanted to stand up and cheer.

With wonder in her heart and the spirit filling her soul with warmth, she heard her grandfather say, "I was wrong, you know."

"About what?" Alyssa had asked him.

"About Ed. I was wrong about him, and so are you."

"Really? Is that why you conceded that I won the bet, and we're on our way to jump Bald Mountain?"

"Maybe the reason he quit calling is because you wouldn't return his calls."

"No. You know the real reason why he quit calling me."

"You're wrong. I think he quit because it wasn't doing any good."

"September is only two days away, Granddad. It doesn't matter anymore, does it?"

"When your grandmother broke our engagement and wouldn't answer my calls, I finally quit, too. I wrote and told your grandmother that this was my last effort, and if she didn't respond to it, I wasn't going to try anymore."

"He won't write."

"Maybe he will."

"He won't."

"How can you be so stubborn?" he asked.

"I'm related to you."

After another short silence, Alyssa heard the sound of the engine sputtering. "Turn it off!" she said. "Mike, turn it off. I can't bear to go through that again."

He pressed the stop button and looked up at her. "You may not need to hear it, Alyssa, but I do. May I continue? Please?"

Alyssa nodded. "But wait until I'm upstairs."

He nodded and Alyssa escaped to her apartment where she turned on a tape by Jeff Goodrich and sang the words with the vocalist with all her heart and soul. "I heard him come, I saw his very face. . . ." And though she knew the song referred to the Savior, Jesus Christ, for Alyssa, it reminded her of her granddad while the leper in the song became herself. And her grandfather led her back to the Savior, safely, where she belonged. Now the song increased in its urgency and message, "Come, and never leave Him. Just let your heart believe Him. . . ." she sang, filled with the spirit of faith, and the temperance of Job.

When the music concluded, Alyssa realized that Ed had listened to the cockpit recording before he'd sent it to her. After all, Ed was privy to Sky Patrol matters. Ed had listened to her grandfather trying to convince her that Ed had given up trying to call her. And Ed had written to her *after* hearing Alyssa insist he would never write to her. Perhaps more importantly, he had signed his name, "Love, Ed." What had he meant by it?

For a moment she felt a splinter of light pierce a hole in the hardness of her cold heart, and she wondered in amazement that such a thing could actually happen. As that light tried to wedge ajar the armament with which she'd shackled her heart the past three months, she realized she must respond to Ed's letter at once. Fear welled up within her, trying to drown the opening with darkness once again.

Suddenly a thought came into her heart, and Alyssa knew what she must do to thank Ed for the gift he'd sent her. She must do it now or forever lose her courage. Would Ed ever fully comprehend what his kindness meant to her?

Searching through a stack of papers on the kitchen counter, she found the envelope that still held the photos of the Bar M Ranch that she had taken from the Cessna in June. Then she grabbed a piece of stationary and wrote:

> Ed;
>
> *Thank you for the tape. It means more to me than I can say. Yes, it was a miracle, one that I shall treasure all my life.*
>
> *I promised these photos to you quite some time ago, but had forgotten to send them until your priceless gift arrived.*
>
> *I am feeling better. Thank you.*
>
> *~ Alyssa*

It was a giant leap of faith for Alyssa to send the photos and letter to Ed Sparkleman. But he had given her a rare treasure, and this gesture was the least she could do to thank him. With a prayer in her heart, she drove over to the post office in Heber City that same afternoon and sent the package off before she could change her mind.

When she arrived back at A & M, Mike greeted her as she stepped out of the Toyota. "What is it?" she asked, when she noticed the tears in his eyes.

"I'm sorry," he apologized. "All this time and I didn't believe that your grandfather was on the plane. Can you ever forgive me?"

Alyssa threw herself into his arms and laughed through her tears. "That's what friends are for."

"You should listen to what happened after your grandfather dumped you out of the plane," Mike said tenderly, taking her by the hand and leading her to the stairs. "I put it on your kitchen counter. It's set at the right spot if you'd like to hear. . . ."

He left the sentence open, no doubt hoping she would listen to the rest of the tape. Reluctantly, Alyssa went upstairs and into the apartment. Mike did not follow her, and for his consideration, she was grateful. She didn't want anyone around when she listened to the rest of Granddad's tape.

After saying a quick prayer, asking the Lord to help her get through her grandfather's final words, she pressed the play button.

Suddenly she heard her grandfather yell, "Yes, you are!"

Alyssa heard the sound of the wind as it buffeted the inside of the cockpit when Alexander Turner altered course, turning the plane into a sharp right bank, and dumping Alyssa out of it. A faint scream was drowned out by the wind and the rattling of the plane as it descended toward the mountain.

Finally Granddad said, "I'm sorry, Mae. I don't know how I'm going to keep my promise to you. I don't expect this plane is going to land in our rose garden."

Without warning, and with crystal clarity, she heard her grandmother's voice say, "Take my hand, Alex. You can still keep your promise to me. Just take my hand."

After that, there were three or four seconds with just the rattling of the plane and the screeching of the wind, and then complete silence.

Alyssa wept with the knowledge that her grandfather had such a wonderful experience. The love she heard in her grandparents' voices seemed almost tangible. It was a love she prayed for, a love for which she would endure almost anything.

With proof that her grandfather was with her on the plane, she felt she could now share the experience with her parents. Up to that point, she'd said very little to them, only that she was sorry, and she hoped she hadn't caused them too much undue strain when the plane crashed. They hadn't talked about where her grandfather's body had been found, or how Alyssa thought he'd been in the plane with her, but rumors traveled just as fast in Heber City and Wanship as they did in Vernal.

When she made the telephone call to her mother, she was glad to hear her voice. Of course they would love for Alyssa to come home for the weekend. Saturday evening would be fine.

When Saturday finally arrived, Alyssa was busy with students and the day slipped by before she realized it was so late. Around eight in the evening she finally locked up, grabbed the cassette tape and her overnight bag, and headed toward Heber City.

When Alyssa arrived at the Kendal home around nine that night, she was exhausted. The garage door was wide open and her father beckoned her to drive inside. She was grateful for this consideration. He knew she was still trying to avoid Ed, and had opened a space for her inside the garage to ensure her privacy. Before she could open the car door, her father opened it for her, and took her hand, helping her out.

"My, I've missed you," he said, giving her a big bear hug.

"I've missed you, too, Dad."

"Let me carry your bag," he offered, and she willingly let him.

"Hmm," she teased. "You never used to carry my bag when I was coming over every other weekend."

"It's been three months," her father scolded. "And you've had everyone worried sick about you."

"I'm fine," she responded. "I just couldn't face anyone for a while. It was all I could do just to go to work."

He helped her in through the side door, "Mother, look who just arrived."

Mrs. Kendal put down her knitting and stood up quickly. "Alyssa, I'm so glad you decided to come." She gave Alyssa an affectionate kiss on the cheek and a quick hug.

"I've missed you," Alyssa said. "I would have come sooner, but . . ."

"We know, dear."

"I like your hair," said Mr. Kendal, changing the subject. "A much more feminine look than that little bob affair you like so well."

Alyssa exclaimed, "Boy! We have a *lot* of catching up to do!"

They stayed up until after midnight sharing thoughts and experiences. Of course, Mrs. Kendal cried all through the cassette tape. It was proof that her daughter's life was a miracle, and that she had been protected by a very special angel. At last, her parents could believe that Granddad was in the plane with her.

Finally Alyssa told them about Ed. It was the first time she could share her experiences without crying all the way through, and she hoped it meant she was mending. She didn't say that his sending her the tape had softened the edges of her anger toward him considerably, but somehow she sensed that they already knew it.

Chapter Twenty

*E*arly the next morning Alyssa got ready for church, then went into the kitchen for breakfast. When she did, she got the shock of her life. Hans Bridger Clark was sitting at the breakfast table, reading from a Book of Mormon.

"Good morning," he said. "You're looking well, Alyssa."

"What are you doing here?" she asked.

"Reading my scriptures until your parents get up."

"Who let you in?"

He held up a key to the back door. "They gave me this about a month ago so I wouldn't have to wait out in the car."

"Wait in the car?"

"Well, yes," Hans nodded. "A few of us still read scriptures every morning at the Bar M at four-thirty. The ranch hands sleep in on Sundays, but I just can't sleep late anymore. On Sundays I drive over here around five. It's usually 7:30 when I get here, and their meetings don't start until ten, so I have about an hour of quiet time. It's pleasant here, reading scriptures in your mother's kitchen. Sister Kendal gets up and fixes me breakfast about 8:30. I volunteer every time to help, but she doesn't like men cooking in her kitchen. You know, she makes the best whole wheat pancakes I've ever tasted."

Alyssa sat down on a chair before her legs could give out beneath her. "How long have you been coming?"

"I started the second Sunday after you left the Bar M," he explained. "I was disappointed you weren't coming home on Sundays anymore, but your parents took me in like one of the flock. We're actually all quite fond of each other."

"They haven't said a word to me about it!"

"I asked them not to. Though I also asked them to warn me if you were coming home, since I was worried you still weren't receiving guests. We missed seeing you at the funeral. I'm sorry about your grandfather. It must have been terrible for you."

"How's your shoulder and your leg?" she asked, hoping to change the subject. She didn't know who had attended the funeral.

"Unlike Ed's heart," he suggested, "I've mended quite well."

Alyssa felt a strumming motion in her chest with the implications of Hans' suggestion. She wanted to ask him how Ed really was, but now she was afraid to find out. Finally she said, "You're still at the Bar M, then?"

"Yes. We've got all the fence posts driven, and the wiring is going up quite fast now. Another week and we should have it all fenced."

"And the herd?"

"Next month, or longer if the weather holds, we'll take them down to the winter range."

"Are you going to help with that?"

"It's a genuine cattle drive," he said with a smile. "I wouldn't miss that for anything."

"How long does it take?"

"Ed says it will take about six days, barring complications."

"It sounds exciting."

"Doesn't it? Who would have thought that a man with four doctorates and not a clue where he belongs in the world, could gain so much pleasure in simple things, as I have this summer?"

"You're a curious man," Alyssa said. "I would never have thought you could enjoy the real world so much."

"The world's a remarkable place," Hans observed. "All that studying in text books, and pieces of paper that say I'm a very smart man, and I find that they don't mean much when I'm out on the ranch. Perhaps my heart wasn't happy before now because I had no reason for being, as you so aptly put it."

"I didn't mean to imply—"

He interrupted. "No, that's what I like about you, Alyssa. You say exactly what you think, no excuses for how you feel. With me, I've had to internalize everything all my life. You're braver than I. You just speak your mind, then go about your business."

"Hans Bridger Clark," she said with a shy smile. "You may finally be growing up."

"Enough about me," he complained with a quick smile. "How are you feeling?"

"Physically, pretty good. But emotionally, well, let's not even go there, all right?"

Hans nodded, though she noticed the disappointment in his blue eyes.

      ૎ ૎

Later that afternoon, after Sunday services and a hearty dinner, Hans and Alyssa sat on the patio glider together to visit. He'd been very attentive and careful not to talk about Ed, except with the reference earlier to Ed's broken heart, and she was grateful.

She wasn't ready this morning to talk about Ed, but being with Hans again brought all her feelings for Ed tumbling to the foreground. Alyssa realized that she loved Ed more every day.

Hans had confided that he was thinking about joining the church, but he wanted to wait until he was back in San Diego and could talk his feelings over with his twin.

Alyssa was not only grateful to hear this news, she was thankful that Hans had come. She needed a friend she could talk with, someone who'd been at the ranch and knew the tender feelings in her heart. Hans had been able to make her smile again, at least a little. Somehow her heart softened. She hoped she could talk to Hans about Ed. Perhaps if she shared her pain with him, she would feel better. But she didn't quite know how to begin.

As though sensing her thoughts, Hans looked tenderly at her and asked, "Do you still love Ed?"

Alyssa thought about the question seriously before she answered. Knowing that Hans was much closer to his Father in Heaven than he'd ever been, she decided to share her feelings, and just knowing that she could do so, seemed to comfort her somehow.

Clearing her throat and trying not to cry, she said, "Remember when you told me that you knew I loved Ed by the look on my face that day in the meadow after I kissed him?"

"Yes."

"The night before," she confessed, "I had pleaded with the Lord to show me, in a way that I could never deny, that when I had found the right man, I would know it. That's exactly what the Lord did. Every symptom that I asked the Lord to give me, He did. I'd asked for that mountain top feeling, I wanted to feel dizzy, I'd asked for my knees to buckle, I'd even asked to faint. I asked that the Lord give me that sweet burning in my chest and let it stay with me until I could no longer deny that I'd found the right man. The Lord confirmed, with that one kiss, that I should love Ed."

"I thought that's when you figured it out," said Hans.

"I know the Lord gave me my answer the way that he did so that I could never deny it. But when I woke up in the wagon I was so disappointed to learn it was Ed, I couldn't stop crying. I didn't want to be in love with Ed. I didn't think I could ever fill the void in his heart created by the haunting love he has for Kayla. I felt so inadequate, but I reconciled myself to the idea, and after I went to the temple the next day, there was no doubt in my mind that I love him."

She hesitated, waiting to see if Hans could possibly understand what she was feeling. When she saw the compassion and empathy in his blue eyes, she continued. "Ever since that horrible night when Ed asked me to leave the Bar M, I tried to hate him, or at least to dislike him for breaking my heart, but I can't. I still love him and that isn't likely to change. I tell the Lord I love him, and ask if I should, and the Lord always says yes. Every single time I ask, He says yes."

"Then don't you think it's time to forgive Ed, and let him back into your life?" asked Hans. "Hasn't he been punished enough?"

Alyssa smiled broadly at Hans' question. "Ed sent me a tape of the flight recording when the plane crashed. When I received it, I smiled. I think it was the first time I'd smiled since leaving the Bar M."

"You didn't answer the question," he reminded.

Now Alyssa laughed. "Right to the point, Hans. That's so like you."

"Well?"

"The real question isn't whether or not Ed has been punished enough. I haven't been punishing him by not answering his calls. I've been trying to find myself. Before I met him, I was in love with flying, and I loved nature and soaring with the birds and the angels. When I thought I had hope of finding a place in his heart where Kayla wasn't,

I became invincible. I couldn't be beaten. Ed lifted me up so high I could have flown to heaven without a paraglider. Then he took heaven away from me, and now, even with a paraglider, I can't find myself there. Not anymore."

"But you've been flying all the time," Hans persisted. "Every time we've called for you, you're up in the sky. You're still flying."

Alyssa tried to explain, "You don't understand. I don't fly anymore because of the joy it used to bring me. I fly because I'm still searching for that piece of heaven that I used to find up in the sky, Hans. Though I fly and I fly and I fly, I just can't find heaven because it's not up there anymore. Now there's nothing in my vision but fields of gray. All the alfalfa and straw and wheat is gray, for as far as I can see, and there's no magic in the flight. It's gone. Ed broke something inside me the day he asked me to leave the Bar M, and I don't know how to fix it." Alyssa dabbed at her eyes with a tissue. "It's just gone." She shrugged, realizing that all the flying in the world wasn't going to fix what was broken inside her heart. Then the tears came once again.

Hans put his arm around her to comfort her. She leaned against him and let him cradle her with his shoulder. Tears dripped down her cheeks, and Hans wiped them away with his fingertips.

"Would you be terribly mad at me if I broke a little confidence that you shared with me?" he questioned.

"What confidence?" she asked, stiffening, pulling away from him.

"Will you ever forgive me, Alyssa?" he begged. "I told Ed how you feel about him. . . ."

Alyssa's eyes widened and her mouth dropped open. "You did what?" she demanded.

He lowered his head, as though he regretted making such a mistake, but then he brought it right back up again in his own defense. "You broke your promise to me," he accused. "You promised to stay at the Bar M for your full vacation, and you promised to let me come visit you on Sundays after you went home."

"Oh, Hans," she moaned. "How could you?"

"I knew what Ed had already been through with Kayla. I wanted him to have a sliver of hope that you might forgive him."

"He doesn't need me to forgive him. Forgiving is easy. It's love that's the final betrayal. If he could make me believe that he loves me more than he loves Kayla, we might stand a chance together."

"But he does!" Hans protested.

She defied him. "He loves Kayla! He told me he did!"

"What about Mike? Do you love Mike?"

"Of course I love him. He's my very best friend."

"That's how Ed feels about Kayla. They grew up together, too, only much more literally than you and Mike. He was two years old when she was born. They played together in the meadow all their lives. They ranched and fished and danced and sang and watched stars together all their growing up years. Unlike you, who only saw Mike at school and an occasional evening or weekend, Ed, Will, Tom and Abbot lived just across the meadow from Kayla. There were no picture shows to see, no ice cream shops and no sidewalks on which to roller skate. All those five children had were each other. Is it any wonder he grew up loving her? You spent probably one tenth the amount of time with Mike as Ed did with Kayla, yet you love Mike. Do you begrudge Mike taking a wife and making her his best friend?"

"No."

"Neither does Ed begrudge Kayla marrying Josh. The only difference is that when he was a teenager, he was in love with love, and he thought he loved Kayla romantically. It turned out he was wrong."

Alyssa stopped listening for a moment and started remembering. She and Mike both thought they would grow up and marry each other, but when they finally matured, they realized they didn't love each other as man and woman, but as best friends.

"Alyssa, give Ed another chance. It's you that he loves. It isn't his childhood chum and best friend."

Still, Alyssa had to admit that Ed had failed her. "If he had phoned me once, just once in August, while Kayla was at the ranch, I might have had hope. But he didn't, Hans. He pursued me for five weeks and then Kayla showed up and I was history. My whole family was praying for him to make one contact, just one little call is all it would have taken."

"He gave up because you wouldn't return his calls. It had nothing to do with Kayla arriving. Besides, she came the middle of July, and stayed six weeks instead of the usual three."

"She was there in July?" Alyssa asked. "Are you sure?"

"Yes. Abbot had accepted a job offer in Seattle and was trying to get on with his life, and Ed wasn't returning Kayla's calls. She was so worried about the riff between Ed and Abbot, she finally decided to see if she could bridge the gap between them from this end."

"I didn't know this," Alyssa shook her head. "Ed was still calling me in July."

"Kayla and Josh left the Bar M the same day you left the hospital. Ed didn't even go to the airport to see them off. The whole time you were in the hospital he slept in the waiting room. He wouldn't even leave the building except to get breakfast across the street at the deli, and then only because he hates hospital food."

"He called me seven times during the last two weeks of July," she remembered.

"Return his calls, contact him, give him hope, Alyssa."

"I want to, Hans," she responded. "But how can I trust him until I've fixed what's broken inside me? If I can't mend whatever it is that tore apart inside me when Ed asked me to leave, how can I trust anyone with my heart a second time?"

"Give him another chance, Alyssa. You gave Abbot a second chance after he'd hurt you," he reminded her. Then he amended, "Frightened you, I believe is how Abbot put it. And you didn't even love him. Alyssa, you love Ed. Doesn't he deserve at least as much consideration as Abbot?"

Alyssa found her mouth curling in a smile. Then she suddenly burst out laughing. It felt good to know that she could laugh again.

"What is so funny?" he asked.

"You are," she said. "You're sitting here trying to convince me to give Ed another chance, and it occurred to me that I couldn't see your bow and arrow or your little cupid wings."

"Now that is a picture!" he exclaimed.

🐚 🐚

On his way back to the Bar M Ranch, Hans put the cassette into the player and listened, wanting to be certain he hadn't said anything to Alyssa he shouldn't have. Hans didn't want Ed Sparkleman to have any reason to resent him.

He cringed as he realized he'd come awfully close to losing Alyssa's friendship and her trust. Since he'd already told Ed that she loved him, he had wanted to see her reaction. She didn't seem too disappointed with him. Now that he knew she would forgive him, he could give the tape to Ed with a clear conscience.

Recalling the past nine weeks at the ranch, and the sheer torture it had been for him to hang on, made Hans wonder if it was going to be worth all the time and effort he'd expended, not to mention the physical injuries. But he'd made a commitment to Ed that he would stay the full summer, and unlike Alyssa, it wasn't in his nature to run away from a problem.

Ed had been moody ever since Alyssa left and moodier still since she was released from the hospital. Hans much preferred the gentler Ed who ran the ranch when Alyssa was around.

If Ed's temper wasn't bad enough, the new men Ed had hired arrived the Tuesday after Alyssa left, and they were a rowdy bunch.

Hans had refused to move back to the cabin, which was now nothing more than a glorified bunk house, and he had started sleeping at the lodge.

The rapport Hans had tried to develop with Ed had vanished almost completely within two weeks of Alyssa's departure. He was still surprised that Ed had invited him along in the helicopter the day her plane went down. It seemed that they were on better terms now than they'd been before that awful day, so Hans was feeling particularly lucky.

In addition to all the other complications in Hans' once peaceful life, Sidekick had been pestering him about his disappearances on the Sabbath. Sidekick claimed he was going to find out where Hans was going and inform the boss if he thought it would benefit him.

Of course, Ed knew nothing of Hans' visits to Heber City, and Hans wasn't about to tell him. This was the very first time that Alyssa had been there, but would Ed believe it? There were enough problems between the two men without adding fuel to the fire. He only hoped he could get the tape to Ed privately somehow, before Sidekick found out about it.

Hans realized now that Kayla had received her inspiration from God, but it took him more than six months to admit it. Of course, neither Hans nor Kayla had any idea that Alyssa would figure into the equation at the time Hans arrived at the Bar M Ranch. In breaking one brother's heart, Alyssa had fallen in love with the other. Hans had to admit that no one knew the elaborate plans God had formulated in his effort to lasso the heart of Ed Sparkleman.

Humbled, Hans realized his efforts would not be wasted. He felt as though he were a special missionary, sent forth by God to accomplish a mighty work. And that was exactly what Hans intended to do.

Hans smiled to himself. He'd offered more prayers for other people in the past few months than he had prayed in his entire life. He wasn't certain that it meant anything particularly spectacular. *But it was significant*, he decided.

Perhaps he could still go on the cattle drive, and live to enjoy it!

Chapter Twenty-one

*E*d rolled out of bed, dropped to his knees and said his morning prayer, but the words sounded automatic and rehearsed. Sometimes he wondered how the Lord could ever listen to the same intonations day in and day out.

As soon as he was dressed, Ed pulled the piece of paper from his wallet and held it in his hands. He liked the crisp feel of it, and he unfolded it again and read Alyssa's letter. The photos had no real importance to him, but the letter. . . .

She hadn't signed it with an endearment. There was no "love" at the end, or "your friend." But it was more than she'd offered at the hospital three weeks ago.

After Alyssa left the Bar M, Ed went to bed each night feeling as though his heart had been yanked out of his chest and flung through the sky where it crumbled into pieces so small they were almost non-existent. For a long time it seemed as though he didn't have a heart at all. He awakened every morning unhealed. It had been three months since she left, and still all he could think about was Alyssa.

He realized more each day that he'd never felt this way when Kayla left the Bar M to pursue a career in marine science. The strongest and most predominant emotion he had felt all those years apart from Kayla had been raw, unadulterated anger. When she finally married Joshua, the hostility changed to sadness.

With Alyssa gone, his feelings were completely different. It felt like she took his heart with her, and sometimes he didn't know if he could even make it through one more day. It wasn't an empty heart that she left behind her, it was no heart at all.

Now that he had her letter, he wasn't sure that it meant anything more than a thank you for the cassette tape he'd sent to her, but it was a new beginning. It was the only real hope he'd had in months.

When Alyssa hadn't returned any of his calls, he'd finally given up. Yet, even at the hospital he'd let false hopes carry him away, until the nurse told him she didn't want to see him. Trembling with the memory, he recalled the day she left the hospital, when she told him she had nothing to say to him. He knew then that he'd lost the only woman he ever really loved. And he still felt powerless to do anything about it.

Finding the cockpit voice recorder had been the answer to many prayers and several days of frustration and searching. When Mike told him about the circumstances regarding her grandfather's death, Ed knew it would prove Alyssa's case.

She had not gone off on some crazy tangent and flown the plane herself, as Mike had assumed. She might be impetuous, but she valued human life, her own included. Of this Ed was certain. Nor was Alyssa suffering from post-traumatic stress to the extent that she would not know who was in the plane with her. No, Ed believed Alyssa's version of what had happened the very moment he heard it. After all, he had witnessed some mighty miracles in his life.

Finding the black box would prove to Alyssa's family that her grandfather *had* saved her life, and for his sacrifice, the Lord had granted him a miracle. To Ed's great relief, the Lord heard his prayers and answered them. He was able to recover the recording himself. After he'd listened to it and had heard the conversation between Alyssa and her grandfather, he prayed that his sending the tape to her would soften her heart toward him.

He had to admit that it had taken every ounce of courage he had to write to her . . . and sign his name with an endearment. How he had prayed over sending her that letter!

After reading Alyssa's response one more time, he put it back in his wallet. It was probably best not to get his hopes up. He'd tried about everything he could think of and nothing had worked so far. Only a fool would read more into her letter than what was in it.

Skipping breakfast, he went out to the stable and saddled up his palomino stallion. Within minutes he was sitting atop Breeze on a full gallop through the dawn haze on his way toward the camp.

The aspen leaves were just beginning to turn from green to a brilliant yellow-gold, and the crispness in the air gave the promise of fall around the corner. High in the mountains, the seasons didn't wait upon a calendar. Though trees in the valley would not change for another month, on the Bar M, winter would come early and stay late.

Marcus would be up fixing breakfast by now. Ed was still amazed at how much Marcus loved sleeping under the stars at night, even when the earth was blanketed in frost upon his arising. Then Ed remembered the daybed he and Alyssa had made up on the deck at the lodge, and how he'd felt when they'd stretched out on it together and he'd held her if only for a moment.

He shuddered. Everything he saw, everything he touched turned his thoughts to Alyssa. He couldn't ride down the trail without seeing her ride in front of him. The stars above reminded him of her love for them. He couldn't even look at Porcupine Ridge without seeing Alyssa free-fall from the Cessna.

Pompanoosuc porridge reminded him of Alyssa's concerned expression when he choked on it, and he could feel her patting his back and feel her nearness. She had worn that lovely cream-colored dress, that somehow shocked him into submission. Ed was a broken man. If he thought he was a goner that morning, he feared it even more now.

When he arrived at the camp, he wasn't surprised to see Marcus cooking pancakes. To his surprise, there was a pot on the fire filled with pompanoosuc porridge as well. Ed swung down out of the saddle and tied the reins to the hitching post.

"What's this?" he asked as he put his hand in a thick glove and removed the porridge.

"Morning Sun told me you weren't eating breakfast no more, Boss. I figured that was part of the reason why you've been growling at the men lately."

"Morning Sun should learn to keep her mouth shut," Ed told him, but it didn't have the usual bark from days gone by.

"Eat your breakfast," said Marcus. "Then you and me are gonna' talk."

Ed opened his mouth to protest but Marcus glared at him, so he poured some milk and honey on the porridge and ate it straight out of the pot. When he was finished, he said, "You happy now, Ma?"

Marcus almost smiled, but Ed was not amused.

"What's on your mind?" Ed finally asked.

"I've been hearing talk ever since I got back, and I'll tell you what I've come to think."

"Not that I'm interested," growled Ed. "But I'll humor you."

"I figure Miss Alyssa put a big ol' hole in your heart, and you don't know whether to keel over dead or just live the rest of your life like a zombie in a saddle." Marcus looked up at him as he flipped the last of the pancakes onto a plate, then poured warm honey over them, and forked into them with zest.

"Go on," said Ed, curious about Marcus' description of him.

"I've come to believe you're nothin' but a coward," Marcus said between mouthfuls.

"What?" asked Ed in surprise, his voice gruff, his temper kindled.

"Sure you are, Boss," Marcus shrugged. "You let Kayla go without putting up a fight, and you've suffered for that mistake ever since. What if you'd followed her to California and helped her with her studies? What if you'd learned how to sail that boat of hers? What if you'd stayed by her until she was through with school and had her job? What if you'd left the ranch and stretched your wings a little? Would you be any worse off than you've been all these past years?"

"You don't know what you're talking about!" snapped Ed. He rinsed the empty pot in a bucket of soapy water Marcus had put near the tent, his back to Marcus now.

"You just don't get it, do you, Boss?"

Ed set the pot in a draining pan and stood up, then turned to face him. "Kayla and I are kin, just like brother and sister. I believe that now, and there's nothing more to it."

"I ain't saying it didn't work out for the best for her, Boss. I was saying, what if?" Marcus finished another mouth of pancake and took a swallow of milk, then wiped his lips on a paper napkin.

"This ain't about Kayla," Ed glared.

"That's my point, Boss. And all I'm saying is . . . what if?"

"You think I haven't tried, Marcus? I called Alyssa Mae every day for over a month. She never returned a single call."

"Did you go see her, try to talk to her face to face? Phoning is a coward's way," observed Marcus.

"I tried talking to her at the hospital. She had me thrown out on my ear! And when I finally caught her unguarded, she told me she had nothing to say to me. If she won't take my calls, and she won't talk to me face to face, and she has nothing to say, what the blazes am I supposed to do next?" Now his anger had ignited, and it seemed to him that's just what Marcus was counting on.

Marcus smiled as though he had caught a feisty old polecat in his trap. With deliberate subtlety, he said, "Miss Alyssa's only seeing Hans because he goes over there every Sunday. That's why I'm asking you, Boss. What if . . . ?" Marcus left the sentence open.

"Hans?" Ed hissed. The skin on his neck prickled as though he'd come across a rattlesnake coiled to strike at him.

Marcus shrugged.

"How do you know Hans has been seeing her?" Ed demanded.

"Sidekick mentioned it the other night around the campfire," Marcus explained. "He said he followed Hans last Sunday and saw him go to church with Miss Alyssa and her folks. He thought maybe Hans was just getting religion with them, so he waited around a while. Said he saw Hans and Miss Alyssa snuggling together on a patio bench."

Ed didn't say a word. He didn't need to say anything. All those months thinking Hans had no interest in Alyssa, thinking he could trust Hans, had been wasted on a traitor! Ed mounted his horse and ground the spurs into the stallion's flanks. Breeze gave a mighty leap and galloped away, leaving Marcus in the dust.

"That's it, Boss!" called Marcus as he laughed heartily. "You go fight for the woman you love!"

When Ed arrived back at the Bar M, he could see the men were still strapping the saddles on their horses across the meadow. Hans was leading a chestnut stallion, saddled up and ready to go, out of the stable. Ed made no effort to slow down, but galloped Breeze straight toward Hans.

Some of the men saw Ed coming and no doubt figured something was wrong. They began yelling for everyone to come quick.

Hans looked up, saw it was Ed and Breeze racing across the meadow in a big rush, and handed the reins to one of the men. Then he walked towards Ed Sparkleman and his palomino stallion.

When they were no less than ten feet apart, Ed yelled, "Whoa! Whoa!" He swung down out of the saddle in one swift movement and left the horse standing untethered.

Crossing the gap between himself and Hans, and without giving any warning, Ed swung out and landed one mighty fist against Hans' left eye, knocking him flat out on his back.

The men grabbed Ed and tried to restrain him, but he was too angry. It took five of them to finally subdue him. There were shouts, yells, and some cursing, too, but Ed was too furious to care about the foul language.

Hans came back up, mad as a mother bear. He, too, had to be restrained. "What's this?" he yelled. "After all I've done for you, what's this all about?" he demanded.

"You and Alyssa Mae!" Ed hissed. "Go ahead, deny it!" He noticed Sidekick trying to slink away by the horses. "Sidekick, tell him what you saw!"

Suddenly Hans eyes brightened, and Ed saw the truth written plainly on his face. He knew that Hans couldn't deny that he'd been with Alyssa. "You were with Alyssa last Sunday!" Ed growled. "Have you been there every Sunday, Hans?"

For no apparent reason, the anger seemed to seep out of Hans. He relaxed and the men restraining him did, too. He shook one arm free. "I won't fight him," he told them. "Release me." When they did, he looked steadily at Ed and his eyes narrowed.

Deliberately, Hans walked over to Ed and stood almost nose to nose with him. "I've been with Alyssa's parents every Sunday," he admitted. "But until this last week, Alyssa was still in hiding."

"I ought to rip your heart out!" Ed growled, straining unsuccessfully against the men holding him back.

"You ought to get your facts straight before you strike out!" Hans yelled. "Tell him everything you saw, Sidekick! Did I kiss her? No. Was she crying? Yes. Was I comforting her? Yes. What's the matter, Sidekick, the truth isn't shocking enough so you invented something to make our meeting sound really juicy?"

"Sidekick?" asked Ed, relaxing a little. But the ranch troublemaker shook his head, pulled his hat down to shade his eyes, and walked away without saying a word.

"What's this all about?" Ed demanded, still unable to quell all of the anger inside him.

Hans smiled, as though triumphantly completing some task he had long awaited. "When you're through, I'll expect a full apology," he said. "I'd have given this to you sooner, but I was waiting to present it to you in private. It would have meant more that way. Just remember, you chose the time." Hans removed a miniature cassette player from his shirt pocket, then tucked it into Ed's.

Backing up, he said to the men, "There's not going to be a fight today. It's over. Let's get to work. This isn't a side show."

Hans headed toward the lodge as the men quickly dispersed, each one going to their assigned duties.

Walking past Sidekick, Hans glared. "I should have expected this from you!"

Ed just stood there . . . numb with shock. He removed the cassette player from his pocket and noticed that it had a tape in it. Hans had brought him an audio recording, and he wanted an apology from Ed for hitting him. His mind whirled as he realized he may have made a terrible mistake.

Seeking privacy, Ed walked up to the clearing where the basement had been poured for his house. The floor for the main level had already been installed, and the walls were up, as well as the framework for the roof. Logs had been cut, stripped and stacked nearby, awaiting his handiwork.

Sitting down on one of the porch footings, Ed felt an awful remorse settle within him for what he'd done to Hans. It made him shudder.

With a lump in his throat, Ed pressed the play button on the cassette player and listened. Alyssa's voice sounded like sweet music to his ears. As she and Hans conversed, he was disappointed to hear mostly small talk at first. Then Hans asked Alyssa if she still loved Ed.

Ed felt his heart pound wildly within his chest, his body tensed, his mind fearful to hear her answer.

Alyssa told Hans about her prayer: how she'd asked the Lord to give her a mountain top feeling, or make her knees weak, or make her faint, so she would know when the right man came along. Ed was delighted to hear that these feelings had occurred the day she kissed him in the meadow, and how she hadn't expected it. She told Hans how disappointed she was when she revived from her faint and realized that Ed was the man she loved. She had agonized because Ed was still haunted by the love he had for Kayla, and how inadequate Alyssa felt in comparison. Then she talked about how she'd felt since the day he invited her to leave the Bar M, no questions asked. He felt sick inside when he heard her say she wanted to hate him, then he was filled with relief when he learned that she couldn't. However, the greatest joy came when she explained how the Lord kept telling her, every single time she asked, that she should still love him.

Then she said something that made Ed's mind reel and his heart lurch. When the tape ended, he rewound it, and played that part again.

"Dang!" he whispered to himself, "How am I gonna' fix what I've broken inside Alyssa Mae?"

His first thought was to get down on his knees. Responding immediately, he poured his heart out to the Lord:

> "Father in Heaven,
> I ain't much of a talking man. I lean toward action more.
> But Alyssa Mae is hurting, and I'm the cause of it.
> Help me know how to help her, Father.
> Help me to do and say what I must to get us through this.
> And thank you for Hans . . ."

For a moment, tears welled up in Ed's green eyes and he struggled to continue:

> ". . . He's been a true friend!"

After closing his prayer, Ed stood up and received an impression to play a part of the tape again. He rewound it until he found the part he wanted. When he pressed the play button this time, he tried not to listen with his ears, but to listen with his heart. It didn't take long until his heart found the things he needed to hear Alyssa say:

> "I'm still searching for that piece of heaven that
> I used to find up in the sky, Hans. Though I fly
> and I fly and I fly, I just can't find heaven be-
> cause it's not up there anymore. It used to be,

before I met Ed. Now there's nothing in my
vision but fields of gray. All the alfalfa and straw
and wheat is gray, for as far as I can see, and
there's no magic in the flight. It's gone."

Ed pressed the stop button, rewound the same part and played it
over another time, searching his mind and his heart for answers. And
then Ed smiled gratefully. Removing his Stetson, he slapped it against
his thigh. He had a plan and he was anxious to begin.

"Thank you, God. And you, too, Pa," he whispered.

Then he hurried down the mountain toward the lodge. Ed was
determined. He had a blessing to fulfill and nothing was going to stop
him this time. *Nothing!* Hans looked up when Ed came rushing through
the back door.

He glanced at Hans for only an instant before he said. "I ain't
much for apologies, but I am truly sorry! Will you forgive me?"

Hans nodded feebly.

Ed gave him a mischievous grin. "Somehow I expect this other
form of apology will mean more to you, though."

He paused to watch Hans' expression. He hadn't noticed, when
he first came bursting in, that Hans had an ice pack over a swollen eye.
A flame of guilt burned through Ed's conscience.

"What is it?" Hans questioned.

"Will you help me, partner?" asked Ed. "We've got a heap of work
to do to make your cupid wings start growing."

⠀⠀⠀

The following Sunday, since Alyssa had been assigned a talk
during sacrament meeting, she hadn't gone over to her parents' home.

She hoped Hans hadn't been too disappointed, but her parents assured her over the telephone that Hans got along well enough without her.

On Monday morning Alyssa debated whether or not to fly the paraglider that day. She looked out the window and realized it may be the last perfect day before autumn brought colder air in to ruin paraglider dreams.

She turned on the computer and logged onto the weather report. Although she learned that it would be clear and warm all day, Alyssa knew that she may never see blue skies again. She'd been trying for almost three months to recapture that feeling of soaring with angels that she used to have, with no success. She decided to try again. *For all the good it will do me!*

Remembering her promise that she would find those sweet, familiar sensations, or die trying, she whispered to herself, "Maybe one last time."

After dialing the telephone number quickly, before she could change her mind, she waited only a moment for Shauna to answer.

"Hello."

"Guess I'm going up today. You want to go?"

Shauna hesitated. "I don't think Mike will let me go up anymore this season."

"Okay," said Alyssa, "but this might be our last good day of the whole year."

"I know. Maybe Mike will go. Let me see."

Alyssa waited only a few seconds. Then Mike answered. "You're nuts, Alyssa. I just can't go up every day like you can. Maybe fatherhood is making me feel old."

"You're not even a fath— Mike! Are you pregnant?" she asked, hoping with all her heart.

"Not technically," he teased, "but Shauna is."

"I can't believe it! You've both wanted a child so much!"

He laughed, and she could hear Shauna giggling in the background.

"That news made my day!" Alyssa smiled, grateful that she could finally do so. "Congratulations!"

Mike said, "Go ahead up. We'll come over and watch you. Would that be all right?"

"Great! I'll get my gear ready and head on up. Just signal me when you get here."

"Right on," he said. "Have a great flight."

Alyssa put her harness and canopy bag in the back of the Toyota truck, then drove the switchback road up to the ridge just below Porcupine Peak. When she reached the top, she spread the canopy, ran the tethers and control lines to the harness and buckled herself in. She looked far below her to the building that had A & M written boldly across the roof. Three flashes from Mike's mirror hit her right in the face. She put the helmet over her hair and secured it. Flipping on the radio transmitter, she said, "Can you hear me okay?"

"Loud and clear!" Mike's voice came over the micro-speaker inside her helmet. "Don't worry about the truck. We'll pick it up later."

"Thanks," she responded. "I appreciate it."

"Have a great flight!" Mike encouraged.

"Eat your heart out, Mommy and Daddy!" she teased.

Then she lifted the control lines to let the canopy fill with air. *Patience!* she said to herself, feeling a surge of warm air rush toward her. When the canopy was filled, she pulled on the control lines and watched as it lifted up and over her head. Placing the toggles in her hands, she stepped quickly forward, then jumped off the top of the mountain ridge. The wind was a little brisk, but the sun was well up in the sky, and she could feel the temperature warming as the sun drove the cold air down, while sending the warm air up in a thermal that would enable her to soar all day.

The canopy overhead held firm in the warming air current, and Alyssa watched the canopy for a time, hoping to feel that *angels are with me* feeling that she used to love, but it didn't come. She pulled on the toggles, maneuvering back and forth in a figure eight, hoping to gain some altitude.

"I see you're in the first thermal," came Mike's voice over the speaker.

"I am!" she replied. "Baby Roberts, this one's for you!"

Then Mike said, "No, Alyssa, this one's for you."

"What?" she asked, uncertain what he meant.

"If you'd get your line of sight off the skyline and a little more down to earth, you'd know what I'm talking about, girl," Mike scolded.

Alyssa turned her eyes toward the land but she didn't see anything except gray oat and wheat fields. "What are you talking about, Mike?" she asked.

"Stay on course," Mike told her. When she complied, he said, "Okay, just go around the bend and look down."

Alyssa shuddered. She didn't want to go around the mountain bend. She would see her granddad's alfalfa fields over there, but now there were too many sad memories at seeing them and she was unable to wave to her grandfather anymore. Besides, those fields no longer looked green and vibrant to her. They weren't beautiful like they were before Ed.

"Alyssa, you have to do this," Mike coaxed. "Trust me."

Reluctantly, she obeyed Mike and flew the paraglider around the bend, even though she was afraid to look down, afraid that all she would see was gray alfalfa. She closed her eyes tightly, frightened and terribly sad.

Then she heard another voice, a gruff, familiar, loveable voice that made her tremble inside. "Maisey, you don't need to wave to me, girl. You need to wave to him."

"Granddad?" she whispered, turning off the radio receiver. "Granddad, is that really you?"

"Open your eyes, Maisey," he persuaded. "Come on, you can do it."

Alyssa shuddered, but she finally obeyed her grandfather's voice and opened her eyes wide to see what he wanted to show her. Then she blinked, thinking something was wrong with her vision. What she saw made her gasp in astonished wonder. She maneuvered the paraglider farther over the field, staring down as though her very life depended on what she would see.

Below her, in the second alfalfa field around the bend, the hay had been mowed in a pattern of letters with some kind of message, and the mowed areas had been blanketed with white dust.

A burning sensation that began in her heart started spreading through her entire body as she flew directly over the field and read the message far below her:

Alyssa Mae,
I love YOU. . .
and ONLY YOU !!!
~ Ed

Tears filled her eyes and she started crying and laughing all at the same time. The gray of the alfalfa field seemed to change from drab to a brilliant, emerald green. The oat fields turned from brown to glistening gold. The sky turned from gray to blue again. She glanced at her canopy, judging how much air to let out of it in order to lower herself down. In amazement she watched the sun snag the sparkles in the blue and silver design of the fabric. She looked around her and felt the presence of angels in the air about her, guiding her down toward the message.

But the most amazing angels of all were the ones flying on each side of her. Her grandma and granddad looked upon her lovingly and guided her down, down . . . down.

Then Granddad gave her an endearing smile and said, "Ed brought you a whole truck full of rose bushes, Maisey. Now go find a nice spot somewhere on the Bar M Ranch and plant them together."

When Alyssa looked more closely, she saw Ed's white truck drive into the field, followed by several other vehicles. In the back of his pickup the entire bed was filled with live rose bushes, their root masses wrapped in white and red plastic, forming a heart shape. The procession of cars, with Ed's truck in the lead, drove in a pattern, until the shape of a heart was formed around the message.

When the white truck stopped, Ed got out. He was wearing his Stetson, wranglers, western shirt and cowboy boots, just as she had remembered him every waking moment since they'd been apart.

As she drew nearer, she saw Ed remove his hat and wave at her, swinging it in a wide arc above his head. The courage it must have taken him to do something so impetuously spontaneous struck her with full force, but his unmistakably familiar voice came wafting up to her as she heard him shouting, "I love you, Alyssa Mae! I love you!"

Alyssa couldn't get down fast enough. She was listening, laughing, crying and reading all in one happy, colorful blur. Carefully she spilled as much air out of canopy as she dared, so she could reach the green field faster than normal.

When her feet finally touched the solid earth, she unbuckled the harness and leg straps swiftly, and didn't bother to watch if the paraglider took flight behind her. She could no longer focus on anything or anyone but Ed. She removed her helmet and dropped it beside her on the ground. Then Alyssa froze.

Ed stood less than twenty feet away from her. His emerald eyes glistened in the morning sunlight, and so did the tears dripping down his cheeks. His sand-colored hair was wind-swept across his forehead.

Just seeing him again made her feel dizzy. But Alyssa had resolved three months ago that if they ever kissed again, Ed would have to initiate it. She stood her ground, regardless of the pounding in her heart that chanted, *run to him, run to him.* Alyssa waited and watched.

Ed looked at her as though he'd just found heaven. He crossed the distance and took her in his arms, kissing her so thoroughly she felt her knees weaken. When he released her, and gazed into her sparkling brown eyes, she nearly fainted.

"Whoa, there!" he exclaimed as he swooped her up and twirled her around, planting a hundred kisses all over her face, from her forehead to her cheeks to her lips, and back again.

Then he put her down tenderly, and let her stand in front of him, close to him, as he looked down at her. "Are you an angel's gift sent straight out of heaven?" he asked.

Alyssa nodded as she realized how much he was struggling to keep his emotions in check.

Tears spilled from his eyes when he said, "I love you, Alyssa Mae."

"You said you love Kayla," she reminded, wanting to make certain that he had no more longing for his childhood sweetheart.

"Who?" he asked, gazing at her as though there could never be any woman in his life but Alyssa Mae.

She put her hand against his cheek, and he responded by putting his hand tenderly against hers.

"I love you, too," she whispered through tears of her own.

Then she kissed him exactly as she did that warm June day in Mountain Meadow. His arms pulled her close to him, as he responded eagerly, relinquishing almost three months of desperate longing.

Alyssa melted against him, finally content that Ed Sparkleman's heart belonged to her, and her alone.

When he finally released her, people started getting out of their cars, laughing, cheering, and coming toward them: Her mother and father, Hans, Luke, Sidekick John, Mike and Shauna, and a half dozen men she didn't even recognize.

"You brought everyone with you?" she asked in amazement.

"No," Ed answered with a twinkle in his emerald eyes. "They followed me here."

"Why?" she wondered.

"They wanted to make sure you got the message."

Epilogue:

*N*ine months later Ed removed the blindfold from Alyssa's eyes and watched her expression carefully. He'd waited for this moment for so long, he could hardly contain himself. Except when they planted the rose bushes together last fall, Alyssa hadn't seen the new house, and he had to admit that their log home looked handsome among the pine trees and the quaking aspens.

Her brown eyes sparkled in concert with the delicious smile on her lips when she saw the wide wrap-around porch. "Oh, Ed," she sighed dreamily. "It's just how I had pictured it in my mind."

She took one step toward the porch, but he stopped her. "No, you don't, Mrs. Sparkleman," he insisted. "Tradition still rules here. I get to carry my bride over the threshold."

He lifted her up into his arms and pushed the door open with his foot. "See," he said quickly. "No furniture!"

"I want to help pick out the furniture," she reminded.

"That's probably why there is none!" he teased. Then he kissed her and let her stand up in the huge gathering room, with stairs off to the right, and the dining room straight ahead, next to a large country kitchen.

Leading her down the hall, he said, "A big den for me, since I know how you hate bookkeeping."

After stepping across the hall, he opened another door to reveal a dandy sewing room. "But I think you'll like this room. It's for someone in our family who has a knack at making canopies for paragliders."

"Mmm. . . ." She lifted her shoulders as she inhaled contentedly. "Our family . . . I like the sound of that!"

Ed took her by the hand and led her to the curved, hand-hewn stairway. "My own special design! And look what we have here!" He pointed to two brand new Stetsons hanging from hooks next to the stairs.

"Matching hats," she murmured dreamily.

When they went upstairs, he said, "Now you have to close your eyes."

Alyssa did as instructed. Ed kissed the tip of her nose and led her down the hall and into the master bedroom. "Okay, Alyssa Mae," he said. "You can look now."

The master bedroom was empty, as well, but it had wooden-framed glass doors that opened onto a private deck. She pushed the doors open and found an oak bed made up with fresh bedding, waiting for them outside. Several large vases filled with her favorite roses stood on a matching oak dresser nearby.

"I hope you don't mind keeping my parents' bedroom set," he said. "I just couldn't part with it."

"It's beautiful," she murmured. He noticed that her eyes filled with tears, but she turned her head away.

"Alyssa Mae?" he asked.

She took in a deep breath of the clean mountain air as she stepped across the deck and looked below the pine trees to the Bar M Ranch road, where it ran past the Sparkleman cabin.

When she didn't respond Ed began to worry. He stepped up behind her and asked again, "Alyssa Mae?"

Tears dripped down her cheeks when she turned to him. "Do you know what I wanted for my wedding gift?" she asked.

For a moment he thought he had forgotten something.

Alyssa smiled at him and the love he saw in her beautiful eyes made his heart quiver inside his chest.

"This," she said, stretching her arms out wide. "I wanted to sleep with my husband under the stars, looking out over the Bar M Ranch. How did you know when I never told you?"

He took her in his arms and kissed her tears away. "It was a selfish act on my part," he confessed. "It's what I wanted."

Later, as they snuggled in the king size bed out on the deck and looked up at the stars, Ed stroked Alyssa's hair and decided that he was the luckiest man in the solar system.

"Do you like Kayla?" he asked, no longer afraid to mention his sister's name to his bride.

"She's the sweetest woman," Alyssa admitted. "I should never have feared her, or your feelings for her."

"I'm glad," he said, pulling her close against him. "I was astounded when she showed up at the temple ceremony with Josh. She never told me that they'd gone through together."

"She said Josh made her promise to keep it a secret. He thought it might add to the joy of our wedding, having you learn the truth today."

"It did!" he said in amazement. "I'm still in shock!"

346

346 ✌ Sherry Ann Miller

"Hans left early today," Alyssa reminded, changing the subject. "Did he say why?"

"He and Tom had something they wanted to do."

"What?"

"He wouldn't say, but I suspect it has something to do with Abbot."

"I thought Tom was in Texas."

"He stopped by the ranch early this afternoon. I guess the filly he'd met down there wasn't the blessing he hoped for."

"I wish I'd met him. He's the only one in your family I haven't met."

"Aw, he'll be back someday. Ranching is in his blood."

"Do you suppose Abbot will ever forgive us?"

Ed smiled. "He already has."

"But he didn't come to the reception," she persisted.

Ed kissed her soundly, hoping she'd let her concerns over his brothers and Hans slip away from her. When he let her up for air, he saw that dazed look in her eyes that he loved, and knew his kiss had worked its magic.

It was time to tell Alyssa Mae about the special blessing that the bishop and his father had given him eighteen months ago. He had waited until after they were married, and this perfect setting was the place he'd chosen to relate that sacred experience to her. He wanted her to know that she was promised to him the day God sent Ed's father to bless him.

Clearing his throat, he said, "Alyssa Mae, there's something special that I want to share with you tonight."

"I have something to share with you, as well," she said. She came up on one elbow. Her long brown hair glistened as the light of a full moon made it glow like an angel's halo about her face.

"You go first," he said. "I want to go last."

"Okay."

Alyssa kissed him tenderly, then straightened a little and gave him that special expression that said she belonged to him . . . and him alone. Her diamond-bright eyes seemed to smile also, reminding him of one of the many reasons he loved her. He knew that tonight they were gleaming just for him.

"Last Sunday night," she began, "Granddad came to see me from across the veil. He told me that a dream I'd been having for quite a while was about to come true, and he brought a special visitor with him who looked a lot like you, only his eyes were brown, and he was older. He had black hair with silver flecks in it, and a bit of a beard. But he was quite handsome."

"Sounds like Pa," whispered Ed.

"I thought so, too, from the pictures I've seen. When Granddad introduced him, I was thrilled to meet your father."

"Go on," he coaxed.

"He asked me to tell you something very important. He even made me memorize it."

"What is it?" Ed asked as a lump grew in his throat. Somehow he sensed what she was going to say, though he could hardly believe it.

She gazed down at him, and he could see love radiate from her eyes. Her voice sounded like an angel's voice when she said the exact same words he had written down after his special blessing eighteen months ago:

"Edward Davis Sparkleman,
I love you with all my heart.
I will be faithful to you all of my life.
I will bring you joy and rejoicing as your

eternal companion and as the
mother of your children."

"Dang, Alyssa Mae," he groaned playfully as he pulled her close
to him. "I really am a goner!"

*S*herry Ann Miller is quickly earning her reputation as the "writer of miracles" and the Gift Series is proof of her belief that she has lived from miracle to miracle during her sojourn on earth.

To improve her health, Sherry Ann recently moved to Port Ludlow, Washington, where she hopes to spend more time writing, doing genealogy and sailing. She continues to gather twelve hundred family names each year for ordinance work, a goal she has met and exceeded for the past fourteen years; she also continues to write Latter-day Fiction, a genre dear to her heart.

Reader response is welcome and encouraged. Please write to Sherry Ann Miller in care of Granite Publishing & Distribution, 868 North 1430 West, Orem, UT 84057 or e-mail her at FDM2Ent@aol.com (If e-mailing, please put the title of the book you are writing about in the subject line). Readers whose responses are printed in Sherry Ann Miller's next book will receive a complimentary copy of that book, autographed by the author. Please keep the letters coming!

Reader Comments regarding *Gardenia Sunrise:*

"I just finished reading *Gardenia Sunrise* and had to let you know how wonderful it was! You are a fantastic writer! . . . your book brought me such joy. May Heavenly Father continue to bless you as you write. You help to strengthen testimonies." ∼ Anamarie Roy

"I loved your story. I bought *Gardenia Sunrise* two weekends ago and fell in love with it. I think you are a wonderful writer and I look forward to reading more." ∼ Ruth Brewer

"Your book (*Gardenia Sunrise*) arrived yesterday afternoon! I got up early this morning and did not stop until I had read the whole book! I was so glad I did not have any pressing obligation because it was hard to put down! It was nice to have a book that conveyed our church's views and standards. My daughter asked if it made me cry . . . that is an indicator in this family if something is good and I had to tell her it did! You have a gift—which I thank you for sharing!" ∼ Doloris Dutton